CHAUCER
AND THE
HOUSE OF FAME

CHAUCER
AND THE
HOUSE OF FAME

PHILIPPA MORGAN

CONSTABLE • LONDON

Constable & Robinson Ltd
3 The Lanchesters
162 Fulham Palace Road
London W6 9ER
www.constablerobinson.com

First published in the UK by Constable,
an imprint of Constable & Robinson Ltd 2004

ISBN 1-84119-817-X

Printed and bound in the EU

1

From a distance and with the morning sun behind it, the castle looked like an extension of the cliff itself. At first all that Machaut could see between the trees as he rested his horse after the climb was the keep with a stretch of turreted wall to one side, and beyond that the slow, glinting swathe of the Dordogne. Although the nearer parts of the castle were in shadow, when Machaut hooded his eyes he was able to make out a cluster of roofs and the bell-tower of a church further down the opposite slope.

There was birdsong all around him. No sound apart from that and the scramble of the other horses uphill. He listened as the two riders came into the clearing after him and reined in. He didn't have to announce that they had arrived, or as good as arrived. Instead he looked round at them and nodded. The whole two-day journey had been like this, a matter of nods and gestures with the minimum of words. Machaut had not known his two companions before they set off together from Bordeaux. They'd met him on the quayside immediately he disembarked. They exchanged the agreed sentences, crossed the Garonne, collected their horses and departed straightaway without preliminaries.

Made uneasy by some fear which stretched beyond his normal wariness, Machaut did not trust the two men who were his escorts. He was not sure whether they were guarding him or waiting for the opportunity to rob him of his possessions –

or something worse. No, the something worse would be to be robbed of what he was carrying. Losing his life would be of little consequence by comparison.

One of his escort was a short man with a boyish face stuffed full of freckles. His name was Guilheme. The other was whip-thin and wouldn't meet his gaze. He was called Gerard. But they were not on familiar terms. Nothing had happened on the journey from the coast, however, nothing that would have caused Machaut to be watchful and suspicious – or more watchful and suspicious than he was by nature.

At the inn where they lodged on the first night, Machaut had been sick after supper. He puked up helplessly in the stable-yard as the sun slipped down the sky. And at once he jumped to the conclusion that one of the pair – freckle-faced Guilheme, probably, because he looked the more innocent – had sprinkled some powder into his drink or his food. Even while Machaut was shaken by the retching he glanced about continuously through teary eyes, waiting for either or both of his companions to sneak up on him and cut the cap-case from the cord that secured it to his wrist. His free hand hovered above his sheathed knife. But freckled Guilheme and thin Gerard left him alone with his misery and, going back inside, he felt better when he saw that they seemed unconcerned about his state. In fact they didn't look too good either and Machaut decided that this was no attempt at drugging or poisoning, but more to do with the quality of the landlord's food.

Machaut snugged the cap-case under his bolster that night in the inn and every time he woke up, which was often enough, he tightened his fist around the leather cord. Now, sitting on horseback in a clearing in the woods opposite the castle of Guyac, he tugged again at the cord for reassurance and glanced down to where it snaked inside his saddlebag. Still there, still safe.

Now they were nearly at their destination, the other two drew closer on their horses. Machaut looked round once more.

Guilheme pointed across towards the castle and almost brought himself to manage a freckly grin. Machaut hoped that he wouldn't have to endure their company on the way back to the west. They'd done their job by getting him here. They weren't needed any more. The countryside was simmering with discontent but it wasn't at the boil yet. He'd feel safer without this particular escort, more comfortable relying on himself alone. Safer and more comfortable too without the burden of what he was carrying in his cap-case. He reminded himself to stop at a different inn on his return.

A darting movement caught his eye and he glanced down at a slab of rock which stood in the sun on the edge of the clearing. The rock was as four-square as a table. In the centre there crouched a greeny-brown lizard. Machaut had a sudden desire to dismount and spread his ungloved hand on the warm stone, but he did not move.

Before urging his horse forward and on to the downhill stretch, he gazed at the view for a final time. Sunlight flickered on the floor of the glade as a breeze passed through the branches overhead. The castle, framed by the trees, looked as though it had stood on the cliff-top for centuries, a natural outgrowth of the promontory which it crowned. The stronghold of Henri, the Comte de Guyac, was positioned above a bend of the river, commanding the view for several miles in both directions. Machaut observed a couple of broad-bottomed barges, their sails furled, drifting companionably downstream. Perhaps he should forget about riding back to Bordeaux and take a boat instead. Once his mission was finished, there was no great hurry over his return.

Another gust of wind shivered through the clearing and Machaut was about to nudge his horse into motion but stopped himself.

Something was wrong.

Something he could see? No, nothing unusual was visible, nothing out of the ordinary.

3

Or was it something that he *couldn't* see, an absence of what ought to be there? He didn't think so.

A sound? Not that either.

He couldn't place it. His neck prickled. He looked down at the stone table. The lizard had gone. He looked back for the third time at his companions. They were regarding him expressionlessly, waiting for him to start on the final stage of the journey. Their hands were loose on the reins, away from their weapons. They were several yards to his rear. He should not have stopped for so long with his companions at his back. For most of the journey he'd taken care that they should be in the lead, although not too far ahead. He'd grown careless as he approached his destination, spurring ahead up this final slope.

But it wasn't Guilheme and the thin man, anyway. They weren't the immediate danger, he realized, it was something else.

And then he had it.

The birds had stopped singing.

There was only the clinking of the bridles, the uneasy movement of the animals scuffing at the leafy ground.

Machaut made to press his own horse forward, to get out of the forest glade and on to the rocky track down the slope facing the castle. But it was already too late.

The black-clad figure fell on him from almost directly overhead. He'd sensed it was there a fraction of a second before the shape launched itself from the branches, knocking him out of his saddle. Machaut landed hard on the ground, all his weight coming down on his left leg. He registered a snapping sound, surprisingly loud in the silent clearing, but did not have time to wonder what caused it. The cord which tethered him by the left hand to the contents of his saddlebag now turned into a dangerous impediment. His hired horse – a stolid bay cob – was not used to surprises. It reared, and Machaut was jerked and dragged towards the edge of the clearing, banging against the flank of the panicked animal. The black figure had landed on

4

the ground but was up in an instant and moving towards him, crouching, holding its arms outstretched like a crab's claws. The figure's face was muffled apart from the eyes. A dagger protruded from a gloved fist.

The surprise of the attack, despite the instant of premonition, left Machaut winded and confused. The awkwardness of his position meant that he was almost defenceless. Even as Machaut twisted about, trying to grasp his saddle pommel and regain his seat, other black shapes were falling like crows through the sun-spangled air, landing close to his two companions. The crows landed on their feet, folding up to absorb the impact. Meanwhile Machaut saw Guilheme and Gerard slip unhurriedly from their own mounts, and understood that they had betrayed him. From their position riding in front of him, they'd pointed the way up the hill to the ambushers, knowing that any rider would pause at the top to rest his horse and look at the view. Or perhaps the trap was set long before, and the ambushers had been lying in wait for hours.

Well, no help would be forthcoming from Guilheme and the other one. There was a grim satisfaction in this. He'd been right not to trust them. He was on his own.

Struggling to keep his balance, he unsheathed his knife with his right hand. Machaut was used enough to danger – he was a veteran of Poitiers and the survivor of a dozen lesser battles and skirmishes – but he was not as quick as he'd once been and he was hampered by the cord that connected him to his saddlebag. His horse skittered about at his back and he was incapable of getting a firm purchase on the earth. His left arm was hoisted up in the air while he attempted to manoeuvre his hand about the pommel of his saddle. At last he grasped it and made to push himself off the ground but there was no strength or firmness in his leg, no strength remaining in it at all, and he realized now the meaning of that sharp crack and was surprised to feel no pain.

The figure with the crab-like arms inched forward, awaiting an opportunity. Only the whites of his eyes were visible in the muffled face. Behind him the others were grouping, ready to join in for the killing strokes but, aware of the risk from Machaut's eighteen-inch dagger, they were more than willing to give the first blow to the first assailant.

He knew he was done for. There were too many of them. Sweat ran down his face and his vision started to blur.

Abruptly, Machaut slashed at the leather cord. Keeping hold of it now was useless. They would kill him and get the contents of the cap-case in his saddlebag, both. Let them kill him, then, but perhaps the horse and the bag with its precious contents would elude them.

With both hands free now, he turned about and struck the horse, yelling at it to move. He called out its name. He cursed the cob. But the horse perversely refused to budge. In desperation, Machaut dug the tip of his dagger into its rump. And, at the same instant, the crouching figure saw his moment and leapt at Machaut's own flank. The attacker's dagger flashed in and out, finding an easy passage through his opponent's tunic and undershirt. Instinctively Machaut slashed out with his own weapon and caught the fellow across the forehead. Blood welled through the new slit in the dark material covering the man's face. His attacker fell away but only for an instant. Then the horse jostled Machaut violently and he tumbled forward on to the ground.

Somewhere in the fall he let go his dagger. He had another which he carried for emergencies, tucked into his belt at the back. But even as he reached for it three or four of the black-clad creatures huddled round him. One jumped on to the small of his back and blocked his arm from the second dagger, while the other crows pecked away at Machaut with their own knives. The one who had been wounded by Machaut – and from whose forehead blood oozed so that he had to wipe at it every few seconds – set to work with a will.

On the edge of the clearing Guilheme and Gerard stood and watched without intervening. They had followed their orders by bringing Machaut to this particular point. Nothing else was required from them, or rather they chose not to get their hands dirty.

After the murderers had finished with Machaut, they rolled him over on to his back. Blood pooled from a dozen wounds in his sides. He was still alive but not for much longer. As if he was gazing up from the bottom of a great shaft he saw the tops of the trees which surrounded the clearing. The leaves fringed an unclouded morning sky. The sun hurt his eyes but otherwise he felt calm, almost drowsy, although he had the peculiar sensation that he had grown to a great size and that his limbs were as distant from him as islands in a sea. He closed his eyes to shut out the light.

Nearby stood the sturdy brown cob, its earlier panic gone. Guilheme said something to one of the black-clad ambushers, who walked over to the horse and, mouthing soothing words to the animal, unbuckled the saddlebag from which the leather cord still dangled like a mouse's tail. He took it across to Guilheme and showed him the cap-case inside the bag. Guilheme nodded but said nothing. He held out his hand for the bag and took it.

Then the two escorts mounted their horses and crossed the clearing towards the path which descended the hill in the direction of the castle. The black-clad figures tugged Machaut's body into the undergrowth at the edge of the clearing. They pitched it far down the slope, where it landed with a crash among the dead branches, before they themselves disappeared among the summer trees. One of the attackers had taken care to retrieve Machaut's dagger, the eighteen-inch one. He glanced at it in quick appraisal and, stooping to wipe it on the ground, tucked it into his belt.

Machaut's cob stayed still, waiting to be told what to do next. Patches of sunlight moved across the clearing, sliding over the scuffed-up piles of leaves and the darkening pools of blood which were already drawing the flies. After a time the birds began to sing again.

He was looking for the last time at the view from the window when he heard Philippa come into the room.

"They are outside, Geoffrey," she said. "They're waiting."

"I know."

"I went out. I wanted to tell them what I think."

"I saw you speaking to them."

"Don't worry. I didn't say anything. We only talked about the weather in the end."

"I expect your expression was stormy enough."

They hadn't looked at each other yet. He hesitated a moment before turning round to face her. He was almost afraid of what her expression would be – his "stormy" description wasn't entirely a joke – and he wanted to be out on the road and away. It was a fine, fresh morning. They'd come close to quarrelling the previous evening over his journey and he half expected her to raise the same questions all over again, the same objections.

So when he did finally look at her he tried to keep his own expression fixed. But he softened as he saw, instead of anger, her subdued distress. He moved towards her and took her in his arms.

"I'll look out for myself," he said. "I promise you I'll do that."

"You fool," she said, not altogether gently, "it's not you I'm concerned about, it's myself and Elizabeth and . . ."

As if on cue, a baby started crying downstairs.

" . . . and Thomas, as well as this one . . ."

She rested a hand on her stomach, already well rounded.

"Then your mind will be full," he said. "And I can think of no better things to be concerned about than yourself and the children."

The comment sounded elaborate rather than straight-forward, as he'd meant it to be. He brushed her cheek, and she clung briefly to him and then released him.

He passed out of the chamber before she should see his own discomfort. He clattered down the stairs. At the bottom Meg was standing, cradling little Thomas. He'd stopped crying as abruptly as he'd started. His daughter Elizabeth was standing near the wet-nurse and the baby. She looked as though she was there by chance. He bent and kissed the baby, inhaling a soft milky smell.

"Aren't you going to tell me to take care too?" he said to the wet-nurse.

Meg looked down, embarrassed.

"Take care of your mother, Elizabeth."

The little girl nodded, her expression serious. She wasn't yet four years old but everything she did was grave and intent. He kissed her too then turned away.

Before going into the open air he stepped into a shadowy spot in the lobby and from his pocket took a leather wallet attached to a cord. He slipped the cord around his neck and tucked the wallet out of sight beneath his shirt. It nestled against his chest, like a cross.

When he was ready he went out of the gatehouse and into the street. Alan Audly and Ned Caton were waiting, as his wife had said they were, and his horse was standing between theirs. He swung himself into the saddle and they rode off down the street together.

He glanced back at the upstairs window and saw Philippa leaning out. She wasn't waving. He was already too far off to read her face or his eyes were not sharp enough. He was quite glad not to be able to read her face.

The road towards Charing Cross was crowded. It was a fine morning on the very edge of summer, with business and pleasure stirring together. For his own pleasure, and to distract himself from the pain of parting, he itemized his two companions, building them up from the outside since he knew so little about them.

Alan Audly and Ned Caton were part of John of Gaunt's extensive retinue – more on what you might call the executive than the fighting side – but they must have been on the fringes of Gaunt's household otherwise he would surely have encountered them before. From their tone and manner Geoffrey knew that they were well-born, probably university-educated. Fledgling lawyers maybe, or perhaps just in training to be court-moths, a post for which the qualifications were smoothness, pliability and a dash of cynicism. Dispensable creatures, easily burnt up if they got too close to the centre of power. Why had the Duke of Lancaster wished these two young men on him?

Alan Audly had coal-black curls which tumbled out from beneath his cap. A prominent nose and brows were anchored by a heavy jaw. Like Ned Caton, he wore a heavily embroidered coat which signified a follower of fashion rather than a practical traveller. Caton had a wide, ingenuous face topped with a thatch of hair so pale it was almost white. When they were off their horses, Alan Audly was a tall, rather gangly figure, while Ned Caton was shortish and compact.

When they made their first halt of the morning, Alan Audly said to him, "Wife trouble, eh, Master Chaucer?"

Chaucer wondered whether Philippa had talked to them about more than the weather. He could have taken exception to the impertinence but he chose to smile slightly and say nothing. To Audly this enterprise was probably something between a joke and an adventure. A trip to Aquitaine, a kind of holiday now that the good months had started. In desultory conversation the two young gentlemen questioned Chaucer a little about his time in France almost a dozen years earlier, but it was plain that they regarded those campaigns as so much ancient history.

The first night they stopped at a dingy place near Chatham. Summer had withdrawn after the promise of the morning. The wind blew off the river as an evening of grey skies closed in. The inn was cheap. They didn't talk much though Chaucer discovered a little about his companions. Alan Audly was the son of a man distantly related to John of Gaunt's late wife Blanche, while Ned Caton was apparently the product of a January-May marriage, although both his parents were now dead (and at this point Chaucer remembered hearing court-talk of Anne Caton, a fair-haired beauty). On the surface, then, there was nothing particularly unusual about his two companions.

The ice wasn't broken until the next night when a typical thing happened to them, or something which Geoffrey Chaucer feared might be typical of these two youngsters.

The condition of the roads was good, even considering the time of year, so they had already reached Canterbury by the second evening. They lodged at an inn on the edge of the city rather than at one of the smarter establishments near the cathedral church. Because he wanted to avoid crowds and the risk of his companions blabbing as they might have done in more salubrious surroundings, Geoffrey chose the Phoenix Inn. It was a dilapidated place, sagging between the buildings on either side like a drunk held up by reluctant bystanders. Alan Audly and Ned Caton wrinkled their noses at the accommodation. As they left the street, Chaucer glanced round. He felt uncomfortable, without apparent reason. There were a few passers-by on foot or horseback. No one appeared to be paying them any attention.

The landlord was a bald-headed individual called Sampson, with a soft insinuating manner. He owned – or was owned by – a full-blown belly that seemed to pull him along like the sail on a boat. After they'd discussed terms (a single room of course, but with two beds in it) and were almost all smiles, Geoffrey waited for Sampson to be tugged away by his belly but the landlord hung about.

"What's your business, if I may ask?" he said. "You've come to pay your respects at the shrine of the blessed St Thomas?"

"That's right."

"Early is best with St Thomas."

"My friends and I are intending to leave early."

"Before the crowds get there, yes. Are you also intending to make an offering at the shrine, sir? Perhaps you're travelling on somewhere else, somewhere overseas perhaps, and want to ask for St Thomas's blessing before you depart."

If the landlord wanted to believe they were going to the shrine, let him. But their travelling bags were too large and too heavy for the quick round trip from London to Canterbury and back again. In good weather Canterbury could be the last overnight stop on the Dover road. The landlord would have noticed the size of the bags while he saw to the stabling of the horses. It would be an incurious landlord who didn't notice such things. But a landlord's curiosity doesn't have to be satisfied.

"Perhaps we are travelling on elsewhere," said Geoffrey Chaucer. "But Master Sampson, hear me, it is best that we go about our business while you go about yours."

"Of course, sir."

Bald-headed Sampson had a wife who was even larger than her husband. And there was apparently a daughter who was somewhere between the two in point of size.

"Did you see her, Master Chaucer?" said Alan Audly, later that evening. "The offspring of mine host whatsisname? Simpson?"

"His name is Sampson. No, I didn't see her," said Geoffrey.

"But I did, in the back quarters of this hole that passes for an inn."

"What were you doing there, my friend?" said Ned Caton.

"Poking around."

"Oh-ho."

The three men were finishing off their wine in front of a dying charcoal fire in the hall where they'd just eaten. There seemed to be no other guests staying at the inn. From the kitchen of the Phoenix the wife of Sampson had brought them their wine, supposedly a claret, and their food, unquestionably a mutton stew. She was attentive, with a share of her husband's ingratiating manner, and she leaned close over their shoulders while she placed the pot and the trenchers on the table.

"She gave me the glad eye," said Alan.

"That one?" said Ned, jerking his thumb in the direction of the departing landlady.

"Not *her*. The daughter."

"They always give you the glad eye," said Ned.

"This one really did, trust me."

"A looker?"

"Depends where you look."

"And where did you look, Alan?"

"Where do you think? Tits like a sow," said Audly, cupping his hands and spilling a little drink down himself as he did so. "I told her they were like pomegranates."

"What did she say?"

"Nothing much, because we came to an arrangement beyond mere words. She giggled mostly. Her name is Alison."

"'Pomegranates'. We'll make a poet of you yet, Alan. Eh, Master Chaucer?"

"A pair of pomegranates won't make anyone a poet," said Geoffrey.

"Nor will Alison make a fitting heroine for our story," said Ned. "That name'll have to change. It's too low for a romance. Can't she be an Emily now?"

Geoffrey drained his cup and swilled the wine round his

mouth. He grunted and pulled a face, hoping to distract them from the subject of the girl. The last thing they needed was an altercation over some girl.

"Something wrong with the wine, Master Chaucer?"

"There's a touch of Spain in here," said Geoffrey, although he'd realized this from the first mouthful.

"But we commanded the French stuff."

"It's a funny thing with Bordeaux wine," said Geoffrey. "It often finds itself stored next to wine from Cadiz, let's say, and by magic the contents of the Spanish barrel will creep their way into their more expensive neighbours."

"Then whatsisname Simpson has cheated on us," said Alan. "We ordered claret from Bordeaux."

"I will deal with it tomorrow when I settle with *Sampson*."

"Why don't we deal with him now, since he's given his betters a bastard sort of wine," said Ned.

"Settle with him by hand," said his friend, "so that he feels what it is to cheat those on a royal commission. One bad turn deserves a worse one. We are entitled to settle with him."

"And after you've settled with him, then we will certainly have to find ourselves somewhere else to stay for the night," said Geoffrey. "No, tomorrow will do."

"You're a vintner's son, aren't you, Master Chaucer? Born with a nose for wine?"

And not university educated like us, Alan meant. *Not the sons of lawyers or court-men like we are.*

"I don't know about a nose for wine but I have my mother's nose, I think – at least in its capacity to smell trouble," said Chaucer. "You are not to make any reference to royal commissions again, either of you. I know nothing about any royal commission. We are travelling on different business."

"Which is?"

A spasm of irritation shot through Chaucer at the high-handedness and indifference of these young men. He wished he could ride on next day and leave them behind. He kept his voice even and patient, as if explaining things to children.

"I am carrying a letter from Nicholas Bember which authorizes me to negotiate with several wine shippers in the Bordeaux region. Bember used to live near my father in the Vintry Ward. He is an old friend to my family. He was good enough to supply me with a reason for my journey."

"So you are a true expert on the grape," said Alan.

"No poem was ever written by a drinker of water," said Chaucer. "The Roman poet Horace said that first, but plenty of poets would agree with him."

"And you're a poet as well?" said Ned.

"The title should be reserved for the great Italians," said Chaucer. "I would be content to be a maker."

That seemed to silence them, or it might have been that they were tired or simply uninterested. Geoffrey was tired. He expected to fall asleep straightaway in the upstairs room. The wine should help, whether it came from expensive Bordeaux or cheaper Cadiz. Alan Audly and Ned Caton were sharing a bed while Geoffrey slept apart in a thin crib a couple of feet away from them. There was a cluster of little rooms up here, perhaps half a dozen upper chambers opening off a gallery which was reached by a simple stairway and which looked down into the hall where they'd eaten. The fire was out, but a moon that was half full poked her fingers through the ill-fitting shutters.

Chaucer could not sleep however. The wine did not help him after all. He watched as a line of white light crept up the restless limbs of his companions like an unearthly tide. Occasionally Alan and Ned whispered to each other or giggled like lovers. Then after a time one of them, Ned probably, started to snore.

Still Geoffrey could not sleep. He thought of Philippa and his family. He thought of Rosamond de Guyac, and of how it seemed they were destined to meet again after a dozen years. He thought of his meeting with John of Gaunt a few days before, and of the importance of what he'd undertaken and he felt unequal to the task, before telling himself that the worst time to reach an opinion on such a matter was during the night when you can't get to sleep. He reached for the cord which he wore about his neck, day and night. Secured to the end of the cord was the leather wallet. The feel of that wallet against his skin, day and night, was more a threat than a comfort.

One of his neighbours rose from the shared bed but quietly, not like a person getting blunderingly up for a nocturnal piss. Then the door to the room scraped open and was pulled to again. Chaucer wondered why Alan, if it was him, was bothering to close the door, and why he was going outside to relieve himself when there was a perfectly good jordan in the corner, placed there for the convenience of the Phoenix's guests.

He waited several minutes for the young man to conclude his business and return. But there was no sound. Geoffrey sat up in his crib. He felt uneasy. He cursed Gaunt for landing him with these two travelling fellows. Cover and company, that's what they were supposed to be – not a liability.

He swung out of bed and crept to the bedroom door. It was not completely closed after all. He slipped through the gap and stepped out into the gallery. Spokes of watery moonlight radiated across the ground floor. Chaucer stood absolutely quiet. There was a noise coming from one of the chambers to his left. It was a subdued but urgent noise. No words were discernible, but it was human utterance of an unmistakable kind. All too human, he thought, and wished Sampson and his wife an enjoyable session together if they were managing to meet round the corners of their bellies, and then he thought again because he realized the landlord was not in bed with his wife but standing at the foot of the stairs.

Sampson was standing with his head down, as if he too was straining to hear the sounds from the upper room. He was holding a candle but shielding the flame with his hand. The deflected light caught the tip of the man's belly and the top of his head, which gleamed whitely. At first Chaucer thought he was wearing a nightcap but it was only his baldness. In fact the landlord appeared to be dressed in his day-gear.

The sound from the nearby room continued. Chaucer wondered how long Sampson was going to let the noises run on. Why didn't he go back to bed? Or if he meant to take action, then why was he waiting when it was obvious what was going on under his own roof?

Suddenly Sampson, still carrying the candle, started to tread up the stairs. He moved lightly, considering his size. At the top he turned left and then left again until he was positioned outside the door of the busy chamber. He was concentrating so much on what was happening within that he was unaware of Geoffrey's presence. Chaucer was puzzled. There was no detectable indignation in Sampson's posture, no outrage, no anger waiting to bubble over. Instead there was a kind of expectation.

Geoffrey didn't understand. There were, to the best of his knowledge, four men and two women in the Phoenix tonight. One of the men was sleeping or pretending to sleep in the room behind him. Two more were stationed on the landing, listening to the activities of the fourth man with one of the two women. However you sliced it, the landlord had a share in this loaf. Surely he ought to be concerned about his women. Why wasn't he doing something? Why was he hanging about?

And suddenly it all became plain to Chaucer.

The landlord waited for a momentary pause in the muffled groans and creakings emanating from the bedchamber and then, raising his candle high in his left hand, he stretched out his right to unlatch the door. But before he could shove it open, Chaucer was by his side. He reached around Sampson's belly and grasped the landlord's thick, hairless wrist.

"No, Master Sampson."

He had the advantage of surprise. Sampson almost dropped the candle. His mouth gaped.

18

"You should leave them to their pleasure," said Geoffrey.

"My daughter's in there."

The soft insinuating tone was gone but he did not raise his voice. Nor did Chaucer.

"How do you know she's in there?"

"Because I – "

Sampson stopped, realizing that whatever he was about to say would reveal more than he intended. There was silence now, inside the room as well. Either the couple had concluded their business or, more likely, been interrupted by the hissed exchange of words outside.

"My property, I believe," said Sampson.

He wrenched himself free of Geoffrey's grip and unlatched the door. It swung open. A combination of candlelight and moonlight, of dirty gold and pale silver, revealed portions of a narrow bed, the top end of which remained in the shadows. Principally illuminated was a pair of long thin buttocks, belonging, Geoffrey Chaucer assumed, to his travelling companion, Alan Audly. Alan's arse was stationed between a pair of much larger female hams. There were cavernous dimples in the woman's upraised knees. The male buttocks and the female hams seemed to be cowering in the candlelight, like a litter of half-blind puppies.

"Time to express your outrage, Master Sampson," said Chaucer, since it appeared that no one else was going to say anything. It was evident that Geoffrey's arrival on the scene had disrupted the smooth running of this drama, which had probably occurred often before.

Reluctantly, Sampson moved forward, preceded by his belly. He lifted up the candle once more. Audly at least had the grace to keep his head turned to one side so that only his coal-black curls were visible.

"You silly fellow," the landlord said. "You bed-violater. You seed of Satan."

Sampson did not speak with conviction. He might have been reciting lines learnt by rote. Audly didn't move his head though his buttocks twitched as if under an invisible lash.

"Well now, Alison – " said the owner of the Phoenix, seeing that he was not getting anywhere with the bed-violater, the seed of Satan.

Sampson stopped in mid-sentence. Now the glow from the candle was lighting up the face of the woman. He stooped forward in disbelief. The woman would not meet his eye.

"*Wife!*" said Sampson. Now he did sound shocked.

"Oh husband," she said.

Alan Audly's black head shot up. Seemingly for the first time he took in the identity of the woman between whose thighs he'd been nestling. He sprang away as if he'd been lying next to a plaguey corpse. Her nightgown was entangled with her great breasts while Audly's own smock was bunched up around his chest, scrawny by comparison. Chaucer noted that, however far Alan Audly had travelled along the road to satisfaction, the shrivelled state of his equipment showed that he'd not be reaching his destination in the near future.

"But I thought . . ." said the landlord.

"But *I* thought . . ." said Audly, tugging down his smock to cover his newly public privates.

Mistress Sampson said nothing. She was perhaps the only one of the three not to have behaved in error.

"Master Sampson, come outside and hear what I think."

Almost gently, Chaucer took the man by the upper arm and led him out of the chamber. Sampson followed without objection. Whatever drama the landlord was playing in, whatever lines he'd learned to follow, had gone quite askew.

Once the two men were outside in the gallery, Geoffrey said, "I don't know what went wrong in there, Sampson, but it wasn't what you planned to go wrong."

"What do you mean? I have found my wife in bed with another man. My wife!"

"Whereas you expected to find your daughter."

"I know what I found."

Behind the other's back Chaucer saw Alan tiptoeing out and going towards their shared room. He was shortly followed by Sampson's wife, her hams, knees and dimples well concealed by her voluminous nightgown. She headed in the opposite direction to the young man, pausing briefly at the top of the stairs before scuttling down them. Chaucer thought it as well to go on the attack and to keep the landlord distracted.

"You assumed it was your daughter – Alison is her name, yes? – because she is in the habit of visiting your gentlemen guests at night."

We came to an arrangement beyond mere words, Alan had said.

"Bollocks."

"Just as you're in the habit of waiting at the bottom of those stairs for the, ah, action to start."

"Pigswill."

"Then explain why you're fully dressed, candle in hand?"

"A man may do as he pleases in his own establishment."

"It's so you can creep up here and burst in on the couple, playing the outraged father. Your daughter is your lure. The gentlemen are the hawks, drawn by her bright feathers. Say what you like, Master Sampson, but it's true."

"I'm a patient man," said Sampson.

"Too patient, considering the provocation to you. How much do you squeeze out of them? What do they offer you to avoid complications? Particularly when they're hurrying off the next day to Dover and will pay to get out of trouble. That's why you're were so curious about our intentions tomorrow."

Sampson sighed. The sound was like air oozing from a pricked bladder.

"I'm not to blame if I can't control my daughter. Although I might have beaten her once."

21

"You cannot control your wife either, it seems. She took the place that should have been the daughter's and hopped into another man's bed without your knowledge. Therefore you would appear to be a cuckold."

The landlord did not answer.

"A cuckold by *arrangement*, Master Sampson? A pander who holds open the door to his own bedchamber."

Still no reply.

"I'll take that for a denial. So if you're not a cuckold by arrangement, this is an honest mistake."

"Oh, it's a mistake all right. My wife'll find out just what an honest mistake it was. I'll learn her."

"Honest mistakes don't interest the law, provided they don't damage others. The alternative is that you are a procurer while the Phoenix Inn is a house of ill-fame. If that's the case, then this is no mistake, and the law will be interested. Sleep on it, Master Sampson."

The landlord slunk away, escorted by his uncertain candle, and Chaucer returned to his chamber. Alan Audly was sleeping shamefully or pretending to sleep shamefully. But of his fair-haired companion there was no sign. Ned must have slipped out sometime during the business in the other bedroom. There came a clattering from another part of the inn, and the sound of voices, a man and a woman's.

Mother of God, thought Geoffrey, if that one has got into trouble as well, I am not going to assist him. Let the innkeeper catch him in bed with one of his women and cut off his cullions if he can get at them. Let him turn Caton into a capon, I am not going to lift a finger to save him or his member. His irritation with the innkeeper was nothing like as great as his anger at his companions. Let the young man lie with both of his women, for all I care. Though lying in the middle of Mistress Sampson and her daughter Alison would be like being between the grinding stones in a flour mill. Geoffrey Chaucer tried to

22

please himself with images of Ned Caton being squashed and pulverized. Then he must have fallen asleep.

The next morning they set off early, as Chaucer had announced to the landlord that they would. He settled up with Sampson, who avoided any reference to the previous night. Of his wife and daughter there was no sign. One of Sampson's eyes was blackened, though, and Geoffrey remembered the noises he'd heard in the night. Perhaps the landlord had been giving his wife a learning in honest mistakes, and come out of the lesson somewhat the worse for it.

Alan Audly was subdued, or as subdued as you might expect a man to be when you have caught a glimpse of his compromised buttocks. Ned Caton, by contrast, was as bright and chirpy as a bird in spring. He took pleasure in his friend's discomfiture and kept dropping broad hints that he had managed a successful engagement with Alison – "The *young* woman, that is, not the old one, you may tell them apart by certain characteristics, you know. The young ones are not so flumpity." This liaison had apparently taken place in another quarter of the Phoenix while the rest of the household was occupied.

Chaucer didn't know whether to believe his story, and didn't much care. Alan did not *want* to believe his friend's story, and did care, until in exasperation he told Ned Caton to shut up. They were riding away from the city. Soon the Canterbury walls dropped out of sight over their shoulders. It was a fair day, with soft clouds moving aimlessly along. There were other travellers behind them on the road but, among the nearest, no one that Chaucer could recognize from the previous days' journeying.

They had not gone to pay their respects at the shrine of St Thomas the Martyr in the cathedral church. Time was pressing. Chaucer vowed that he at least would stop there on the return journey. He had visited the shrine once before on his first voyage

23

into France when he was nineteen years old and setting off on campaign. The monk who showed Thomas's tomb to the group of pilgrims, most of them departing soldiers, had taken them first to the high altar and pointed proudly to the martyr's blood which was still visible on the stone flags in front of the holy place. The blood looked fresh to Chaucer's eye, rather than two centuries old. But then it probably was fresh, he had thought, touched up regularly in the same way that the stall-traders in Mercery Lane outside the church miraculously renewed their unique relics and irreplaceable gewgaws when stocks began to run low.

For all that, the shrine itself was a solemn and eloquent spot, crusted with jewels like the barnacles on a boat. A dozen years ago, Geoffrey had made an offering and then knelt to say a prayer for his safe return from France. He was eager enough to prove himself in battle but he lacked the hot-headedness of some of his companions. He could not help reflecting that he would witness more blood – and blood which was casually spilt rather than carefully painted on the ground – before he was allowed to come back home. If he was allowed to come back home . . . But St Thomas had kept his side of the bargain, you might say. That return had been delayed by captivity, but he'd eventually been restored for the unprincely sum of sixteen pounds. He'd be worth more now.

"What?"

Alan Audly had just said something.

"Did you deal justly with our Master Sampson in the matter of the wine which was Spanish and not French?"

"Did I pay him less, you mean?"

"Yes."

"No, instead I gave him something over the odds."

"I don't understand you, Master Chaucer. He deserved to have his nose rubbed in it."

"He could have caused trouble about last night. He didn't cause trouble."

"I thought *you* were going to cause him trouble from what I heard."

So Alan had been listening to their whispered conversation in the gallery.

"I was more concerned to get you out of trouble."

"We have all been victims of imposture," said Ned cheerfully. "We have been passed goods under false pretences, wine or women. A Spanish wine for a Bordeaux, a wife for a daughter. Tell me, Alan my friend, was the human item just a little vinegary as well? Mine wasn't."

Alan Audly turned his horse to ride at Ned Caton but thought better of it. Instead the humorous aspect of the business suddenly struck him, and he laughed aloud.

"Properly seen," said Geoffrey, "this has been material for comedy. It is best seen in that light, a little relief before the main enterprise."

"I am glad that Master Chaucer takes the long view," said Ned.

After that some of the unease between them evaporated and they rode on, stopping briefly at midday to rest and water the horses, and eating the bread and cheese they had purchased before leaving Canterbury. Eventually, as the sun was slipping down to their right, they climbed out of a sparsely wooded valley and saw – beyond the springy turf of the downland and the white track which snaked across it – the distant blue of the sea, all scattered about with sails hurrying to make the port of Dover before nightfall. In clear conditions you could see English Calais, but now the opposite coast was hazed over, as unreadable as the days to come.

3

The man was standing outside what had once been the town gate for the road from Canterbury. The gate no longer existed and the walls were dilapidated, as if the great castle on the facing hill had taken away the need for additional defence. The man assumed that the travellers would arrive by this route. They might cross the bridge further up and go to the other part of town on the east bank of the river. But no respectable traveller would choose to stay across there. It was a fishing settlement, knee-deep in guts and hooks. The smell wafted across to the west side when the wind was in that direction. If Geoffrey Chaucer wanted to attract attention to himself and his little party then the surest way to do it would be to go looking for accommodation on the east bank of the Dour. They'd stand out like pike in a tank of minnows, well-dressed and with their arrogant London voices. Not Chaucer perhaps but Audly and Caton.

He'd noted Geoffrey's careful choice of lodging the previous night in Canterbury. From a distance he'd watched as the three men entered the Phoenix Inn. He'd observed Chaucer looking round with that bland absence of curiosity which seemed to characterize him. The man waited until the three were well settled inside the Phoenix before finding himself a room and a shared bed in an equally unpromising place down the street. He didn't care. He was indifferent to where he slept. He paid his landlord in advance. At first light he'd saddled up and spurred towards Dover.

The safest way to follow someone is to be a little ahead of the quarry, always ready to stop or turn when they do. The risk for the man was that he was so far ahead that he might have lost them altogether. Since arriving in Dover, he'd had time to sell the horse which he had bought in London for the journey. He carried nothing with him except for a grey sack which he sometimes tucked into his belt and sometimes slung over his shoulder. So now here he was standing in the shadow of the town walls of Dover, waiting for the trio to catch up with him.

There were other people hanging about on this spot, the usual flotsam that collects at the entry points to any town. Men and women and some infants, touting for business, looking for alms, or just observing the arrivals and departures. But no one approached *him*. He had a trick of discouraging attention, which was to smile. His smile was pleasant to begin with, but he kept it going until it started to seem mocking. His bared dog-teeth gave him the appearance of a death's-head.

Now he kept his eyes fixed on the track that looped down towards the town. It was late afternoon, time for travellers to reach their destination and fix their accommodation for the evening. He needed to know where they were staying that night in order to track them from their lodgings to the harbour the next morning. Plenty of ships scudded between here and France every day, weather and winds permitting, and it would be easy for Chaucer's little group to slip aboard one of them without much notice. He could not afford to lose his quarry.

If the three reached Dover tonight, there was no reason why they shouldn't set sail tomorrow. The sea glittered under the afternoon sky. It was calm. The man with the smile glanced towards the other side of the river. Over the shabby fishing village loomed the great castle, well out of the slime and fish-hooks. He looked up the road again. Plenty of people were travelling along it, on foot and horseback and in carts, but there was no sign of the ones he was waiting for. He wondered if he was wrong. Maybe Chaucer had decided to stop for the night somewhere between Canterbury and Dover. Not likely, though, since the weather and the road were relatively clear. And Chaucer's mission was urgent.

He felt a tug at his sleeve. Looked down. An old woman had her hand held out. She mumbled something. She was blind. She must have found him by instinct, or perhaps have been directed towards him. There was a ragged knot of beggars in the empty gateway. He shook the hand off but she persisted, reaching out for him again. He would have smiled his dog-tooth smile but it was no use with a blind woman.

"What is it?" he asked, though of course he knew.

"Alms. Alms."

The term bubbled up from an otherwise incomprehensible stew of words.

Out of the corner of his eye the man saw three riders cresting the hill above the town. Almost certainly they were the ones he was looking for. He bent down towards the old woman's be-whiskered ear.

"If you do not leave me alone this instant I will break your wrist. Feel."

He put one hand round the woman's wrist and squeezed. He could have snapped it with a single twist. It was like a dry twig. She tried to snatch her hand back.

"Maybe I will break it anyway and teach you not to come bothering honest men."

Even as he said this, he was looking away. Yes, it was them, Chaucer and Audly and Caton. He recognized their bright coats as they cantered down the final slope towards the town. He held fast to the woman's wrist, giving it a final wrench before releasing it. She moved back without uttering a sound though her mouth twisted in pain. There was a horse and cart immediately behind her but by instinct she avoided them, keeping her sightless eyes fixed disconcertingly on his face. But the man had no interest in the old beggar-woman. He was watching the trio of horsemen draw nearer the gate. They slowed down to pass on the other side of the cart and Geoffrey Chaucer, in the lead, turned his head and looked at the man, who was by now bending down towards the ground in search of something he'd dropped.

As Chaucer and the younger men ambled past, he glanced up from his crouching position. Chaucer's eyes flicked over him without concern. Geoffrey looked like what he was – or so the smiling dog-toothed man thought – he looked like a civil servant who spent most of his time sitting on his arse and poring over papers in a bad light. There was already a little plumpness in his comfortable face. A touch of self-satisfaction too perhaps. The man felt a tremor of contempt.

He pretended to pick something out of the mud and straightened up as the three horsemen disappeared through the gateway. Moving quickly, he brushed past the knot of beggars and idlers. The horsemen veered to the left. It was easy to keep them in sight. The coats that Caton and Audly were flaunting made them stand out. Chaucer was wearing a more subdued garment. The town lanes were crowded in the late afternoon and the riders' progress was slow.

Not far from the harbour stood a large monastic-style building inside its own walled grounds, with stables and an orchard of fruit trees losing their blossom, and (on the evidence of the smell) a brewery. Chaucer and his companions rode into the courtyard that fronted the building. The man did not need to see a couple of black-garbed figures flitting about the place to realize that this was a religious house.

He watched as the riders climbed down from their horses and stretched their limbs. A stable-hand with lank hair ambled across to help them unsaddle their bags. Chaucer spoke to him and then handed something over. Money, judging by the way the stable-hand took hold of it and nodded several times. The man waited while the three travellers went inside the building and the ostler led the horses away. He allowed some more time to go by. He tucked his grey sack into his belt. Then he walked into the courtyard himself, choosing a moment when it was empty. He found the lank-haired ostler returning from the stables. The ostler, little more than a boy, scuffed along with his eyes on the ground. The man stood in his path so that he was forced to stop.

"Tell me the name of this place, my friend."

The stable-hand looked up at the man, who had the sun behind him.

"Who wants to know?"

"I want to know."

Something in the man's tone or appearance prevented the boy from putting the question again. Instead he said, "This is St Mary's. This is the Maison Dieu."

He said *Dee* for *Dieu* but the man knew what he meant. It was a hospice run by monks for travellers and those in need (often the same thing), a cross between a monastery and an inn.

"Which order?" said the smiling man.

"Order?"

"Who runs your Maison Dee?"

"The Brethren of the Holy Cross, sir."

"And who lodges here?"

"All sorts. Soldiers, sailors. Pilgrims from across the water."

The stable-boy jerked his thumb over his shoulder in the direction of France. The pilgrims would stop here on their way to St Thomas's shrine at Canterbury.

"I am particularly interested in those men who have recently arrived," said the man. "The ones whose horses you have just stabled."

"You are, sir?"

"I am. What's your name?"

"Peter."

"Can you read, Peter?"

Surprised by the question, the boy shook his head. From his cloak the man drew out a parchment and pointed to the lead seal at the bottom.

"Whether you can read or not, you have eyes. See this. It means that I am on the King's business."

The boy swallowed audibly but said nothing. The death's-head man was conscious of their exposed position, standing in the courtyard in front of the main entrance to the hospice. At any moment one of the black-clad Brethren might appear and start asking questions. He slipped the document out of sight again.

"On the King's *secret* business, I say. But this place is too open to discuss all that."

He grasped the boy by the upper arm and ushered him in the direction of the stables, which stood to one side of the hospice and slightly behind it. The boy allowed himself to be led off without comment. The two entered the comparative seclusion of the stables. Soft scuffling and champing sounds emanated from the stalls, and the air was pleasantly warm and dungy. Finally the boy found his voice again.

"What do you want from our house?"

"I want nothing from your house. You should be grateful I am here. I am protecting your Maison Dee from harm," said the man. He smiled very slightly, half reassurance, half threat. "Those men who have just arrived are agents of the French king. Do you know who the French king is?"

The boy shook his head.

"He is called Charles and these people are his spies. They are on their way back to France."

For a moment the boy stood undecided in the dimness of the stable. Then he said, "We must tell Brother James. He'll know what to do."

The man's hand shot out to detain him by the arm, although the boy hadn't moved.

32

"We'll do no such thing, Peter. There must be no whisper of this. This is a weighty affair of state beyond the reach of your priests and your monks. Do you understand that?"

The boy shook his head before deciding it was safer to nod. The man, standing close, sensed his unease turning into fear.

"Show me their horses," he said.

The boy gestured towards one end of the stable.

"I said, *show* me."

The man was still holding on to Peter's arm. Before releasing it he tightened his grip, not by very much but sufficiently to make the boy uncomfortable. Peter walked to the far end of the building. Three horses were stalled side by side down there. The man recognized them as the ones which Chaucer and the others had been riding since leaving London.

"What were his instructions, the older man's?" he said. "He gave you some money so he must have told you to do something."

"He told me to look after the horses."

"For how long?"

"A month or two, maybe longer, until he returned. If he and his friends hadn't returned within three months we could sell the horses, but the money must go to this house. Or we could keep the horses, he said. Whichever we preferred. He was going to tell Brother James that."

"Did he say anything else?"

"Only that his life was in God's hands."

"He's right enough there," said the death's-head man.

"But if he's a French spy, sir, he won't be returning, will he? So why did he say he would be?"

The boy was quicker and brighter than he looked.

"To trick you into believing that he and his friends were ordinary travellers."

But Peter could not quite keep the doubt out of his face. The man began to regret approaching the lad. He might have to deal with him later. A bell began to chime from the Maison Dieu.

"Where do you sleep at night, Peter?"

"With the horses of course, sir."

The stable-boy raised his eyes to a platform affixed to the wall. It was scarcely more than a ledge in the air, like a bird's eyrie. Judging by the dirty straw which protruded over the edge, the boy shared his charges' bedding. There was a rickety ladder propped against the platform.

"Why all the way up there?"

"So I can keep an eye on everything, sir."

"Large enough for two?" said the man.

"I can sleep in a stall," said the boy promptly.

"Of course you can sleep in a stall," said the man. "But first I want you to get some food and drink. Not from your house pantry though. I don't want anyone wondering why you're picking up extra supplies. Go to the nearest ale-stake and buy some bread and some cheese and beer. Don't draw attention to yourself. Here."

He handed over a few halfpennies.

"There'll be more for you when you bring what I ask. But, Peter, not a word to anyone. This is the King's business, remember."

This time he grasped the boy by the shoulder, again exerting a little pressure. Peter sped off from the stable. For a moment the man stood staring after him. He considered following the stable-hand to ensure that he didn't go into the main house to report on him or the "spies" but thought better of it. Then, clutching his grey sack, he clambered up the ladder to the little platform. A couple of dirty pieces of cloth were spread out over the straw which served for bedding but there was no other sign of human occupation. He lay down on his back and gazed at the rough-hewn timbers which slanted above his head. Early evening light squeezed through the gaps in the planking. The air was dusty. The snuffles and shufflings of the horses in the stable had quietened. If you sprawled or turned carelessly on this ledge you'd risk dropping the dozen or more feet to the ground. This didn't trouble the death's-head man. He'd slept in worse places, and more dangerous ones too.

He must have fallen asleep – the result of an early start that morning, saddling up in Canterbury at first light – because the next thing he knew was that someone was prodding him in the shoulder. It was a gentle prod but even so his hand flew to his dagger before his eyes opened, and the tip of the dagger was at the boy's throat before he was fully awake. Peter's head and shoulders were on a level with the man. The lank-haired boy was leaning on the ladder, holding up the food in one hand and an earthenware flask in the other. Instinctively the boy jerked backwards and almost fell. But the man was quicker and seized him by the shoulder with the hand that wasn't grasping the dagger.

He put down the dagger and relieved the boy of what he was carrying. He placed the bread and the flask on a clear patch of straw. He was hungry and thirsty but didn't touch the food or drink.

"There was no cheese left," said the boy.

The man said nothing. By the alteration in the light which came through the gaps in the roof he knew that some time had passed since the boy first left.

"What took you so long?"

Peter was still perched on the ladder, looking at the individual who occupied his sleeping quarters. He hesitated before answering.

"Brother James stopped me."

"When?"

"Just now, as I was coming in."

"Why?"

"He wanted to ask me about the horses. Two of the horses in here may be sick. Their piss is clear, see, and the piss of a healthy horse should be yellow . . . or it should be whitish and not clear but not too dark neither cos if it's clear it means – "

The dog-toothed man gestured impatiently. He wasn't interested in horse piss and what it signified. The boy was talking too quickly. Was it because he was on familiar ground when it came to horse diseases or was he trying to distract the man's attention from something else? All the time the man kept listening out for other sounds, apart from the stable noises. But there was nothing.

"Did your Brother James have anything else to say? Did he ask why you'd been out? Did *you* say anything to him?"

Peter hesitated again before shaking his head. He shouldn't have hesitated since it suggested to the man that he might be lying. Now the man shrugged and sat up, letting his legs dangle over the edge of the platform. He stuck his dagger in the bread and brought it towards him. He carved off a chunk and handed it to the boy, at the same time inclining his head to show that he could join him on the ledge.

The stable-hand paused a moment then scrambled up and sat next to the man. He seemed less apprehensive now. He bent over the chunk of bread, tearing off a mouthful. His long hair fell away from the nape of his neck. Despite the dimness of the light, the man could see the line of little bumps that were the top of his backbone.

"You said something about more money – when I brought the food back," said Peter, still chewing.

"I did too," said the man.

He moved his hand to his side where his purse was situated. By touch he located and drew out a couple more halfpennies. He grazed the boy's free hand with the coins. The hand opened and closed, swallowing the coins. The boy laughed slightly and said, "I'm sorry there was no cheese."

"It doesn't matter," said the man. "This is enough."

He picked up the flask and pulled out the stopper with his teeth. He tilted his head back and drank from the flask. When he had drunk about half the contents he put the flask down and listened to the background sounds of the stable. He heard nothing out of the ordinary. The boy spoke.

"What did you say?"

"It's good, the ale?"

"I've tasted worse."

"Can I see that parchment again, the one with the seal on it?"

"Why?"

"Just think, the King's seal. I've never seen it before."

"That's nothing to seeing the man himself."

"You've seen the King?"

"What do you think?"

"The Queen, she is dead, though?"

"Yes," said the man. "Queen Philippa died last year."

"Can queens die?" said the boy. "Let me see that seal again."

"Have a drink first," said the man, passing over the flask. He waited until Peter was drinking from the flask, head tilted back, oblivious and glugging away. Then he swung his hand out and across, keeping the fingers taut. He struck the boy hard on his exposed windpipe. The earthenware flask flew out of the boy's hand and shattered somewhere out of sight. Ale spurted from his mouth together with fragments of bread. His arms flailed and the coins which he'd been holding in the other hand were scattered in the gloom. He writhed on to his side, his breath wheezing as he struggled for air. The man gave him a push, almost a delicate one, so that he rolled off the platform. He landed on the ground with a thud.

The man peered down. Peter lay curled up and unmoving, his head at an angle which suggested he'd never move again of his own volition. The man swung himself around and down the ladder. He jumped the last few feet to the ground. He bent over the stable-boy's body and checked it for signs of life. There were none. He made to drag the body away but realized that that would leave scrape-marks across the dirt and straw of the floor. He lifted up the dead stable-boy. Peter was surprisingly light and as warm as life. His head lolled. The front of his tunic was spattered with ale and sopping crumbs of bread.

The man had earlier observed that several of the horse-stalls were empty. He intended to put the body in one for the night in case anyone came snooping about the place while he was sleeping up in the boy's eyrie. As he carried the body through the stables, the animals snuffled and shifted uneasily, as if they could sense that something was wrong. The man found one of the unoccupied stalls. He deposited the boy on the ground and heaped straw over him. It was mostly dark in here anyway.

He was just straightening up, his hand still touching the warm body, when he heard footsteps approaching. He ducked down out of sight in the stall. The footsteps halted at the entrance to the stable.

"Peter!"

There was a pause then the voice called from closer to: "Peter! Boy! Are you up there? Are you asleep?"

Someone from the hospice, someone who knew that Peter slept on a platform in the stables.

"Where's this person then, the one who was asking questions? Where is he?"

A few yards from you, thought the death's-head man as he crouched in the stall with the boy's body. If this one starts looking around he will have to be dealt with as well.

There was a scrabbling sound followed, a moment later, by a thunk as an object hit the roof at the far end of the stables. There was a further stir from the stalled horses. The man understood that the newcomer – Brother James? – was trying to attract Peter's attention by throwing a stone or a chunk of mud in the direction of his perch. The man couldn't see Brother James but he imagined him as fat and idle, too fat and idle to climb the ladder and see for himself whether the lad's sleeping quarters were occupied. When there was no answering call or yelp from up there, the other said, "It's lucky Brother Stephen didn't catch you absent from your post. He'd have thrashed you for it."

Then the footsteps receded. The man waited a few minutes longer before slipping out of the stall and returning to the far end where he climbed the ladder and, once again, stretched out on the straw and rags that had served Peter for a bed.

It did not weigh heavily on his mind or his conscience that he had killed Peter, since the boy had disobeyed instructions and talked about him to Brother James. It was what he'd suspected from the boy's hesitations, and the monk's words a moment ago had confirmed it. In one way the boy's death had saved him from having to deal with the monk since, if Brother James had turned up a little earlier while Peter was still babbling on, the man would have had some awkward questions to contend with, questions about French spies and the King's business. He guessed that the boy had been eager to lay his hands on a couple more halfpennies before one of the Brethren of the Holy Cross appeared to relieve him of the responsibility for this stranger. He guessed also that the request to see the document with the seal affixed to it was an attempt to distract the man until help arrived.

The man sat up once more and drew the document from beneath his cloak. He cleared away the muck and straw from a patch of planking and smoothed out the parchment on it as best he could in the near darkness. He felt the outline of the seal with his fingers. The parchment, and particularly the leaden emblem at the bottom of it, were worth their weight in gold to him. The image – which showed a knight on horseback, his left side on view – was not a copy of the King's seal. Being caught in possession of that would have been very dangerous. In fact the man was always careful to avoid claiming that it was the King's seal, but said rather that it showed him to be on the King's business, a different matter altogether. If anyone chose to assume that it was the King's seal which they were being shown, then that was their lookout . . .

The parchment and seal passed as the real item when shown quickly to the ignorant, like the stable-boy. Likewise the writing on the parchment was impressive since the penmanship was in what the educated referred to as "document hand", often used for legal and administrative purposes. In addition the words were in Latin, a further bar to the ignorant and the illiterate. The man wasn't sure what they said either, but nor was he about to show them to anyone who might know.

He rolled up the document and returned it to an inner pocket. No doubt it would come in useful again. He lay back once more. The last dregs of light were disappearing from the sky, glimpsed through the gaps and holes in the wooden roof. There was a rustling from down below and then what sounded like someone breathing. For an instant the man thought that Brother James had returned, perhaps with others. Maybe he'd suspected something was wrong all the time and his earlier departure had been a feint. Or maybe the boy wasn't dead after all, and was even now crawling out of the straw which covered him. Or was coming back from the dead, like Lazarus. The man had once watched a play about Lazarus and thought that, if returning to life ever caught on, then his trade would no longer be so secure. But, underneath all these fears, the man knew that the boy was dead as surely as he knew that night was coming on, and within a moment he had mastered his fear and no longer heard the breathing sound.

He slept fitfully. Soon after first light he climbed down from the platform. The air was chill. He retrieved the body of the stable-boy from the stall where he'd concealed it. He carried it back to the foot of the ladder and positioned it approximately where it had lain the evening before. What had seemed warm and light was now cold and heavy as clay. Finally the man clambered a little way up the ladder and, using his dagger, hacked away at a couple of the topmost rungs until they were sufficiently splintered for him to snap them with a blow from his elbow. A cursory look would indicate that the rungs must have given way under Peter's weight and that the boy had fallen to his death in a straightforward accident, while the state of the body, growing stiff and cold, would suggest that this had happened some time during the previous night.

Then the dog-toothed man slipped out of the stables. Since this was a religious house people were already stirring and the bell had chimed for mattins. He waited to make sure that the courtyard in front of the main building was empty before walking across it and out of the gate. The day was dawning fine and the sky was streaked with pink clouds. There was a clump of trees nearby on a mound. The man found himself a position among the trees from which he could keep watch on the entrance to the Maison Dieu but which hid him from view. He did not expect Chaucer and his companions to emerge for some time but he was taking no chances that they might not be making an early start for France. He'd saved a bit of the bread which the boy had brought for him the previous day, and he took small bites out of it while he waited.

4

As the boat battered its way through the water, the people on deck clung to whatever was nearest to hand. The rounded prow came down like a hammer on the waves. The passengers were jolted about, as well as being stung by the spray and the wind. There was a tattered awning of canvas stretched overhead on hoops to protect them from the worst of the weather, but the weather got underneath anyway. Nevertheless being out in the open air, among the ropes and the leather buckets and other deck-clutter, was preferable to being shut up in one of the dungeon-like cabins.

Geoffrey Chaucer noted that Ned Caton and Alan Audly were putting a brave face on things but it was plainly their first time at sea. They'd been lucky, with a favouring wind, and so their ship the *St Thomas* – her name a good omen? Chaucer hoped so – had set off early from Dover. Barring a change in the direction of the wind, barring storms and pirates and acts of God, they ought to be in Calais by the end of the day. A storm looked unlikely, while pirates usually operated in the more open waters to the west. That left acts of God.

Rather than think about dangers over which he had no control, Chaucer kept an eye on his fellow travellers. He wasn't worried that Audly or Caton would do anything foolish, as they had in the Phoenix Inn at Canterbury. There was limited opportunity on a boat, especially if you weren't too comfortable on your legs or in your guts. But in his instinctive way he had rapidly noted the three dozen or more individuals who were out on the deck, apart from the shipman and his mariners. Had noted and dismissed most of them.

Several were part of the English administration in Calais, he judged, civilians based in the castle and working in the tax office or for the wool staple. They had a kind of government stamp or seal on their features – sober-faced, a bit superior – and they kept to themselves. There was a small company of soldiers on their way to the castle garrison which, given the current situation, was most likely being strengthened. Talk of war was in the air. The French were making noises about what they were pleased to call the English "occupation" of Calais, although this might just be their way of diverting attention from what was happening much further south in Aquitaine. The possibility of war did not seem to have deterred visitors, however. There was a brace of women who were chatting with the shipman and whose red and yellow dresses were barely adequate for a wind-blown crossing. Chaucer guessed they were hoping for better pickings on the other side of the water but it might be that they'd hooked an early piece of business. The older of the two woman was fingering a dagger that hung from a cord about the shipman's neck. The master of the vessel was leaning his bearded face in between the two women's. He had a large mouth – like a whale's mouth must be, Chaucer imagined – as if he wanted to swallow the women up wholesale, Jonah-fashion.

But it was the late arrivals on the boat whom Chaucer had been interested in. Several ships were leaving for the French coast more or less at the same moment, taking advantage of the fine morning and favourable wind. For Chaucer, who was no judge of boats, choosing a particular craft had been a matter of impulse. In fact he was heading towards the *Christopher*, a large cog, before he suddenly veered in the direction of the smaller *St Thomas*, moored fifty yards off. Alan Audly said nothing but Ned Caton asked him what he was playing at, irritated at having to carry his luggage any further. What was wrong with the first boat, anyone could see that it was more solid and seaworthy? Chaucer didn't answer. He was too busy watching to see whether anyone else changed direction for the *St Thomas* at the same time as they did. But there were too many people on a quayside which was already crammed with barrels and woolpacks – too many travellers, too many harbourmen, sailors, fishermen, sightseers – for him to be certain whether anyone was following them.

The suspicion had grown in Chaucer over the last couple of days that while they weren't exactly keeping company with anybody, somebody might be keeping company with them. The feeling had been strong on the evening when they'd arrived in Canterbury, only to be driven out of his mind by his companions' antics. Then, on the next day's ride to Dover, it had faded and he'd more or less forgotten about it until they were riding into the port itself . . . Then he felt uneasy once again, even though the gateway was crowded with no more than the usual beggars and idlers. The sensation had persisted as they rode into the forecourt of the Maison Dieu and it had lingered throughout the evening.

It was when they were leaving the Maison Dieu in the early morning, with the sun in his first dazzle, that Chaucer was most conscious of being observed. Others were departing at about the same time as he and Audly and Caton. There was a stir in the area of the stables and Chaucer gathered that there'd been some sort of accident, someone slipping off a ladder. Several black-garbed members of the order were striding or even running in the direction of the stables. However, there was nothing for Chaucer or his companions to do – and experience had taught him that a crowd at accidents often makes matters worse – so they continued through the gate.

A few townsfolk were already out on this bright May morning. There was a clump of trees, almost fully leaved and with dark bands of shadow, which stood on a mound at a little distance from the Maison entrance. If anyone was going to keep watch on the comings and goings from the hospice, that would be the spot to pick, he told himself. Whether it was because he'd jumped to this conclusion or whether because there really was a person in the trees gazing at them – not likely, he thought, not likely at all – Chaucer experienced a prickling on the back of his neck. He ignored it and did not look behind him.

This was the reason Chaucer had changed his mind about the boat at the last moment, and the reason he was especially interested in the passengers who had boarded after he had negotiated their fares with the bearded, whale-mouthed ship-man. Half a dozen pilgrims had scrambled on later. Then there'd been a portly, wheezing merchant – Chaucer knew what he did for a living, he'd heard him attempting to make conversation with the government types when he recovered his breath – who was overseeing a shipment of hides to Calais.

There was also a monk wearing the order of the Holy Cross, the brethren who had charge of the Maison Dieu. Chaucer wondered what he was doing on the *St Thomas*. He thought to ask him about the person who'd slipped off a ladder. Who was he? Was he all right? Was he badly hurt? But the monk was attending to a devotional book and leaning in a particular way against the side of the ship. He looked as though he didn't want to be disturbed but wished himself back in the cloister. A monk out of his cloister was like a fish out of water, they said. If that was so then there were more fish floundering on land than swimming about in the sea these days. Perhaps the Brethren of the Holy Cross had a sister house in Calais. Apart from these obvious passengers there were three or four others he couldn't account for.

Of course he might be absolutely mistaken and there was no one following them. Or, if there was, that unknown individual might have boarded another boat and taken the gamble of arriving in Calais around the same time as the *St Thomas*. He said nothing to Ned Caton or Alan Audly of his suspicions. Meantime the *St Thomas* battered through the waves as if the boat was trying to get them to submit.

Geoffrey Chaucer remembered this crossing on the way to his first campaign in France many years ago. That was the occasion when he had visited the shrine of St Thomas the Martyr in Canterbury. It was already October and the days were growing colder. He remembered his first glimpse of Dover harbour which seemed to contain more boats than water. Chaucer had the sensation of being part of some great river of men flowing in stops and starts down towards the sea. There were unexplained delays, broken by flurries of movement when it looked as though they might be embarking in the next hour. Then, without any order being given, it was understood that they wouldn't after all be leaving for an afternoon, then for a whole day at least and maybe another night as well. They shrugged off their kit and settled down to eat, to talk and tell jokes, to play games, to speculate, to sleep.

Geoffrey Chaucer had been part of the retinue of Lionel, Duke of Clarence (one of King Edward's sons – he was dead now), but a very junior, inessential part. Not quite twenty in the autumn of 1359, he was older than his years. He already knew that those who talked most confidently, even boastfully, about the coming campaign were the ones whose expectations were likeliest to be overturned. He kept his own counsel. He listened to the talk swirling round him about the chances of booty, the prospect of ransom, the spoils of war.

For himself, he was excited and frightened in equal measure. He watched some of the boats being loaded with their oddly domestic gear – little hand-operated mills for grinding corn, ovens to bake the bread in, whole kitchens it seemed – together with all the animal accessories required by the nobility, not for their fighting but for their hunting. The falcons and coursing-dogs were handled with kid gloves while the ordinary enlisted men were treated like animals. The soldiers' equipment, their helmets, hauberks and the rest, was casually piled in carts along the sides of which clanked rusty cooking pots. If you closed your eyes it sounded like an army of tinkers. Chaucer was curious to see little flat boats with leather skins being embarked on the larger craft, and was told that they were for fishing on the French lakes and rivers, so that the King at least would be assured of a supply of food during Lent. It was mid-autumn now, and Geoffrey suddenly saw how long this campaign might last.

King Edward was angling for bigger fish than could be found in country ponds, since he intended to dredge up the French crown itself from the murky mud of claim and counter-claim. The French king, who was known as "John the Good", was in England during that period, living the luxurious life that was fitting for a royal hostage. But his son the dauphin was still in Paris. Charles was a tougher nut than his father, unwilling to give way to English demands. Accordingly Edward had announced his intention to march on Rheims, there to be crowned in the cathedral like a regular king of France.

It didn't work out like that of course. They beseiged Rheims but never even got into the city, let alone celebrated a coronation. The expedition petered out in a quagmire of sickness and hunger and filthy weather. Chaucer himself had been captured and, briefly, been a prisoner. Captivity wasn't necessarily to be feared. A prisoner was spared outright battle or the almost daily skirmishes between the two sides. Prisoners, at least well-born ones, were treated almost as respectfully as the king's falcons and coursers. Noble captives who could be ransomed were as good as money under the mattress. And the brief time in captivity had brought Geoffrey Chaucer close to Rosamond de Guyac. So when it came time to leave – the ransom of sixteen pounds having been paid by the Keeper of the King's Wardrobe – he quit France with plenty of backward glances.

Shortly afterwards an uneasy peace broke out between the two neighbours. But the easygoing John the Good died and the harder-nosed dauphin Charles took over, wanting to kick out the English altogether. He proceeded by guile and diplomacy, rather than the open warfare which was the resource of honourable kings like his father. Guile and diplomacy seemed to be working, albeit slowly. So now, more than ten years on, England was struggling to hold on to the great swathe of territory in the south-west known as Aquitaine or Guyenne. It turned on the loyalty of a few Gascon lords, and how willing they were to maintain their links with the "old country". How much the lords felt they owed to her. How much she could still do for them.

One of these lords was the Comte de Guyac. Chaucer remembered him clearly and with some fondness, since it was the Comte who had, indirectly, received him as a prisoner during the siege of Rheims. Geoffrey Chaucer, son of a wine merchant, had become the prize of a nobleman whose domain in western Aquitaine covered an area equivalent to many Londons, a man who could have bought out all the merchants in the Vintry ward without noticing the difference to his exchequer. It was this old connection between the famous house of Guyac and Geoffrey Chaucer that had led directly to his present mission.

Chaucer's capture at the seige hadn't been a glorious fight-to-the-finish. Geoffrey, together with half a dozen others, was a couple of miles from the city of Rheims, whose unbroken walls were visible in the intervals between rain and mist. It was a day or two before Christmas Eve. The English nobility were feasting as if there was no war on, taking turns to play host to each other in their tents or requisitioned houses. But the other ranks were frequently left to their own devices. So Chaucer found himself with four or five companions from the fringes of Lionel's retinue crouched round a meagre fire, made from the charred timbers of a torched barn, and roasting whatever they'd managed to forage. It was only mid-afternoon but growing dark. Maybe they didn't expect enemy action – after all, their own leaders were preparing to celebrate the birth of Our Saviour as if peace and goodwill had genuinely broken out on the earth for ever – because one moment they were joking and recalling somewhat bitterly what they'd be doing in England if they weren't on this godforsaken campaign (already they knew it was doomed, this attempt on the French crown) and the next a ring of armed men had sprung up from the gloom of the surrounding trees.

Chaucer and his fellows had taken off their sodden mail and were swaddled in cloaks and blankets that would soon be just as sodden. Their weapons were more carefully wrapped, to protect them from the rain. One of their number made to resist and was run through within seconds. Another tried to flee but was tripped and fatally wounded in the thigh. Then the leader of this French band of irregulars called on them to surrender. He might have had them killed, a bunch of bedraggled English youths sitting round a cooking fire, but since they were wearing some important man's insignia he must have worked out that they were valuable even if he didn't recognize the badge of Lionel, Duke of Clarence.

For an instant Chaucer considered resistance. But in the gathering dark he saw the fellow he'd been talking with only moments earlier lying face down on the ground and another fellow, still alive but with red pumping from his upper leg as if his body wanted to get rid of the blood as fast as possible, and he decided that this was not the moment to resort to arms.

They'd spent the night shivering in the ruins of the nearby barn, the dozen or so captors and the four surviving captives. The man with the leg wound had been left to die in the dark on the marshy ground. Either it did not take long or else he was tough for Chaucer heard no sound other than a single cry. Then as soon as dawn broke, with the sun shivering behind mist, they were marched the few miles westwards to Cernay, a town still under

French control. There the prisoners were split up and Chaucer found himself in the hands of the Comte de Guyac who was taking temporary refuge in the town. Through some complicated system of obligation which Chaucer didn't understand at the time, the leader of the band of irregulars was under the direction of a local landowner who was related to the Comte. The landowner would have expected to make a small profit on Chaucer by ransoming him but Guyac offered to "look after" the Englishman until the ransom was forthcoming. And so Geoffrey Chaucer was handed over to Henri de Guyac, while the other three prisoners were surrendered to the marshal of Cernay.

Within a day Chaucer was moving south with Guyac and his retinue. He had given his word not to try to escape and so was lightly guarded. It took them several days' hard riding to reach Guyac's stronghold in Aquitaine. They rode over Christmas Day, stopping at a chapel in the morning, and arrived at Guyac on New Year's Day. Chaucer wondered at the nobleman's interest in him, since it must stretch beyond the matter of ransom (which would in any case not be paid to Guyac but to his French kinsman). The Comte de Guyac had evidently recognized some affinity with his young prisoner. Early maturity perhaps. He was ten or more years older than Chaucer. His father had perished during the plague of '49 and, with no brothers living, he had taken on the responsibility of Guyac and its estates.

Maybe he was also predisposed in favour of Chaucer and his countrymen because he had spent some time in England himself. Indeed, his father had died while he was cutting a fine figure in the English court. By his own account, Henri de Guyac had indulged himself, cuckolding other men with abandon, sowing his seed in fertile ground. He hinted at worse things besides. But the death of his father (and the realization of new responsibility) sobered him and, as he told Chaucer, this was compounded by what happened on his return. He had

51

almost drowned when his ship went down. By chance, he was rescued on the Brittany shore, the sole survivor from his craft. A man – an ordinary, humble fisherman – had risked his own life to rescue Henri from the waves. "I tell you, Geoffrey, that I made a promise to God that if I was saved I would lead a better life in the future. Unlike many men who forget such promises once they are safe, I have kept my word." Chaucer didn't doubt that once de Guyac had determined on something he would stick to it. Any promise made wasn't so much to God as to himself.

Standing on the pitching deck of the *St Thomas*, Geoffrey Chaucer recalled Henri de Guyac. His Gascon captor was not a handsome individual. Short and almost swarthy, he'd reminded Chaucer of one of the labourers who unloaded barrels of wine on the Thames wharf near his family home. Guyac was most comfortable in the saddle. Hunting was his passion. He was a resolute man, a proud one, sensitive about his honour and the honour of his house.

And then there was Rosamond de Guyac . . .

But Chaucer didn't have the leisure to remember Rosamond just at that moment. A violent motion of the boat caused him to grip hold of a halliard and brought him back to himself, back to years later. The *St Thomas* was a clumsy, clunking vessel, like a plate thrown on to the water. He noticed that Alan Audly and Ned Caton had disappeared, although most of the other travellers were still on deck. The pilgrims were in conversation with the merchant, the monk was still reading his devotional book, the whores were airing the goose-bumps on their bare shoulders. The soldiers had lain down on deck and were trying to sleep. France was no longer a thin line on the horizon but had begun to take on irregular shape.

The sensation of being followed, which had persisted with him for a couple of days, had grown as familiar as a mild ache, always there if nothing else was occupying his head. But he shook off the feeling and looked out towards the growing coastline.

On the other side of the deck the man in the monk's habit observed Geoffrey Chaucer once more inspecting his fellow travellers. The watcher watched. Maybe the civil servant wasn't as bland and incurious as the man had assumed, maybe he was a little more cautious and vigilant. He'd gazed slightly too long at the clump of trees where the man was hiding that morning, a gaze that had had consequences, although not for Chaucer. Even so the man did not think there was anything out-of-the-ordinary in the other's manner at the moment. No suspicion or unease was showing in Chaucer's face.

Meantime the man took care to keep his own face hidden, with the hood of his cowl up. He couldn't afford to be seen bare-headed. He had no tonsure of course, and its absence would immediately reveal that he was not a true religious. Even so the risk of the disguise was worth it, since the monk's habit was as effective as a suit of armour when it came to repelling attention. The talkative merchant had tried to start a conversation with him, but the man had merely looked up, smiled enough to show his bare teeth and resumed his reading. He'd found a book in a pocket of the habit and, assuming that it was a volume of prayer or devotion, was scanning it intently. Like the fraudulent King's seal and document which he carried, it appeared to be in Latin. Perhaps it was not a devotional book at all but a book of dirty rhymes. He'd heard stories about those monks. The idea amused him but he kept his eyes on the page, glancing up from time to time at the breakers which battered continuously against the prow of the *St Thomas*.

It had been a providential moment when one of the monks from the Maison Dieu had wandered in the direction of the copse where the man was lurking. It was just after he'd heard shouting from the courtyard (he couldn't hear the words but guessed that they'd found Peter's body) and after Geoffrey Chaucer and the two younger men started off with their baggage towards the harbour which lay a few hundred yards off. The man needed to keep them in sight but he could not afford to step out from cover too soon, in case Master Chaucer turned his head and noticed him. So it had indeed been providential when the monk strayed by the edge of the copse. Not for the monk though. What was he going to do there? God knows. Have a piss, say his prayers?

"Brother James?" said the man, stepping half out of the shadow of the trees. Before he knew it, he had a plan. The best plans were like this, the ones that arrived in his head from nowhere.

The monk started. He squinted at the speaker. The sun was in his face.

"Brother James? No, I am Brother Hubert."

"No matter who you are," said the other. "I need to speak to Brother James or Brother Stephen straightaway."

"I don't understand," said the monk called Hubert, putting up his hand to shield his eyes. His cowl was down. His head was freshly tonsured. He was quite young and about the same height as the man.

"There is a boy called Peter who works in your stables?"

"I – I think so. What's wrong?"

Evidently the monk didn't yet know about Peter's death. That was good.

"Something terrible has happened to him," said the man. "Come and look."

He glanced about to make sure that no one was watching then reached towards Brother Hubert and almost tugged him into the trees. Whether because the monk was taken by surprise or because he was reassured that this stranger knew the names of several members of his house, Brother Hubert allowed himself to be pulled into the damp, chilly copse. The monk looked at the ground. His eyes hadn't yet adjusted to the shade.

"Something terrible," repeated the man, although the smile on his face contradicted his words. "Poor Peter."

"Where?"

"Not down here, up there."

He raised his left arm and pointed to where the sun was bursting through the branches and the new leaves. He waited until Brother Hubert was looking up, almost directly overhead.

"Surely you can see him?"

"See Peter?"

"Yes."

"In that tree?"

"No, in heaven. See for yourself," said the man, swinging his right arm round, the hand flat and the fingers extended, so that it struck the monk's exposed throat.

Barely two minutes later, the man stepped out of the copse. He travelled light, it was easy for him to assume another's costume, another's identity. He walked briskly, making adjustments to Hubert's habit and cowl as he went. Soon he was in sight of Chaucer and the others. If Master Chaucer had been suspicious before, then he wouldn't think twice when he turned round to see one of the Holy Brethren also walking in the direction of the harbour. The man, who'd decided that until nightfall at least he'd go by the name of Hubert, *Brother* Hubert, was almost disappointed when Chaucer did not turn round to look.

He observed the three men board the *St Thomas* – although not before it seemed that they were going to board a different vessel – and waited his own turn until a gaggle of pilgrims were about to embark. Then he moved ahead of them, strode up the shaky gangplank, paid quickly and took up his position near the prow while the shipman was distracted with the new passengers. The book in Hubert's pocket was a godsend, literally a godsend, giving him something plausible to occupy his hands with during the voyage. His right hand throbbed from where he had struck Brother Hubert and, earlier, Peter the stable-boy. But the new Hubert had almost forgotten those deaths by now and his mind was working on the next few hours even as he attended to his devotions or glanced up at the rolling waves.

5

The *St Thomas* arrived at the English port of Calais in the late afternoon and, because the tide was coming in, she was able to navigate the channel between the sand dunes which protected the town like a pair of folded arms. If the tide had been out the ship would have been forced to wait in open waters until the morning. At the southern end of the channel and guarding the entrance to the harbour stood a fortified tower which Chaucer did not remember from his last expedition more than a decade earlier. In the crisp light from the sea the battlements of the tower seemed to have been cut out of white paper. Soldiers were visible on the parapet. They watched impassively as the cog slid by below them, with her sails furled and her mariners equipped with pole-like oars that helped to push the vessel along and also to keep her off the sandy banks on each side. Once through the channel, the *St Thomas* traversed an estuary on the far side of which were the walls of Calais port.

The harbour, full of boats including several warships as well as merchantmen like the *St Thomas*, lay immediately under the town wall and seemed to be clinging to its shadow. Compared to the ramshackle sprawl of Dover this was a tight little town, an embattled island with marshes on three sides and the sea on the fourth. The surrounding area for several miles in each direction was in English hands. The English Pale, it was called. It was where Chaucer's countrymen had left their mark. But a mark can be erased and this was what made so precarious the position of Calais and half a dozen other castles on the edge of the Pale such as Sangatte and Marck. All it took was one French king determined to recover what he regarded as rightfully his. This precariousness must have accounted for an atmosphere which you could sense before you got off the boat, an atmosphere that was half fear, half excitement.

Chaucer waited for the others to leave the boat before disembarking with Audly and Caton, who had emerged from below decks with an air that suggested they were out for an afternoon stroll. Their sickly complexions indicated otherwise. Chaucer oversaw the departure of the government officials, the merchant, the pilgrims, the monk and the rest of the passengers. He felt happier, or at least more secure, if there was no one behind him. Even so he was unable to shake off that sense of being observed.

"What now, Geoffrey?" said Alan Audly when they were standing on solid ground once more. He sounded subdued.

"We wait."

So they waited amid the bustle of the quay, with its cries in English and French and Flemish. Waited and watched as the merchant fussed about the little crane which was hoisting his canvas sacks up from the hold, to the evident irritation of the men operating the mechanism. Waited while the garrison soldiers assembled themselves into some sort of order under one of their number and marched themselves through the town gate. Waited until the ship's captain, the man with the whale-mouth, awkwardly descended the *St Thomas* gangplank with the two whores wreathing their arms about him.

"Master Chaucer?"

A man with a mournful expression had appeared on the quay in front of them, as if from nowhere. Without waiting for an answer, the man then said something that struck Audly and Caton as odd. He spoke emphatically.

"*Flee from the crowd . . .*"

" . . . *and dwell with truthfulness*," said Chaucer with less emphasis.

The two shook hands after this exchange.

"My name is Roger Holly," said the stranger. "You have had a good journey?"

"No disrespect, my friend," said Chaucer, "but ask me that question when we're back at home."

"I have found a room for you. Not so easy, the town is filling up at the moment. It was the last I could get. The Mouton may not be one of the best places in Calais – but it's not one of the worst either."

"Then we shan't stand out."

"You may not stand out but I don't know about your friends," said Holly, looking at Audly and Caton. They were still wearing their embroidered coats, by now somewhat travel-stained.

"They are well behaved," said Chaucer. "There is an innkeeper in Canterbury who can vouch for them."

He introduced Holly to Ned and Alan, who looked a little uncomfortable at the reference to the Canterbury inn, and the three men shook hands.

As they walked through the gate and into the town, Holly explained that he'd also made inquiries about the next boat departure to Bordeaux. He talked too much and seemed eager to please. That eagerness and his large, mournful eyes gave him a dog-like quality. Chaucer and his friends were in luck, he said. Not only was there a ship – the *Arveragus* – due to leave the following morning but it was part of an armed convoy that had escorted a fleet up from Bordeaux and was due to return imminently.

"Escorting the wine fleet?" said Alan.

"No, sir, the wine fleet arrives in October," said Holly. "This was a special convoy. Some of the ladies and gentlemen who live down south are growing a little . . . uneasy at the way things are developing. They have precious things which they wish to transport to England for safe-keeping."

"That's not such a good omen," said Chaucer.

Holly was right about the town. The streets were full, with soldiers swaggering everywhere and energetic trading from the stalls and shops despite the lateness of the day. Holly led them by a roundabout route to a side-street containing their inn, Le Mouton à Cinq Pattes. The faded inn-sign showed a sheep with a grimy fleece.

"Well, at least it doesn't pretend to be anything it's not," said Geoffrey Chaucer, looking at the warped and pitted walls and the clumsily patched roof. "Not mutton dressed as lamb but simply as mutton."

"Look more closely at the sign, sir," said Holly. "Look at the legs on it."

"Why, there are five of them," said Ned Caton.

"Just so," said the short man, tapping the side of his nose. "It was the old landlord's joke, I believe. He was a Frenchman. A five-legged sheep is unique, you see, as he hoped that his inn would be unique. Now the landlord is English but he chose to keep the name."

"A five-legged sheep is *rara avis*, a rare bird," said Ned Caton and laughed at his own joke. Alan Audly did not smile. He hadn't quite recovered from the Channel crossing and looked as though he expected something more comfortable than the Mouton, whether it had four legs or five.

Roger Holly made a show of greeting the innkeeper, whose name was Burley. Despite the name, and against the run of landlords, he was a wisp of a man. Holly explained that these men were the important visitors from England he'd already mentioned. Then Holly insisted on accompanying them to their room, which stood at the end of a passageway. The room was mostly filled by a large bed. A little daylight from a yard penetrated the parchment-covered window.

"Is there anything else I can assist you with, Master Chaucer?"

"There is, Master Holly."

"You have only to say it."

"We are not important visitors, I and my friends. We're on our way to Bordeaux for reasons of trade, the wine trade and nothing else. If anyone asks you what we're doing, that should be your answer."

"But can I ask what it is you are really about?"

"I am about the wine business, Master Holly."

"Very well."

It was obvious from the man's tone that he was offended. Chaucer hastened to mollify him.

"Thank you for what you've done for us so far, Roger. And if you wish to do more, then you may secure us three berths on the *Arveragus* tomorrow."

"Very well again, Master Chaucer. *Delighted* to be of service."

And he walked out, a little less eagerly than when he'd first appeared to them on the harbourside.

"Who was that man?" said Alan Audly.

"Holly is one of Gaunt's agents," said Geoffrey.

"Agents?" said Caton. "Why does he need agents in a place that belongs to the English?"

"This place was French until twenty years ago when they were driven out. There may not be very many of them left here but you can be sure they're not all well disposed towards us. So it is prudent for the King or one of his sons to employ someone to keep an ear open for whispers of discontent."

"Why don't we just go and get the berths on this boat for ourselves?" said Ned Caton.

"Because I don't want to be seen around this town more than I can help," said Chaucer. He said nothing of the sense of being followed. "Calais isn't London, with a whole sea dividing us from our French friends. We are on the border and they are only a few miles off. What we shall do is to have some supper and then some sleep since we don't know how early we'll have to start in the morning."

61

"You sound as if we're on campaign, Geoffrey," said Caton.

"Last time I was in Calais," said Chaucer, "I was on campaign."

Hubert bought Roger Holly another drink. The man with the mournful face was well away. They were sitting in a tavern a few streets distant from the Mouton à Cinq Pattes. Hubert had removed his monk's garb in an alleyway, although he hadn't yet discarded it altogether, not knowing whether it might not come in useful once again. He had bundled Hubert's habit into the grey sack which now sat, plumply, at his feet. He appeared to Holly as an ordinary civilian.

For his part, Holly had already reported to Geoffrey Chaucer on the successful completion of his errand. He'd found them three berths on the *Arveragus* and confirmed that it was leaving for Bordeaux with two other ships on the following morning. Chaucer and his companions were having a meal at the inn where Holly had found a room for them. They didn't invite him to join them. Feeling unappreciated – these Londoners didn't know what it was like for an agent in the field, didn't know what it was like to work alone and unthanked – Holly left the Mouton, head down and brooding.

Within a few minutes he collided with a tall, smiling man. Literally walked into him. The man didn't seem bothered, however, and even claimed that it was his own fault. He was a stranger here, he said, not attending to where he was walking as he should have been but looking around for a decent tavern. Did they have such a place in Calais, did they have a decent tavern? Minutes later Hubert and Holly were side by side on a bench in the Goutte d'Or.

"What are you doing in Calais, sir?"

"Business," said Hubert.

"Oh business, everyone's here on business. So they say. The wine business?"

Hubert shrugged but said nothing.

"It's a convenient cover, the wine trade."

"I expect it is."

"'Smatter of fact, I've just been on an important piece of business," said the other, tapping the side of his nose.

"You have?" said Hubert.

"Hush hush," said Roger.

"Then I won't ask you. Call me Hubert."

"And I won't tell you . . . Hubert. To be honest, I couldn't tell you. Kept in the dark, I am."

"Given the run-around," said Hubert, smiling slightly in sympathy.

"An errand boy, finding rooms for them, getting them their passage on a boat. Gentlemen from London!"

"Which boat would that be?"

"That would be the *Arveragus*."

"Oh, I know it. Bound for Cadiz."

"Bordeaux, my friend. Leaving first thing tomorrow."

"Where are they staying, these gentlemen from London?"

"Why do *you* want to know?" said Roger Holly, his large eyes narrowing slightly. Hubert realized that he wasn't as well oiled as he appeared to be.

"Why do I want to know? Because they're comfortably lodged no doubt, being gentlemen from London. Somewhere I might like to stay myself. I'm from London too. A big and crowded city. Sometimes I want to *flee from the crowd* . . . "

Hubert let his last words hang in the air. He was gratified to see the other pause with his tankard on the way to his lips. Roger Holly turned and gazed up at the man beside him on the bench. Hubert watched him gulp, his Adam's apple bobbing in surprise.

" . . . *and dwell in truthfulness*," added Holly eventually. "Why didn't you say so earlier?"

"Just a test. To see how much you would give away without any prompting."

"I didn't give anything away. Only the name of a boat."

"No more did you, Roger Holly. You can be pleased with yourself. I shall report back favourably."

"So you're with this Geoffrey Chaucer and his friends, are you?"

"Not so much *with* them as keeping an eye on them. They're not to know it though. Orders from across the water. You understand?"

"Oh, orders from across the water is one thing I do understand," said Roger.

"But I do need to discover where they're staying."

"If you're keeping an eye on them, Hubert, why don't you know where they are already?"

"Because, Roger, I lost sight of them in the crowd on the quayside," said Hubert, smiling outwardly and reflecting inwardly that this was the first accurate statement he'd made since the two of them had sat down together in the Goutte d'Or. It also occurred to him that Holly was on the alert now. Maybe it had been a mistake exchanging the password sentence. He glanced once again at the man's Adam's apple, bobbing this time because Holly was taking a swig of ale while pondering whether to answer the other's question about their lodging. If Hubert had been planning a longer stay in Calais, then it might have been necessary to take preventative action against Master Holly. As it was, after what he'd heard, he intended to be out of town before daybreak.

Roger put his tankard down on the table and said, "You've heard of Le Mouton à Cinq Pattes?"

"It sounds familiar."

"You can recognize it by its sign. Rather a strange sign it has."

"Describe it to me, Roger."

A half-hour or so later Hubert was looking at the very sign. He could not make out anything of the five-legged sheep other than a pale smudge on a board which creaked slightly in the gathering dark. He tucked himself into a doorway on the other side of the street. The street was empty and narrow enough that he could almost have touched the wall of the inn opposite by stretching out his arm. The curfew bell had rung. If discovered out of doors by the watch he would have had to answer some questions. But he would not be discovered. Hubert did not have much respect for the watch, whatever town he was in.

He'd found out that Chaucer and his companions were lodged on the ground floor at the rear of the inn. He hadn't asked Holly any more questions. The man was balanced between eagerness to help and a simple suspicion. Before leaving him in the Goutte d'Or he'd enjoined him to silence. "Lives depend on it," he said. He meant Holly's life. It was fortunate for him that he'd bumped into Master Holly since he had in fact lost the trail of Chaucer and the others in the crowded streets of the town. He would have tracked them down sooner or later but it was a task made easier by seeing again the little man whom he'd already spotted talking to Chaucer on the harbourside.

Hubert considered the possibilities for action.

He favoured fire. Fire was clean and decisive, fire was a smoker-out of secrets. Once he had been commissioned to steal some jewels from a London widow who lived in a fine house near Ludgate. He'd inveigled his way into the house as a servant. The widow kept the jewels hidden in a particular room in her house. He couldn't find out which room though. So he had started a small fire. He used dirty rags in a bucket to produce as much smoke as possible. By the time it was over, he knew where the jewels were, since the woman had run to their hiding-place (behind a wall panel) to retrieve them. The widow had returned the jewels afterwards when she realized the house was safe. Hubert – although that was not his name at the time – had covertly observed all this even while he was among the household members dousing the fire, which had spread beyond its original site in the bucket. He waited several days before taking the golden brooches, pins and necklaces from their place behind the panelled wall. An hour later Hubert was handing over the valuables to the widow's brother, who had commissioned the theft, and receiving his cut.

Hubert had employed fire on other occasions. He liked the clamour it provoked. He relished the difference between fire's silent creeping and the uproar when people scented the smoke. The confusion and panic. So now, crouched in the doorway opposite the Mouton à Cinq Pattes, he considered that the best way forward would be through flame. He didn't think it would be as straightforward this time as it had been with the widow. Chaucer might be carrying what Hubert was looking for. But there was a chance that he'd secreted it somewhere in the inn-room, and would scrabble to save it from the flames. That would be best.

Hubert slipped down an alley beside the inn, which was hardly wide enough to accommodate his shoulders. His eyes were used to the dark by now. He clambered over a wall into a yard. No dogs here. His luck was holding. It was his experience that if you believed yourself lucky, you generally were.

At the far end of the yard nearest to the inn the glow of a candle was visible through a small ground-floor window covered with stretched parchment. From Holly's description of Chaucer's lodging, he guessed that was where they must be. Once again, he settled down to wait, sitting with his back against a wall and his legs stretched out. Shortly afterwards the candle was snuffed out. Some time later a back door into the yard opened. Hubert had not been asleep, not even nodding, and he was on the alert at once. The figure of a man emerged uncertainly into the yard. Hubert tensed, then relaxed as the figure halted outside the back door and stood with straddled legs, fumbling at his garments. Just someone pissing. One of the two younger men, Hubert thought, Caton probably from his height. The pisser finished, looked up at the emerging stars then went back indoors. The door creaked shut.

Still Hubert waited. There was no sound apart from the intermittent barking of dogs and someone shouting, both in the far distance. Then even that stopped. A late moon, growing towards the full, began to rise. A cat paced deliberately across the yard. If he'd been superstitious he would have taken that as a bad sign. It was growing colder, with a wind picking up from the sea, but Hubert did not move. These moments he enjoyed, when everyone was dead to the world and he was alone and wakeful and bent on mischief. Last night he had been in the stable of the Maison Dieu with the body of Peter hidden under the straw of a stall, while this morning he had been in the grove with the monk dead at his feet, and now here he was in the yard of a Calais inn, on the other side of a sea but under the same moon, about the same trade.

Hubert unfastened his grey sack, which still contained the dead monk's outfit. Underneath that were various items which he always carried, such as a long cord and a selection of daggers. With practised hands he placed a couple of little leather pouches on the ground. If it had been daylight and sunny, he would have simply used a burning-glass. Night-time called for special measures and was more difficult. On the other hand, a fire after dark was always more . . . productive.

Hubert had already observed that the yard was littered with scraps of wood from the place where logs were split, as well as other waste. Moving silently, he assembled a little mound of the stuff underneath the window from where he'd glimpsed the candlelight. He went back and brought the leather bags to this point. He pulled at the drawstrings of each and reached inside. From one he extracted a flint and a piece of steel shaped with a hand-hold. From the other bag he carefully drew out a small segment of material with the stiffness and texture of a sliver of charcoal. This was charred cloth – ordinary cloth treated by being heated in a sealed pot – which would take fire at the slightest spark. The spark would progress from flint to cloth to wood shavings to the timber of the house, as nimbly as a cat jumping. An old building like the Mouton à Cinq Pattes was built mostly of timber which, dry and warped, should catch nicely. Hubert did not intend to kill anyone in their beds – although if that happened it could not be helped – but merely to roust the occupants of this room and to take advantage of the confusion which followed.

Kneeling over the pile of waste matter, he gripped the steel in his left hand and the flint in his right. He scraped the flint against the steel. Sparks showered on to the charred cloth which after a moment glowed red. He bent down and blew on the cloth until it flared up. The little flame seized on the surrounding fragments of wood and very soon it had grown into a useful fire as big as a man's fist, then two fists. Using a larger chunk of wood Hubert shoved the flickering mass up against the wall. Then he eased open the back door to the inn and slipped inside. Once in the passage he crouched on his hams. This should not take long at all.

Inside his room in the Mouton à Cinq Pattes, Geoffrey Chaucer turned uneasily in the shared bed. There was scarcely space for the three of them. He was on the outside. Ned Caton and Alan Audly were sleeping soundly – soundly in every sense, he thought, with their quota of sighs, snores and farts. No wandering off in search of Calais landladies and their daughters tonight. No picking of quarrels over the quality of wine they'd been served at supper. Away from the security of home ground, they seemed less full of themselves. Chaucer was glad that they were subdued. His task was difficult enough without being required to act as a restraint on two hotheads. Why had John of Gaunt landed him with these two?

I can travel alone, he'd said to Gaunt. I'll find a local guide.

You can't travel alone, said Gaunt. Aquitaine is dangerous territory now. It's on a knife-edge. French Charles said last year that he intended to confiscate Aquitaine. Nobody knows why he hasn't repeated the claim yet. It's only a matter of time before he does.

I know, said Chaucer, thinking that he didn't need a lesson in recent history and what the French king had or hadn't said.

My brother Edward's losing his grip down there. You need protection, that's why you can't go alone. I can't afford to lose my poet.

I'm not a poet, I'm a maker.

Whether you call yourself maker or poet, I would not want to lose you – either of you.

Then don't send me, said Chaucer before adding as an afterthought, My lord.

There is no one else to send, Geoffrey, said Gaunt. You alone have the connections to the Comte de Guyac . . . and his family . . . and the skills of rhetoric to make sure he doesn't throw in his lot with the French king. The gift of persuasion. You're a poet, for God's sake! What else do poets do except persuade us of things that never were nor ever shall be? They can achieve the impossible.

Is this an impossible task?

Not for someone of your genius, said Gaunt.

Flattery, said Chaucer.

Yes, use flattery, use whatever it takes.

That wasn't what I meant, my lord. But if you're going to despatch me to Aquitaine with an escort then at least give me people who can take care of themselves as well as me.

And what had he got? Alan Audly and Ned Caton, two young bloods who'd already behaved like characters out of some bawdy fabliau of bed-hopping and mistaken identities. They were a liability. Unless there was something more to their

69

presence . . . Instinctively he felt round his neck for the wallet which he had not taken off since leaving his Aldgate house. Gaunt had entrusted its contents to him, telling him to use them only as a last resort.

Some disturbance beyond the cramped bedroom brought Chaucer out of his reverie. A quick scraping from the outside. Once, twice, three times. Then no more. It sounded like a flint. After a short while, there came the noise of the outer door being opened. Someone going for a piss in the yard as Caton had done earlier? But you wouldn't need a light for that.

Chaucer half sat up in the shared bed. He was growing impatient with these nocturnal disturbances. Lie down and go to sleep, he told himself. You've an early start tomorrow to catch the tide. Then it occurred to him that the opening door could mean someone coming *into* the building, not leaving it. Next, a sweetish scent filled his nostrils.

Chaucer was out of the bed before he was aware of it and into the passage. The door to the yard was half open. He ran outside, wearing only his shirt and leggings. Flames were licking at the exterior wall of the bedroom and sparks shooting into the air. He looked about the yard for buckets, for a water barrel but, after staring at the darting flames, his eyes were dazzled and he was able to make out nothing clearly. He raced back inside and seized the blanket off the sleeping forms of his companions, at the same time shouting at them. He couldn't have said afterwards what words he shouted, whether it was their names or a command or a warning.

Outside again, he made to throw the blanket over the fire to smother it. But before he could do so he was encircled by a pair of arms. For an instant he thought it was one of the others playing a joke, but only for an instant. He felt hot breath on the back of his neck as an arm moved up and folded around his throat. The fire danced and sparks shot upward ever more frantically. He felt the heat of it on his face. Chaucer's hands were impeded by the blanket and it took a moment before he threw it to the ground and freed his hands. By this point, the other man's fingers were fumbling with the cord which hung in a loop from his neck. If his assailant hadn't already had his other arm wrapped around Geoffrey's throat he would have found it easier to tear the cord away – the cord and the leather wallet which was attached to it.

Geoffrey felt the pressure on his windpipe grow even as he fastened both his hands on the other's fingers while they were picking and twisting at the cord. By bending back one of the man's fingers he succeeded in prising all of them loose. But this only made the situation worse, since Hubert now employed his unoccupied hand to reinforce the other arm angled across Geoffrey's neck. Chaucer's head was being forced up and back. His assailant was taller than him. Certainly he was stronger. The poet heard the crackling of the burning wall. He felt sick and dizzy. An uncomplete moon swam across his blurred vision. He thought, I shall not live to see her at the full again. He could feel the heat of the fire on his knees and now a roaring in his ears had replaced the sound of burning wood.

His attacker was shaking him from side to side, as a dog might shake a rat. He seemed to have grown several arms, all of them waving about in the night air. Then the grip around his poor neck loosened before falling away altogether. Geoffrey tumbled down backwards on the ground.

A little time passed. He lay there, concentrating on forcing air through his windpipe. It hurt to breathe but he was still alive. Faces loomed over him, lit by flickering flames.

"Geoffrey, are you all right?" said Ned Caton.

"What happened?" said Alan Audly.

Even in his discomfort he noticed the concern in their voices. Maybe I've wronged them, he thought. They are good folk, Ned and Alan, good souls. Instinctively he reached for the cord and the wallet round his neck. Still there, thank God.

He tried to speak but no words came out, only a wheezing sound. He raised his head. There were a group of people dancing in front of the fire. Why were they dancing? No, not dancing but trying to douse the flames. Water arced through the smoky air, expelled from hand-held buckets. People raked at burning chunks of wood so the flames had less to feed on. Sparks flickered like fireflies. A large blanket was thrown over a portion of the blaze. The blanket sizzled and steamed, and Chaucer realized that it must have been immersed in water.

It wasn't surprising that so many people were ready to attend to the fire, as well as knowing what to do about it without being told. Towns and fires went together. You could not get through a six-month period without an alarm in your street. Most city blazes were quickly quenched because they had to be. You did your utmost to save a neighbour's house from the flames because you knew that yours would be next if you didn't. At least it was so in London, and Chaucer saw that it was the same in Calais, perhaps especially in this district of old wooden dwellings.

Audly and Caton helped Chaucer to his feet. By now the fire had been brought under control. Men were stamping out smouldering pockets of flame with a kind of gleeful relief. The three Englishmen stared at the blackened, gaping side of the room where they had recently been sleeping. The whole business, Chaucer realized, had lasted only a few minutes, from his hearing the scraping of steel and flint until now. He looked around the yard. It was full of people in their night garments. Inn servants, travellers staying the night, no doubt a scattering of neighbours as well. Was his attacker among them?

"Did you see him?" he said, surprising himself with how normal he was able to make his voice sound.

"We were woken by your call," said Ned. "We ran out here."

" A man had you by the throat," said Alan. "We beat him off."

"He got away," Caton said, gesturing towards the wall that

bordered one side of the yard. "I saw him jump over it like a dog in heat. Who was he?"

"I don't know."

"What was he after then?"

This, Chaucer almost said, fingering the wallet that hung beneath his shirt, *I believe he was after this*. But he turned the movement into a random, scratching gesture.

"I don't know," he repeated. "Trying to burn down this inn, I suppose."

"We could have died in our bed," said Alan.

"While I almost certainly would have died out here," said Geoffrey Chaucer. "It was lucky you two turned up when you did. Thank you."

By this time the fire was thoroughly extinguished. The side of the room in which Chaucer and the others had been sleeping was a mess of blackened wood and plaster but, thanks to the prompt arrival of help, the flames had spread no further. Richard Burley, the landlord of the Mouton à Cinq Pattes, could turn his attention to where it had started, how it had started. The usual cause was to be found indoors in a carelessly dropped candle or a kitchen accident. Since this blaze had begun in the region of Chaucer's room, he or his companions might have been blamed. But the signs were obvious enough on the ground of the yard. Someone had deliberately attempted to fire the inn from the exterior. It was arson, and it was a wicked crime. If caught, the perpetrator would have been summarily hanged by the city authorities. The watch was summoned and made a search of nearby streets but it was for form's sake only.

Chaucer explained that he had smelled burning, come outside and been set on. No, he had no idea who his attacker was or what he'd been after if it was anything other than confusion, ruin and destruction. That's enough, isn't it? To his credit, Richard Burley was more concerned for the welfare of his guests than the damage to his inn. Maybe he recalled Holly's words that these were important visitors. He lamented the fact that their clothing and baggage had been thoroughly smoked. He found them another bed in his own quarters at the inn. He wished them a good sleep for the few hours that remained until dawn and then went off to attend to the damage.

They were unable to sleep. The realization that they had been close to death, in different forms, banished sleep. For himself, Chaucer was confirmed in his suspicion that they hadn't been unaccompanied in their journey so far. For Audly and Caton, the fire and the attack on Chaucer turned what had been a kind of jaunt into something earnest and dangerous.

They rose early the next morning and made their way to the harbour. Three armed boats with high forecastles – the *Arveragus*, the *Dorigen* and the *Aurelius* – were waiting for the tide to begin the long haul back to Bordeaux. They boarded the *Arveragus*.

6

The voyage to Bordeaux was expected to take more than a week, if they were lucky. Without luck, the shipman told them, it might take twice that. That's if they got to their destination at all, he said. There's luck, there's bad luck, and then there's disaster. Get there at all, what with the pirates . . . and the Spanish . . . and the rocks . . . and the French . . . and the winds and the waves . . . and the monsters who lived under the sea. Always assuming of course that, before any of these contingencies, the *Arveragus* didn't spring a leak because the seams hadn't been properly caulked. Or that a fire didn't break out on board and burn them all to cinders. Or that the gang of soldiers and archers they were transporting didn't up and slit their throats one fine night.

The shipman of the *Arveragus* was Master Jack Dart. He had a face like crumpled parchment.

"Why does he do it, Geoffrey?" said Ned Caton. "Put the wind up us like that, telling us we'll most likely never reach our destination. He likes saying that worse things happen at sea."

Chaucer was reading, sitting not very comfortably with his back against a bulwark. It was a method of keeping out of the spray and the occasional sun. He wasn't so bothered about himself as concerned to protect the little book which he was holding in one hand. The pages were not covered in beautiful script but in a sometimes scrawled handwriting that only he could read with ease. The book was cheaply bound. It wasn't valuable but it had taken him a long time to copy it out from the original, a task he would not relish doing again. Chaucer looked up. He'd already noticed Audly and Caton being lectured by the shipman.

"Maybe he enjoys putting the wind up you," he said. "Or maybe this is his way of warding off trouble, to talk all the time about the worst in the hope that Fortune will take pity on him and deliver the best – or at least the bearable."

"Fortune isn't so easily deceived," said Alan Audly sagely. "What are you reading, sir?"

"As chance would have it, I am reading about Fortune," said Geoffrey, holding up the small volume. "This is Boethius and his *Consolation of Philosophy*. You've read Boethius?"

They hadn't.

"I recommend him," said Geoffrey, "especially when you're on a voyage. Boethius puts things in perspective when you're all at sea."

He stood up, placing the compact volume carefully under his clothing. A breeze was blowing from the east and the high-ended *Arveragus* rolled slowly down the Channel, the coastline of Picardy to their left. Running slightly astern were the other ships in the convoy, the *Dorigen* and the *Aurelius*. There was strength in numbers and the shipman of each would do his best to ensure he stayed in sight of the others. All three vessels were designed to carry troops and, if necessary, to fight on the water. The forward and stern areas of the *Arveragus* were raised high above the deck, and protected by shield-like fixtures which gave them the appearance of little castles. The deck itself was cluttered, not just with men-at-arms, but with military equipment being transported down to Bordeaux, principally new-fangled bombards for projecting stone balls over a distance. These were shrouded under canvas and guarded by the bombard-men, who tended to swagger because they were associated with the latest "secret weapons", as one of the bombard-men referred to them. Chaucer, who'd done a bit of campaigning, was amused by the expression.

Whatever scepticism Chaucer showed concerning these secret weapons was as nothing compared to the mockery heaped on them by the detachment of archers which was also being transported to Aquitaine in the *Arveragus*. The archers huddled towards the fore of the boat, a class apart under the command of a fat, pocky-faced bowyer and fletcher named Bartholomew. The archers talked shop, comparing the shapes of feathers and boasting of how they'd single-handedly won every battle since the days of Adam. Ned Caton said that the enemy must have died not of flights of arrows but from a hail of boredom, and when he was overheard by one of the archers a fight broke out between the two of them. Chaucer was privately impressed by the way Caton handled himself in the scrap, though he helped to separate the combatants and rebuked Caton afterwards. But relations between the archers and the bombard-men were even worse. Some days it seemed as though the war might break out prematurely on the deck of the *Arveragus*. Jack Dart showed himself a skilful diplomat, however, and frequently brought peace between the two factions. For all his gloomy talk, he was no bad master.

It was a wearisome, sometimes tense voyage. Chaucer and the rest of the better-off passengers were lodged in the after-castle which contained a group of tiny, shared berths as tight as a honeycomb but by no means as sweet. They retreated to this fuggy, rat-infested accommodation only to sleep or to escape the weather. The enclosed smell was made worse by the frequency with which the little terracotta pots – for the night relief of passengers or for the use of those afflicted by seasickness – were knocked aside by careless feet or spilled by the rolling of the ship. The bombard-men slept on the breezy deck while the archers lay down in the stench of the forecastle, a place inferior even to the after-castle. Each group believed that the other was worse accommodated and so was satisfied.

Twice a day a trumpet tooted and the passengers would crowd round a table fixed to the deck near the after-castle. There, those who had the cash could buy garlic and onions, bread and cheese, walnuts and dried meat. None of this proved very appetizing even at the beginning of the voyage. The bread was hard and the walnuts were stale, the blocks of cheese were largely a habitation for maggots, while the strips of meat had the consistency of leather. Only the wine was of any quality, and that not very high.

Time hung heavy as they crawled down the coast first of Picardy then of Normandy, sometimes out of sight of land. At first Chaucer used the enforced idleness to read his beloved Boethius. Quite often his mind turned to Philippa and Elizabeth and little Thomas. By the time he returned there should be an addition to his family. He remembered the milky smell of the last baby, held by the wet-nurse. He thought of his wife's unhappiness at his departure and wished he could go back and relive the moment and say the right things.

And he thought too of Rosamond de Guyac, since every breath of wind pushed him closer to his destination.

Although he had been her husband's prisoner, Chaucer spent much time with Guyac's wife. She was several years younger than Henri but taller than him, and her skin was fair where his was weather-beaten. Chaucer was entranced. They talked of books and poetry. Whereas with the man, the conversation had been about honour, with the woman the talk turned to verses about love, beauty and romance.

Chaucer remembered in particular Rosamond reciting a poem which she had off by heart. Ostensibly she spoke it to show the superiority of verses written in French to verses written in English. It wasn't a point which he would have contested anyway, and certainly not after hearing her speak. In the poem she detailed the fine features of an imagined girl who, after referring to her delicate eyebrow or her white breasts, asked at the end of each stanza: "*Suis-je belle? Ah, suis-je belle?*"

The words were provoking but, underneath the tease, there was a note of appeal as if the girl – or as if Rosamond herself – was seeking reassurance. The final line of the last verse was *"Etais-je belle? Ah, etais-je belle?"*, and a different note entered her voice as she acknowledged the inevitable fading of her beauty, not tomorrow perhaps, but all too soon.

Chaucer had fallen in love with Rosamond. It was almost his duty as a young man to fall in love with a beautiful married woman, only a year or two older than himself. It was what knights did in days of yore, as they said in the stories. But his passion was quite as hopeless as a knight's in some story. More hopeless since in romances a happy ending was usually guaranteed or, even better, a tragic ending. The outcome here was neither happy nor tragic. For one thing Rosamond had children – indeed she had just borne her first son after two daughters – and children are an issue that don't usually feature in romances. For another, Chaucer wasn't even a knight, merely a squire or a jumped-up yeoman, while Rosamond de Guyac was a woman who had grown used to looking out of any window in the castle at Guyac and seeing a view which revealed no end to the lands controlled by her husband. A woman married to one of the most powerful men in Aquitaine.

Nevertheless, when Chaucer was ransomed and so had to leave the domain of Guyac he wrote a poem for Rosamond. The poem was about a man released from captivity who finds himself still in thrall to love. Since he knew that he would probably never see her again, he felt more able to speak his mind on paper. He grew ingenious, balancing the paradoxes of freedom from confinement and captivity in love.

He left the verses in Rosamond's chamber, where she would not find them straightaway. He wondered afterwards how often she read his lines, whether it was many times or whether she had simply glanced at them and then put down the paper, even torn it to pieces.

Geoffrey didn't know what had happened to Rosamond de Guyac. Of course she would be older, like him, older and wiser maybe. He had little idea of her feelings – never had had, perhaps – and he wondered if there was still a flicker burning within him. He would soon find out, though this voyage seemed to be taking an eternity.

For a time, sailing down the coast on the way to Aquitaine, they were driven along by fair winds and distracted by the incomprehensible cries of the sailors to the ship's boys, who did most of the actual work – "Haul in the bowline!" "Hissa!" "Ware the sheet!", that sort of thing. But after rounding the Cape de la Hague the weather turned and they found themselves in more dangerous waters, a sea dotted with rocks like little islands. Nevertheless there was something reassuring in seeing even this evidence of dry land. For Chaucer and his companions, the open sea – once they'd lost sight of terra firma – was a vast expanse of liquid, with nothing to grasp hold of. The *Aurelius* was out of fresh water so the little fleet moored off a larger island where there were plenty of springs. Jack Dart told them that they were lucky to be part of a well-defended convoy since the inhabitants of neighbouring Sark were in the habit of preying on vulnerable ships. And for once he was not exaggerating. Looking through the drizzle across the few hundred yards of water which separated them from that island, they could see figures standing on the edge of the high granite cliffs, figures still and watchful.

It was some time afterwards that Geoffrey Chaucer found himself telling a tale to his companions. Ned Caton had asked to borrow his copy of Boethius. Chaucer was reluctant to lend the precious book to anyone and used as a pretext the difficulty Caton would have in reading his handwriting.

"Even I have difficulty making this out," he said, holding up a particularly scrawled page. "Anyway, why do you want to read it, Ned? Are you after the consolations of philosophy?"

"Ned was looking for something a bit lighter," said Alan Audly.

"Well, there's not much that's light here," said Chaucer with relief, tucking the book away.

"A story for example," said Alan. "A tale of bawdy or a romance. Something to while away this tedious journey."

"Oh, a story . . . if it's a story you're after now . . ."

That was what they expected. He was a poet, wasn't he, a maker. The ship was beginning to wallow in rough seas, the sky to grow darker. It might be summer on land but not on the sea. Geoffrey Chaucer cudgelled his brains.

"There was once a young man who . . . no, a young woman who . . . lived on that shore over there," Chaucer began. He gestured in the direction of the coast of Brittany, a low black line to their left. "Her name was . . . let us say, her name was Dorigen."

"Like the boat?" said Alan, jerking his thumb over his shoulder at the vessel that wallowed in their stern.

"Yes, it's as good a name for a woman as for a vessel. Better maybe. In fact my other characters will also be named after our boats. Dorigen was a lady, and recently married. The man who'd wooed and married her was a knight called . . . Arveragus, like this vessel."

"Naturally," said Ned Caton.

"Arveragus had great difficulty in winning her hand in marriage, she was so difficult and stand-offish, he thought. But she was merely behaving as a lady was supposed to behave in those days. Everything changed when they were married."

"For the worse?" said Ned.

"That's the usual way, isn't it, Geoffrey?" said Alan.

"In this story it was for the better and not the worse. They truly loved one another, you see, Arveragus and Dorigen. And when they married they made a promise to each other. The promise was – "

But he was interrupted by a call from the lookout platform in the top-castle. Several ships had been sighted ahead of the convoy and nearer to land, their sails already lowered against the worsening weather. Now there was danger not merely in the weather but in the strange ships. Everybody on deck, including Audly and Caton, crowded to the bulwarks or climbed up on the forecastle to get a better view. The archers talked hopefully of the French while Dart the shipman gloomily referred to pirates. But when they got among them, they found that it was a convoy on its way up from Aquitaine, a mixture of merchant ships and armed vessels. Shouted greetings were exchanged, whipped away by the rising wind.

The *Arveragus*, the *Dorigen* and the *Aurelius* ploughed on through lines of black waves rolling endlessly out of the west, each boat labouring heavily in the water, their hulls seeming to dip out of sight below the waves only to be thrown up the next instant so that the rigging stood out sharp against a yellow-tinged sky. The deck of the *Arveragus* was swept by spray and perpetually aslant. Even so, Chaucer preferred to remain outside as long as he could. He felt a hand on his shoulder. It was Alan Audly. His black curls were all bedraggled.

"What happens next, Geoffrey?"

"It's out of our hands, Alan. We can only pray."

"I mean what happens in your story?"

"Oh, the story," said Chaucer. "I'll have to look for a more suitable moment to start it."

"Will it end happily?"

Somehow his words applied to more than just the story.

"End? It's only just begun."

He spoke truer than he knew. The next day and night were the most miserable of the voyage. The three boats made little progress but wallowed in heavy seas. To be out on deck was to be buffeted about and soaked through, with the real danger of being swept overboard by a particularly violent wave. Even the bombard-men were forced to couch with the archers in the forecastle. They were too busy puking and groaning to think of arguing. The shrouded shapes of the bombards, the empty table from which provisions were sold in calmer conditions, the deck-jumble of ropes and buckets – everything looked infinitely frail and insignificant against the wind-torn sky and sea.

But to stay inside was to be thrown about in a pinched, stinking berth, listening to the coughs, groans and retching which encompassed you. It was hellish – or certainly purgatorial. Chaucer tried to gain consolation from Boethius and his philosophy but, on this occasion, the book did not work. Well, he thought philosophically, even the highest philosophy cannot relieve the toothache.

Then the bad weather cleared and they enjoyed several days of uninterrupted sailing. Master Dart, who had been cheerful during the worst of it, returned to his customary gloom. A different territory now lay on their left. This was no longer Normandy or Picardy or Brittany – all of which were either in English hands or disputed between the English and the French – but enemy territory, France herself. Then it was not so long after that they were passing the place near the mouth of the Gironde, Notre-Dame-de-la-Fin-des-Terres, where pilgrims bound for Compostela were accustomed to disembark and give thanks for a safe journey. The convoy did not stop but as they passed the church most of the travellers offered up a prayer to St James for having brought them this far.

The wide mouth of the river marked another dangerous stage, since between the two shores lay a shoal across which the water rippled with deceptive calm. The *Arveragus* carried a pilot who was employed solely to navigate this final stretch and, with the *Dorigen* and the *Aurelius* following suit, he now took the tiller to steer the boat down the channel between the sandbank and the south-westerly side of the estuary. There was a moment when the boat seemed to stick at a shallow spot, quivering like a bird's heart, and then an almighty grinding sent echoes resounding through its frame. But the *Arveragus* eventually shrugged off the obstacle and almost fell into the deeper, faster waters of the river on the far side. The other two vessels slipped through in their wake, unscathed.

There followed a passage of calmer sailing, tacking down the Gironde. On either side of the river, the sun glinted white off the salt-pans while everything beyond was hazed in a gentle heat. Geoffrey Chaucer marvelled again at the size of this great river, dwarfing the Thames even in its least wide stretches. He filled his lungs with the strange, indefinable scents blowing off the land. A land that was indisputably other, indisputably foreign, for all that it belonged to the English. There were boats everywhere, from lumbering cogs and carracks to little dinghies, and he caught occasional cries thrown to and fro. He remembered that they spoke their own tongue down here, close to but not quite French. Some fragments of the language returned to him.

"Well, we've arrived," he said to the shipman who had come to stand nearby.

"Never say so until your feet are on dry ground, Master Chaucer," said Jack Dart, crinkling his parchmenty face. "Worse things happen at sea and ships can sink even in port. We may have sustained some damage crossing the bar back there."

He jerked his thumb over his shoulder. Chaucer wasn't altogether sure what was meant by crossing the bar but assumed the master was referring to the shoal at the river mouth.

Getting confidential and more gloomy, Dart continued, "I once knew a man who slipped as he was descending the gang-plank to his native soil. He cracked his head open on that same soil. And this was after a perilous voyage that provided him with plenty of opportunities to lay down his life, all of which he had neatly side-stepped."

"He died?"

"No, but it was touch and go. See."

Dart took off his cap and lifted up the hank of greying hair that hung halfway down one side of his face. Chaucer saw a queerly shaped hollow in the side of Dart's head as if the bone there had melted.

"I was young and eager. I wanted to get back and see the child which my wife had borne in my absence. You've got children, Master Chaucer?"

"Two, with another on the way."

"I never saw mine. Baby and mother died – died in that order, one after the other – while I was still at sea. I did not know they were dead and ran down the gangplank to plant my feet on dry land. I thought I would be at my house within five minutes. Instead I fell into a black hole of my own carelessness and did not climb out of it for several weeks."

"I am sorry to hear it," said Chaucer.

"It was many years ago, but it taught me that the time when things seem most secure is when they slip from your grasp," said Jack Dart.

"A good lesson."

"I have had another wife since, God rest her. I have had other children too, God rest some of them. What is your business in Bordeaux?"

"What else but the wine business?"

"I prefer the red from further north, from Niort or Rochelle."

"At one time you would have been right, my friend, but Niort produces white wine these days."

Geoffrey had the obscure feeling that the shipman was testing him but at this point Dart was called away by the pilot. Passing a series of barren islands which lay like an exposed spine in the centre of the river, the three-ship convoy swung from the Gironde into the Garonne. Eventually they dropped anchor in front of the great port of Bordeaux. The pale city curved along the western shore of the river, reminding Chaucer of his native

London if only because there were almost as many towers and clanging spires to this place. Smoke from the town forges plumed into the air. The elaborate gables of the private houses nearest the river could be glimpsed over the wall. But then, Chaucer reflected, there was an obligation on Bordeaux to appear prosperous and powerful since this was the place where Edward, Prince of Wales and Aquitaine, most frequently held court.

Audly, Caton and Chaucer were grouped together at the bulwark. Behind them the bombard-men were unshrouding their machines before disembarking. The archers were collecting their more portable gear. On the riverside the city walls were pierced by three vast water-gates and the area between their mooring-place and the walls was busy with dozens of smaller craft.

"Well, we've arrived," said Alan Audly.

"Safely arrived," said Ned Caton.

"Never say so until your feet are on dry ground," said Chaucer. "A wise man told me that."

The three of them were travelling comparatively light and so were off the *Arveragus* in advance of the soldiers, climbing down into the lighters which clustered underneath the larger vessels. At the same time the other non-military passengers were disembarking from the *Dorigen* and the *Aurelius*. Chaucer did not look carefully at the occupants of these other boats. If he had, he might have spotted the man who went by the name of Hubert clambering down the side of the *Dorigen* and settling himself into the stern of a rowing boat which presently pushed off for the city.

7

The first place they stopped at beyond Bordeaux gave them an inkling of the hostile atmosphere of Guyenne or Aquitaine. Chaucer reflected that troubles seemed to arise when they halted for the night. They got off comparatively lightly this time – no farce of swapped beds, no attempt to roast them alive. Still it was worrying, despite the efforts of Jean Cado to brush it off.

Jean Cado was their guide from Bordeaux, a garrulous fellow. A Gascon, he spoke English and French and the local *langue d'Oc*. With his round face and heavy brows, and permanently hunched shoulders, he had a rather owlish look. By pre-arrangement Cado had met them near the Minster of St Andrew's in the middle of Bordeaux. This was the place where Prince Edward held his court. Chaucer and Cado had exchanged the necessary half sentences – *Flee from the crowd . . . and dwell with truthfulness* – and Cado explained that he'd been assigned to them by the Prince's household. His responsibility was to see they reached the stronghold of the Comte de Guyac safely. Chaucer was slightly surprised that their escort was to consist of only one man, but assumed that it was safer to travel unobtrusively rather than surrounded by soldiers. They'd stayed in the city that first night at the hotel of the Twelve Apostles and then hired horses the next day on the far side of the river. All this – being ferried across the Garonne, negotiating over the horses – took so much time that they'd journeyed only about twenty miles east of the city before having to put up for the night at an unprepossessing inn.

Jean Cado had told them to wait outside while he established whether there were any beds, claiming that it was better for him to do this by himself. Moments later he was back to say he'd procured a room for all four of them. They saw their horses stabled and went indoors for some supper.

Inside the inn there was a long table, one end of which was occupied by peasants eating chestnuts and black bread and drinking cheap wine. They looked up with the incuriosity of grazing animals as the door opened. But a more prosperous drinker, discerning that these newcomers were English, made a show of holding up the silver coin with which he was about to pay for another bottle of wine. He hissed something in Occitan, so that Chaucer could catch only the gist of it, but his feelings were apparent enough from his tone and the way he spat on the coin before handing it over to the innkeeper. The innkeeper pretended not to notice this – as though it was a local custom for his patrons to gob on their money – but surreptitiously wiped the coin on his apron (silver is silver, after all) before handing over the drink. Clutching his bottle, the spitting man returned to sit by the fire in a corner with a couple of similarly dressed companions.

The three drank and talked hard among themselves, frequently casting glances at the opposite corner of the tavern where Geoffrey was sitting with Ned and Alan and their guide. Through Jean Cado, the Englishmen ordered some supper. It came after a long time – greasy bowls containing some nameless meat set off by a bitter sauce – and would not have been worth a tenth of the wait or a quarter of the money. They required wine and then more wine to wash away the taste. All this time the other gentlemen in the far corner drank even more deeply but took no further action. Eventually they swung out of the place, slurring and clattering. "*Gafet de putan!*" said one of them. "*Viech d'ase!*" said another, as they exited.

Ned Caton leaped off the bench.

"What was that? What was that?"

He would have looked comical, with his pale hair in tufts, and his movements awkward through drink, had there not been a real fury in his eyes. Chaucer put out a restraining hand.

"Nothing much," said Jean Cado. "Merely the child of a whore."

"Whore! No one insults my mother!" said Ned.

"That insult is so usual down here it's almost a compliment. It was intended for me, I am sure," said Cado. "The other comment was for you, Master Caton."

"What does that one mean then?"

"*Viech d'ase*? Why, the cock of a donkey!"

And Ned Caton sat down again, his anger blown away in laughter.

"You should be complimented," said Geoffrey, admiring the way in which Cado had blunted the edge of a dangerous moment. Nevertheless, he reminded himself not to go into the yard that evening, just in case . . . and to tell the others to stay indoors as well. Meantime the peasants continued to munch their bread and chestnuts and to slurp their vinegary wine, oblivious.

Jean Cado leaned forward and spoke softly: "As you get deeper into Aquitaine, sirs, you'll notice that feelings run higher against us. Against the English, I mean. Against Prince Edward especially. They say he is arrogant and extravagant."

"He's the Prinsh of Wales, for God's sake!" said Alan Audly, rapping on the table with the bottle.

"Prince Edward captured the French king at Poitiers, the old French king," said Ned Caton. "Would that he could get his hands on the new one!"

"Hush now," said Cado, looking over his shoulder.

But the peasants at the long table were still rootling around in their food and drink while the landlord was turning a politic deaf ear to their conversation even if he could understood it (silver is silver, after all, and the Englishmen were already on to their fourth bottle). Cado dug into his purse and extracted a small silver coin. He handed it to the others.

"This is local currency. See here on the front. That is the Prince."

With the aid of a pair of scraggy candles, they scrutinized the coin. One side showed a figure with a crown, pointing with his left hand to a sword which he held in the other, as if to leave the viewer in no doubt of the source of his power and authority. On the back of the coin was a design of fleur-de-lys and leopards, quartered by a cross.

"It goes against the grain with some people in these parts to have to pay with *this*," said Cado, tapping his forefinger on the image of the Prince and then pincering the coin between finger and thumb before putting it back in his purse.

Alan Audly yawned.

"And then there's the *fouage*, you see. The *fouage* is not making things any easier, I'm telling you."

"*Fouage?*" said Chaucer.

"Hearth tax. It's been set at the rate of ten sous for each household for each year . . . "

Audly yawned more prominently.

" . . . and some of the local lords object to the fact that the Prince is trampling on their own right to raise taxes . . . "

Audly yawned as if he would like to engulf the table, greasy bowls and all.

"I think we realize that there are grievances, Master Cado," said Chaucer, ever the diplomat.

"Not that I agree with them. I'm simply reporting what's being said and, well, you can see for yourself just now the attitude of some towards you English." Jean Cado gestured towards the corner of the room recently vacated by the three drinkers. "At the moment it's words, mostly words."

"Of course it's only words, because they are *French*," said Caton.

"Thass very true, they are French," said Audly.

"But they're more Gascon than they are French down here – or so the English would say," said Chaucer.

"There you have got to the root of the trouble," said Cado. "You see – "

But he got no further since Alan Audly pitched forward on to the table, knocking over candles and bowls. A couple of the peasants looked up and grinned through gummy, dough-filled mouths. The landlord turned away, perhaps disappointed at the loss of one of his best customers, but did not come to their aid. Chaucer and the others helped their companion up the stairs. Fortunately their room contained four separate beds so Audly would be able to sleep it off without undue disturbance to the rest. Remembering the hostility of the three drinkers, Chaucer ensured that the door was secure. Before lying down himself, he looked out of the window. The inn lay at one end of a sorry straggle of houses. A single candle was visible in the window of one of the houses, shining out against the dark like a good deed in a naughty world.

The next morning Audly, looking very sorry for himself, gave a single shake of his head when offered wine at breakfast. He clambered into the saddle like an old man. He rode like an old woman, and Caton mocked him for being like a young girl, since he was incapable of holding his liquor (until Audly threatened to void whatever was still in his guts over his friend). All this time Chaucer rode ahead with Jean Cado. They'd reached a crossroads which Cado identified as one of the pilgrim routes for Compostela, when the guide suddenly said, "You aren't the first to try to persuade the Comte de Guyac to keep his allegiance."

Chaucer said nothing. They hadn't yet discussed the purpose of his errand.

"There was a man called Machaut who journeyed to Guyac in the spring," said Cado.

"What happened to him?"

"He never arrived."

"An accident on the road?"

"There are accidents and *accidents*, if you know what I mean, Master Chaucer."

"I think I do, Master Cado."

Until this point they'd been moving across relatively open country, with the bright straggle of new vines ascending the slopes to their left. On the other side the terrain fell away and broadened out into a plain alongside the river Dordogne. Patches of this flatter land showed the pale green of the lenten crops. Now the road they were travelling on narrowed and plunged in among trees.

Chaucer pondered Cado's words. John of Gaunt had said nothing to him about any previous attempt to influence Guyac. Or rather he had said nothing about the disappearance of a man called . . . what was his name? . . . Machaut. Had Machaut been betrayed? Had he been bought out by the French? Chaucer was aware that defections to the French king were growing by the day. It was only a few significant noblemen and landowners who were holding out, or who had not yet been offered sufficient inducements to switch their allegiance. Perhaps Gaunt didn't know about this man Machaut. Why should King Edward's younger son be aware of all the diplomatic machinations and covert actions that were going on hundreds of miles away from home?

Chaucer's hand went to the wallet which hung on the loop round his neck. The movement had become almost automatic. To reassure himself that the wallet was still there.

They rode deeper into the woods. Sun flecked the track, the air glowed and the birds sang. It was the kind of early summer's morning that made you dream of living in the wilds for ever, feeding off berries, drinking from cool springs. But, of course, for most of the year the wood-dweller would be couching on rocks, searching fruitlessly for food and hurting his hands as he shattered the ice on the streams.

It was towards the end of that afternoon when they first heard the sounds. They had been riding all day – stopping only briefly to eat some stale bread and cheese (bought in Bordeaux) – and hadn't yet emerged from the great wood through which the way, now reduced to little more than a path, was lazily winding. They were travelling in single file, with Audly half asleep in the rear. Cado, who was in the lead, estimated that they should arrive at the domain de Guyac towards the end of the following day. There was an inn a couple of miles ahead, he thought he remembered. They should stop there for the night. It was called Le Chat Qui Pêche. He announced all this over his shoulder.

"I hope it'll be better than last night's," said Ned Caton.

"What's that?" said Cado, cupping his hand to his ear.

"I said I hope – "

"No, not you, sir. Listen."

Now Cado held up his hand and they reined in. Listened. From somewhere up ahead came the piping of a flute and the rat-tat-tat of a drum. The sound was fitful, sometimes clear but then fading away again as if it were pursuing its own meandering course through the air. Some mournful quality to the noise, all solitary in the middle of this green wood, made the hair on the back of Geoffrey's neck stand up.

"There is surely no danger in that music," said Jean Cado.

He urged his horse forward, the others following. They had encountered no one since crossing the pilgrim route that morning. As they drew closer the sound of flute and drum ceased, to be replaced by a peculiar medley of barks and neighs. After a few minutes the path emerged into a wide clearing.

Cado and Chaucer halted and gazed at the spectacle, as did the other two.

A large four-wheeled cart had been drawn up on a level patch of ground. A grey-bearded man was standing in the middle of the cart. He was wearing a white shift. Around his feet crawled several people on all fours. The cart shuddered to their movements. The animal sounds were emanating from them. They held their heads up to the bare sky and barked and brayed. They waggled fingers above their heads in imitation of pointed ears. A small dog was lying in the shade of one of the cartwheels while a mud-coloured horse was hobbled and grazing nearby, both creatures indifferent to all this human activity.

Suddenly a red-faced woman in an equally red dress rushed across from the far side of the clearing, waving her arms. She looked like a fishwife.

"What do you think you're doing, husband?" she shouted. She sounded like a fishwife too.

"I am doing God's will," said the grey-bearded man in a resonant voice. "The end, it is nigh, with doom from the sky. Learn how the world goes, look beyond your nose."

"God's will, pigswill," bellowed the woman. "While we sweat on our knees, you do as you please. When our table is bare, you don't turn a hair."

With surprising agility, given her size, the woman sprang on to the cart with a single bound. Ignoring the crouched "animals", she seized hold of the man with one hand and cuffed him repeatedly round the head with the other. She was bigger than he was and soon had him on the floor of the cart without difficulty. Then she sat on him.

"Should we intervene, Master Chaucer?" said Jean Cado.

"I don't think so," said Geoffrey.

"No, no, no."

The four riders turned as one towards the direction of this new voice. A man came striding across from the edge of the clearing to the centre. They hadn't noticed him before now, partly because he hadn't moved or spoken and partly because he was dressed in a mixture of greens and browns which blended with the colours of the trees.

"No, no, Martin. And no, Margaret."

The woman got up from where she'd been sitting on the man. He clambered to his feet. The other people, three men and a woman, who'd been adopting animal postures also sat up. The individual wearing natural colours stood in front of the cart. He gave no sign of noticing Chaucer and his companions.

"This isn't a knockabout comedy, Martin," he said to the greybeard who had been sat on.

"It's always got a laugh before, Lewis," said the woman he'd called Margaret.

"It's a tradition," said the greybeard.

"Remember we're playing to the quality now," said the man standing in front of the cart.

"Just one cuff, Lewis?" pleaded the woman. "One teensy little tap to his stupid head."

"All right, my dear, but only one. And no falling down from you, Martin, and no being sat on. It's not dignified."

"If you say so."

The other people on the wagon accepted the judgement without enthusiasm. Lewis turned towards the horsemen.

"Gentlemen, you must agree, it's not dignified."

He was a narrow fellow, with a narrow face. He'd been aware of their presence all the time.

"Maybe not, but your friend over there is right," said Chaucer. "It is something of a tradition that Noah should be hen-pecked by his wife."

"Being hen-pecked is one thing, being beaten up by her is another altogether."

"Oh, this is a play," said Alan Audly, who'd suddenly come awake, "and these people are mummers."

Ned Caton clapped ironically at his friend's quickness, and the narrow man inclined his head.

"Yes, this is my band. We prefer to be called players and not mummers. My name is Lewis Loup and we are Loup's troupe."

"You're English," said Caton.

"Indeed we are, like yourselves. But we have not been home for over a year."

"What do you do now?"

"What do we do now? We practise the story of Noah and his flood. He is boarding the animals on his boat. His wife doesn't understand. She thinks he is neglecting his family."

He swept his arm round and the half-dozen players standing on the cart bowed raggedly.

"Noah is just one item in our repertoire, you understand. We cover everything from the fall of Lucifer to Doomsday. We do a fine Expulsion from Eden, we do a bloody Cain and Abel and a duplicitous Jacob and Esau, we do a heart-rending Abraham and Isaac, we do a . . . well, you get the picture."

"You ought to play something for us now," said Ned Caton. "Something light if you have it."

"No offence but I prefer it when the audience is bigger than the cast," said Loup. "And it's not just a question of profit either."

Chaucer dismounted and stretched.

"Who do you play in this Noah's flood, Master Loup?" he said.

"Whatever we play, I am always God."

Geoffrey was curious to know what this group was doing in the wilds of Aquitaine, since the usual home for travelling players was the inn-yard or the market square, any place where crowds naturally congregated. They'd get no revenue from the birds and the trees.

"And who are you practising for?"

"An audience of quality, sir, in a place called Guyac."

"That's our destination too," said Jean Cado, slipping off his horse.

"Oh, is it?" said Loup. "Well, we are going to play before the Comte de Guyac and the Lady Rosamond. It is our first visit to the place."

"Rosamond. The Comte's wife?" said Chaucer.

Something in Chaucer's tone caused Loup to say, "You know the Lady, sir?"

"A long time ago."

Loup opened his mouth, hesitated then spoke in a different tone. "What I was saying just now, about preferring it when there are more people in the audience than on the stage. Well, that's generally true. But we can make exceptions. So if you would like us to put on something here and now, we could probably oblige . . ."

He gestured to his band, who had resumed their positions on the cart. They ambled over, four men and two women.

"This is Martin. He plays our older and more reverend parts, like Noah and Abraham. And this is Margaret." He indicated the red-faced woman, the wife to Noah. "She plays all our shrewish roles. There is always a proper shrew in a decent play."

In proof of this Margaret cuffed the speaker round the head but it was a light blow, a teensy little one. Rapidly, Loup went on to introduce the other three men as Bertram, Simon and Tom. Standing slightly behind them was a dark-haired girl who glanced up shyly from time to time.

"And who is *this*?" said Alan Audly.

"This, sir, is our Eve in the Fall of Man, although her real name is Alice. She is also our Delilah, our Jezebel, our temptress."

"I can see that."

"And she is our daughter," said Lewis Loup.

"Daughter?" said Alan.

"Our?" said Ned.

"This lady is my wife," said the leader of the players, putting a fond arm round Margaret.

The players and the four travellers shook hands and exchanged names. Chaucer's group tethered their horses at the edge of the clearing. Then they settled down together on the grass to pass round a couple of bottles of wine which Lewis Loup generously produced from a pannier stored under the cart. As well as the shared wine, it might have been the shared language which brought them together. Or it might have been that Chaucer and the others were tired after riding all day and welcomed a short break before pushing on those last few miles to the inn. Or it could be that they welcomed company after a day's solitariness, especially the company of the easygoing Loups and their attractive daughter.

It turned out that the Loup troupe was a family enterprise. There were the husband and wife, Lewis and Margaret, together with their dark-haired daughter Alice. The grey-bearded Martin was a cousin to Lewis while Tom, one of the junior players, was his son. The other two men, Simon and Bertram, the first youthful, the second closer to middle age, had been recruited in England. All of them had more or less fled from England after some disaster which wasn't specified.

"Why do you do it? It must be a hard life," Chaucer asked.

Lewis Loup looked surprised, as though he'd never been asked the question before – or asked it of himself.

"Because it makes us free. We live by our wits and owe no man a living."

"And do you make a living?"

"A good one. Pretty good. Well, not too bad anyway," said Lewis Loup. "Better than in England, latterly. Now we are on our way to Guyac to play before the quality. A step up from some rain-swept town square or an inn-yard stinking of piss and puke, which seems to be the general condition of those in our native land."

"Talking of inn-yards, you are familiar with this particular route, you said," said Jean Cado to Loup. "There is an inn up ahead, is there not? Le Chat. I remember – "

He broke off, seeing the expression on Loup's face. The player explained, "I'm afraid the Cat is no more. It was burnt to the ground in the spring. A careless cook, I heard."

"I don't think there's another inn between here and Guyac," said Margaret Loup. The sun, beginning its descent towards the tree-tops at the edge of the clearing, gave an even redder glow to her face as if she too were the victim of a careless cook.

"So what are we going to do for lodging, eh?" said Ned Caton.

"I've just remembered," said Martin, the older player. "I do know of some excellent accommodation in the area after all."

"But you said there was nothing."

"This is spacious and airy accommodation," said Alice Loup. Her voice had a huskiness which contradicted the shyness of her expression. No wonder she was invariably cast as the temptress.

"The landlord of this particular place never overcharges and you can stay as many nights as you like," said Lewis.

Chaucer noticed Simon and the other players grinning. He guessed that this was a little routine banter among them and joined in.

"I suppose there's a plentiful supply of food for supper too," Geoffrey said, "provided you search for it."

"What are you on about?" said Alan Audly.

"When I was in northern France many years back," said Geoffrey, "we had a saying which went, 'Whoever has not slept in wind and rain, he is not a worthy companion.' I think we're about to find many worthy companions."

He looked round at Audly and Caton and Jean Cado where they were sprawled on the grass, taking a little pleasure as the realization sank in that they were going to have to spend the night out in the open. There were still some hours of daylight left but no one travelled on until the brink of night unless they were certain of arriving at a fairly secure destination.

It was soon established that Chaucer's group would remain with Loup's troupe and that they would travel on together through the territory that belonged to an individual called Gaston Florac and then into the domain de Guyac. The players, more accustomed to roughing it, were prepared for those times when they might not find a roof for the night. Suspended in sacks underneath the cart, which served as their playing platform, were not only their costumes but blankets and other domestic gear like pots and cutlery. There was even a bird in a cage swaying from the underside. It was fortunate that there was sufficient feed not only for the players' muddy work-horse but for the newcomers' mounts. Loup had purchased oats at their previous stopping-place, intending that they should last several days. Now he was happy to cater for the hired palfreys, at a premium. Chaucer willingly paid him.

The younger players busied themselves with various tasks. Alice Loup saw to the horses while Simon gathered kindling and broken branches for a fire in the centre of the clearing. Bertram and Tom disappeared among the thorn bushes at the edge of the clearing, carrying a bundle of small nets and a couple of leather buckets. They were accompanied by the terrier-like dog which had been sleeping all this while. Bertram called him Cerberus. Chaucer was amused by the name, since it belongs to the three-headed hound who guards the entrance to the underworld. This terrier was about as far from that grim guardian as could be imagined.

The older players continued chatting with Chaucer's party. They were not so much curious about the latter's reasons for visiting Guyac as eager for news from England. They knew that Queen Philippa was dead. Was the King going to find himself a new wife? And was it true that John of Gaunt had been widowed too? What about him?

Quite soon Bertram and Tom returned with several rabbits, lying broken-necked in the nets, and with their buckets slopping with water from one of the numberless streams that flowed down through the woods from the chalk uplands. Cerberus, his snout caked with dirt but his duty done, calmly resumed his position by the cartwheel.

"*Coneys!*" said Alan Audly as the dead rabbits were extracted from the nets by Margaret Loup, who promptly set about skinning them with her broad, competent hands.

"What's wrong with the coney?" said Ned Caton, glancing at Alice Loup who was within earshot but talking to Simon. "The most delicious food – in the right company."

The sun sank down below the trees and shadows poured into the bowl of the clearing. The fire was lit. Margaret Loup finished preparing the coneys for the spit and rinsed her hands in one of the water buckets. The others contributed the remnants of their bread and cheese, far from fresh now after two days' storage in the saddlebags but better than nothing. More wine was miraculously discovered. A mess of beans was reheated in a rickety skillet. Whatever Audly's view of coneys, Chaucer noticed that he ate his share readily enough. Ned Caton kept trying to catch the eye of Alice but she seemed oblivious to his glances. At the end of the meal Martin produced a cittern and plucked its melancholic strings while Jean Cado sang some interminable song about a knight who went in violent pursuit of another knight.

By now they were all on first name terms. Content, they bedded down under the moon and stars. Without anything being said, the women slept on the back of the cart – a touch of chivalry here perhaps – with the men lying underneath or on the edges. Owls hooted, the terrier whimpered as he dreamed of rabbit-snaring and intermittent snorts came from the horses on the fringe of the clearing. The fire gradually grew dimmer and the dark grew stronger.

Geoffrey recalled how only that morning he'd been indulging in the townsman's fantasy of living in the wild. Well, this was it. The ground was hard, and the night already cold. He was getting too old for this kind of expedition, he told himself. No longer a boy in his teens setting off on campaign, but a married man with two children and a third on the way, a man with a certain rank and position in society . . .

From the greater darkness under the trees the man who had killed the monk called Hubert and taken his name as well as his garments watched as the fire started to die out. If he had been the kind of person to feel loneliness, now would have been the moment to feel it most acutely, while he gazed on the circle of travellers gathered in the night for safety and company, seeing them as they ate and laughed and slept together. But it would not have occurred to him to feel lonely. Nor did he envy them their scant food or the little warmth provided by the fire. He was used enough to going hungry and quite satisfied with the shelter provided by his own clothes and skin. He settled on the ground and pulled his cloak about him.

Geoffrey Chaucer must have fallen asleep because the next thing he was aware of was that he was looking at the pale remnants of the fire. Wisps of mist were rising from the ground. It was altogether quiet and cold. Dead of night. No snoring, no whimpering, no grunting or snorting. They might have been the last people on earth, the last animals on earth. If they had been on Noah's boat they would truly have been the last people, the last animals, no doubt about it. God would breed a strange new world out of us lot, Chaucer thought. One dog, five horses, and ten humans, only one of them capable of bearing children.

A twig snapped somewhere on the edge of the wood and for an instant Chaucer came fully awake. Some animal out there?

A wolf or boar? Some *person* out there? Dead of night, dread of night. He strained to hear more but there was nothing. After that he fell asleep again.

8

The players were accustomed to making slow progress through the countryside. One or two of them might travel in the cart but their speed was necessarily governed by the walking pace of the remainder. Besides, the players weren't like most travellers, looking forward to a stopping-place for the evening and the chance of rest. Rather, that was when their working day began and they must stage a Biblical tale in marketplace or inn-yard. Therefore they had to conserve energy moving about from place to place, and be fresh for when they leapt on to the cart to present the Fall of Man or the Ruin of Sampson. If the players were well received in one location they might stay for a bit but, except in the largest towns, they had to move on after a few days when the audiences thinned out. It was a precarious existence, but no more precarious than the general times, perhaps.

The wordly wealth of the Loup troupe was contained in and under the cart which was now being laboriously towed uphill by the work-horse whose name was Rounce. In consideration for the horse – or in consideration of the fact that, without him, they'd have to pull the cart themselves – no one was sitting on the cart although Cerberus the terrier had positioned himself up there on a pile of costumes. Lewis Loup was leading Rounce, making gentle clucking and tutting noises to urge the animal onwards. The rest of the playing company was pacing beside or to the rear of the cart. Geoffrey Chaucer and Jean Cado were riding ahead, while Alan Audly and Ned Caton brought up the ambling rear. Caton had offered his horse to Alice Loup but she had made it clear that she preferred to walk, thank you. Preferred to walk with Simon, it seemed. Out of gallantry, Cado had made a similar offer to Margaret Loup but she merely laughed. With her thick legs and powerful arms, she was the largest and perhaps the toughest of the players.

During a pause in their journey Chaucer, who enjoyed hearing people's stories, learnt from Lewis Loup the reason why his company had left England twelve months earlier. '69 hadn't been a good year for the travelling players. It hadn't been a good year for the entire country, come to that. There'd been filthy weather followed by crop failures, there'd been outbreaks of plague and the rumblings of war with France. Lewis and Margaret Loup found themselves barred from market squares and inn-yards in case they had already journeyed near infected places. If they were permitted to stage one of their Biblical pieces they found the audiences were not only smaller but rowdier and less generous. In one place they were accused of lewdness – Alice had been all too effective in a temptress role – and driven out of town. Finally, when they were playing at Winchelsea in Sussex the mayor had taken it into his head that the figure of Noah as depicted by Martin was a poorly disguised version of himself, since everyone knew that old Winchelsea had been inundated by the sea in the previous century. In addition, the mayor claimed, Margaret's version of Mrs Noah was obviously intended as a slur on his wife. He'd threatened to confiscate the players' gear and throw the lot of them into gaol. Loup's troupe sneaked out of their meagre boarding house at first light and jumped on the first boat they could find, which happened to be going to Bordeaux. Since arriving in Aquitaine or Guyenne they had never looked back but strove to make a living in the towns and villages which were scattered along the Dordogne and other rivers. In all of this, Lewis gave great credit to his wife as the real guiding light of the company. "You wouldn't think so, Master Geoffrey, but she was a mere slip of a girl when I knew her first in Rochester. But I have been with her ever since through thin and thick, you might say."

They went forward at an easy pace for most of the day. Earlier in the morning they had ridden past a burnt-out house which Jean Cado identified as the site of Le Chat. There was no other inn on this road, and little sign of human habitation apart from charcoal-burners' shacks and the shepherds' bories, mounds of white stone in the shape of beehives. They passed occasional travellers on foot or horseback, never more than two or three of them at a time. Both sides exchanged wary greetings.

At one point there'd come a rumbling along the track behind them. Lewis Loup called on the party to halt. Noises were muffled in the still air under the trees but the sound of hooves and wheels was sufficiently clear and drawing closer.

"Soldiers?" said Lewis.

Chaucer, perhaps the only one of the group with the experience of standard warfare, shook his head.

"The tread of their horses is not heavy or regular enough," he said. "Brigands?"

"Unlikely," said Loup. "We're in Florac's territory now. He has a short way with any bandits or mercenaries."

Realizing that they couldn't outrun whoever was behind them, the players pulled off the track and waited for their followers to show themselves. Presently round a corner there appeared a liveried escort. They were armed but only lightly, with swords in ornate scabbards, for show rather than use – Chaucer was right, these were not soldiers. In the centre of the escort was a covered wagon, as different from the players' cart as silk from sackcloth. This conveyance was painted in reds and blues and yellows, and was pulled by a pair of white horses under the guidance of another liveried fellow sitting up on his perch with the assurance of a farmyard cock. The occupant of

107

the wagon was concealed behind dark blue curtains. In a city street the carriage would have been imposing. In the middle of a forest, its transit was like someone shouting in a church aisle.

The escort scarcely bothered to glance at the group of travellers who'd pulled off to one edge of the track. Then Chaucer saw Bertram dart forward and snatch something from under the wheels of the wagon. The player flung himself to one side just in time, as the rainbow blur of spokes spun past his prone body. When he stood up again, he was clutching the squirming dog Cerberus to his chest and whispering reassurances in his ear.

As the convoy disappeared round the next corner, leaving the branches shivering and the air ringing, Loup said, "If I'm not mistaken that was Gaston Florac himself."

Apart from this they saw nobody, although Geoffrey Chaucer was conscious that the surrounding woodland offered plenty of cover for those who might not want to show themselves. From time to time the path broke out into the open and in any direction the view was of thick pelts of trees covering the cliffs and hills which bordered the river valley. The river itself was visible in stretches that glittered like pewter. Sometimes they could see tiny barges and *couraux*, floating downstream with the current. The sound of a shout or the clack of wood striking on wood would reach them, diminished by distance but still audible.

As they were crossing one of these open spaces, Jean Cado pointed ahead.

"Look, Master Chaucer. The castle of Guyac."

There was an odd tremor in his voice. Geoffrey squinted to where Cado was pointing – his sight wasn't quite as sharp as it had been once – and he saw a small square shape on the skyline. It was not exactly as he remembered it. When he was taken captive, they had approached Guyac from the north rather than the west. Also, that had been in the middle of winter. Now they were approaching in all the fullness of summer.

"You know this region well?" he said.

"Why, I was brought up in these parts," said Cado. "It was on account of that I offered to be your guide."

They'd had further glimpses of the castle from open areas of the wood. For a long time it seemed to grow no closer until, at once, Chaucer could make out the battlements of the great keep and the white and ochre tints of the stonework. It was as if the place had jumped forward to meet them, like a rook in a game of chess. The castle was situated on a high bluff overlooking the river. One flank was protected by a cliff which dropped almost sheer to the water while on the other side the land fell away, making a natural defence.

Now the road wound further inland and deeper among the trees and, after a time, they came to the bottom of a stony slope that ascended through the wood. From this point Lewis Loup grasped the bridle and urged the horse gently on. His wife Margaret walked up with ease, her voluminous red dress billowing about her. Simon and Alice still kept company together. The climb was steady but lengthy. The centre of the track was thick with leaves pressed into black furrows by the passage of many wheels. The players' own cart swayed from side to side and the terrier sat up, alarmed. Margaret shouted to her husband to take care. The cart was even more important than the horse to the players. It was their Eden, it was their Ark, their whatever they wanted it to be. On the track the horses of Chaucer and his companions sometimes fumbled for a foothold.

Because they were in the lead, Chaucer and Cado arrived first in a level clearing at the top of the slope. It was a natural place to rein in and rest. From here they had a view of the castle through a fringe of trees. Behind them they could hear the heavy breathing of the horses and the creaking of the cart. Something drew his eye. Chaucer looked down. In the centre of a slab of rock crouched a greeny-brown lizard, the length of his hand. Chaucer was close enough to see its pulsing throat and lidded eyes. The lizard pretended not to notice that it had been noticed. Chaucer knew people who were like that. He looked out towards Guyac's stronghold. The rock outcrop on which it was based merged imperceptibly with the foundations of the great walls. The sun picked out the finials on a building which he thought was the great hall. In the valley that lay between this clearing and the castle was a cluster of houses, as well as a church, more than enough buildings to constitute a village. The air in the valley was dusty and golden. In the clearing the birds were singing.

He looked down again for the lizard on the rock but it had taken advantage of his inattention to make itself scarce. Cado's reference to a previous emissary to the Comte came to his mind. Machaut, wasn't it? He wondered if Machaut had got as far as this place. Surely not, otherwise what was there to prevent him from covering the last half-mile to the castle? Geoffrey looked round for Jean Cado. But the clearing seemed to be empty. Coming up from below the edge on the far side, he could hear the scuffle of the horses and the lurching of the cart but no one else had yet emerged into this open space. For an instant, he felt alone and vulnerable. Then he caught a flickering movement in the corner of his eye, and Cado rode into sight. He'd been off in the shade of the trees and Chaucer had somehow overlooked him.

"What is it?"

"Nothing," said Cado. "But I thought . . ."

If he'd meant to add anything his words were drowned by the tolling of the bell in the church tower. The others arrived in the clearing. They crowded to the edge opposite the castle and wordlessly looked at their destination. After a moment they set off down the slope towards Guyac. Chaucer felt a tightening in his guts.

In the shadows, Hubert watched them picking their way down the slope. He'd almost been worried when that fellow who was leading Chaucer and the rest had started to scour the edge of the clearing. Even Chaucer was looking alert, a change from his usual plump, self-satisfied posture. But there was nothing there, he'd distinctly heard the guide say that. He waited until the scuffling of horses and the creaking of the cart had faded. Turning to retreat deeper into the wood, Hubert came face to face with a stranger.

It was a man with ragged hair and a face covered with scratches and scars. Hubert must have been off his guard not to to have sensed company. Instinctively he went into a protective crouch, his arms tensed. His grey sack was on the ground beside him. He had a dagger attached to his belt, but it was behind his back. He rarely used it, relying instead on his hands. And, as he gazed at the stranger in the dappled light under the trees, he realized that most likely he wouldn't need the dagger anyway. Hands would do. For the shag-haired individual possessed only one arm.

9

Her hair was golden, with little love-locks; her eyes blue and laughing; her face most dainty to see, with lips more red than ever was rose or cherry in the time of summer heat; her teeth white and small; her breasts so firm that they showed beneath her vesture like two rounded nuts; so frail was she about the girdle that your hands could have spanned her, and the daisies that she crushed with her feet in passing showed as if black against her instep, so white was the flesh of this fair young lady.

The castellan saw all this beauty of the lady's as he entered the room. He greeted her with sighs and said, "Lady, God give you health and joy." She replied, "God give you pleasure and peace." Then he took her by the hand and made her sit down near him. He said nothing because he was too moved to speak straightaway. He grew pale and distracted and sighed frequently. The lady noticed this and apologized for her husband's absence. She said that he was out hunting in the woods and would return soon. The castellan did not acknowledge her words but replied instead that he loved her and that if she did not have mercy on him, then nothing mattered to him. The lady reminded the castellan that she was married and that he must not ask her for anything which would soil her honour or that of her husband or their house. He replied that nothing would keep him from serving her all his life.

"One glance from your eyes could kill or save me," said the castellan, gazing at her blue, laughing eyes. "One word from your cherry-red lips could preserve me or condemn me for ever," he said, *gazing now at her lips which were as red as rose or cherry in the time of summer heat.*

Rosamond de Guyac snapped shut the book entitled *Nicolette and the Castellan.* She stood up and laughed. It was probably wise of this particular romance-writer to hide himself behind the cloak of anonymity, she decided. She took up a hand-mirror from the table and went near the window. Staring at her face, she itemized the number of ways in which she failed to live up to the writer's notion of female perfection.

It was unfortunate, thought Rosamond, that she fell short of perfection from the very beginning. Her hair was dark and the love-locks were distinctly lacking, while her eyes were brown and, at the moment, they were squinting rather than laughing. Lips like roses or cherries? Well, they were red enough to fit her name, she supposed, but it would be odd if lips were any other colour. The same could be said of her teeth, which were naturally small and as white – or as whitish – as regular cleaning with sage and twigs could keep them. But it was when the writer lowered his eyes to the lady's breasts that things really went awry as far as Rosamond was concerned . . . "rounded nuts"? What was he thinking of? Thinking of a boy, most likely, or – let us be charitable here – a girl with a boyish figure that might remind him of his squire. It was only between the pages of a book that most men would prefer "rounded nuts", Rosamond considered, and certainly not in a bed.

She put the little mirror back on the table and stood, hands on hips. Her waist, even after a clutch of children, was not thick but it definitely wasn't frail enough to be spanned by a couple of hands. And then there was the general question of her white flesh, to say nothing of her white instep. Whiter than a crushed daisy? As a noble lady married to a noble lord, she had inevitably avoided the kind of outdoor life that would have coarsened and reddened her complexion. So her cheeks were quite pale and, if necessary, she could make them paler with pastes and powders. Further she would not go. For instance, she had heard of a noble lady in England who applied leeches to draw the blood from her cheeks before appearing at great occasions. The loss of blood had the additional effect of causing her to swoon regularly, and that always makes a lady interesting.

She remembered reading the anonymous romance of *Nicolette and the Castellan* when she was eleven or twelve years old. She remembered wondering if her life would be like Nicolette's. It had not been, of course, and now the gap between the book and real life seemed amusing rather than poignant. Romances were all very well, but here in Guyac she had a household to run, children to see to – or, to be accurate, she had to oversee the people who oversaw the people who saw to these things. Yet, like Nicolette, she had her admirers . . .

She didn't think that she'd picked up the book of *Nicolette and the Castellan* from that day to this. The reason why she'd taken it out of the chest where it was stored seemed obvious enough to her. It was because she knew that Geoffrey Chaucer would soon be arriving at Guyac.

She remembered her husband saying to her, all those years before, "I have brought you home a poet."

It was a New Year's Day. Henri de Guyac had been absent for several months in northern France where he owned further estates. And now her husband, newly arrived, stood by the window. He was looking at the bare branches of the trees which perched on the base of the cliff three hundred feet below. Beneath the branches the river slid by like unsheathed steel. There was a great fire in the hearth but his breath still frosted on the glass.

"I have brought you home a poet," he said.

"I have brought you home a son," said his wife Rosamond.

In Guyac's absence in the north Henri had been born, a first son after two daughters. Rosamond was sitting over a backgammon board. She'd been playing with one of her women,

115

who'd flutteringly withdrawn when Henri was shown into the chamber.

"Where is he?" said Henri.

"Where is *he*? His name is Henri and he is sleeping," she said. "Where is your poet?"

"Washing and changing after the journey. He is all travel-stained."

"You are all travel-stained, my lord. You have not changed – or washed either, my nose tells me."

"So eager was I to see you," said Guyac, moving from the window and coming across to kiss his wife. It was the first time they had touched for six months. They were a little awkward in each other's company.

"You were winning," he said, glancing down at the back-gammon board.

"Tell me about the poet," she said.

"Tell me about my son. Tell me about Henri."

"All babies are alike."

"Not to their mothers."

"Then let us say that he has your nose and eyebrows. But his eyes are my colour."

"Then he's lucky."

"And the poet?"

"I have been travelling with the poet for several days and yet I couldn't give you a precise description of his appearance. He's just . . . average," said Henri.

"But then you couldn't give a precise description of me if your back was turned for five minutes," said Rosamond, although she spoke fondly. Henri bent forward and kissed her once again. She stood up. She was taller than him by a couple of inches. They embraced.

"I must change," he said. "Wash and change. Then see my son."

"No," she said. "Wait. Not yet."

"Not see my son?"

"He's asleep while I am awake."

"What about your nose? What about my smell?"

"I didn't say I didn't like it," she said.

When Geoffrey Chaucer was presented to her, Rosamond saw at once what her husband meant. The Englishman was quite ordinary to look at. He was a little younger than her, about nineteen or twenty, with a roundish face and eyes that were attractively hooded. She invited him to sit opposite her. They spoke in French. Outside it was getting dark. Inside the chamber there was light from the fire and from candles and oil-lamps. The backgammon board was laid out on the table between them, with its interrupted game. Chaucer toyed absently with one of the ivory pieces.

"You're winning," he said.

"We can complete the game if you like."

They completed the game. She did win but only just. She complimented him on almost salvaging the situation. Chaucer said something about luck.

"But you also had some poor throws of the dice and only skill can make anything of those," said Rosamond.

After that they met almost every day to play backgammon and to talk. Rosamond was curious about London. Was it as great and grand a city as Bordeaux? What were the newest fashions there? Was the river Thames as wide as the Garonne?

She was curious about his poetry too. What were his subjects – lovelorn poets and cruel ladies, she supposed? Yes, he had to admit that those were his subjects at the moment. Not to deal with such topics would be perverse, like the apprentice carpenter who refuses to pick up his hammer and bang in nails with it. Lovelorn poets and cruel ladies were the basic tools of the trade – the cruel lady was the hammer while the unfortunate poet was the nail, repeatedly bashed over the head as he was driven not into a plank of wood but deeper into despair.

117

Once you'd mastered these stock subjects, Chaucer said, you could move on to something more elaborate, more interesting perhaps. Surely nothing could be more interesting than love? she asked. The very language they were speaking was framed to deal with questions of love. It was the language of romance and of romances. Ah yes, said Chaucer, romances such as *Nicolette and the Castellan*. She clapped her hands, delighted. You know it, you know the story of *Nicolette*? I read it when I was twelve, read it again and again. I've read it, said Chaucer, but only once. Oh, you dry English, said Rosamond, with your dry tongue, which grates like a squeaking axle on an ungreased cart. Even your insults, said Chaucer, are like poetry. Yes, she said, even when spoken plain, our language sounds like a song. To prove her point, Rosamond recited one of her favourite poems to him. It had the refrain *"Suis-je belle? Ah, suis-je belle?"*

She was aware of course that Chaucer was falling in love with her. Like the love poems that were to be expected from an apprentice poet, falling in love with the married noblewoman was only to be expected of the young squire. Yet Chaucer couldn't merely be dismissed as a green, inexperienced love-poet. He might have been all that, but there was also a self-mocking quality to him (as in the comment about the lady and the hammer and nails). He gazed at her with the right measure of devotion but at the same time there was an attitude about him which seemed to say, "Well, what else would you expect? It's the done thing, isn't it?"

When it came time for Geoffrey Chaucer to leave Guyac – because his ransom had been paid to her husband's kinsman in the north – Rosamond was genuinely sorry to see him go. She found the poem that he'd left for her almost straightaway, it wasn't very carefully hidden. She read it several times, then folded it away only to retrieve it half an hour afterwards. Maybe these lines were what he meant by something more elaborate, more interesting. There was no cruel lady here, but there was a lovelorn poet certainly. In the poem Chaucer lamented that he was being freed. He was going from liberty to servitude because he would no longer have the sight of the lady whom he loved. A nice conceit. It was written in English. He'd complained that it was only his inadequacy in the French which prevented him writing in that language and he even included a line or two about squeaking axles. The first part wasn't true of course. He could have composed in French if he'd chosen to. Was the rest of it true, the love and so on?

And now, more than ten years had passed. She had scarcely thought of Geoffrey Chaucer in the intervening period, or not much. And then she had discovered that he was arriving at Guyac, not as a captive this time, but as an emissary from John of Gaunt, the son of the English king. It would be . . . interesting to see him again. And she'd found herself rummaging around in the chest and digging out the romance entitled *Nicolette and the Castellan* and reading it with that amused tolerance you bring to something – or someone – you were fond of, a long time ago.

There was a tap at the door.

"Yes?"

It was Avice, one of her women. She said, "He's here."

Rosamond didn't have to ask who it was that Avice meant.

"Tell him I shall come down soon," she said.

When Avice had gone, Rosamond gazed for some time at her chamber without seeing anything. Then she picked up the book again and opened it at the same page.

The lady Nicolette returned the gaze of the castellan. Despite herself, she was touched by his pleading. The castellan was here as the guest of her husband, and was owed all the dues of honour and courtesy. He was a well-made man, tall and bright of eye. She could not help contrasting him with her husband, and the contrast was not to her husband's advantage. Nevertheless she let nothing of this show in her face and continued to regard the castellan with her blue eyes.

The castellan said, "Whether you accept or refuse me, my lady, be assured that I will serve you for ever. You have only to command and I will lay down my life at your feet. Tell me, will you receive such a sacrifice?"

"Thank you, my lord," said the lady Nicolette, "I am honoured by your words."

"I should prefer to honour you by my deeds," said the castellan.

"Provided that no harm comes to my honour or to my husband's honour or to my house's, then you may," said the lady.

And the castellan, seeing that he would get no further at this interview, withdrew from his lady's presence. He sighed and lamented at his lot but was secretly pleased to have won from her even this much agreement.

10

The community of Guyac lay to the north and west of the
great castle on the bluff above the river Dordogne. In the
time of Henri de Guyac's grandfather it had consisted of a
handful of ramshackle dwellings that were more like huts. But
now it had grown into a fair-sized village – almost a town – of
two- and three-storey stone houses separated by steep alleys,
and containing its own church and wine-shop and inn as well
as various workshops. It looked naturally to the castle for
protection and, particularly when the weather was bad and the
rains lashed down in November or the snows fell in February,
seemed to huddle under the fortress walls like a fledgling under
a mother bird. But although the villagers were literally in the
shadow of the castle, they had more independence than the
peasants and smallholders who occupied the plains on either
side of the river. They saw themselves as broader-minded than
those fellows who lived on the flat. For one thing the village
welcomed, or at least accepted, visitors from the wider world.

Vistors such as the troupe of players led by Lewis Loup who
were currently setting up their cart in the village square for a
performance. It was the evening of their arrival. Loup didn't
believe in wasting time before exploiting the excitement of their
arrival in a fresh place. You're a novelty today but when tomorrow
comes you're yesterday's news.

Chaucer's party had already been admitted to the private,
privileged areas of the castle. After crossing the bridge which

led to the gatehouse, all the travellers had stopped in the lower bailey. Chaucer and the others dismounted. The players clustered round their cart. Various lackeys in Guyac's livery (yellow and green) strode or slouched about, pretending not to notice the newcomers, perhaps because they assumed that all of the visitors were mummers and other riff-raff. Eventually the chamberlain appeared. He was profuse in his apologies to Geoffrey and was about to lead them to the seneschal, but Geoffrey told the chamberlain to attend to his friends first.

"Friends!" Lewis Loup overheard that and wouldn't forget it. That Geoffrey Chaucer possessed true *gentillesse*, he was a born gentleman. The chamberlain informed Loup that he and his gang would have to be content with quarters in one of the out-buildings. Fine, said Loup, but we are due to play before your lord and lady. Yes, yes, the same chamberlain assured him, casting anxious glances towards Chaucer and the other impor-tant visitors, you will perform inside the great hall in a couple of days' time in the presence of the lord and lady. It is all scheduled. Meanwhile, you are free to polish and perfect your act in front of the good people of this village.

The plays for the evening had been decided on by Lewis and Margaret Loup: the story of Noah and his flood, followed by a light-hearted interlude concerning a wicked bailiff who in-advertently gives away his soul to the devil, and to conclude with, Margaret suggested the old tale of Jacob and Esau. Lewis knew why his wife was eager to present the tale of the two brothers. It wasn't so much to do with the violent spat between the brothers – although fraternal hatred always makes for good drama and has done ever since the days of Cain and Abel – as because Rebekah, the mother of Jacob and Esau, was a strong woman as well as a cunning one. Like Noah's wife, it was a part that Margaret Loup considered had been made for her.

The villagers of Guyac had already been drawn out by the signs of preparation and, when the evening came on, a good number were assembled in the public square – although it was not so much a square as a space which had never been built over on account of the well which occupied a corner. On another side was a great chestnut tree, its pale candles at their fullest. Here the players set up their stall. The day's business was over, the evening air was mild, the wine-shop customers were ready to be entertained provided they could carry on drinking. There was a scatter of children playing, and two or three sleeping curs – surprisingly plump, these dogs – as well as bedraggled chickens pecking, all alike in the dirt.

Everything went smoothly to begin with. Tom juggled with his multicoloured clubs, while Bertram sang to Martin's accompaniment on the cittern. Cerberus the terrier got up on his hind legs and did a perfunctory jig which interested almost no one. Alice Loup and Simon collected the money, without which no performance would have been forthcoming. Word went around that this girl, with her innocently teasing face and an older, more experienced woman's voice, would be appearing as Delilah the temptress on the following evening – provided receipts were good enough for this one.

Loup's troupe sailed through Noah and his flood. Martin in the guise of Noah was instructed by Lewis playing God to build his boat. The "animals" barked and neighed as they clambered or leapt on to the cart, only to tumble over the far side and re-emerge round the corner as different beasts, growling and hissing this time. Margaret earned appreciative hoots and cackles when she clouted her stage-husband and sat on him – that bit of business had been restored by her, whatever her real husband said about dignity. Even the wine-shop customers forgot their drinks while they watched Noah release the white pigeon from his boat and wait for it to return (which it did, promptly – the pigeon was accustomed to a plump life in its cage under the cart), whereupon an olive twig was produced by sleight of hand from the region of its beak.

123

The trouble came when they reached the interlude or rather came afterwards. The interlude was about a bad bailiff who encounters the devil. This is a joke because in real life bailiffs are even worse than the devil. Nobody likes bailiffs, not even the lords who employ them to collect rents and confiscate property. Who could be offended by a satirical dig at a bailiff? Nobody but a bailiff, surely?

Loup's troupe played in the Occitan tongue but, in truth, they could have played without words since the action of the Noah play and the bailiff-devil interlude were well known to their village audience, with the exception of the children who weren't much interested anyway. The last little piece was well received, with boos and groans and a burst of ill-natured laughter when the bailiff got his come-uppance.

There was a break at the end of the interlude before the final staging of the evening, the story of Jacob and Esau. The players were gathered to the rear of their cart, where a makeshift shelter had been constructed by tying a tarpaulin to the lower branches of the chestnut, and were refreshing themselves with wine and ale.

Suddenly Lewis Loup felt a tug at his sleeve. In the person of God, he had no part to play in the story of Jacob and Esau but he was overseeing the final costume and cosmetic touches for his company. For example, the kidskin which Simon would drape round his neck when he impersonated hairy Esau, or the white paste that would be applied to the eyes of Martin who took the part of blind Isaac.

Loup looked around. To one side stood a short man with a boyish face full of freckles.

"My master wants you," said the man. "No questions, come quick."

"I can't come. I'm in the middle of a play," said Loup.

"You'll get no further with your playing unless you come now," said the man, gesturing towards the flank of the castle which loomed over the square and which apparently gave weight to his statements.

Loup sighed. Telling Margaret that the company should proceed with the story of Jacob and Esau if he hadn't returned within a quarter of an hour, he followed the short man away from the playing area. He'd expected to be led up the slope towards one of the postern gates of the castle but instead they simply walked round the edge of the square, where the villagers were milling about, before turning down an alley. After a few yards they came to a door in the wall. The man opened it and ushered Lewis Loup inside. Then he slipped in himself and shut the door.

It wasn't dark but it took a few moments for Loup's eyes to adjust to the gloom. Before that, the thick, musty smell which hung in the air told him that this was a store-room for wine. There was a barred window high up in one wall and the evening was still light outside. Barrels were stacked to one side and through that same wall there came talk and laughter. Loup realized that this place was at the back of the wine-shop. A fat man was sitting behind a table. He had a heavy, florid face.

"Here he is, sir," said the short man.

"You are the leader of the players?"

"Lewis Loup at your service."

"I have been watching you."

Any player ought to be complimented by such a remark but the individual behind the table turned it into a warning. Lewis Loup wasn't particularly intimidated, however. He and his company had received many warnings over the years. He didn't reply to the man behind the table but simply nodded. There was a stool in front of the table but he was not invited to sit down.

"This last piece you played, you have no authority for it."

"Begging your pardon, sir, the chamberlain said we could – "

"I don't mean that kind of authority," said the florid man, "but a higher authority. Where did you find written down the meeting between the bailiff and the devil?"

"Written down? Nowhere. It is a story well-known to all."

"There is no sanction for it in Holy Writ."

"Well, no . . ."

Uneasily, Loup wondered if he might have encountered here some pedantic church official who objected to players presenting anything which was not to be found in the pages of the Bible.

"It is dangerous to question the rights of a lord's man going about the lord's business."

"A lord's man?"

"The bailiff in your piece."

So that was it! This individual didn't care for the portrayal of the bailiff in the interlude. Well, it was never intended to be flattering. Nevertheless, Loup kept silent.

"It is never wise to stir up the people concerning their obligations to their betters, and especially at the present."

"It was only meant to be light-hearted, sir, a bit of a diversion."

"You've been in Guyenne for a long time, Loup?"

"A year only."

"I could have you whipped and pilloried. I could have you deported, like that."

The man snapped his fingers. Still, Lewis Loup was not unduly worried. Any man who says, *I could do this, I could do that*, is at least a couple of steps away from taking action. The chances are fair that he won't do what he threatens. At the same time Lewis was trying to work out who this person was. Not Henri, the lord of Guyac, he was fairly sure, since the owner of this great domain would hardly hold court in the back of a wine-shop. Yet he must be someone superior to the chamberlain, who had already given them clearance for their performances.

"May I ask whom I have the honour of addressing, sir?"

There was a cough from behind Loup, as if the freckled man by the door was cautioning against such a foolish question. The florid person stared at Loup for a moment before answering.

126

"I am Richard Foix, the seneschal of Guyac."

"Of course, sir," said Lewis, inclining his head. "I have heard you spoken of with respect but did not expect to encounter so great a man in such – such inadequate suroundings."

Outside a silence had fallen and he guessed that the performance was about to start once more. Now he had an inkling of why this Richard Foix (of whom, by the way, he had never heard) should have taken offence at the bailiff-devil story, since a seneschal – despite the resonance of his title – isn't much more than a jumped-up steward or bailiff.

"I choose my own surroundings," said the florid seneschal.

There was a pause. Loup understood that he'd been brought here for a reason, not just so that this pompous individual could carp on about an interlude. That was simply a way of getting some leverage under the players' leader.

"If we have offended in any way, sir, I beg that you will accept my humble apologies."

Foix waved his hand in a gesture that conveyed impatience rather than indifference.

"If there is any way that I can atone for our actions . . ."

"There is, Loup. You travelled here with four men, did you not?"

"They met us on the way."

"By arrangement?"

"No, no. Never seen them before."

"But you talked with them? Especially to the man called Geoffrey Chaucer."

"We talked . . . quite a lot," said Lewis, judging that was what the man wanted to hear.

"Then you must tell me everything about him," said the seneschal.

The plays were finished. The villagers of Guyac had been suitably edified by the story of Jacob and Esau, since it demonstrated various irrefutable facts to do with the cunning of women and the duplicity of younger brothers. Lewis Loup reappeared just before the end of the action.

"Where have you been, husband?" said Margaret.

"Making friends," he said.

"We have important spectators," she said. She gestured towards the edge of the square which faced the postern gate of the castle. A gaggle of finely dressed individuals was standing there. Without being told, Lewis knew that they must be from the castle. He thought he saw Geoffrey Chaucer in the group.

"Did they watch us in action?"

"They have only just arrived. I suppose they've come to see whether we're good enough for them."

"The Comte de Guyac and the Lady Rosamond, they're there too?"

"Oh yes," she said.

"Are you well, wife?" said Lewis, detecting a strain in her voice.

"I was thinking how I would prefer to play before the ordinary people," she said. "You know where you are with them."

"The nobility pay better."

"Their hearts are not so warm," she said.

Ignoring his wife's sudden scruples, Lewis Loup mounted the cart and, in practised fashion, briefly advertised the players' wares for the following evening. The chief attraction would be the story of Samson and Delilah, featuring Alice as the temptress and Simon as the strong man who in the end destroys his enemies along with himself. Alice looked demure at the announcement but took care to rub her hand languorously along her thigh.

The sky was turning a deeper shade of blue and swallows were swooping above them. The high-ups from the castle turned back and filed through the postern-gate. The villagers were more reluctant to leave the scene but the square gradually emptied so that the wine-shop was closed and the house-shutters drawn by the time the first stars were coming out. The players returned to their quarters in the castle outbuilding. At some point during their return they noticed that Bertram was no longer with them. Nobody worried unduly, however. The players were independent souls, capable of looking after themselves.

If they'd known Bertram's whereabouts at that moment, however, they would have been more than worried since he was fighting for his life in the river Dordogne. Bertram was unable to swim but in one respect at least he was lucky. Had he been in the river at almost any other time of year he would have been overcome straightaway by the rapid, swirling current. But during summer, without the spring floods or the autumn rains to top it up, though the water flowed fast it was at less of a break-neck pace. While the player flailed around – his garments already pulling him down as if they were made of lead, his boots clinging to his ankles like fetters of iron – while he flailed around – sometimes surfacing for an instant before being thrust back under the surface once more, kicking and lashing out with all his limbs, his mouth and nose and eyes crammed with water – during all of this, Bertram thought that his last moments had come. On one of his periodic surfacings, he opened his mouth to shout for help but all that came out was a despairing gurgle before he was pulled down once more.

He couldn't understand it, couldn't understand exactly how he'd come to this dire situation. Images flickered through his head. There'd been a monk standing on the edge of the crowd in the square, his face hidden by his cowl. At the conclusion of the Jacob and Esau story, the monk had moved towards Bertram and said urgently, "Your dog is like to drown."

"What?"

Bertram looked around for Cerberus in the ebbing light. The

dog was his personal property rather than the company's and would not stray more than a few yards from his master unless he was chasing a coney or a squirrel.

"Where is he?"

"Down by the river. Come quick!"

Bertram pursued the monk out of the square and down a rough track that led around the flank of the castle and towards the river. As they neared it, the rumbling and creaking of a mill-wheel grew louder. The monk ran ahead, his black garments flapping. Bertram didn't have time to wonder how this had come about. All he knew was that he didn't want to lose Cerberus. To the band of players the dog was useful as a rabbiter and an indifferent dancer of jigs but, to Bertram, he was a companion.

Following the monk's lead, Bertram veered off the path and reached the river's edge at a point where the bank fell sharply away. The river slid past, showing silvery streaks in the places where it was interrupted by snags or sandbanks. From further upstream came the clacking of the mill. Downstream was a landing stage.

"Where is he?" said Bertram again.

The monk pointed down towards his feet. Bertram moved to the edge. He heard scrabbling sounds before he saw the terrier clawing at the almost vertical face of the bank. Cerberus was standing on a narrow ledge of mud beyond which the water flowed with glinting speed. The dog was unable to get sufficient purchase to scramble up the bank.

Bertram called out the dog's name and swung his legs over the edge. Seeing salvation at hand, the dog yapped. The drop was a dozen feet or more. Bertram clung to tufts of grass on the brim before letting go. He landed, awkwardly, on the mud ledge. He almost toppled backwards into the water. He teetered but saved himself by grasping at a root that protruded from the bank. He grabbed the dog, which was soaked. There was scarcely room for him and Cerberus on this tiny patch. Down at this level the river seemed to run wider and deeper.

He felt something brush against his shoulder. He looked up. The monk was kneeling on the edge of the bank above, visible only as a dark outline. A rope was dangling from his hand. Bertram seized hold of the other end. He wondered where the monk had obtained the rope.

"The dog first," he called. "I'll manage."

Gripping Cerberus between his knees he fastened the cord behind the dog's forelegs, checked that the knot was secure and told the monk to pull away. The wriggling animal disappeared from view. Bertram explored the bank in front of him, more by touch than sight. He discovered he could wedge his feet into the soft mud at the bottom of the bank and use the protruding root as a handhold. He lost his footing several times and it was more of a scrabble than a climb, but by the time the monk's head and shoulders appeared once more against the darkening sky to check on Bertram's progress, the player had hauled himself over the lip of the bank.

Taking the man's outstretched hand, he clambered upright. It was a firm hand, a surprisingly strong hand for a man who spent his life in a cloister. He heard the terrier yapping with pleasure at his return. The monk had tied the dog to a tree, presumably in case he should try to throw himself into the river again. Bertram stood for a moment, recovering his breath.

"Thank you," he said.

The monk, who was still wearing his cowl, bowed his head so that the white oval of his face disappeared altogether. For some reason Bertram, breathless and wet and muddied as he was, found this unsettling.

"Who am I thanking?" he said.

"A Brother of the Holy Cross. Who have I saved?"

"My name is Bertram. I would not have lost Cerberus for the world."

"You call him Cerberus?" said the monk.

"After the dog that guards hell-mouth. I could not have followed him into the water. I'd have sunk like a stone."

"You can't swim?"

"Of course not," said Bertram, thinking that it was an odd question. He didn't know anyone who could swim.

"Well, if God had meant us to swim, I always say," said the monk, "he would have given us fins and a tail."

Bertram's unease deepened, not so much at the comment – which might have been meant piously – as at the other's manner. He suddenly realized that they'd been speaking in English, rather than French or Occitan. This man was a fellow country-man. What was he doing here? The monk had lowered his cowl by now and Bertram observed that he wasn't tonsured. It was almost dark but the final dregs of daylight revealed a full head of hair, cut short but lacking the shaved patch that denoted the true religious. Whatever this noddle contained, Bertram doubted that they were holy brains.

"Who are you?" he said.

The monk gave no reply. They were still standing on the river bank, Bertram with his back to the water. Too late, the player realized the exposed danger of his position. Too late, because by then the other man had shoved him violently in the chest and Bertram was tumbling backwards into the water. He landed with a great splash, went under and resurfaced, floundering helplessly. Instantly the current picked him up and carried him towards the middle of the river. The monk was relieved at that. He'd worried that the player might be carried towards the landing stage downstream, might be able to grasp at one of the wooden supports and save himself. But the current, as if in obedience to the monk's wishes, took him straight out.

The man in the monk's habit watched for a long time. His eyes were accustomed to the dark and, against the background of the silver-grey river, more shadowy objects could be discerned, objects both fixed and moving. Smooth spurs of rock, branches of trees. He saw the flailing arms of Bertram, he saw the ball of the man's head bob up above the surface a couple of times, a long way out by now, a long way off. Then the head appeared for a third time. What did they say about the number of lives a drowning man was permitted before the water swallowed him up for ever? He heard a human cry, a meaningless noise carried over the water. He watched until he could see nothing more. Then he turned back towards the tethered dog, which had fallen silent but presently growled and bristled as he approached.

Cerberus had reason to feel apprehensive of the man since, not half an hour before, he had been snatched from where he was peaceably napping against the bole of the chestnut tree in the square, while everyone's eyes were fixed on the play-action aboard the cart. Originally the man had intended to throw him into the river, to give colour to his story of a drowning dog, but the terrier's accidental landing on the mud-bank worked even better. For himself he couldn't have cared less about the dog and was minded to chuck him into the river after his master, but a way of exploiting the rescue of the animal had suddenly occurred to him.

For the moment the man ignored the growlings of Cerberus. Swiftly he retrieved the grey sack from underneath a nearby bush and stripped himself of the monk's habit. He was wearing his own clothes underneath. He thrust the garment into the sack. He untied the dog from the tree and, bending down, grasped him firmly round the middle. The man tucked the wet bundle under his arm. Cerberus squirmed for a moment but then thought better of it. Slinging the sack over his other shoulder, the man set off up the path towards the castle.

Loup's troupe was settling down in the wooden outbuilding which served as their quarters in Guyac. The barn-like space was used to store farm carts and ploughing implements waiting repair, such as broken whiffletrees and blunted coulters. The stable-marshal had provided palliasses for them at the direction of the chamberlain, who had overall control of the great hall where they would be playing in front of the lord and lady of Guyac. The players had sometimes enjoyed better accommodation but they had more frequently suffered worse, as on the previous night in the forest. Here at least they were dry and safe, with only the odd rat for company. Similarly, although the food brought out from the castle kitchen hadn't been first-rate, it had been an improvement on roasted coney and stale cheese.

Lewis had said nothing to the others about his encounter with Richard Foix, who outranked both chamberlain and stable-marshal in the castle pecking order. The red-faced seneschal seemed very interested in the English visitors, particularly Geoffrey Chaucer. Loup was not able to tell him much but, being a good actor, he made the most of what little information he had. On the key question, though, of why Chaucer was at Guyac, Loup could only surmise that he was visiting because he was an old friend of the Lady Rosamond. This didn't satisfy Foix, and even Loup thought privately that there must be more to the excursion. Foix told him to keep his eyes and ears open. There'd be a reward, he said, if Loup discovered anything. Loup didn't suppose that he would find out anything else, but there was no reason to let Foix know that. A seneschal might be no more than a jumped-up steward but he still wielded considerable power within the confines of the castle.

It'll probably turn out all right, thought Loup. He was a perpetual optimist, and this was an asset in a company of travelling players whose condition was always precarious.

Loup had just commented favourably to Margaret on the evening's takings but she seemed preoccupied.

"What's the matter?"

"I was thinking that people are not going to be so interested in our playing tomorrow. There's a hunt."

"The hunt is in the morning. By the evening people will be ready for diversion."

When Margaret didn't reply, Lewis said, "That de Guyac's a brave fellow. He will take on the boar single-handed if need be, they say."

But Margaret Loup still didn't reply, and Lewis pressed her to say what was troubling her.

"Very well, husband, I am worried about Bertram," she said. "Where has he got to?"

Their fellow's absence was unusual but, as Lewis told Margaret, he was a grown man, able to take care of himself.

Meanwhile Simon and Alice were talking and giggling in one corner of the barn, while Martin and Tom, father and son, were dicing nearby. The only light came from a couple of small oil-lamps on the ground. Suddenly a dirty white shape scooted across the ground. Recognizing her voice, it made for Alice.

"Ugh, Cerberus, you're all wet," she said.

"He was the lucky one," came a voice from the door.

The players stood up. The figure came forward so that his feet and legs entered a circle of light. His face was still in shadow. A bag swung idly from one hand.

"Where's Bertram?" said Lewis Loup.

"A gentleman with grizzled hair, is he?"

"Yes," said Margaret Loup. "What's happened to him? Is he all right?"

"Alas, madam, I have bad news for you and for your company. He is drowned, I fear."

Someone gasped, someone else said simply, "No", but that was all.

And, sitting down cross-legged on the floor, the stranger proceeded to explain how he had been present at the company's fine performance in the village square scarcely an hour earlier. He'd been a mummer himself in his time, he said, so he knew what he was talking about. Deeply affected by their rendering

135

of the tale of Jacob and Esau, and the deception of good old father Isaac (here the stranger nodded in the direction of Martin), he had walked down to the river bank to enjoy the last moments of the evening. There his ear had been caught by the sound of frantic barking, which seemed to be coming up from the river itself. Looking over the edge he'd seen this wretched cur trapped on a spit of mud, baying at the water. Within a few yards of the shore a man was struggling with flailing arms to keep his head above the current. But even as he watched, an invisible hand pressed the man's head down and when it next emerged the head had been carried many yards further off. The man waited and called and waited again but saw nothing more. Eventually he clambered down the bank and rescued the cur which, by the by, didn't appear very eager to be rescued.

"Bertram was devoted to Cerberus, and the dog was devoted to him," said Martin.

"He must have been trying to save the dog and fallen in . . ." said Lewis.

"Just so," said the stranger. "The bank is slippery at that point. It would have been better to let the animal drown than lose a human soul."

"Yes," said Margaret.

From the darkness came a single sob. It was Alice. The man said, "I should have tried to save your friend but I can swim no better than he could, poor fellow."

"You did your best," said Lewis, reaching over to pat the other on the shoulder. The man flinched slightly. To cover the movement he said, "If God had meant us to swim he would have given us fins and a tail, I always say."

There was a silence and he gathered that he'd struck the wrong note. Now he said quickly, "A mass must be said for the poor fellow. I shall see the priest myself tomorrow. They already know of this up at the castle for I encountered the chamberlain on the way here and he told me where you were."

"Thank you, friend," said Lewis.

"Who are we thanking?" said Margaret, unknowingly echoing Bertram's question before he went into the river.

"You should call me Hubert," said the stranger.

"You say you've been a mummer, Hubert?"

"In my time."

"We prefer to call ourselves players," said Martin.

"Well, I've played many parts," said Hubert.

11

Some hours before the meeting between Hubert and the players, Geoffrey Chaucer and his company had entered the castle of Guyac, as you've heard. The welcome offered to them was a little more elaborate than that given to Loup's company, once their identity had become plain. These were, of course, no ordinary travellers but emissaries from the son of the King of England. In normal circumstances they would have arrived with a heavy escort and plenty of ceremony but the times weren't normal. A fresh outbreak of war between England and France was imminent, and whether England hung on to Guyenne depended on the decision of great lords such as Henri de Guyac.

Chaucer had been pleased to hear that the players, received first by the chamberlain at his insistence, were being lodged halfway decently and not left to search out another roof under the stars. He'd taken a liking to Loup and the others in the day or so since they'd met. He overheard the chamberlain assuring the players that they would perform, as arranged, in the presence of the lord and lady in the great hall.

The chamberlain then bustlingly ushered Chaucer and Audly and Caton, together with Jean Cado, up an enclosed stairway. At the top was a kind of lobby where the seneschal himself, a large red-faced person called Richard Foix, was waiting to receive them. He accompanied the visitors to their second-floor chambers. Cado, as a mere guide, was relegated to the back quarters, but the others were lodged in adjoining solars over-looking the river valley. Chaucer's room contained a curtained bed, a chest and a stool. On the wall hung a tapestry depicting a boar-hunt. The animal, larger than any of the human figures who were pursuing him on foot and horseback, was crouched in a thicket in the left-hand corner of the scene, brought to bay but determined to take plenty of men down with him. Its tusks were whitish-yellow and monstrously large. Geoffrey recalled Henri de Guyac's passion for the chase.

He crossed to the window. Immediately below was the castle garden with its separate beds for flowers and herbs. A vine was splayed against a south-facing wall. The scent of roses and of sun-baked stone suffused the evening air and filled his nostrils. Further off lay the glinting eye of the castle pond, no doubt well stocked with trout and pike. And all the time, far below, the river ran its soundless course.

He thought of another river many hundreds of miles distant, and of the house in Aldgate where he dwelled with his family. He recited their names several times over like a comforting phrase from the litany: Philippa, Elizabeth and Thomas. Philippa, Elizabeth and Thomas. He trusted that all was well with them. He prayed that his wife had not miscarried. By now she would be in her – let me see – sixth month or even the early stages of her seventh. Odd, that he had not dreamed of Philippa in his travels. He wasn't certain what had filled his dreams but, whatever it was, he did not believe that his wife was in the habit of appearing to him.

He must have been concentrating on his thoughts because when he next took in the view from the window he saw that a man and a woman, both elegantly garbed, had appeared in the garden. They were walking round the edge of the fish-pond. For an instant he assumed that the well-dressed man was Henri, but this individual was perhaps taller and certainly not so old (de

140

Guyac would be well advanced into later middle age by now). There was a kind of bounce in this one's step and he was inclining his head towards his companion, following her every word.

The woman, quite slender and graceful, was wearing a pale yellow mantle. Her head was wimpled so that Chaucer was unable to see her face directly. She was pacing along, talking and looking at the ground in front of her rather than at her companion. Chaucer assumed that this couple were also guests at the castle. Then a boy opened a door in the wall beyond the pond and approached the two. About him there was something familiar, very familiar. He was stocky and dark-haired. Then it came to Chaucer in a flash that he was surely staring at Henri the younger, the first-born son of Rosamond and the Comte, who had been a mere baby when he was last here. The boy looked about right both in terms of age and appearance. Then, as the woman raised her head at the lad's approach, Geoffrey saw that she was Rosamond herself. He recognized her now. Why hadn't he done so before? Although it was absurd, he felt cheated. This was the woman who, for an intense space of his youth, had filled many of his waking (and sleeping) moments.

A brief conversation followed between mother and son, very brief indeed on her side. Chaucer had the impression that Rosamond was impatient at being interrupted. Soon the lad turned sharply on his heel, showing his own kind of impatience perhaps, and disappeared again through the door in the wall. The man and woman resumed their pacing round the pond, but without the absorption in each other that had characterized the scene so recently. Then a woman emerged from a different quarter of the garden and spoke to Rosamond. From her dress and bearing she was an attendant. The man who was keeping company with Rosamond removed himself a couple of yards off, as if whatever was being said was of no concern to him. Rosamond nodded at the woman, who walked away. And a few moments after that yet another figure came out. This individual, comparatively short and thickset, was dressed in green and brown hunting gear. Although it had been more than ten years since he'd last set eyes on him, Geoffrey at once recognized Henri de Guyac, his present host and his one-time captor. And yet he reminded Geoffrey of someone else . . .

Guyac kissed his wife and embraced the man. The three of them talked for a time, talked easily to judge by their postures and the occasional burst of laughter. At one point, Henri de Guyac drew his sword from its scabbard – it was a sword designed for boar-hunting, having a thin shaft and broad point – and Rosamond playfully took it. She jabbed down and sideways with it. There was no female squeamishness here.

"Something interesting, Geoffrey?"

Chaucer looked round to see Ned Caton standing in the entrance to his room. He wondered how long the other had been there.

"I have been looking at our hosts."

He moved aside from the narrow window. Caton came across to see for himself.

"Which one is Henri de Guyac?" said Ned.

The eagerness in his tone surprised Geoffrey.

"Which one? Let me look again. The man in hunting clothes is Henri. The woman is Rosamond de Guyac."

"And the other man?"

"I don't know. I'm only a guest here, Ned, like you."

Alan Audly entered the room and said, "We are bidden to supper tonight."

"No elbows on the table, my friend," said Ned, talking quickly and to little purpose. "No burping and no talking with your mouth open. And Alan must be sure to scrub under his fingernails before he sticks his claws into a dish, eh, Geoffrey?"

"What? Oh yes. We are bidden to a feast, you say. Good."

Chaucer's attention was still held by the trio near the fish-pond. They chatted for a moment longer then the man he'd identified as Henri de Guyac walked away. Almost as soon as her husband's back was turned Rosamond reached out a hand to grasp the other man's arm. Geoffrey was unsure what to read into her gesture: reassurance? warning? simple friendship, or something more?

It was a fast day and so supper in the great hall of Guyac was to be without meat and comparatively modest in scale. Yet, for Chaucer and his companions, it was an experience far superior to anything they'd enjoyed or endured – whether in a tavern or on board ship or by the roadside – for many days. Being early summer, there was no fire in the great hearth. Evening light penetrated the high windows like the spokes of a great golden wheel. It glinted off the salt-dishes and the silver cups and spoons on the table. Bright tunics or hose emerged into the shafts of light, and the crimson or blue cloth took fire for an instant before the wearers disappeared into the relative gloom of the hall. Hounds crouched on a floor which had been newly swept and strewn with fresh rushes. The dogs were the favoured ones from the pack which had been out that day. Pages wearing the green and yellow livery of Guyac stood by discreetly holding ewers of water and small towels for hand-washing.

Before the meal they had met their hosts. Geoffrey was warmly embraced by Henri de Guyac, no longer in his hunting gear but dressed to receive guests. The Gascon had a few more lines in his face and his hair was shot through with grey but the strength of his grip was undiminished and so was the cordiality of his welcome. In deference to his guest, he talked in English.

"Master Geoffrey! It is an honour to have you under our roof again."

"The honour is mine, my lord."

"Long life to your house."

"Long life to the wisher," said Chaucer.

"Besides all that, it's good to see you again," said Guyac. "I hear that you came with some players."

"Yes. They call themselves Loup's troupe."

"We shall go and look at them in the square after supper," said Henri. Then, standing back to gaze at the Englishman, "You've put on a bit of weight."

"And now I can expect to put on a little more, unless the contents of your table have changed."

"You've caught us on the wrong day, Geoffrey. No spiced ortolans, no beccaficoes, none of our specialities, nothing that flies or walks or runs on the surface of the earth, just fish and more fish. Still, we shall make up for it tomorrow."

"Make up for what, my lord?"

The question came from Rosamond de Guyac, who had overheard her husband's final words. Geoffrey had observed her over Henri's shoulder making towards them. At the same time he saw Ned Caton observing the three of them closely. He bowed low and said, "My lady."

"So formal, Geoffrey," she said, smiling. "Don't I get a kiss?"

So Chaucer smiled and they kissed. They looked at each other. Close to, had she changed? Yes, slightly. Did it matter? No. Was she beautiful still? She was.

Rosamond turned towards her husband and said, "And what is it that we must make up for?"

"I was talking about the shortcomings of our table on a fast day, my dear."

"It is our guests make up for any shortcomings. They are the sauce to our meat."

She smiled gracefully at Geoffrey before moving off to greet other guests. Among them, Chaucer recognized the man who'd been walking and talking with Rosamond by the fish-pond. Henri's wife was gracious with all her visitors; wherever she went she left a circle of smiles and gratified expressions.

"We shall meet later, Geoffrey," said de Guyac. "Meet this evening."

Chaucer inclined his head. Of course, Henri knew why he was here, or if he didn't know then he'd certainly guessed.

A demure horn was blown to announce the start of the meal, the diners trooped to the table to be seated in order of precedence and, once grace had been said, the meal began with the customary procession of servants. The pantler and his assistant brought in the bread and butter, then the butler and *his* assistant appeared clutching slopping jugs of wine, to be followed by other attendants with dishes of whole fish and salvers piled high with mortrews and pasties, as well as bowls containing a variety of sauces, honey for sweetening, and all the rest of it.

Geoffrey listened to the mixture of English and French and Occitan floating around the table, a verbal equivalent of the medley of smells – of ginger, vinegar, cinnamon, almonds – wafting up from the dishes. There was much talk of that day's (unsuccessful) boar-hunt. It was not the season but a particular beast had been spreading terror in the neighbourhood and had killed two – or was it three? – peasants. It could not be allowed to run rampant any longer.

Chaucer's speculation that the boy he'd seen out in the garden was the Guyacs' son was right. Young Henri served his father, as the well-trained squire should do. If there'd been meat on the table he would have done the carving. As well as the son there were present two attractive young women who were the daughters of Henri and Rosamond. When Chaucer had been a captive at Guyac they had been little children, kept out of sight.

There were a handful of noble guests who took precedence over the English visitors, and who therefore sat closer to the lord and lady of Guyac. Geoffrey was particularly interested in the man who sat on Rosamond's left, the one he'd already seen in her company in the garden. On the other side of this man was another lady, an older one. Chaucer turned to serve his neighbour from their shared dish and, at the same time, asked if she knew who it was that occupied such a privileged position next to the Comtesse.

The neighbour – a woman fairly advanced in years but with quick blue eyes set in nets of wrinkles – said, "You are referring to her husband?"

"Him I know," said Chaucer. "But the other man . . ?"

" . . . is Gaston Florac. He is the castellan of the next territory but you would not think it, to judge by the amount of time he spends here."

Geoffrey remembered the carriage and escort which had swept past them in the woods earlier that day.

"Perhaps he is drawn by the chase?"

"You might say so," said Chaucer's neighbour in a tone that suggested that she wouldn't have said it.

"Is that his wife sitting next to him, on the other side?"

"You are very curious for a stranger – an English stranger."

"I spent time here once," said Chaucer.

"No, it's not his wife. Florac's wife is dead. That is another lady altogether, and a little on the old side for him, wouldn't you say?"

"I would be too gallant to say anything of the sort, madam."

Chaucer's neighbour – who was considerably older than the lady she'd just mentioned – jabbed in his direction with her spoon.

"Nonsense!" she said. "I can spot a gossip at a hundred paces, let alone one when he is right under my nose. Admit it, you like a bit of gossip."

"You've found me out," said Geoffrey.

"Aha," said the woman, spooning a gobbet of *quenelle* into her mouth. She paused to pick up her napkin and dab away a spot of grease on her chin. Then she said in a conspiratorial way, "You'd like to know more?'

"Of course."

"You talked of the chase, Englishman. Then you should know that gossip has it that the quarry which Gaston Florac pursues here is a human one, and female, and already mated."

Chaucer looked towards the centre of the table. Rosamond de Guyac was inclining her head towards her guest. They looked as confidential together as they had earlier this evening in the garden, except that now it was Florac doing the talking.

"You say he had a wife until recently," said Chaucer.

The old woman abandoned her spoon and stabbed with her knife at a dish of shrimps in vinegar. Chaucer hastily removed his own hand from the region of the shrimps. Like everyone, he'd heard of people getting their fingers cut off by accident while they and others were scrabbling in the same dinner platter.

"Oh yes, Gaston Florac had a wife," said the old woman, just before the shrimp disappeared into her pursed mouth. Geoffrey waited while she chewed, with relish. "She died after a great feast, they say. A surfeit of something, they say . . . "

"What do you say?"

"Nothing," said the woman, patting her lips with the napkin, either as a mark of silence or satisfaction. "I say nothing."

"Not even to a fellow gossip?"

"Florac is a powerful man, almost as powerful as Henri de Guyac. Gossip can be dangerous."

"You leave me eager for more, madam."

"What a thing to say to an old lady!"

She darted a look at Geoffrey before spearing another shrimp. Then the music struck up. As they'd been eating, a singer with a viele had established himself in the gallery. The singer scraped tentatively at the strings of his instrument before launching into a sweet tune containing a hint of sharpness, like many of the three-quarter-empty dishes which now littered the table. While he sang a silence fell in the hall. Chaucer watched the last of the sun's beams inching up the stone wall facing the west

147

windows. When the song was finished, and the singer had played the tune over once more, the pages came forward to light the candles and oil-lamps. The shadows in the hall grew deeper.

"You understand the song, Englishman?" said the old woman.

"Not altogether," said Geoffrey.

"It is a tribute to a woman," she said and then, in a voice that was surprisingly firm, she began to sing.

"Vous estes le vray saphir
Qui peut tous mes maus garir et terminer.
Esmeraude a resjoir,
Rubis pour cuers esclarcir et conforter."

The whole table, which had started to talk again, quietened to listen to her. When she had finished the unaccompanied verses they clapped or rapped gently on the board. The old woman's eyes almost disappeared into their wrinkled setting as she turned her head from side to side, acknowledging the applause.

"Now I understand, madam," said Geoffrey. "You are the true sapphire that heals and ends all my sufferings, the emerald which brings rejoicing, the, er . . ."

" . . . the ruby to brighten and comfort the heart . . ." she said.

But she was not speaking to Chaucer. She was looking down the table to where Rosamond was sitting with her husband on one side and Gaston Florac on the other.

When the party, or some of them, had been to inspect the players in the town square they returned to the castle and settled to their various diversions. The chamberlain came to Henri de Guyac to report on the news of the drowned man. Henri nodded, made some remark about the dangers of the river, then indicated to his seneschal, Richard Foix, that he was ready to see Geoffrey Chaucer.

Back in her own chamber, Rosamond picked up the story of *Nicolette and the Castellan* and resumed her reading.

That night the castellan dreamed of Nicolette. He was once again talking to her in her chamber. He was urging his love on her, as he gazed at her fair face and blue eyes. This time his words seemed to be having the effect he wished for. She no longer talked of honour but smiled sweetly and put her hand on his arm.

"So you will accept my love?" he said.

"I give my word to love you," said this fair lady, "but only when my husband is dead."

At that moment, as if by a magical summons, the door to the chamber opened and in strode the lady's husband. He had been out hunting and was still dressed in his huntsman's garb. He carried a spear that was stained with a boar's blood. The castellan – whose heart had leaped high when the lady first pledged to love him and then sunk as low when she gave as a condition the death of her husband – stood up to face the lord of the castle.

"O castellan of Domfort," said the lord of the castle, "what are you doing in my lady's chamber? Is it to my honour and the honour of my house?"

The castellan did not reply and the lady turned her head away. The lord needed no further answer. His eye flashed and when he spoke there was anger in his voice.

"O lady Nicolette, your averted look betrays you and your cheek is bright with shame. I heard your words outside the door. You wish me dead."

He lifted his bloodstained spear and shook it, then cast it with a clatter into the corner.

"Yet you are my lady, and neither harsh words nor heavy deeds have any place with you."

And with that he buried his face in his hands.

Meantime the castellan, thinking that the lord of the castle meant harm to Nicolette or to him, had seized a crossbow which was in another corner of the chamber. He did not question why such an implement should be in a lady's chamber, for in a dream things come to hand, things which are both wished for and unwished. He raised *the bow and loosed the bolt and struck the lady's husband full in the neck. With a great crash, the noble huntsman toppled to the ground. Blood flowed forth from his wound, blood unstaunched.*

The lady shrieked and almost swooned.

"What have you done?" she cried.

"I do not know," said the castellan.

"See how he bleeds!" cried the lady.

They looked towards the ground where lay her husband's body. A rising tide of blood was issuing from the wound. The blood flowed across the floor, where the hungry rushes soaked it up at first. Then it lapped about the feet of Nicolette and the castellan of Domfort. Who would have thought that a mere man could contain so much blood? By now the tide of red was at their knees and presently reached their waists.

The lady turned towards the castellan and gravely said, "You are at fault in this."

The castellan would have replied but his mouth was full of the other man's blood. He was choking. He could not breathe and so woke from his dream.

From this dreadful dream the castellan awoke, fearful and feverish.

Rosamond was interrupted by a knock on her door. She recognized the knock and said nothing. She would only have spoken had there been anyone in the room with her. After a moment the door opened and Gaston Florac entered.

In the outbuilding where the players were sleeping, the man called Hubert lay on his back and smiled up at the darkness. Around him were snores and little sighs.

This had been more quickly settled than he could have hoped. There'd been some grief at the death of Bertram but Hubert sensed that the drowned man was the most expendable in the group, the only one not linked by blood or attachment to the others. They'd lost a player, they were short-handed. So when Hubert planted the seed in Lewis's mind – "You say you've been a mummer, Hubert?" asked Lewis. "In my time," said Hubert – it was only a matter of time before Loup realized that the solution to their short-handedness was sitting right in front of them.

And so they'd taken him on. After all, he'd rescued their little dog. After all, he'd offered to go to the priest tomorrow morning to arrange a mass for poor, drowned Bertram. After all, he was a player.

You couldn't deny that. As to whether he'd ever need to show his mettle as a player . . . well, that depended on what happened tomorrow.

Henri de Guyac waited for Geoffrey Chaucer. He was sitting in his chamber. The windows were open, it was a fine summer's night. Moths fluttered round the candles, casting agitated shadows that were impossibly bigger than their tiny selves. Around the room were tapestries depicting the hunt, their bright colours dulled and with only the gold thread catching the light. Guyac wasn't alone. His seneschal, Richard Foix, was seated at a desk on the far side of the room.

While he waited for Chaucer's arrival, he recalled his first encounter with the Englishman. It was during Edward's fruitless campaign to lay his hands on the French crown. This campaign, conducted in the north, with its skirmishes and little sieges, was nothing to do with the Comte de Guyac, or nothing very much. As a lord of Aquitaine he owed an ultimate allegiance to Edward the Third but he was also bound by remote blood-ties to King John the Good, currently living in England. As if in a perverse game of chess, the king on each side had been shifted on to the other's territory, the one by choice, the other by compulsion.

151

The Comte de Guyac was more concerned to preserve his lands and his independence. Seeing that Edward's attempt to grab the crown was going to falter, he decided to return home to Périgord before he was called on to intervene on behalf of one side or the other. He took Geoffrey Chaucer with him. It was not on account of the paltry ransom which would be handed over sooner or later for the young man and which, in any case, would be paid not to him but to his northern kinsman. Rather he took Chaucer for the sake of company and conversation on the journey. There was something about this young squire in the Duke of Clarence's retinue that interested Guyac. He was not like most of his peers, all mouth and fine leggings, boasting about his feats in battle or the number of upper-class girls who'd fallen helplessly in love with him or the hordes of servant-women he'd bedded. There was an inward quality to this Englishman. Chaucer thought before he spoke, and often he didn't speak at all. When he did say something, it was generally worth listening to or at least amusing in a quirky fashion.

Guyac recalled the first words he'd heard Chaucer say. The English prisoners were being held in the office of the marshal of Cernay-en-Domnois near Rheims. The town was strongly fortified but the people were jittery (with reason, since it was taken by John of Gaunt a few days afterwards). One of the marshal's men was striding about the guard-room, taunting the handful of English captives. He was asking them what their Edward was doing on this side of the water. No one responded. Why didn't he stay at home in England, minding his own kingly crown instead of bothering about other people's? What was he doing in France? Eh? Respond!

"Our king has come shopping," said Chaucer calmly.

"*Shopping*? Are you saying that we're a nation of shop-keepers?" said the angry Frenchman.

"Trading, you might say, under the sign of Roi John *et fils* – "

The man raised his fist then lowered it. He wasn't sure whether he'd just been insulted.

"King Edward is going shopping for a crown," said Chaucer. "But I tell you he is prepared to take what he will not pay for."

Henri de Guyac, who'd been standing on the other side of the guard-room, stared at the man who'd just been speaking. The Englishman was quite unremarkable to look at, the sort of person you'd pass in the street without more than a glance, perhaps not even that much. Guyac admired the dexterity of the man's answers. He'd insulted his captors by suggesting that they were more at home behind a shop counter than on horseback, but he'd also insinuated that his own king was a violent thief, albeit a determined one.

"What's your name?" said Guyac.

"Geoffrey Chaucer, in the service of Lionel, Duke of Clarence."

"Well, Master Chaucer, you should beware of insulting your hosts with talk of shopkeepers."

"To own a shop is no disgrace," said the man. "My father is a vintner."

"And what are you?"

"A squire in the service of – "

"Yes, yes, I know. But what *are* you?"

"I am a maker," said Chaucer, then, seeing the other's baffled expression, "A poet."

"What have you written?"

"I have written ballads, roundels, virelays. Small beer so far, but I shall go on to do something more worthy."

The confidence, the quiet assertion of this prisoner of war, delighted Henri de Guyac.

Learning that the vintner's son was in the custody of his kinsman, Henri had proposed that he remove him somewhere safe for the duration of the campaign. The kinsman would negotiate over the ransom and receive the proceeds. The kinsman was in no position to refuse him. So it was that Henri and his men rode south with Geoffrey Chaucer, stopping at a chapel on Christmas morning and reaching the domain de Guyac on New Year's Day.

"I have brought you home a poet," he'd said to his wife. Later he had gone to see his new son for the first time. Rosamond was right, babies did look alike. Despite what she said, he wasn't able to discern anything of himself in young Henri. But now the lad was a mirror image of him.

He glanced across the chamber at Richard Foix. The seneschal was sitting with paper and ink in front of him, quill hovering. De Guyac knew the reason for Chaucer's visit. The Englishman was to bring an appeal that he, de Guyac, should throw in his lot with the English Edward.

There was a rap at the door and Geoffrey was ushered in. Henri waved him in the direction of a chair. Chaucer sat down. He felt the leather wallet burning against his chest. He was starting to have an idea of what it contained now. Was guessing at the secret, the information which Gaunt had instructed him only to reveal as a last resort.

"Let us speak in English," said de Guyac, "in honour of our guest."

Geoffrey bowed his head in acknowledgement, before saying, "Thank you – although I am happy in Languedoc, happy in the place and its people as well as in its tongue. To hear it again if not to speak it."

"But the tongue you have acquired is a courtier's, I see," said Guyac.

"If it is so, I learned my first lesson here more than a decade ago."

Guyac placed his elbows on the chair-arms and steepled his hands under his chin, as if to signal that the compliments were finished. Foix's pen stopped hovering and applied itself to the top sheet of paper.

"You have heard the latest news?"

"You are better placed for news than I am, sir."

"Then I can tell you that a man drowned in the river tonight," said Henri. "One of those players who arrived with you."

Chaucer felt sweat break out on his forehead.

"No! Who? Not Lewis Loup?"

Guyac looked towards Foix.

"A person called Bertram. He was trying to rescue his dog. The dog was saved," said the seneschal.

Any man's death was sad enough, but Geoffrey felt curiously relieved, not at the salvation of the dog but because Loup was all right. There was a silence.

"The tide is turning," said Henri.

At first Chaucer thought that he was making some reference to the drowning, but saw after a moment that he was talking about bigger business.

"In whose favour?" he said.

"You aren't so out of touch as to not know that, Geoffrey."

"No, I'm not."

"The Vicomte de Rochechouart and the lords of Chauvigny and Pons have declared their allegiance – for King Charles naturally."

"Also the Comte de Périgord," added Foix.

"But the Comte de Guyac does not have to follow others," said Chaucer. "He is a leader."

"Only a fool resists the tide," said Foix.

Henri shot a glance at his seneschal and the man leaned back so that his face was shadowed.

"You have your answer," said de Guyac.

"Your final answer?"

"We shall talk more, no doubt. But I do not want you to cling to false hopes, Geoffrey."

"I am not one for false hopes."

"Ever the realist, eh," said Guyac in milder tones. "You must

155

be tired after your journeying. I am out hunting tomorrow, but we shall talk later."

"The boar that was talked of at supper?"

"The beast that has already killed three men. It is out of season but he cannot be allowed to run riot any longer. I feel that tomorrow is the day appointed for his death."

As if to underline Guyac's words, there was a sizzling sound from the region of one of the candles and a moth fell, singed, to the rushy floor.

"When I return from the hunt tomorrow, we shall talk again," he repeated.

After Geoffrey had left, Richard Foix said to his master, "You will refuse this embassy, my lord?"

"I shall be the judge of that."

"Gaston Florac is inclined to the French cause."

"I am not interested in Florac's inclinations."

"The Lady Rosamond thinks there is no future in holding allegiance to the English crown."

"What?"

Foix realized he'd overstepped the mark.

"I – I – she happened to mention to me – "

"When I want her opinion I shall ask her direct. And yours also, Foix. Now go."

Sitting alone in the near darkness Henri de Guyac pondered the future. Of course, his seneschal – to say nothing of his wife – was right. The tide was turning against the English in Aquitaine. Sooner or later they would lose their grip on the territory. Self-interest dictated that he throw in his lot with other lords such as Chauvigny and Pons or his neighbour Gaston Florac. Yet there was also the question of honour, the pull of old loyalties and acquaintances (like Geoffrey). On his decision rested the fate of many. His house of Guyac was famous. How would it be talked of in the years to come?

12

The light of a summer's dawn hardly penetrated the thick curtains surrounding Chaucer's bed. Any noises from outside were muffled too. But Geoffrey was already awake. It was the time of year when the young can't sleep, out of love or out of lust, and when the old come unwillingly awake. But in his case, between youth and age, he awoke because he was preoccupied. Brooding on the brief interview with Henri, he had not enjoyed a sound sleep. The situation in the castle was difficult. He had made no headway with de Guyac and, in effect, his mission looked likely to fail. He would make one final attempt to persuade the Comte when the latter returned from his hunting expedition today. He had still not decided whether to use the secret information entrusted to him by Gaunt.

Inside the wallet which he wore about his neck was a sealed letter. John of Gaunt had passed it to him, instructing him to give it to Henri de Guyac only as a last resort. "Do not ask about its contents, Geoffrey," he'd said. "Merely hand it to the Comte if he should seem – unresponsive to our request."

To carry a secret letter, to be denied knowledge of its contents, is an invitation to the imagination. On and off throughout their long journey Chaucer had wondered exactly what it contained. There was no way of knowing, of course, short of breaking the seal and reading it. But he might guess. It was reasonable to suppose that it was information which Henri would not welcome, something that would put pressure on him.

Something from his past . . . his past in England perhaps, since that might lie within Gaunt's field of knowledge . . . ?

Geoffrey recalled the account that de Guyac had once given him of his youthful days in England. Of how he'd spent time at the English court, a dissolute time. Of his shipwreck off the Brittany coast and his vow to live a better life, if he was rescued. Chaucer put this information together with a couple of other things which he'd observed. He'd observed Ned Caton, for example. Fundamentally a good-humoured young man, high-spirited but with a temper on him. There'd been that altercation with a bowman on board the *Arveragus*. And he recalled Ned's outburst in the inn when the young man had flared up at the insult *gafet de putan* – a whore's child. Ned Caton had a mother, the beautiful Anne Caton, whom Chaucer had never met but of whom he'd heard court-talk.

Chaucer thought of the similarity between Henri de Guyac and his young son, also Henri. He'd spotted it almost straightaway when the young lad appeared in the castle garden the previous afternoon. And there was no denying too a . . . certain likeness . . . between Caton and de Guyac. Both were stocky, with a determined way of moving. By itself, that was almost nothing. But family resemblances are often more subtle, things that lie beneath the skin, things you can't put a finger on. Was that why John of Gaunt had foisted the young man on him, together with Alan Audly? Was Caton a by-blow of Guyac's, dating from his time in England more than twenty years earlier, the product of an illicit liaison between the Gascon noble and Anne Caton? Had Gaunt sent the young man down as a kind of "reminder" to Guyac to stay in line? Yet even as Chaucer, lying in bed in the Comte's castle, considered this he came near to rejecting the idea. What nobleman would be shamed by his illegitimate son? Bastards were inconvenient but often a source of pride as well as a complication. If it were otherwise – if shame was the rule – then there'd be no shortage of hung heads and red faces among the nobility of England.

Suddenly he heard the door open, unobtrusively, and footsteps moving towards the bed. His first thought was that it must be a servant but it was surely too early in the day for anyone to be attending to his chamber. Also, this person's tread did not resemble a servant's. Although soft it was too confident, too proprietorial. Through half-closed eyes, he was aware of someone parting the curtains a fraction.

He knew her by her sweet smell, knew who it was before she'd even parted the curtains. She was wearing some mixture of lavender and rosewater. He feigned sleep.

"Come now, Geoffrey. A true sleeper never looks so guarded."

He opened his eyes fully.

"I should have known better than to try to deceive you, my lady."

Rosamond was wearing an embroidered shift. There was a high colour in her face. She sat down on the edge of his bed. He felt it give under her weight. He could have touched her by stretching out his arm a little. He sat up. There was only a small gap in the bed-curtains admitting a half-light.

"Is that all you have been trying to deceive me in?" she said.

"It is too early in the day for this, my lady. You deserve a better reception than I can provide just now."

He made an indeterminate gesture to indicate his night-gear, his sleep-worn state.

"You should call me Rosamond, Geoffrey."

"Where is your husband, Rosamond?"

"He is going to hunt the boar. He has vowed not to return until he has rid the neighbourhood of this scourge. He will not be back for many hours."

"Aren't you worried for him? This beast has already killed at least three men."

"My husband is an experienced huntsman. He will get what he is after."

"And what is it that *you* are after?"

"My question exactly, Geoffrey." She shifted her position slightly so that her scent came fresh to his nostrils. She was close enough for him to be aware of the warmth of her body underneath the shift, or perhaps he merely thought he was aware of it. He observed the swell of her breasts, rising and falling slightly more than necessary.

"Tell me what are you doing here in Guyac."

"What has passed between Henri and me is . . . confidential. He could tell you if he wished."

"Perhaps he already has told me. But I'm interested in what you have to say. Once you would have told me."

Stung by the remark, Chaucer said, "But you would have had the tact not to ask."

"You will be saying next that it is man's talk, not fit for women's ears. But everything to do with Guyac is my business too. This is a very old house, a famous house. Do you believe that its fortunes are not close to my heart? I know that great things are at stake."

Geoffrey found himself unable to return her frank gaze. The light beyond the curtains was growing stronger by the minute. She had not yet made herself up for the day and the high colour in her face was unfeigned. He wondered whether this un-adorned appearance, in the simple embroidered shift, was planned. (But of course it was planned, he thought.) She was no longer the young woman he'd moped over when he was nineteen and she was a few years older, but she was beautiful still and the intervening years had given her a kind of ripeness as well as a greater certainty. He was finding it hard to refuse her and she knew it.

"You know that matters here in Guyenne are on a knife-edge," he said. "The French king has already announced his intention to confiscate the territory."

"While your king has announced his intention to hold on to it."

"You might say that Edward is your king as well," said Chaucer.

"How lucky we are to have a choice of kings!"

She laughed but without humour.

"Kings don't like being chosen," said Geoffrey. "They are too accustomed to choosing for themselves. If they don't get their way they generally resort to arms."

"Edward has fought in so many campaigns," said Rosamond, "he must be tiring of them."

"It is the old lion you should beware of. And don't forget his sons, they are just as warlike."

"The young Edward is not popular here," she said. "Not so young either. He is sick as well. People sense that his grip is weakening."

"There is always Gaunt," said Geoffrey.

"It was he who sent you, wasn't it? And, in order that you should give away no secrets, I will tell you why. You are here to persuade my husband to pledge his allegiance to Edward."

Chaucer conceded defeat. Since she knew or guessed at everything there was no point in evasion. He said, "Yes, to persuade him. In the hope that where Henri de Guyac goes, others will follow. War might be avoided if enough of the nobility of Aquitaine declare for Edward. Isn't that a worthy aim, my lady?"

"Is war unworthy?"

"I've got out of the habit of war. It's years since I've worn armour. I'm getting a little plump for it."

She ignored his self-deprecating attempt to turn the conversation and said, "We used to play at backgammon."

"I remember."

"Luck with the dice isn't enough in that game, you need skill as well, and more even than that – something in reserve. Gaunt wouldn't send you here, depending only on luck or your silver tongue. There's something in reserve."

"I don't understand you, Rosamond."

"Oh you do, Geoffrey." She moved closer to him once again and he was conscious of her warmth. "You have something in reserve. What is it? Tell me."

The players watched the chase depart. They'd heard about the dangerous wild boar which had already killed three peasants. The villagers talked admiringly of Henri de Guyac's prowess as a huntsman, of how he would strike out by himself into the woods in pursuit of his quarry. The scene was a scrimmage of dogs and horses and men, mounted and on foot. Cerberus, cradled in Alice Loup's arms, squirmed in his eagerness to be among the other dogs and on his way. Alice kept hold of his ruff and whispered in the dog's ear to tell him that he was better off where he was, he'd be trampled beneath the horses' hooves, or a mere mouthful for the great alaunts once they were un-muzzled. The dogs, well disciplined, were still but their ears were pricked and their eel-like heads were directed expectantly towards their human masters. There was also a pack of running hounds, similarly muzzled. Fewer in number were the tracker dogs, the lymers. Bred, beaten and bribed into the habit of silence, they didn't need muzzling. The mounted men included Henri de Guyac accompanied by his son and Gaston Florac as well as Richard Foix, the seneschal, and Alan Audly and Ned Caton. A large number of men stood by holding spears and crossbows.

Alice said, with a mixture of excitement and fear, "They look more like an army than a band of hunters."

Simon was next to her. He said, "The boar is the most dangerous of all creatures. And this one is the very devil."

She looked at him and he quickly added, "That's what the villagers call him. They say that a man who is killed by a boar loses his soul."

The "army" of hunters started to move out of the castle

precincts. There was an air of grim purpose to the men, although the morning was bright and clear.

Simon nodded towards Hubert who was standing out of earshot.

"Have you talked to that man?"

"No."

"I don't trust him."

"But he rescued Cerberus," she said, giving the wriggling dog a squeeze.

"Not Bertram though."

"You would've done better, I suppose."

"I'm not claiming that. I just don't like him. Why has your father taken him on?"

"We're short of a man. He says he's a player."

"He says."

"You really don't trust him, do you?"

"Where's he off to now, for instance?"

They watched as Hubert walked at a relaxed but steady pace in the direction taken by the hunt.

Simon had never hunted but he was right when he claimed that the boar was the most formidable quarry in the chase. Solitary, ferocious and cunning, he demanded a plan of battle if he was to be tracked down and killed.

On the previous day Henri de Guyac had come close to his quarry but the beast had outrun his dogs. He was taking no chance of that happening again and had commanded his huntsmen to arrange relays of hounds for today, so that any exhausted, wounded or killed animals should be promptly replaced. The normal pattern would have been for one of the lymers, accompanied by its master, to search out the boar's bed. Once found, and if the bed was still warm, the running hounds were released to give chase. Sometimes the boar would turn and face his canine pursuers, perhaps wounding or killing a couple, before making off once more into the woods. Eventually, though, he would be brought to bay. And then a combination of dog and man would drag him down, using teeth and claws and spears and swords.

But this beast was different. For one thing, the "devil" would not be occupying the bed from which he had been ousted the day before. He'd have moved on to a new resting place, although he was unlikely to have gone very far. Henri did not doubt that they would encounter the "devil". He had meant what he'd said to Geoffrey Chaucer the previous evening: that this day was the one appointed for his death. But de Guyac did not trust to fortune alone. Preparation both of body and mind, unremitting alertness, the willingness even to lay down his life, all of these things were necessary too.

Henri de Guyac led his party on to the wooded upland that lay opposite his castle and village. One of the huntsmen who'd gone on ahead with his lymer returned to say that the dog had picked up a possible scent.

Gaston Florac, who was riding near Henri, suggested that the running hounds be released. Guyac shook his head.

"Why not?" said Florac.

"It's not time."

They cantered deeper into the woods. Henri's senses could not have been more alert if he had been the hunted rather than the hunter. For some time nothing happened. Despite his earlier confidence, Henri began to fear that the boar was sulking, refusing to poke his head out of shelter, refusing to take up the challenge. If on hearing the distant hunt – and his hearing was very acute – he decided to secrete himself in the deepest reaches of the forest, then he would stay hidden, unflustered by all the trumpeting and halloo-ing in the world. And the hunt would be done for the day.

But eventually the moment came that de Guyac had been waiting for. His favourite lymer, a heavy-headed dog named

Ravault, returned with the huntsman whose instincts de Guyac most trusted. This particular combination of dog and man – *his* name was Bauderon – was on the mark nine times out of ten. Henri dismounted to consult with Bauderon. They talked briefly, the huntsman pointing to an area of woodland to the east and mentioning the signs he'd observed (recent tracks of the beast, fresh smears of mud on the trees which he had rubbed himself against). Henri nodded. The dog stood close by, waiting for the words of acknowledgement and praise which Henri bestowed before he remounted.

He rode on, followed by Florac and the others, including Alan Audly and Ned Caton. Some way to the rear were the spearmen and the huntsmen with their coupled hounds. This was a more inaccessible area of the forest, though close to where the boar had first been detected the previous day. Henri wasn't sure whether to attribute this to the animal's cunning or to his defiance – both most likely. The villagers referred to the beast as a "devil". De Guyac, though properly fearful of his opponent, thought of him less harshly. For him the beast had the qualities of a hero, an *eros* in the local tongue. It was hardy, proud, undaunted. He'd had no more than a couple of glimpses of the thing, a black bulk crashing through bushes and underbrush, but each time he felt himself in the presence of a worthy adversary.

Without signalling to the other riders, de Guyac directed his horse on to a side-track and spurred off into the depths of the forest. He couldn't have explained why he did this. But it was a manoeuvre he'd performed before on the chase. It was as if an invisible thread connected him to his quarry and that one or both of them – hunter and hunted – suddenly started pulling on the thread. Though there were upwards of two dozen men behind him and double that number of dogs, he experienced an acute – and pleasurable – sense of isolation. He recalled those tales in which the hunter was led by his quarry out of the real world and into a strange landscape inhabited by monsters. The hairs on his scalp stirred and his grip on the reins tightened involuntarily.

Geoffrey Chaucer stirred uneasily in his bed as the lady repeated her demand.

"There is a secret here. What is it? Tell me."

This time she grasped his wrist. She had a strong grasp.

"No secret, lady."

"The Geoffrey Chaucer I knew once would not have refused me."

"We are neither of us as we were," he said, conscious of the feebleness of the reply.

"No, you are married for one thing. For another you have children, I dare say . . ."

"Thomas and Elizabeth."

"You should hear how your tone softens to say their names. And your wife's name?"

"Philippa."

"Is she beautiful?"

"In my eyes."

"Oh, is that a poet's answer? You can do better than that."

"No man is a poet inside his own house."

"Not even in the bedroom?"

"Rosamond, what is it that you seek? Your husband is not the only one in the chase."

"No, he has taken your young friends with him. We are alone here."

"And Gaston Florac?"

Chaucer noticed the renewed colouring in the lady's face when he mentioned the name.

"He too has gone hunting. A gallant gentleman."

"So I am lounging in bed on a fine summer's morning while they are all engaged as men should be."

"There are other sports men can profitably engage in."

"I should be with them."

"It's already too late, Geoffrey."

Seized with a sudden unease, he flung back the blankets and pushed aside the curtains which shrouded the bed. Rosamond stood up. He strode to the window and opened it. In the far distance he could hear the yelping of hounds.

"It sounds as though they have found their quarry," he said.

Henri de Guyac spurred on after the *chiens courants*. He hadn't given the signal after all. Florac must have ordered their release. Henri would have felt angry if he'd had the leisure. The dogs might set off on a false scent if released too early.

Now, off to another side, he recognized the sounds of the alaunts, the dogs reserved for the kill. From their baying he knew that they were close to the mark. He took a different path. It was narrow and tortuous but he trusted his horse – a broad-chested, sure-footed mount called Brun – to negotiate its twists and turns. By instinct the horse eluded outcrops of rock and decayed stumps of trees. Henri kept low in the saddle to avoid the overhanging branches but even so he was lashed repeatedly across the face and upper body by twigs and foliage. He hardly noticed. His mind and temper were keyed up to the approaching encounter. He had already outrun the others. The only living things ahead of him were the dogs – and the boar. He preferred it this way.

The barking and baying grew louder and then, mingled with those sounds, Henri recognized the howls signalling that the dogs had indeed brought their quarry to bay. Now moving at little more than a walking pace, man and horse were emerging from the shadows of the track and into an open area. In the centre of the clearing was a wide pond produced by a stream whose clogged progress had filled up a natural depression in the forest floor. The pond was round, like a great eye in the centre of the forest. The edges were slick with mud and a mush of weeds and rushes.

Still half in the shadows, Henri reined in. He felt Brun quiver beneath him but otherwise the horse stood its ground. This was where it counted to have a mount that was not merely courageous and sure-footed but above all possessed of an equable temper. For the sight that confronted the two of them would have been enough to cause a highly strung animal to turn tail.

The boar was on the far bank of the pond. He was standing on a patch of relatively uncluttered ground that sloped up from the water. In this position he had the advantage over the dogs which hadn't yet managed to encircle him. Henri had arrived at a momentary pause. There was an eerie silence. The first blood had been spilled and every creature was drawing breath. Wiping away the sweat that was streaming down his face, he saw that some of the alaunts – heavier and stronger than the running hounds – had grouped themselves in a semicircle below the boar. In fact there was no sign of the running hounds. They must have set off on a false scent. Several other alaunts were swimming across the pond, eager to take the most direct route to their quarry. Two of the dogs lay tossed to one side, many yards from the boar but gored and thrown across the distance by the infuriated swings of his mighty head. One of the dogs was already dead, the other lay still moving but with its innards spilling out on to the reddened earth. In other circumstances de Guyac could have spared a moment's pity for the loss of two of his pack. But now all his attention, his whole being, was fastened on the great boar which crouched on the other side of the water.

He recognized the signs of a likely attack. The boar was about to take the fight to the dogs. He had his snout close to the ground and his ears flattened against his head. Then, alerted by some movement on the opposite side of the clearing, he looked up at the man on horseback. De Guyac had faced (and killed) a good many boar in a lifetime of hunting but he did not think that he had ever confronted such a formidable opponent. The devil. The *eros*.

This one was in his sixth or seventh year, long used to living a singular life in the forest, consorting with the sows only in autumn. His tusks were a dirty white, and his coat had an absolute blackness as if he had absorbed all the shadowy places of the wood. For his part, the boar could make out the rider, a dim figure on the other side of the pond. His sight was not good but he sensed an enemy more dangerous than the hounds crouched before him.

De Guyac's eyesight might have been superior but in every other respect (apart from brains, and they are not always a match for brute cunning) he was the boar's inferior, and the man knew it. Knowing that fact was the only way to have a chance of success.

Henri listened for the rest of the hunt but the wood to his back was silent. Surely the others would soon catch up, would shortly burst into the clearing. Then this "devil" might retreat further into the trees that clustered above the pond. Either that or he would choose to take on all his enemies, dogs and men, all at once. He'd die eventually through sheer weight of numbers but the glory would go to whoever delivered the finishing stroke, and not to Henri de Guyac who – in his own eyes at least – would have failed the final test because he had waited for help.

Quickly, before he could debate the matter further with himself, he urged his horse along the margins of the pond. Without being told to, Brun kept away from the mud-slick banks and paced sedately round the water's edge. Henri sensed the horse's fear, a reflection of his own, but to an observer they might have been out on a morning exercise. The boar's head shifted slightly as he followed the progress of man and mount. His eyes rolled, the hair on his neck bristled like a crest, his teeth and tusks were a fence of bloodied bone.

169

Taking advantage of the boar's momentary distraction, one of the more reckless alaunts leaped for him. The dog managed to sink its teeth into the other's flank but its purchase wasn't sufficient or secure. It was thrown off in an instant, and sent spinning down towards the bank of the pond where it collided with one of its fellows emerging from the water. If the hapless dog had kept its grip it would have been joined in the attack by half a dozen more, but instead the others, hackles bristling, teeth bared, remained in a semicircle out of reach of the gnashing tusks and the ponderous head. By now Henri de Guyac was only a matter of yards from his quarry. Brun was brave enough to have ridden on but the rider halted him with a squeeze to his flanks.

Then slowly, almost nonchalantly, he dismounted.

At some distance from the pond where the boar was at bay, Gaston Florac and Richard Foix were trying to decide which direction de Guyac and the dogs had taken. Alan Audly and Ned Caton had reined in behind them while Guyac's son, young Henri, was between the four men. From one quarter of the forest there was a kind of charged silence, broken by the occasional yelp or cry. But the bulk of the sound came from a different quarter.

"There, I think," said Florac, indicating the second direction.

But he seemed in no great hurry to move.

"With respect, sir . . ."

Florac looked down at Bauderon, the huntsman whose lymer had originally scented the presence of the "devil" boar. He was on foot. Without eagerness, Florac waited to hear what the servant had to say.

"My master is over there."

And Bauderon pointed towards the silent quarter.

"You've scented out your master, have you?"

"Not me but Ravault. He knows by instinct."

It was true that the attention of the dog was angled towards the less active area of woodland.

"What do you think, Foix?"

"I defer to your judgement, my lord."

"Then I say we should split up. Take the two English with you, Foix, and Henri. Half the men as well. I shall set off this way."

Without a word more he turned his horse in the direction he'd first indicated.

Geoffrey Chaucer hurriedly dressed and, ignoring the Lady Rosamond, almost ran from his chamber. It wasn't so much that he felt his place was outside in the woods with the hunt. Geoffrey had no great liking for the chase. But he was troubled by some apprehension which he couldn't put his finger on. What had Rosamond meant when she said that it was already too late?

It took him some time to locate his horse in the unfamiliar stables, to get it saddled and to ride out of the castle precincts. The village square was full of idle people, as if this was a feast day. But they were queerly silent, standing with their heads cocked as though they were listening for sounds of a distant battle.

As if his own passage was a cue for action, the people in the square started to move after him in the direction of the surrounding woodland. They wouldn't have wished to be present at the kill – even a badly wounded boar was a ferocious danger – but they wanted to be in on the aftermath, the ceremonial cutting-up of the beast. Then this ordinary working day would truly become a feast day as they celebrated the demise of an enemy.

He spurred downhill and then off to the right towards the faint whoops and halloos echoing through the summer leaves.

Like the villagers of Guyac, Geoffrey himself had no desire to be in at the very kill. Unlike them, he did not have much taste for its aftermath either. This entailed the severing of the boar's head, the burning-off of its bristles, the ritual unmaking of its carcass, with the liver and spleen reserved for the castle kitchen and the rest of the innards going to the dogs as their reward. No, Geoffrey thought, he'd never had a taste for those pursuits which in an odd way united the nobleman on his hunter and the peasant behind his plough. He was too much of a townie, born and bred in a place where, if you wanted to see the surrounding countryside, you had to climb a church tower.

In any case, if he was serious about getting close to the action, then he ought to have obtained a better horse than the one he was currently astride, hired in Bordeaux. Like him, it was a townie at heart. At the first whiff of a boar's scent, it would take fright and probably throw him. So why was he riding deeper into the woods, lured by the distant cries? Simply a sense of unease which he couldn't shake off.

And then his horse swerved abruptly and Chaucer was almost knocked out of his seat as an outstretched branch struck his shoulder. Gripping hold of the cantle, he hung on and calmed the animal, suppressing his curses. What the devil . . . ?

There was a man on the path. He must have emerged from the undergrowth and startled the animal. It was a man with long hair and sunken cheeks. His face was scored with unhealed scratches, as if he pushed his head into thorns or perhaps tore at himself in mortification. That was as much as Geoffrey could see in the uncertain light. From his dirty, ragged clothes, he looked to be a forest-dweller. There were scavengers who lived just far enough from human habitation not to be troubled by people but close enough to pick up their leavings. Sometimes they were dignified by the name of hermit. For sure this was one of those fellows. There was no visible danger but he might be concealing a knife under his rags.

Geoffrey did not dismount. Neither did the man shift but continued to occupy the middle of the narrow path as if he required something, alms most likely. Geoffrey gently urged his horse forward. It moved with reluctance, frightened by this apparition with staring eyes and gaunt features. Then the man did a strange thing. He stood to one side and held out his right arm like a signpost. His forefinger tapered into a claw-like nail. Mutely he was indicating the direction in which Chaucer was travelling anyway. But the man's stance, the rigid arm with its hanging rags, the fingernail which protruded like a little dagger-point, all seemed to say, "There is what you are looking for."

It wasn't this that disturbed the rider, however. Anyone, even a forest-dweller, might have helpfully pointed the way to the hunt. It was rather something that Geoffrey hadn't observed until he was almost level with the man: that this individual possessed only one arm. The stump of his left protruded from his shoulder. Raising his own arm in the slightest of acknowledgements, Chaucer rode past the man in the woods.

De Guyac's plan was straightforward. It was to use what was offered by this stretch of terrain, with its wide pond and tree-fringed clearing. He'd dismounted from Brun when there were still a good few yards separating man and horse from the boar. Since the last dog had been flung off, none of the others had dared approach. The wounded alaunt was still flailing around on the edge of the pond but those who'd been swimming across it had now emerged, instinctively shaking themselves before going into the posture of attack. The boar snorted and tucked his head closer to the ground.

Once Henri was on his feet he took his sword from its sheath. He carried a boar-spear with his saddle-gear, but it would be no good for what he had in mind. Sending up a prayer to St Hubert, who protects hunting dogs and their masters, he stepped sideways nearer the water. Now he stood with legs braced and sword poised. He spoke to the boar.

"Avant, maistre," he said, "avant."

He spoke almost in encouragement, in a whisper.

The boar tensed on his haunches. Now his eyes were rolling.

"Or sa, sa!" said de Guyac. Still he did not raise his voice but uttered with greater urgency, "*Avant, maistre, avant.*"

He took one step closer to the water's edge, keeping his gaze fastened on the boar's writhing, foam-flecked mouth. For an instant it seemed as if time were suspended. Henri was conscious of the contrast between the sky, where summer clouds sauntered across a bowl of blue, and the dark mud which clung to his boots. He saw himself as if from above, approaching the blue eye that lay in the centre of the clearing.

Without warning it happened. The boar launched himself at de Guyac, driving through the scatter of dogs that lay between man and beast. There was a cacophony of howls and squeals as several of the alaunts threw themselves at the boar. The beast paid them less attention than a man would give to a cloud of midges but, as Henri had expected, the dogs nevertheless slowed the boar sufficiently for him to get to the water's edge. For an instant they almost halted the beast altogether.

Moving as quickly as his uncertain footing would allow he half walked, half stumbled into the pond. He'd feared it wouldn't be deep enough but he was soon up to his chest and had not even reached the middle. He stopped to establish a stable footing – or as firm as the slippery, clogging bottom would permit. The water filled his boots and made his hose cling to his legs, and the rank smell of rot and weed penetrated his nostrils. But de Guyac was oblivious to all this. He was aware only of the boar.

Tearing a path through the dogs, the great beast crashed into the pond, sending up a fountain of water and causing a violent disturbance which nearly knocked Henri off balance. Sensing rather than clearly seeing the whereabouts of his enemy, the boar paddled furiously in his direction, the ridge of his back bristling above the waves, his head like a black tun of wine. Henri settled into position. He felt something solid against his heel – a rock, a submerged tree stump – and braced himself against it.

The one physical advantage the man had over the boar was in the length of his legs, not much use on dry land where the animal can easily outrun the human but significant in water. The advantage for de Guyac of being up to his chest in the pond was that he could land a blow on his opponent while the beast, needing to keep afloat and lacking anything which might have given him the purchase to strike, was less well placed. But Henri needed all his nerve to hold fast while the snorting, tusked head propelled itself through the rough water. The temptation to turn away, to flail desperately towards the bank was almost overwhelming. So too was the contrary desire to lash out at the boar before the animal was truly within range.

But Henri de Guyac stood firm, grasping his sword with two hands. He was a proper hunter. He was a true member of the house of Guyac, undaunted by man or beast.

The boar in the water might have no purchase for a charge or for a swing of his tusks but he remained a dreadful danger on account of his bulk and his teeth. When he was almost on top of Henri – his reeking breath and jaws were like a trapdoor into hell, and his tiny eyes rolled frantically – the man shifted to one side and, gripping the sword as if it were a monstrous dagger, he plunged it with all his might into a point between the beast's neck and foreleg. The sword sunk into the slot, as if into a preordained place, piercing bristle and hide and flesh and brawn. By main force, the boar reared out of the water, and in a spume of spray and blood, screamed out in his agony, in his rage.

They heard that terrible cry in the woods, all of them heard it, and the hair rose on the nape of their necks. It was heard by Gaston Florac and Richard Foix, who were travelling on diverging paths. Heard by Alan Audly and Ned Caton, who were supposed to have attached themselves to Foix's party but had somehow gone on separate tracks and had indeed lost sight of each other as well. Heard by Jean Cado who had taken himself off into the woods. The one-armed man who had pointed out the way to Chaucer, he heard it too. He grinned to himself. Further along the track Geoffrey Chaucer urged on his horse. The scene of the kill was further off than he'd thought. Even the English players and the Guyac villagers, straggling on foot in the wood's by-paths, heard the sound.

And, elsewhere among the trees, the man who'd called himself Hubert (though not after the patron saint of hunting) was alerted by the boar's cry and hastened in the direction of the scene.

There was a ringing noise in his ears but overhead the sun was still shining and clouds drifting past as if nothing had happened. Henri de Guyac swayed and almost tumbled backwards into the water. He regained his balance just in time. He wasn't sure whether, if he had fallen in, he still possessed the strength or the will to drag himself out again. He was sodden from head to foot, and smeared everywhere with mud and water-weed. He was panting. Blood was flowing freely down his face and he was unable to move, or even to feel any sensation in, one of his arms, yet experience told him that his wounds were not serious. Anyway they'd be attended to soon enough.

And, irrespective of the damage to himself, what a prize he had taken!

The boar lay on the edge of the pond, surrounded by yelping alaunts with bloody paws and muzzles. Several of their fellows lay dead or dying around the boar. From his flank protruded the thin shaft of the boar-spear which Henri had seized from his saddle-carriage and plunged into the beast once he was on land and surrounded by the dogs. After Henri had pierced him with the sword, the boar had uttered that dreadful cry and leapt up from the pond like the devil himself, dragging Henri through the water and almost wrenching the man's arm from its socket. But he'd regained his sword at least. The dogs, regrouping and given new heart by their master's stroke, swarmed over the boar and wore him down by sheer weight of numbers, though at considerable cost. Henri discarded his sword and retrieved his second weapon, the boar-spear. Seeing an opening among the mass of dogs, Henri delivered the final blow with the spear's broad point. He drove it home as if his life, his whole world, depended on that single thrust.

Now he stood, barely conscious of his surroundings, as feeble in his limbs as a baby. Henri's task was finished. He was not even armed. His sword, its blade slimed with red, lay in the grass while the shaft of the boar-spear quivered as the dogs tugged at the boar's carcass. Where the devil were they, the chase? The men were required now to light a fire, to sharpen their cutting implements . . .

His ears were still ringing so he couldn't tell whether the hunt was approaching. He thought he saw a movement on the edge of the clearing, a shiver among the bushes. He moved forward. He might have called out, but couldn't be sure that any words passed his lips. Perhaps they didn't because no one emerged from the bushes in response. With his good arm, his left one, he wiped away the sweat and blood that clotted his vision. No one there, only the breeze. Nevertheless, swishing his way through the long grass, he walked towards the place where he'd glimpsed the movement.

Suddenly the bushes parted and a figure darted straight out at Henri. The figure was holding something in its hand. Henri had time to recognize the object as a hunting sword. Perhaps, in his exhausted state, he did not understand the meaning of what his eyes told him. By instinct he raised his good arm, half in acknowledgement, half to ward off any attack. He opened his mouth to say . . . to say what? He never knew, because he felt a mighty blow in the chest which knocked all the breath out of him. He fell backwards and his head struck the ground. As he lay defenceless on the earth, he had a moment in which to reflect that the deadliest and most dangerous animal in the forest is the human animal. Grass fronds waved above his head. One was tickling his nose. Absurd that he should experience something so slight, so insignificant, when he had real hurts to attend to . . . Because the sun was dazzling his eyes he closed them. But he need not have done so because the figure stepped between Henri and the shining sun and raised the sword it held.

13

Suddenly the clearing was full of men and dogs and horses, pouring in pell-mell like latecomers to a celebration. Shouts and yelps replaced the silence which had momentarily fallen after the figure had brought down the sword on Henri de Guyac before slipping back among the trees. Because the body was lying in the long grass at the edge of the clearing, the hunters didn't immediately detect it. Rather they saw the alaunt-hounds clustered about the boar's carcass. Some of the men were sorry that they hadn't been in on the kill, others rejoiced in de Guyac's success – for there was no doubt that he'd been the first on the scene. Excited by the sight of the carcass and preoccupied by the need to get the dogs off it, no one stopped to consider what had happened to the Comte.

Eventually the dogs were shooed and beaten away from the boar which lay by the pond's edge. When the carcass was exposed like this, the wounds inflicted by de Guyac in the beast's shoulder and flank, from which the spear protruded like a battle standard, were plain to all. Gaston Florac publicly regretted that he hadn't been present for the boar's killing and Richard Foix, who made the same claim (though less convincingly), dismounted and examined the beast.

Alan Audly and Ned Caton, reunited after their brief separation in the forest, looked on from a distance. They'd hunted in England of course, even the boar, but never in pursuit of a quarry as large and dangerous as this one. Nevertheless they talked knowledgeably about the way in which de Guyac – where was he, by the way? – must have cunningly employed the existence of the pond to lure his opponent into the water so as to slightly redress the odds against him. Meanwhile young Henri de Guyac, truly his father's son, paid close attention to the bloodied tusks of the beast, the foam-encrusted jaws, the little eye which was now dulled.

It was one of the foot huntsmen who discovered Henri. He'd been foraging at the edge of the clearing for kindling to light the fire so that the boar's bristles could be burnt off and his innards broiled for the benefit of the dogs. He all but stumbled over the body in the grass. His call soon brought the party crowding round the corpse of the Comte de Guyac.

Death during the chase, quite apart from that of the quarry or the pursuing hounds, was hardly unknown. Any man who chose to go up against the boar by himself, equipped only with sword or spear, would be very fortunate to emerge unscathed. To perish in such circumstances was almost as honourable as death on the battlefield, a source of grief but also of pride. So the reactions of the huntsmen were muted, even those of Gaston Florac and Richard Foix. Young Henri de Guyac looked, bit his lip and turned his head away from the gaping wound in his father's chest. Richard Foix the seneschal put his hand on the boy's shoulder.

The real distress was shown by some of the villagers who now streamed into the clearing together with Lewis Loup and the rest of the players. Any liking or affection for their lord was out of the question but de Guyac had been respected and feared by those who owed their well-being (or otherwise) to him. In such uncertain times, his violent departure tore a hole in the future. There were cries and groans. Several villagers dropped to their knees and held their hands up to the blue skies.

Geoffrey Chaucer, who had reached the clearing a little earlier and spent some time surveying the scene, now dismounted from his horse. He regretted Henri's death, but he did not yet feel it. That would come later. His first thoughts in fact, were for the new widow, perhaps because he had so recently seen her.

Lewis Loup said, "What do you think, Geoffrey?"

"I don't know what to think. Except that fortune is a great goddess. I am sorry to hear of your loss."

"My loss?"

"I heard that Bertram drowned."

"That is so," said Loup, looking grave. "We are all irreplaceable − and yet we can all be replaced. There is already another man come in his place. What did you mean by fortune being a great goddess?"

"I was referring to Henri de Guyac," said Chaucer. "Here was a man who was at the top of fortune's wheel, with great wealth and estates, and now he lies in the long grass, the lowest of the low."

"Ah, the long grass," said Lewis.

"Out with it, Lewis. What's on your mind?"

The player leaned his lank face towards Geoffrey. Even though they were talking in English, he glanced round to make sure no one was in earshot.

"I'd rather you said it. I'm a outsider here, this is nothing to do with us players."

"I'm a outsider too," said Chaucer.

"Very well, I shall say it then. Why is this man's corpse lying at such a distance from that − that thing?" Lewis Loup indicated the space between the body of de Guyac and the boar's carcass. "I'm no hunter but is there is any beast on earth who could toss a man from there to here?"

"Maybe the attack took place by the trees and then the wounded boar returned to the water, where he was set upon by the dogs."

"In that case . . ." said Loup, obviously unwilling to state his doubts openly.

"In that case, my friend, you're wondering why there is so little disturbance on the ground where Henri de Guyac met his end."

Loup again glanced round nervously. People were scattered in little knots between the trees and the pond, with the largest groups near the two bodies, human and animal.

"Just so," he said. "They didn't see him straightaway, he was concealed by the grass."

"Perhaps," said Chaucer, more to himself than to Lewis, and following the line of his own reasoning, "perhaps the Comte de Guyac was mortally wounded over by the water, where there *are* signs of a great tussle, and then he managed to stagger closer to the woods. Maybe he was looking for help or shelter – or simply trying to get away. He had enough life left to pace out those few yards and no further. Blind instinct could have carried him so far."

"That must be it," said Loup. There was relief in his voice but he did not sound wholly convinced. "Blind instinct. Anyway it's none of my business."

"As you say, that must be it," said Geoffrey, stroking his beard.

"Ah husband! There you are."

It was Margaret Loup, striding towards them. Her heated face was nearly the same colour as her dress.

"Where have you been? I lost you in the woods."

"As well say I lost you," said Lewis, glancing round uneasily.

"This is a bad business," said Margaret, sweeping her arm round to encompass the whole scene and almost striking Chaucer in the face. There was anger in her large brown eyes. Geoffrey moved off to examine the body. There were others standing or kneeling round it, and wondering what to do next. De Guyac was lying on his back. One arm, his right, was stiff by his side. The other, with its heavily ringed hand, was clenched across his chest as if to try and stop his life from spilling out. The front of his hunting-coat was saturated with blood. The centre of his chest had been stove-in by the boar's tusks. There was a minor gash on his forehead and the blood from that wound, which must have been sustained before death, had dried on his face.

Geoffrey Chaucer gazed on the visage of a man he had liked and admired. The dead man's expression was unreadable – rage, fear, a grim satisfaction, it might have been any or all of those. The Englishman sent up a silent prayer for the peace and rest of his soul. Henri had, he supposed, died in one of the two places he would have chosen: the hunting field or the battlefield. But so much was left unresolved!

Geoffrey looked again at the gaping wound in the man's chest. There was something about the injury that troubled him, although he couldn't pin it down. He broadened his examination. The coarse, stalky grass was flattened in the area where Henri lay but, following Lewis Loup's prompt, he confirmed that there were no signs of a pitched battle between man and beast. A boar can weigh several times more than a man, and he cannot move without leaving traces. There were no such traces to be seen. That, and the absence of any weapon, was significant since it suggested that Henri must have received the fatal wound in another place.

As if he merely wanted a space for reflection, Geoffrey moved away from the region of the corpse. He kept his head down, apparently lost in thought. He cast about with his eyes. His sight wasn't as sharp as it had been. Still there was no sign of anything much.

Except . . .

He lifted up his head. A line, faint to the point of being invisible, seemed to run through the grass from the place where the body lay to the nearest fringe of the wood. Despite the warmth of the day, Chaucer shivered. Pacing about apparently at random, he circled nearer the trees. Thorn bushes and under-brush formed a natural hedge in front of them. The line of bent grasses ended at a gap in the bushes. Chaucer looked round. No one was watching him. Nevertheless he unlaced the purse from his belt and dropped it. Bending down to retrieve it, he looked more carefully at the gap. It wasn't wide. A boar would burst through it, leaving shattered branches in his wake. A more delicate animal like a deer – even a man at leisure – might squeeze through without leaving a mark. But a man in a hurry would be likely to tear or bend twigs and foliage on either side. And, sure enough, there were twigs hanging thread-like from the larger branches, and leaves that looked new-fallen strewn on the ground. Once again Geoffrey felt cold.

He straightened up. He edged into the shade of the trees. Making a little circuit he returned to the same spot, this time on the inner side of the straggly line of bushes. At a distance of thirty yards or more lay de Guyac's body, still surrounded by kneeling and standing figures. Beyond that he saw Gaston Florac, the lord of the neighbouring domain, giving instructions to a handful of huntsmen. One of them seemed to be disputing some point with him. A dog howled briefly before being silenced. In the middle distance and slightly to one side was the body of the boar. And beyond that lay the pond which, through some peculiarity of the angle from which Geoffrey was viewing it, had taken on a blackish, glinting quality.

For the second time he deliberately let fall the purse which he was clutching. For the second time he bent down to pick it up. Down here, in the shelter of the bushes, he thought he was concealed from the crowd in the clearing. Yet he could see them, could see the huntsmen at last moving to shift Henri's corpse from where it lay while others in the party attended to the boar.

Chaucer scanned the ground. The area was in shadow and it was hard to tell whether anyone had been lurking here. The earth was bare and crumbly with small roots running across it like veins. Yet there were marks that might have been the impress of the toe-end of a pair of boots and, close by on the left, an odd cluster of tiny indentations in the soil. Animal prints? No! Chaucer suddenly had it. The marks had been left by a human hand. Someone had been crouching here, squatting on his hams. His weight had fallen on the front part of his feet and he'd spread his left hand on the ground to steady himself. It was the position you'd adopt for a few moments if you were waiting to leap up, to emerge in a hurry from the shelter of the bushes.

Yet who was to say that these human traces hadn't been here for some days? Supposing you were a peasant forager in the wood, like the one-armed man he'd encountered earlier, then this would be a useful place from which to observe any animals coming to drink at the pond. And, even if the marks were fresh, there was no necessary connection between whoever had been crouching here and Henri de Guyac, whose body was even now being hoisted on to the shoulders of several huntsmen and carried in a half-ceremonial fashion towards his horse.

No necessary connection between a hiding place in the woods, a line of bent grasses and a gored body. Yet Geoffrey Chaucer was certain that these things were connected. How could they not be? The darkness of the overhanging trees seemed to enter his head, and he felt the presence of a dark shape concealed among the bushes, the heart of this person full of thorns and hatred. A shape poised on his toes, steadying himself with his left arm. Why the left? Because, of course, the right would be required for –

All at once he was conscious that he was not alone. Still crouching, he twisted round and saw a man behind him under the trees. The man was accompanied by a smaller figure. Chaucer shot upright.

"What are you doing?" said the man in Occitan, then in English, "Oh, it's you, Master Chaucer."

It was Richard Foix, the castle seneschal. His ruddy face was dulled by the shadows, like a banked fire. Standing next to him was de Guyac's son, young Henri. Foix had his hand on the boy's shoulder, either consoling him or restraining him.

Geoffrey held up his purse.

"I dropped this and now I've found it."

The answer appeared to satisfy Foix, or at least he didn't ask any further questions. Instead he seemed eager to justify his own presence in the wood. Coming closer to Chaucer, he spoke in a half-whisper. "I wanted to get the lad away from all that."

He nodded towards the action in the clearing. By now the body of Henri's father had been laid across the saddle of his mount. The "unmaking" of the boar was also proceeding apace. The beast's head had been severed and his carcass opened up. Yet there was none of the jubilation which normally went with the process. Rather, there was a ponderous silence broken only by the commands of Gaston Florac, who had taken charge of the scene. On the far side of the clearing, Geoffrey glimpsed Alan Audly and Ned Caton. At this moment, he wished that they were with him. He felt uncomfortable, as though he'd been caught out in some wrongdoing.

Without any further word being uttered, the two men and the boy made their way into the open. Gaston Florac saw Richard Foix and beckoned him over. He was holding a bloodied sword with a broad tip. Evidently he'd retrieved it from the grass, but lying at a distance from Henri's body. Chaucer was left with the young Henri. He wanted to say something in condolence and was turning over different sentences in his head when the boy surprised him by speaking.

The first surprise was that he spoke in English. The second was what he said.

"I have seen death before."

Chaucer looked at him. He was much closer in appearance to his father than his mother, short and stocky, with a determined expression that in normal times would be offset by a mobile, good-humoured mouth.

"You've seen death during the chase?" said Geoffrey.

"I have been present at the chase, oh, for several years."

His English was oddly formal but his words sounded like a man's, and his voice was beginning to lose its boyish timbre.

"That was a formidable opponent," said Geoffrey, vaguely indicating the dismembered carcass of the boar. "Your father was a brave man."

"There was none to equal him," said the boy with simple pride. "You were his friend?"

"I hope so – though we had not met for many years."

"I do not think that everyone here was his friend."

The remark was left hanging in the air. Then Richard Foix returned and indicated to young Henri that it was time to return to the castle. A group of huntsmen and dogs remained behind to deal with the boar's carcass but the rest – the other huntsmen and villagers, even the players – formed up into a somewhat ragged escort to accompany the body of de Guyac, draped over Brun's saddle. Chaucer fell in at the rear of the column which had taken on the air of a funeral procession. He was joined by Audly and Caton. They retraced their path through the woods, leaving behind the sun-filled clearing and the glinting pond.

"A terrible thing," said Ned.

"There will be trouble," said Alan.

Of course there will be trouble, Chaucer thought. A powerful man has died, and died unexpectedly. There's generally trouble when that happens. But there was more to Alan's tone than straightforward foreboding. It was the latest in a string of cryptic observations made by the bystanders to this event and Chaucer said with a touch of irritation, "What do you mean?"

"There's a dispute between the man called Florac and one of the huntsmen. His name is Bauderon, I think. We heard them arguing."

"What about?"

187

"Don't know. They were speaking in their own tongue."

"It must have been to do with the injury to the Comte de Guyac," said Ned. "When they were getting ready to lift up the body, this fellow Bauderon kept pointing to here." He thumped the centre of his chest. Geoffrey saw again the gaping wound, with the dead man's left arm folded across it.

"The huntsman had tears in his eyes," said Alan. "His dog was howling until Florac shut them both up."

Chaucer recalled the howling dog. He was obscurely pleased that someone should have shown public grief at Henri's death, even if it was a mere huntsman and his hound. His mind jumped and he wondered how his death would one day be received by his son Thomas. He wondered how he would respond in time to his own father's death. John Chaucer was still alive, but frail.

They completed most of the rest of the journey in silence, each man wrapped up in his own thoughts. Above the canopy of trees the day continued bright and clear. Geoffrey, though, was preocupied with all that he'd seen and heard. Why had the huntsman Bauderon been so troubled by the fatal injury to his master? He must have been more than used to violent death. It was a tribute to his devotion that he was tear-stricken but was there more to it than that. . ?

Chaucer reviewed again what Lewis Loup had said. The player, with his quick wits, had spotted something odd about the scene of Henri's death while Geoffrey had confirmed with his own eyes the fact that an individual had most likely been spying from the edge of the clearing. He might have discovered more if he hadn't been interrupted by Richard Foix. The faint line in the grass which led from the gap in the bushes towards the corpse was like a thread – a clue – linking the dead man with his unknown watcher. It seemed odd that the boar, the apparent cause of de Guyac's death, should be lying many yards to his rear. Was it plausible that a man so badly wounded should have staggered towards the trees in search of help or shelter? Would he have had the strength? But he would have had the strength – Chaucer had no doubts on that score. He'd seen men mortally wounded in battle achieve astonishing feats before they expired, facing down and even killing the opponent who'd delivered the fatal stroke to them. Then the two enemies would fall together and lie on the field, entangled like brothers in death.

That wasn't the case here, for there was only one corpse (if you discounted the boar). Suppose, though, that Henri de Guyac hadn't been fatally injured by the beast, but had sustained only those relatively superficial wounds to his head and right arm which Chaucer had observed. That would mean that the finishing stroke had been delivered not by the animal but by . . . whoever was concealed in the bushes. He'd been taken by surprise. He wasn't expecting another attack. That would explain his defenceless state, the way in which the sword had been discarded by the pond, as well as accounting for the signs that "someone" had emerged rapidly from the bushes. Was this the cause of the dispute between the huntsman and Florac, the reason why he'd been indicating the wound in Henri's chest? That, with his experienced eye, he had realized that his master had *not* been killed by the boar's tusks.

Chaucer recalled too the son's words, *I do not think that everyone here was his friend.*

As they neared the little township of Guyac, Geoffrey said to his two companions, "You gentlemen are experienced in the hunt. How does the boar kill his victims?"

"Some peasants say that he has the evil eye," said Alan. "One look from him over a distance is enough to turn a man to jelly."

"Leaving magic aside, how does he kill at close quarters?"

"Your boar is like a well-armed knight," said Ned. "He has a choice of weapons. There is first of all his weight when he's charging – that alone can smash a man's bones."

"But it's his teeth and tusks that are the very devil," said Alan. "He uses his top tusks for no other purpose than to sharpen the lower ones. He can split you open from the nave to the chops."

"With a single stroke, like a man with a knife," said Ned.

"Except that no man possesses the beast's strength," said Alan.

"Was the wound to Henri de Guyac's chest caused by the boar?"

"What else could have caused it?"

"You didn't look closely."

"There was no need," said Ned promptly.

By this time they were entering Guyac. The news of Henri's death had travelled on ahead of them and those villagers who hadn't gone into the woods after the hunt were standing in silent groups, gazing at the passing file of men and horses. The church bell was tolling.

The outer yard of the castle was also full of people, guests and members of the household. There was no sign of Rosamond waiting to receive her husband's body but her daughters were there. The daughters' heads were bowed and they seemed like little girls rather than the young women whom Chaucer had admired the previous evening. Suddenly Rosamond appeared in the company of one of her waiting-women. The wife looked impassive, although Chaucer did not think he had ever seen a woman's complexion so white. How different had been his last glimpse of her when she came into his room in her embroidered shift and with her face glowing, only a matter of hours before! Could she ever have dreamed that she'd be welcoming Henri's corpse home that very day? She must rue her words. *My husband is an experienced huntsman. He will get what he is after.* Chaucer felt an abrupt stab of discomfort, almost of guilt, even though nothing had passed between them.

Rosamond stood by as the body was lowered from Brun's saddle and carried indoors on a makeshift bier. Then, flanked by her son and Gaston Florac and with the young girls at their heels, she followed it inside. Geoffrey and Alan and Ned dismounted and waited among the outermost ring of mourners.

Chaucer's whole purpose in coming on an embassy to Henri de Guyac had suddenly evaporated. The man he'd been trying to persuade to stay loyal to the English king was dead. He supposed that Henri, as the only son, would succeed to his father's title and estates but the boy was too young to take control of them directly, however mature he seemed. Until he came of age he'd be assisted and advised, by his mother no doubt and by Richard Foix and other senior members of the household like the chancellor. There was always the possibility – no, there was the strong likelihood – that Rosamond would marry again. She was not so old and she was certainly attractive still. Even without the lure of her property.

He pushed the thought away. It seemed indecent to be considering remarriage when her first husband's body was at this moment being laid out in their private quarters. He and his companions had no further role in Guyac. They should stay until the man's obsequies were completed and then unobtrusively slip away from this place.

It was not yet midday but the courtyard was growing uncomfortably hot and, once the body was taken in, the area emptied without any orders being given. The servants returned to their late morning routine – laundering, cooking, cleaning – but with a noticeable absence of the usual gossip, grumbles and whistling. The noble occupants of the castle, lacking the distraction of employment, retreated to their chambers. The church bell continued to toll but after a period that too fell silent. The shadows shrank at the foot of the castle walls. Lizards scurried from crack to crack in the crumbling, sun-baked mortar.

Alone in his chamber, Geoffrey Chaucer retrieved the volume of Boethius from his luggage but could not settle to reading. Frequently he glanced up at the tapestries which covered the walls. On one of them was depicted the boar with his foaming, yellow-white tusks and his leering eyes, that monstrous boar larger than any of the human figures on foot or horseback. He was crouched in a thicket in the left-hand corner of the scene. Chaucer shoved his Boethius into a pocket and went to examine the tapestry figures. He was interested in the weapons which they were brandishing. The boar-swords had broad tips with twin tines. The spears were longer, almost like lances. The weapons looked accurate, as if drawn from life. The skill of the tapestry-weavers had also suggested, in the eyes and tusks of the boar, the killer's cunning and ruthlessness. The concealed killer. Chaucer couldn't help recalling the "evidence" which he had uncovered close to Henri's corpse, the disturbance in the bushes, the foot and hand marks on the ground.

Where did his duty lie in this situation? What, exactly, was the extent of his responsibility? He was not a justice or a crowner, charged with investigating the circumstances of a man's death. Chaucer's instinct was generally to let sleeping dogs get on with their sleeping, to let the world roll by in its own sweet or soured way. He'd observed the world had a habit of doing that anyway, whatever his wishes. Why not do the same here – that is, do nothing? Once back in England, he'd have to give a full report to John of Gaunt. The report would be brief. He'd failed.

But even as he argued himself into doing nothing, he knew that matters weren't so simple. Back at the disreputable Phoenix Inn in Canterbury he'd told Caton and Audly that he possessed a nose bequeathed him by his mother, a nose well tuned to sniffing out trouble. And what he could scent now was trouble indeed, and no end of the stinking stuff. He didn't have to go looking for it. It would arrive of its own accord soon enough.

It arrived that afternoon.

Word spread through the castle faster than fire that their lord and master, the Comte de Guyac, had not been gored to death by the boar. Rather, it was rumoured that Henri's destroyer was a beast of the human variety. The mortal wound to the dead man's chest had been produced by a hunting sword and not by tusks. The experienced eyes of half a dozen huntsmen could attest to that fact. It was old Bauderon who'd first pointed it out to Gaston Florac. In the immediate aftermath of the discovery of the body his objections were brushed aside. But now, as the immediate shock was wearing off, suspicions were being raised. Richard Foix the seneschal was said to be questioning various members of the hunt. It was Jean Cado who burst into his chamber to tell Chaucer this. Cado looked beside himself. Chaucer did his best to calm the Gascon down and thanked the man. Afterwards he stood gazing out of the window for a time.

Chaucer summoned Alan and Ned for a discussion, more of a council of war. He outlined the rumours which he'd heard from Jean Cado. As he looked at Ned's open face, with its thatch of pale hair, Chaucer remembered his speculations of that morning about the young man's parentage. If there was an answer, then it lay in the letter contained in the wallet which he wore about his neck. Now there was no one to deliver that letter to, and it would be returned to Gaunt, the seal unbroken. But in the unlikely event that Ned Caton was the son of Henri de Guyac, then it would surely be best the Englishman never knew of the fact . . . Unless he already knew of course. Was it possible that Caton had an inkling of the truth? He looked tense – but then they all looked tense at the moment.

"Do you believe what they're saying, Geoffrey?" said Alan Audly, interrupting his thoughts.

"There are some strange aspects to Guyac's death," said Chaucer.

"Is that why you asked whether his wounds could have been produced by a boar's tusks?"

"What strange aspects?" said Ned.

"Oh, one or two things which I saw for myself. But that's not the point right now. It is likely that we too shall be questioned by the seneschal."

"What! He has no jurisdiction over us." Alan Audly sounded outraged. "We're English. We've got no obligations to him. I shall answer no questions."

"No doubt you're right about the jurisdiction, Alan. But remember that Guyenne is still in English hands even if it's hanging by a thread at the moment. It would take a lawyer's hand to unpick the niceties of jurisdiction and obligation. The simple fact is that we're visitors to this place. A suspicious death has occurred."

"A murder?"

"Possibly a murder. We were there. How would it look if we refused to answer some questions and took shelter behind our Englishness?"

"He's right," said Ned.

"It may not come to that," said Geoffrey, glad of Caton's calmer response. "Foix may decide he doesn't want to hear what we have to say – "

"Or it may be that we have nothing *to* say," said Ned, "since we saw nothing, we heard nothing."

"Just so. But let us be sure that is the case."

"All right," said Alan. "But first, where were you, Master Chaucer, amid this to-do? I didn't see you out and about on the chase."

"That's because I wasn't there to begin with. I don't like getting up early."

"Not even on a fine summer's morning?"

"Summer mornings are for lovers who can't sleep – or labourers who aren't allowed to." Geoffrey felt evasive because he did not intend to mention Rosamond's visit to his room. "In brief, gentlemen, I was a slug-a-bed while you were out riding."

"But you followed the party? You turned up in the clearing not long after we did."

"Yes. Something caused me to set off on my own pursuit. A sense of unease."

A sense of unease compounded by Rosamond de Guyac's words, *It's already too late.*

"Well, you said once you had a nose for trouble," said Alan.

"Did either of you see or hear anything in the forest? How did you become separated from de Guyac?"

"Ha! It was de Guyac separated himself from us," said Ned.

"Give me more details."

So they told him how Henri had spurred away from them without warning, as if he was engaged on a private pursuit of the quarry. Told how Gaston Florac had given the order for the hounds to be uncoupled and how the woods had suddenly been populated by racing streaks of black and white and grey in full cry. But there must have been a false scent, maybe more than one false scent, because the pack had hared off in different directions and Florac gave the command for the human group to split up as well. Alan and Ned were detailed to accompany Richard Foix and young Henri, in addition to half the men.

"Wait a moment," said Geoffrey. "This man Florac, he had the authority to give the command for the dogs to be unleashed and so on?"

"There was no one to gainsay him," said Ned. "Besides, de Guyac had disappeared. If he was really on the track of the boar, Gaston Florac was right to give the order."

"And when you split up from him, Florac went towards the clearing where the boar was brought to bay?"

"That's not so easy to say, Geoffrey," said Alan with the merest touch of a young man's patronage. "We are on unfamiliar terrain here. Since we didn't know these woods we relied on the noises of the dogs to guide us. Florac might have gone off in the right direction."

"No, he didn't," said Ned. "He started off towards the noisier part of the forest but the clearing with the pond was in another quarter. It was where one of the huntsmen was pointing but Florac ignored him."

"And that was where you went?"

"Well, yes."

"But we got lost ourselves," said Alan.

"Let's say that we didn't make a great effort to keep company with Richard Foix and the boy."

"Why not? Since you were on unfamiliar terrain."

"Alan said he didn't see why we had to tag along at others' heels."

Alan gestured impatiently and said, "However it happened, it's true we got separated from Richard Foix and the hunters who were on foot. And then I lost sight of Ned here . . ."

Now it was Ned Caton's turn to look uncomfortable. Chaucer waited.

"I heard voices . . . which turned out to be the players, or some of them. God knows what they were doing in the woods."

"Turned out to be Alice Loup, you mean," said Alan.

"I heard a woman's voice. I thought she might be in trouble."

"You hoped she might be in trouble so you could ride up on your white charger, Ned. The perfect damsel in distress."

"We know that your taste is confined to matrons, Alan. The fat wives of fat innkeepers in Canterbury."

"Gentlemen, let's stick to the matter in hand," said Chaucer. "The whole world was wandering about in the woods as far as I can see. What did you do when you saw Alice Loup, Ned?"

"I realized she was in no danger. The players were with her. So I turned back to join Alan but by that time he had gone on somewhere else . . ."

"I heard a dreadful cry, an animal cry. I set off in that direction."

"And everyone eventually came together in the clearing," said Geoffrey, stroking his beard. "I too heard the beast's scream. It

196

must have acted as a signal to all the people in the forest. Like an alarm bell. But in another way that scream was helpful."

"*Helpful?*"

"It tells us that Henri was still alive, that he'd just stabbed the boar. How long did it take you to reach the clearing after you heard the cry?"

"I don't know," said Alan.

"Half an hour?"

"Less, rather less."

"But more than just a few minutes," said Chaucer. "That was my impression of how the time went between hearing the beast's scream and arriving on the spot. Yet I was one of the last to arrive. So whoever it was didn't have much scope for action . . . he must have been prepared . . . and very quick. Tell me, did you see anyone else in the woods?"

"Anyone else?"

"A one-armed man for example? Dressed in rags."

"I must have overlooked him when I was distracted by the fire-breathing dragon," said Ned. "A one-armed man! Are we in the realm of legend here, Geoffrey?"

"I'm beginning to think that we are. Yet I tell you I saw such a figure standing in the path."

"What was he doing?"

"Nothing."

"Not even spouting prophecies?"

"He was silent, but he pointed out the way to me."

Chaucer could see that the two weren't sure whether to believe him. He wasn't sure that he believed himself. Perhaps the figure had been a figment of his imagination. He turned the conversation back to more practical questions.

"The seneschal Richard Foix was with Henri's son in the beginning, you say. Did you see them arrive together in the clearing?"

"I don't think so."

"You mean, you didn't see them together or you didn't see them at all?"

"Does it matter?"

"It might. I tell you that our position here is . . . uncertain. We should be agreed on what we saw and what we didn't see."

"Alan was already present when I rode up," said Ned. "Maybe he can answer."

"The man and the boy did not appear together. I remember thinking it was a bit odd."

"Why?"

"Because . . . because I had the feeling that the boy was supposed to be in the seneschal's charge. But he wasn't. Henri de Guyac had already reached the clearing, Henri the son I mean. No one knew that his father was dead then. The lad was standing looking at the boar and the dogs. There was a lot of noise but I heard someone call out his name and the boy looked round. It was Richard Foix. He was on horseback. Then he dismounted and joined the boy. He put his hand on Henri, like so, as if to comfort him."

Alan Audly clasped Ned by the shoulder.

"So they too had become separated in the forest," said Geoffrey. "They were alone for a time."

"Everyone was alone, it seems," said Ned.

At once there came a thunderous rapping on the door of Chaucer's chamber. He called out but the door had already flown open.

On the threshold stood the normally stolid Jean Cado.

"They've got him," he said, his voice rising almost out of control. "They've got him!"

14

The "him" that they had got was the one-armed man. Once Richard Foix, with the help of Gaston Florac, had apparently determined that de Guyac's death had been caused by human agency rather than a boar's tusks, he sent out men to scour the forest. Almost immediately they'd encountered Matthieu, as this individual was known. It appeared that the man had long held a violent grudge against the house of Guyac, since he had lost his arm after being savaged by one of de Guyac's alaunts, though not in Henri's time but his father's. Matthieu had been discovered in a place of his own devising in the wood, a nest of branches and foliage more like a beast's lair than man's accommodation. There were traces of blood on his face and he was clutching a ring – a notable stirrup-ring adorned with a sapphire – which had been identified as one of Henri de Guyac's.

Geoffrey Chaucer might have been made happy by this news. Not only were his doubts about de Guyac's death confirmed, and the perpetrator caught, but his account of having met the one-armed man had proved no dream. But Chaucer did not feel happy even though, once Jean Cado had left the room, Audly and Caton set about congratulating him almost as if he'd personally tracked down the malefactor.

"There's just one problem," said Geoffrey. "This fellow Matthieu didn't do it."

* * *

199

"He didn't do it."

"You're very certain, Master Chaucer."

"As certain as I'm sitting here, Master Foix."

The two men were in the very room where Geoffrey had been told by Henri de Guyac the previous evening that he shouldn't cling on to false hopes. Once again it was a summer's evening but on this night the air was close as if a storm was in the offing. A mere twenty-four hours ago Foix had been in the secretary's position to one side of the chamber. Now he was sitting in the very chair occupied by his late master. He was clutching a goblet of wine. The flask was on a nearby table. He hadn't offered any to Chaucer. Foix didn't look altogether at ease but at the same time there was an obstinacy to his posture as if he wasn't going to be shifted by anyone (let alone an Englishman).

"Your reasons?"

"I encountered Matthieu in the woods shortly before the lord's body was discovered."

"And?"

"There is no way he would have been able to reach the clearing where the – the crime was committed, in that time. It took me quite a few minutes and I was on horseback."

"You are familiar with these woods of Guyac?"

Chaucer shook his head. He knew what Foix was going to say next.

"There are side paths and short cuts known only to the denizens of the woods. Matthieu has dwelt there these many years."

"Why?"

"Some men do not like the company of their fellows."

"I hear he nursed a grudge against the house of Guyac."

Foix shrugged. "Who knows what goes on in the mind of such a man? He lost an arm to one of the lord's hunting dogs many years ago. In Henri's father's time. Matthieu was a child.

His family was paid compensation at the rate laid down, so much for an eye or a leg, such-and-such for an arm. The family could have no complaint."

"No complaint," Geoffrey echoed. "What happened to his family?"

"How should I know?" said Foix. "It was before my time also. Anyway they were peasants. We do not keep count of peasants."

Chaucer said nothing. Foix evidently considered more persuasion was required.

"There was blood upon the man's face, Master Chaucer. Fresh blood."

"His face was a mass of new cuts and scratches when I saw him *before* Henri died. It was as if he was in the habit of mortifying himself like a holy man, with the thorns and briars of the wood."

"You're saying it was his own blood?"

"In my opinion."

"We don't care much about your opinion, Master Chaucer."

Geoffrey wondered who the "we" was. Stung, he said, "There's more. Earlier today you and young Henri found me searching in the bushes by the clearing."

"You dropped your purse, you said."

"I had dropped it. And while I was picking it up I noticed what probably hadn't escaped your eyes either, Master Foix. There were signs that someone had been waiting there, hidden in the bushes."

"Exactly so. It was that savage man of the woods, Matthieu. He was skulking there, waiting to pounce on my lord."

"With his single arm?"

"If a man loses an arm or a leg, nature has a way of compensating him for his loss. He grows stronger than ever in his remaining limbs. Besides, Matthieu was equipped with a sword. That was what inflicted the fatal wound on the Comte de Guyac and not the tusks of the boar, as we first believed."

"How did Matthieu acquire a sword? A wild woodman with a hunting sword?"

"A huntsman reported one stolen this morning," said Foix.

This seemed an unlikely story, or at any rate a convenient one. Chaucer was about to point this out but instead he said, "There were marks on the ground, as I say. Marks like this."

In the half-light, Geoffrey held up his hand, palm outwards, with the thumb and fingers splayed. "He was squatting down, resting one hand on the ground for balance. This left his other hand free to grasp his sword, no doubt."

Richard Foix nodded a few times as if the Englishman was starting to see sense at last. Then suddenly, as the meaning of Chaucer's words penetrated, the nodding stopped. A deeper red seemed to suffuse his face.

"Exactly so, Master Foix. I am holding up my *left* hand. You see?" Again Geoffrey splayed out his fingers and thumb. "It was an imprint of a person's left hand on the ground. The thumb was on the near side, as it would have been if this individual was facing out towards the clearing and the pond. But the unfortunate Matthieu has no left hand or even arm available to him. So, whoever was hiding in the bushes, it wasn't him."

Foix sighed. He reached for a small object next to the wine flask on the table. He held it up so that it glinted in the light. Then he tossed it in the Englishman's direction. Chaucer caught it overhanded, more by luck than dexterity. He opened his palm and took some time examining it, even though he'd realized what it was while Foix was holding it up.

"Conclusive, eh?" said the seneschal. "A quick search of Matthieu's clothing revealed that he had that item secreted in one of his pockets."

Chaucer thought of the ragged individual he'd seen on the forest track. In one of his pockets? The fellow didn't have enough cloth to cover his nakedness, let alone the surplus to produce pockets. Pockets were for people who had something to put in them. He struggled to recall his final sight of Henri de Guyac, lying in the long grass, one arm resting by his side, the other clenched protectively over the bloody rent in his chest. Like most men, especially rich and powerful ones, de Guyac wore plenty of rings on his fingers. Chaucer himself, though not rich or powerful, wore several. In his mind's eye, he conjured up the hand across the body, the hand and the fingers. Had this stirrup-ring, with its finely worked silver and its large sapphire stone, been among the jewels on the dead man's fingers? He thought of the song sung by the old woman at last night's supper. *Vous estes le vray saphir*, it had begun. He held up the ring. The stone was a pure fathomless blue, like the deepening sky beyond the casement window. Still he could not be sure whether Henri had been wearing it when he'd looked at the body.

But the seneschal had no such doubts about the significance of the ring.

"That is conclusive, Master Chaucer, eh? For the Comte de Guyac always wore it."

Conclusive? Yes, Geoffrey supposed it was. For if the ring had been snatched from the dead or dying man's hand then it could only have been by his murderer (having killed a great man, you were hardly likely to balk at snatching a jewelled ring). And if it had honestly been discovered in the unfortunate Matthieu's pockets, in those non-existent pockets . . .

"Why did this wild man of the woods take only one item? Tell me why he didn't help himself to several while he was about it?"

Richard Foix leaned forward in his master's seat. His face seemed to redden further like a man at stool.

"No, you tell me something, Geoffrey. Why are you so eager to exonerate this worthless, savage creature? What do you know?"

"Only what my eyes and my reason tell me."

"You should be careful where your reason wanders."

But Chaucer could not resist one final remark. "Have you asked Matthieu what happened? Maybe he saw something."

"Oh, we would question him if we could, we would subject him to hard questioning, believe me. But it would be no use." Foix sat back with satisfaction. He took a gulp of wine. "He lost more than his arm when he put himself in the way of one of the alaunts. He lost the power of speech as well. He is a mute now and has been these many years."

"So that was that," said Geoffrey to Caton and Audly. "I saw that I wasn't going to get anywhere with the seneschal."

"I don't understand why you're so set on proving that this Matthieu had nothing to do with de Guyac's death," said Ned. "If a murder has been committed then a culprit must be found. One has been found very quickly."

"Conveniently quickly."

"Let justice take its course, I say."

"Anyway," added Alan Audly, "don't they have to send to Bordeaux and request someone from Prince Edward's courts to come and take charge? A justice or some such. We're still under English authority here."

"These great lords of Guyenne are a law unto themselves," said Chaucer. "No one would take kindly to 'English' interference at the moment."

"Then we should let them get on with it," said Ned. "After all, this fellow hated the Comte from what you've said, on account of his armless state. Armless but not harmless!"

Chaucer ignored the joke and said, "It happened in his father's time, so why should he suddenly decide to take revenge on Henri the *son* years afterwards?"

"But he was also found with a ring belonging to the dead man, you say," said Ned with a return of seriousness. "And I remember seeing that very ring on the Duc de Guyac's hand. A fine sapphire ring."

"They found it in one of the woodman's pockets though he didn't even have enough cloth to cover his nakedness."

"In his pocket, in his hand, what's the difference? He might have been wearing it through his nose and it would still show his guilt."

"I fear it is we who are being led by the nose here," said Geoffrey.

The three Englishmen were not the only ones consulting into the night. Gaston Florac and Richard Foix were sitting up late, drinking wine. Foix had thought for a moment, then surrendered the best chair in the room to Florac as a mark of respect. Now he was regretting his decision. He was sitting where Chaucer had sat earlier, and he kept wriggling his wide buttocks in the effort to get comfortable. He felt sweat accumulating in the creases on his forehead and wiped at it with a handkerchief.

"A bad business," he said, not for the first time.

Florac ignored him. Instead he toyed with the sapphire stirrup-ring which, until that morning, had never been off Henri de Guyac's middle finger.

"Your men found this?"

"It was Guilheme found it in Matthieu's possession."

"Guilheme?"

"A short fellow with a face like a wizened boy."

"Oh, that one."

"It is sufficient to hang Matthieu."

"More than sufficient. So when will it be, the hanging?"

"After my master's funeral, do you think? I would welcome your opinion."

"Sooner rather than later. That way everything is cleared up promptly before there is some intervention from Bordeaux."

"In advance of the funeral?"

"I would say so – if you are determined to go ahead with it."

"The Englishman is not content."

"The English are never content. Which one are you talking about?"

"The older one. Geoffrey Chaucer rode into the woods on our tail. I came across him sniffing around in the clearing where my master died."

"Was murdered, you mean."

Foix flinched but managed to nod. He wiped at his brow once more. Christ, it was hot in here. He wished the weather would break. He said, "It appears that Chaucer has some suspicions."

"He's right to have them."

"I did my best to persuade him that matters were in hand. I presented him with the evidence, including that ring you're holding."

"Was he convinced?"

"I don't believe so."

"The English are a perverse lot. If you told them their noses were on the front of their faces, they'd start searching round the back," said Gaston Florac, slumping in his seat and extending his legs. "So what are you going to do about him?"

"What am *I* going to do?"

"You're in charge here – for the moment."

If that was the case, then Foix wished he hadn't given up the comfortable chair. He said, "The Lady Rosamond might have something to say about that."

Florac shifted his shoulders in a way that suggested he couldn't be bothered to shrug.

"You should leave the lady to her grief. But, I repeat, the Englishman . . . ?"

"His presence here is certainly inconvenient."

"You have a gift for stating the obvious, Foix. You want my opinion?"

He was really insufferable, this Gaston Florac, thought Foix. He disguised his feelings by burying his face in his goblet. He drank too quickly and red wine dribbled down his chin. Any answer he might have given was lost in the splutters.

"Let me say this then," said Florac, sinking lower so that his body was almost horizontal with the rush-covered floor. "I know that the English came here on a pitiful mission to sway my lord of Guyac to declare himself finally for the English crown. I myself have had such overtures in recent months. We all have. But I know where my allegiance lies."

To yourself, thought Richard Foix.

"And if when the time comes," pursued Florac, "you understand where your allegiance lies, then it will go well with you. Meantime, in the matter of this Chaucer and his companions, it might be best if they were got out of the way."

"Temporarily?"

"You're in charge," said Florac, folding his hand in a conclusive fashion round the stirrup-ring. "But you've spilled some wine on your front."

And this was not the last of the councils being held in the precincts of the castle of Guyac. While Chaucer and his companions discussed the guilt or otherwise of the man in the woods, and while Richard Foix and Gaston Florac had decided that not only was Matthieu guilty but that he should pay the supreme penalty without delay, the players were talking in their barn-like quarters, talking about this terrible day. They were sitting in a circle, illuminated by a single lamp in the middle.

"I say we should leave now," said Margaret Loup with her usual decisiveness. "There's no call for our, ah, services any longer. We are not going to be invited to play in the castle."

"I don't know," said Lewis Loup. "It's when tragedy strikes that people want to be diverted."

"We've been overtaken by real life," said his wife. "The people here are not going to be diverted, because they're already *distracted*. The lord of this domain has died violently – "

"Murdered, they say," said grey-bearded Martin.

Alice Loup visibly shivered. She said, "We have lost Bertram as well. Two deaths within a day and a night. I don't like it."

"None of us *like* it but Bertram's death was an accident," said Lewis, "a terrible accident."

"Whatever it was, Bertram is gone," said Simon, who in the dimness had his hand on Alice's thigh. "Accident or otherwise, he is gone." He glanced towards Hubert who, as a newcomer to the company, was sitting just outside the circle, his face entirely shadowed.

"What do you think, Tom?" said Lewis, appealing to the member of the group who spoke the least and was usually the most willing to fall in with his point of view.

"I think we should go," said Tom.

"Good lad," said Margaret.

Lewis Loup might have argued that they'd faced tragedy before, that their livelihood as players depended on their rising above little circumstances like violent death and plague and universal warfare. But he had the sense to realize that he could not gainsay his wife. With her, he might have persuaded the others. But without her whole-hearted support . . .

"I agree with my son. I say we should return to the coast, to Bordeaux," said Martin. "At least we're on home ground there."

"You haven't asked Hubert for his opinion," said Simon.

Lewis Loup turned his head towards the figure who was sitting quite still beyond the circle of light.

"Speaking as a newcomer, I am sorry not to have had the opportunity to play yet," said Hubert.

"Oh, there'll be plenty of chances for that," said Lewis, his mind already jumping to the future and what they'd stage when they reached Bordeaux. Perhaps it would be better to go back to the city after all, back to a place that was in so many ways an *English* town under an English prince.

"Where were you today by the way, Hubert?" said Simon, his grip on Alice's thigh tightening although he wasn't aware of it. "We saw you set off in pursuit of the chase."

"Where was I, by the way?" repeated Hubert, as if he needed time before answering. "I was by the way, you might say. Out and about in the woods – like the rest of you."

Over the rest of the castle it was quiet during that short, hot summer night. The body of Henri, Comte de Guyac, was laid out in his bedchamber. The old woman who had been his wet-nurse more than forty years earlier, and who had helped to dress his torn corpse that very afternoon, now sat as a watcher beside the bier. Her head drooped frequently on to her withered chest and just as frequently she would awaken with a jolt and a little cry at her unfamiliar surroundings. Adjacent to her husband's chamber lay Rosamond de Guyac. The first time she heard the watcher whimpering she felt her scalp crawl. Sleep did not arrive for her until the first glimmers of light appeared beyond the casement window. In a nearby room young Henri was sleeping surprisingly soundly. When he awoke to the muffled noises of the household next morning it would take him some moments to remember that his father was dead. It was otherwise with Henri's daughters, who wept and consoled each other through the short night.

Some floors below this exalted level, in one of several rooms that served for stores but could double as cells when necessary, the man called Matthieu twisted restlessly on the bundles of sacking piled on the stone floor. He didn't notice the hardness of the floor or the dankness of the room. The sounds of scratching and scuttling didn't disturb him, they were companionable. He was used enough to the night noises of the forest. But every time he cast his eyes upward he could not at first understand why the stars had gone out, and then his nose would wonder – if noses can wonder – why the air had turned so sour and stale. In his distraction he raked at his face with his remaining hand. The long tapering nails scored new trails and opened up old ones so that the blood flowed fresh.

His only recollections of the day were confused and shapeless. A rush of armed men seizing him in one of the places where he made his bed, hands cuffing and pawing at his body and the rags which scarcely covered it. One of the men gleefully holding up a thing that shone blue in the light, a deep blue like the end of the day. A stumbling progress away from the woods, a walk full of curses (not his curses naturally), a sweating passage through a place with houses and silent onlookers. And then creeping along through great gates and under tall walls and down steps before being shoved into this lightless hole. Like an animal, Matthieu could recall shreds of the past and be conscious of the present. But he could not conceive of the future, any future. He curled up on the filthy sacks, covering his blood-streaked face with his arm.

15

"My God, Geoffrey, what are we going to do?" said Ned Caton.

"Do? Nothing."

Of the three of them it was definitely Ned Caton who was showing the strain of their situation. Alan Audly had huffed and puffed about how it was a disgrace, how it was an outrage that they – as true-born Englishmen, as servants of the King of this province – should be treated as prisoners. But then he'd seemed to resign himself to the situation and gone to stand by the grille which admitted the only air and light to penetrate the room from outside and which looked on to one of the inner wards of the castle. Ned, by contrast, had gone very pale and begun muttering to himself, occasionally shooting comments at Chaucer which suggested that he blamed Geoffrey for what had happened.

As for Geoffrey himself, this was hardly his first time under restraint. Why, on his initial visit to Guyac more than ten years earlier he'd been a prisoner though a prisoner accommodated like a lord. Then, of course, Henri had been in charge and he was being held under the rules of war. Now it appeared that seneschal Foix had taken matters into his own hands, claiming that the Englishmen were being incarcerated for their own protection. According to him, all kinds of rumours were flying about the castle and the surrounding countryside. Although they'd apprehended the individual responsible for de Guyac's death, that hadn't stopped tongues wagging and fingers pointing. Being outsiders, Chaucer and Caton and Audly were in an exposed position. Foix was so pleased with the phrase that he repeated it, "an exposed position". It would be better for everyone if you kept out of the way for a time. So you see, Master Chaucer, you are put in here for your own safety.

Chaucer had been lured from his chamber early that morning as the household was starting to stir. A short man with a disagreeable, freckled face had knocked on his door, none too gently, and said that Richard Foix wished to see him urgently in his quarters. Chaucer had dressed, thinking that perhaps Foix was having second thoughts about their conversation of the previous night. He had been escorted to a distant wing of the castle, along some nondescript passages. He'd just started to think that Foix should surely have better accommodation than a chamber in this ill-lit, ill-ventilated area when he saw a couple of soldiers stationed outside a stout door. One of them rapped on it and the door was opened from within. The light was poor but Geoffrey's eyes had adjusted to it by now. He noticed Caton and Audly already inside, with another pair of armed men. For some reason, their posture – Ned's and Alan's – reminded him of schoolboys who'd been caught out. A trap then. But it was too late to take evasive action. No point in protesting either since Chaucer sensed that whoever had given orders for this tangled business, it wasn't the freckled man who now, with a ironic bow, gestured for him to join his companions. The soldiers exited and the door shut with a thud followed by the turning of a key. The room was furnished with an oak table and stools, and a chest which on inspection proved to be empty. The smell of burnt wood lingered around the stone slabs of a wide hearth. Chaucer peered up the chimney which narrowed and bent out of sight. He smelt dank, sooty air. The walls of the room were bare. The orderly spareness of the chamber made him think it was a guard-room.

After an hour or so, the door opened to frame Richard Foix. He filled the space, blocking most of the little illumination from the passage. With an air that sounded almost apologetic, he explained why they were here. It was only for a matter of hours, he said, a day at most. Then he left.

That was when Ned Caton started on his questions. Why are we here? What are we going to do?

"Do? Nothing," said Geoffrey.

"Nothing?"

"We must make the best of our situation. They mean us no harm."

"How can you say that when we are confined against our will?"

"Because we are not badly lodged. This is no cell or prison, it's cool and shaded in here. You'll be glad of that when it reaches midday outside. You heard what the seneschal said. We'll be out soon."

Caton's only response was to grunt. Alan Audly continued to look through the barred opening. Geoffrey was not as certain as he sounded, yet he did not believe that they could be in any serious danger. To shut away English envoys under the pretext of ensuring their temporary safety was one thing; to go any further would be to invite a iron response from the court over in Bordeaux. Wars have been started with lesser provocation. Unless, of course, someone was looking to start a war . . .

Shortly afterwards they were brought food and plenty of it, as if to compensate for their confinement. Meat and cheese, bread and wine. They hadn't eaten for twelve hours or longer, and for a while they forgot their predicament and became cheerful under the influence of the drink. Then they were taken out, singly and under guard, in order that they might ease themselves in a dank and odorous privy which was situated on an outermost section of the wall so as to empty straight into the river.

When they were all returned, Alan sat down against the wall under the grille. Soon his head slumped forward and he began snoring lightly. Though they'd been locked in once more, Ned tried the door as if he did not trust the evidence of his ears. Then he positioned himself at the table and stared into space. Geoffrey wondered whether there were men posted outside. He wondered what to do next. There was nothing to do, of course, as he'd said to Ned. Accordingly he was delighted when he found his *Consolation of Philosophy* in a side pocket. He must have shoved it there yesterday in his own chamber. Here was a link with ordinary life, a volume written out in his own scrawled hand, a volume which counselled resignation and forbearance in the face of adversity. Boethius, he remembered, had been in prison once. (He suppressed the thought that Boethius had been put to death shortly afterwards.) The barred window was not large, yet so glaring was the midday southern sun on to the ward outside that there was light enough to read by, and to spare.

Chaucer opened the book and laid it flat on the table. He sat down and read. The shadows in the room shifted. For all that they were separated from the exterior by several feet of stone, the air was warm and close. After a time Alan woke up and resumed his watching by the window.

"What do you see, Alan?" said Ned

"Nothing. There's no one out there to see. Where is every-body?"

"What do you read, Geoffrey? The same old book?" said Ned.

Chaucer held up the book so that Caton could see it was nothing new.

"Oh, the *consolation* of philosophy. Ha!"

"Don't speak too soon, my friend. Listen to our author now. 'You think that Fortune has turned against you; but you are wrong to think so. That has always been her habit. Rather, as far as you're concerned, she has retained her proper constancy by changing herself. She was just the same when she deceived you with the illusion of prosperity.'"

"It doesn't do a great deal for me," said Ned.

"Why don't you go on with your tale," said Alan.

"Tale?" said Chaucer.

"The one you were telling on the vessel that brought us to this damned country, the *Arveragus*."

Chaucer shut Boethius up and returned him to his pocket. He had a duty to distract his companions, surely. And wasn't a prison a traditional place for storytelling? Which story was it now . . . ?

"The knight and his lady, Arveragus and Dorigen," prompted Ned.

"Oh, that one."

"What happened to them?"

What happened to them indeed? He'd have to find out. Which was partly the reason he started once more telling the tale to Audly and Caton. Also, it kept their minds off where they were. It kept his own mind off it too.

"Where was I? There was the young woman called Dorigen who lived on the Brittany shore. There was the knight who'd wooed and married her. He was called Arveragus, the same name as the boat. I mentioned the great difficulty he'd experienced in winning her. I mentioned the true love they bore one another, Arveragus and Dorigen . . ."

He paused. It was like making a tapestry perhaps. You picked up the threads you'd abandoned some time before, you started to weave them together once more, and eventually a pattern, a shape, a picture emerged.

"And when they married, Dorigen and Arveragus, they made a promise to each other . . . "

What was the promise now? Whatever it was, it would have to be tested before the end of the tale. Promises in stories are

215

made to be tested, sometimes to be broken. Chaucer's brain laboured, even if laboured as rapidly as a weaver's fingers. Despite this, the brain could only come up with something obvious.

"Dorigen . . . she said that she would always be his true and faithful wife while he promised never to compel her to do anything against her will. And they lived very happily like this for a year or a little while longer. Then the knight had to go away to fight – to England. Dorigen didn't attempt to stop him. He wouldn't have been the man she loved without those knightly pursuits which added to his honour and reputation. But she did grieve at Arveragus's departure, she couldn't stop herself. The longer he was away the worse her grief became. She couldn't sleep, she hardly ate anything, she wouldn't talk to her friends about any subject except her husband's absence and how much she loved him and how worried she was for his safety in a foreign land. Underneath it all, however, she was a reasonable woman and her friends were patient and eventually they managed to calm her down. It helped too that she received letters from her husband, assuring her of his welfare, saying that he loved her and would return as quickly as he could.

"So her thoughts, which had all been concentrated on his absence, now began to turn towards his coming back. When her friends saw Dorigen recovering her spirits they urged her to take some exercise, to get out and about a bit. The castle she lived in was hard by the sea. Dorigen walked with her companions on the very cliffs. Naturally she looked out to sea and dreamed that every boat which she glimpsed was *the* boat – the one bringing her husband back to her. But the boats sailed by, indifferent to the pain of the lady on the cliff-tops. Then Dorigen would sit down on the springy turf at the edge and, instead of gazing out to the horizon, she would look down.

"What she saw hundreds of feet below didn't please her. In fact, it brought her heart into her mouth. The base of the cliffs was scattered with vicious black rocks, like the discarded teeth of some sea monster. Dorigen asked herself why God had put the rocks there, in that particular place at the foot of the cliffs. What good did they do to anyone? They were too exposed and wave-lashed even for the birds. It was as if they were a barrier between herself and Arveragus. Rather as many sailors must have done, she wished the rocks were sunk into hell."

In his mind's eye Chaucer saw the cliffs of the Brittany coast as he'd glimpsed them from the deck of the *Arveragus*, black with a fringe of white at their base. He felt the wind on his face. He heard the regular whisper of the waves. No, the whispering sound at least was real. He stopped what he was saying.

"Can you hear that? What is that sound?"

"That is the sound of people," said Alan, returning to the barred window to listen. "Only people."

"Where?"

"In one of the outer wards of the castle, maybe in the village."

It was a continuous swirl of sound – quite recognizable when you'd identified it – the sound of people in good humour, even a state of excitement. The noise floated over the walls, borne up by the hot afternoon air. Chaucer was reminded of a town fair or of a crowd waiting for a drama to be staged in a marketplace. Perhaps Lewis Loup and the others were setting up to play again. Yet surely not on the day after the death of the Comte de Guyac?

There was only one other kind of crowd he could think of which would display the same mixture of excitement and good humour. He feared the worst. He pushed the thought to one side. Quick, on with the story – although something dark and flinty had now entered it. The lady Dorigen . . . the rocks . . . sunk into hell . . . how she wished them in hell! Through Chaucer's mind there flashed the story of Henri de Guyac, of how in his early days returning to Guyenne on the death of his father he'd been shipwrecked on the Brittany coast, and of how he'd promised God he would lead a better life if saved.

217

"Then Dorigen's highest hopes and her worst fears came true, almost at the same instant," said Geoffrey. "For one morning a ship did not sail blindly on but began to turn towards the very spot where the knight's lady was pacing the cliff-tops. She shaded her eyes to make out the image on the ship's sail. Yes, she thought, it may be his, Arveragus's. And, trying to rein in her racing heart, she turned away and counted to a hundred. She had only reached fifty before she turned back to look once more. It *was* Arveragus's ship. There could be no mistaking the lion, the golden lion rampant, which blazed out like fire on the sail. Arveragus was almost home. But as her husband's boat was trying to steer a course around the rocks, a great wave came from nowhere, from out of the blue sea, and picked up the boat and dashed it against those same black rocks. Before her very eyes, the ship split in two and the passengers spilled out into the waters. Only the roar of the surf and the wind prevented her from hearing the cries of the drowning men. Among them must be her husband.

"Dorigen went white and fell down in a swoon on the cliff-top. It was fortunate for her that she was soon discovered. She hovered on the verge of death for several weeks but eventually she recovered and started to live again. Her friends set about cheering her once more, although this was a much more difficult task since beforehand she had merely feared that her husband might not return and now she knew that he would not.

"Still patient, the friends drew her inland. They took her out of sight of the dreadful rocks and tried to distract her in pleasant gardens and on the banks of peaceful rivers. On one of these outings – accompanied by food and wine, music and fine weather – they were in a garden belonging to one of Dorigen's friends. It was a beautiful day early in May. It was as if the world had been freshly painted. Her friends were enjoying themselves singing and dancing, all innocently of course, because in this story there is no indecency. Dorigen sat it out, though. She didn't feel like singing, didn't want to dance. She was still thoroughly miserable. At the same time there was a young man at this event who was also miserable. His name was . . . what was the name of the third boat in our convoy to Bordeaux?"

"The *Aurelius*," supplied Alan Audly.

"Aurelius, of course," said Chaucer. "Well, he shall become a character in our tale. Aurelius was a squire and therefore handsome, strong, and all the rest of it. He'd been in love with Dorigen for a couple of years but had never said anything to her directly. Instead he gave vent to his passion by singing songs of unrequited love and casting yearning glances in her direction. She was quite oblivious to this because all the time her thoughts were fixed on her husband, more than ever now that he was gone.

"On this occasion, though, Aurelius and Dorigen started talking to each other. Everybody else was enjoying the fine day, the beautiful garden. But misery loves like-minded company. And Aurelius understood that if he was ever to declare himself, now was the moment. It wasn't that he was insensitive to the widow's situation so much as unable to restrain himself. So he burst out with his lovelorn speech. He knows his devotion to her is useless, his only reward is heartbreak, she can kill or save him with a single word. Take pity on me, he cries, or he might as well be buried at her feet. Dorigen is not hard-hearted, far from it, but she is faithful to the memory of Arveragus. So she is about to say no, I will not become your lover. Then she looks at Aurelius. He's not quite at her feet but there is supplication in every bone of his body. Dorigen is not hard-hearted, I say, and perhaps she sees in his despair a pale image of her own. So she sets him a task, one that is apparently impossible to fulfil but one that will allow her to salve her conscience afterwards by saying to herself, *Well, at least I didn't turn him down outright*.

"What she promised him was that she would give herself to him if he retrieved her husband from the sea, so that she could give Arveragus a proper burial rather than one in the maw of a sea monster. Aurelius was dumbfounded. By now the body of the knight must be a scatter of bones many fathoms deep. Dorigen's promise could not be fulfilled. How can you recover a man's bones from out there?

"What Aurelius wanted couldn't happen without the fulfilment of what Dorigen wanted, and since the body of her first husband was beyond recovery he would never be allowed to become her second. Nevertheless, this was Dorigen's way of dealing kindly with Aurelius, since she hadn't given him an absolute refusal."

"Kindly!" said Ned Caton. "A typical woman's trick."

Chaucer held out his hand, palm upwards, as if to say, *Whatever you think, my friend.* This was the moment that he enjoyed, the moment when he had his audience (even an audience of two) where he wanted them. They'd forgotten their surroundings, their predicament, even though the noise from beyond the walls continued.

"Well, Aurelius sank even further into gloom. Like Dorigen he took to pacing along the cliff-tops. He thought about throwing himself from the top of them. He considered drowning himself in the waters where Arveragus had drowned. Then he noticed another ship heading helplessly for the very rocks which had shattered the knight's boat. This was no great craft with a lion on the sail but a mean little vessel, probably containing fishermen. This boat duly struck the rocks and the handful of men on board were flung into the sea. Without a thought, Aurelius ran down a path which – conveniently – zigzagged across the face of the cliff. There was a sailor quite close to the shore, still alive, clinging to the fragment of a spar but only just. Once on the shore Aurelius plunged into the water although he could not swim. What was going through his head? Did he want to kill himself? Certainly he was reckless of his own life. Maybe that counted for more with him than trying to save someone else's – "

Geoffrey was interrupted by the sound of the key in the door. He turned with irritation, expecting to see Richard Foix. But it wasn't the seneschal. Instead, Jean Cado the guide and interpreter stood there.

"Hurry, sirs," he said. "You must come this way."

From the top of a curtain wall in the outer ward of the castle, Gaston Florac and Richard Foix watched the preparations being made in the town centre below. The buzz of the crowd rose towards them.

"The paperwork is in order," said Foix, wiping his brow.

"Paperwork?" said Florac.

"You know what sticklers they are in Bordeaux. Everything has to be properly signed and sealed."

"It hardly matters now," said Florac. "But I'm glad to hear it's all in order. Don't worry, your back is covered."

There'd been a hasty session that morning to administer justice. The evidence against Matthieu had been produced and cursorily considered by a group consisting of Foix, the chancellor of the castle and a couple of other senior members of the household. Gaston Florac had not attended, but his views were clear to them all. Matthieu had seemed hardly conscious of proceedings, as mute and blockish as the stools which his accusers were sitting on.

Of course Matthieu was guilty, as guilty as hell, and now he must pay the penalty. A small cart, with a mule between the shafts, had been drawn up beneath one of the most sturdy branches of the chestnut tree in the village square. Under the direction of Guilheme, the freckle-faced fellow who had visited Chaucer's room that morning, another of Foix's men was sitting astride the branch and holding on with his left hand. His right was clutching at a thick coil of rope. The man had no head for heights and Guilheme was berating him for his timidity. While he sought for the best spot to secure an end of the rope – one that would allow a decent sway and avoid getting snagged on neighbouring branches – little pyramids of blossom were shaken loose or snapped off altogether. Petals floated down like snow on to the mule's back or lodged themselves in Guilheme's hair and clothing.

The village crowd, which had been growing since midday, offered advice and opinions. They ignored the sun beating down and the heavy air which still held the promise of a storm. They forgot about the tasks to be undertaken in workshop and field. A holiday spirit reigned. No one had a word to say in Matthieu's defence. He'd always been the wild man in the woods, a figure to frighten your children with. Now he was a wicked man as well, one who'd killed their lord and master at the moment that Henri was demonstrating his bravery in the boar-hunt. In two or three days de Guyac's funeral obsequies would take place. The whole village would participate in the mourning, albeit at one remove. There'd be a few more hours off work with the promise of ample food and drink at the end of it. But to begin with, there was the prospect of a hanging, like the first course in a feast.

There were no men stationed outside the door. Chaucer looked a query and in response Cado almost spat out, "They've got something more interesting to attend to."

Jean Cado knew his way around this quarter of the castle. He led them into its more distant recesses, past the foul-smelling privy and then stumblingly up some spiral stairs. They emerged into a circular room lit by shafts of afternoon light penetrating the arrow-slits. The openings were arranged close to the ground and longwise so as to accommodate the play of a crossbow. Chaucer realized that they were on the lower floor of one of the south-facing turrets, to judge by the angle of the light. There was a trapdoor in the middle of the floor through which arms and provisions could be brought up, and a corresponding opening in the ceiling to supply the chamber above. There was a large, unornamented chest to one side. From this room a defence could be mounted against attackers and the rest of the tower sealed off since the staircase ran no higher than this floor.

What were they doing in here? Chaucer crouched down and saw tree-tops like the upper segment of a tapestry. He turned towards Jean Cado, turned expectantly since the interpreter must have brought them here for a purpose. He was surprised to see on the man's face an expression almost of anguish but perhaps it was no more than the strain of circumstances.

"You must leave this place, sirs. We all must unless you want to end up like poor Matthieu."

Nobody took up the remark. Alan Audly was squinting through a slit. The upper part of his body was angled along the aperture which narrowed as it reached the horizontal opening. The wall was more than five feet thick. Audly squirmed his way back inside again.

"How do we leave?" he said. "We're a long way above the ground here."

"Why don't we simply walk out of the gate?" said Ned Caton.

"We wouldn't be let through the gate now. They are hanging the unfortunate who killed the lord of Guyac," said Cado.

"Hanging him!" said Alan.

"The poor Matthieu," said Cado. "None of us will be safe."

The circular nature of the chamber gave to his voice a strange resonance. Chaucer felt goose-bumps on his arms. Whatever the temperature outside, the air within the tower was cool, almost dank. Odd creaks and shushing sounds emanated from above and below. *They are hanging the unfortunate*. Geoffrey had the bitter satisfaction of having his earlier suspicions confirmed. That noise from beyond the castle, that excited swirl of sounds. There was nothing like an execution to please people. He thought of the mute he'd met in the forest – an unfortunate indeed – the man with one arm.

Jean Cado beckoned to Geoffrey and together they opened the chest. Its hinged lid struck the stone wall. Inside Chaucer saw coils of rope, hooks, pulleys. Cado fumbled and drew out one length of rope then another.

"How familiar are you with knots, Master Geoffrey? The *cabestan*, the *tête d'alouette*? I don't know their English names."

"I defer altogether to your knowledge, Master Jean."

His hands moving with practised speed, Cado made knots at regular intervals in the two lengths of rope. He tied the sections together and set about securing one end to the ring embedded in the trapdoor in the floor. He tested this last knot by tugging repeatedly at it. Then he gestured for Audly to take the other end and run it out through the arrow-slit.

Chaucer crouched down once more and examined the view from another aperture. A breeze was shoving the crowns of the trees from side to side against a glaring swathe of sky.

"It is not as bad as it seems, Master Geoffrey," said Jean Cado, standing up and brushing the dust off his clothes. "I have already made a surveillance. The wall falls straight downward and then there is a steep slope of rocks and bushes. But this place is built to prevent persons getting in, not to stop them getting out. I would sooner go down than up."

"Just so," said Geoffrey.

But what was bothering him wasn't the climb down the wall, clinging desperately to a rope. Or rather this fear failed to drive out another, more subtle humiliation which might lie in store.

"After we get down?" said Ned Caton. "What then?"

"I have made an arrangement," said Cado.

Caton looked at Chaucer who nodded as if to say, we should trust him. He was already impressed by the resource that the little man was showing. He might have added that they didn't have much choice. The news that the one-armed Matthieu was to be executed for the murder of de Guyac had shaken Geoffrey. He'd said that it would take a lawyer to sort out the niceties of jurisdiction in this domain of Guyac, but even in his ignorance he was pretty sure that Richard Foix – if it was indeed the seneschal who had authorized Matthieu's hanging – was exceeding his authority by doing so. At the very least the death of an important individual like the Comte de Guyac should have been reported to the Prince's court in Bordeaux and a proper inquiry set in train. The fact that this procedure was being flouted told Chaucer that Foix, maybe egged on by Gaston Florac, did not care about consequences . . . or that he was gambling on the English not being in control of this part of Guyenne for much longer. And if that was the case then their own position was more precarious than Chaucer had claimed in the guard-room. What had been a mission to shore up an alliance had become a simpler task: to preserve their own necks.

"Who is the first?" said Jean Cado.

None of the Englishmen immediately volunteered. Cado muttered to himself, turned round and wriggled his way into the aperture that led to the arrow-slit. Lying on his stomach, he went feet first, an awkward process since it involved going at a slightly upward slant. Audly and Chaucer crouched down to push at his shoulders and outspread arms. With the rope running underneath his squirming body, Cado blocked out the light. The Gascon's owlish face was rigid with concentration. He gave a little gasp, something between alarm and satisfaction, as his feet reached the lip of the opening. Then using one hand to get a purchase on the stonework on the inner side of the aperture and the other to cling fast to the rope, he arrived at a point where the weight of his body was almost evenly balanced between its two halves, outside and inside. Almost but not quite. By this stage both his hands were clenched around the rope. With a final shake of his body, Jean Cado tipped himself over the edge. Now only his shoulders and head were visible, outlined against the lurid sky.

"Hold fast and God speed, Jean," said Geoffrey.

The man grunted and disappeared from view. The rope, stretched between the ring of the trapdoor and the arrow-slit, shivered slightly. The others waited in an agony of suspense, waited for the tension in the rope to slacken suddenly, waited for the cry and the distant thump of a body hitting the ground. Eventually the tautness did appear to go out of the rope but no sounds followed apart from the shushing of the wind in the tower. Alan Audly plucked idly at the rope. He shrugged.

"Hard to tell if there's still anyone on the other end."

He attempted to sound careless but there was a tremor in his voice. Geoffrey crawled towards the entrance of the arrow-slit and peered out and down. After the stony gloom of the tower room, the hot air and sunlight struck him on the face like a blow. He couldn't see anything at first. Then he was aware of a diminished figure down below, its arms windmilling. For an instant he wondered who it was. He scrambled back into the chamber.

"He's reached the ground. It's a sheer drop down the walls and then there's a slope which can't be too steep because Cado is standing on it at the moment, waving his arms. Who's going next?"

"Why not you, Geoffrey?" said Ned.

"No," he said, and then quickly added, "I have a special reason for wanting to go last."

"Never let it be said that an Audly is afraid to follow where a Gascon has gone," said Alan.

He inserted himself into the opening feet foremost and soon he too was reduced to a head, a pair of shoulders and a set of hands clutching sweatily at the rope. Then, with the whispered encouragement of Geoffrey and Ned, he dropped from sight.

They waited for perhaps a couple of minutes. The rope gave slightly and a faint shout came up from the exterior. Audly was on the ground. Next was Ned Caton. To Chaucer's slight surprise, he scrabbled without protest into the tapering space and then slipped over the stone lip. To an observer at the bottom, Chaucer thought, the tower must appear to be vomiting men.

Geoffrey waited until the call came once more from below. He heard a single shout showing that Ned too had arrived. Still he listened. Some quality of the tower's interior magnified small sounds. Was that a door slamming down below? The sound of feet on the spiral stairs? No, but someone might come at any moment. He presumed that the castle's occupants were out in the village square or crowding the battlements which overlooked it.

Lacking the litheness of his fellows he squeezed himself into the aperture. His hands were slippery on the cold stone. His feet slid over the edge of the arrow-slit until they were gripping vacancy. It was an unpleasant sensation. He pushed himself further up the incline on his stomach. Despite the coolness of this place, sweat ran down his face and tickled at his sides.

Now, as more and more of his lower half was extruded into the empty air, he was reaching the point he'd feared – not the point of maximum danger but the point of maximum humiliation. True, there was danger here but it was the humiliation which was uppermost in his mind. This was the reason he'd insisted on going last. For Geoffrey had been afraid that the horizontal gap in the tower wall would be too narrow for him to ease his way through. It was all very well for a small man like Jean Cado or for those young fellows, even if Ned was on the stocky side. They might glide through such a opening like warm butter down a gullet. But for a gentleman who was somewhat more . . . who was better endowed, let us say . . . it was an altogether trickier manoeuvre. He'd visualized the possibilities. Of himself, stuck ignominiously half in, half out of the tower,

227

dangling dozens of feet above the ground, his upper half crammed into the stone tunnel. Of Ned and Alan pushing at him with jokes and curses. Going last at least meant that the others were out and – if not safe – standing on solid ground.

Chaucer checked that his grasp of the rough hemp was as fast as fear could make it. He felt himself slipping over the edge like liquid being poured reluctantly – oh how reluctantly – out of a flask. It was a tight fit but he thought he was going to make it through the arrow-slit. One humiliation spared. Strange that he could fear humiliation more than death. Now there was merely death to worry about. His privates, no doubt shrivelled up with terror, bumped over the ledge, followed by his nicely padded waist and guts. And then he was hanging from the very lip of the opening, arms straining from the rope. He thought – irrelevantly – of the tale he'd started back in the guard-room. The tale of Arveragus and Dorigen and Aurelius. Well, he'd abandoned the young Aurelius as he plunged into the sea, into an unknown future. Now here was he, the not so young Geoffrey Chaucer, about to launch himself into the unknown.

The stonework was an inch from his nose, too close for his eyes to focus on. Don't look down, he told himself, don't look up either, don't look sideways, don't look at anything. Climb down instead. And move straightaway before your arms get tired of supporting your great weight. By instinct his feet had entwined themselves with the rope. He lowered himself a couple of yards. His elbows and knees banged against the rough stone. His nose tickled and he concentrated on that to distract himself from other matters. He felt the heat radiating from the wall. The sun was heavy on his back but beyond that he sensed a great emptiness. Below him, nothing . . .

In the village square of Guyac the one-armed man was about to be hanged. Matthieu had been lifted up into the back of the cart.

228

Guilheme and the clumsy assistant had had a debate about what to to do with Matthieu's single arm while the local priest intoned some prayers which no one listened to. It was a problem, that single arm. They didn't want the wild man of the woods lashing out at his executioners with his hook-like hand or scrabbling at his own neck in a futile attempt to unfasten the rope. But the normal recourse of tying a man's two hands together behind his back was unavailable to them. In the end they trussed a length of cord around his torso so that Matthieu was unable to move the upper part of his body. His legs they left free since the kicking of the condemned man was a rightful part of the spectacle on such an occasion. Now Matthieu stood – or rather he drooped, held up by a soldier on each side – with the rope slithering down from the branch of the chestnut and ending in a loop around his neck. Pale blossom garlanded the men's shoulders.

The crowd had fallen silent. One or two among them might even have experienced a pang of pity for this mute and ragged figure. But there were more of them disappointed that the condemned man seemed likely to go so quietly. Why, he might as well have been dead already. He certainly looked it. His eyes were half-closed and his face was a mass of scars and bloody scratches. His clothes looked like scraps of grave-cloth through which his bony body – nut-brown from exposure to the elements and emaciated – could be glimpsed. A yellow sky pressed down on the village square. From over the hills on the far side of the river came clumps of thunder, like someone inside a neighbouring chamber shifting furniture to no purpose.

When the rope had been secured round Matthieu's scrawny neck, the soldiers climbed down from the cart. Now nothing supported him except the hanging rope. Guilheme gave the command and the soldiers prodded and thwacked at the mule which lumbered away, jerking the cart behind it. Matthieu's feet scraped across the boards of the cart before swinging free in the air. He writhed, briefly.

And what did Matthieu think while all this was happening? What did he feel? In truth, he thought nothing and felt little. He had tasted the air – hot and leaden but better than the sour atmosphere of his cell – while he was being dragged across the square and hoisted into the cart. He'd looked up for a moment at the sky. Some part of him registered that this too was preferable to the dark roof of the place where he'd been incarcerated. He felt a stab of fear when one rope was coiled about his body and another when the cord was placed round his neck, but this was more to do with being restricted than from any apprehension about what was to happen to him. The deprived fellow had never witnessed an execution. In front of him was a field of upturned faces, as blank and silent as flowers against the sun. Then there was a tightening in his throat and a scraping sound and the sense of the ground moving underneath his feet and the tightening grew much worse.

But beyond these things, there was nothing . . .

The knots which Jean Cado had tied at regular intervals were a help, providing hand and footholds. After a time Geoffrey Chaucer reached the place where Jean Cado had linked the two segments of rope. He risked a look down. Beyond his knees and feet, stretched the flank of the tower. Figures flickered in the corner of his vision. Someone called out. In the distance there was the sound of thunder. A long way still to go. He remembered as a child climbing a pear tree – but where? – and understanding for the first time how different the world looked even from a little way up. And, more important, how different a few yards could be when you judged those yards with your feet planted on the ground and when you appreciated them as a space to fall through.

He bumped his way down until the massive blocks of the tower merged with the rockface that was its pedestal and then a little further down until his feet ran out of rope to cling to.

He slid until his hands were almost at the same point. There was a drop of a couple of yards from here to the ground. By now, Cado and Caton and Audly were waiting to receive him. He let go and almost tumbled into their outspread arms.

His friends were standing with legs braced on a slope that was half rock, half vegetation, mostly thorn bushes and dwarf oak. Chaucer paused for an instant to recover his gravity. He examined his raw, reddened palms and flexed his legs, one of which was trembling from the descent. He brushed away the dust and fragments of stone from his clothing. He scratched his nose and sneezed.

"Come along, Geoffrey," said Ned.

Without a further word being spoken, they set off at a run down the slope. At the bottom was a path of beaten grass which snaked around the base of this side of the castle. Jean Cado led the way to the left and within a few moments they emerged on to an open area fronting the Dordogne. A wind was ruffling the water. A black mass of cloud was gathering to the west and the thunder grumbled.

Some way upstream was a mill. In the other direction a slanting piece of ground led to a landing stage, a primitive construction of planks and props that projected a couple of dozen feet over the river. A barge-like boat was tied up to it. Its single sail was furled. Near the stern was a square tented shape. Otherwise the deck was empty apart from a handful of people and – less explicably – a horse and cart.

Chaucer recognized the broad-bottomed craft as one of those designed to carry the maximum amount of cargo with the smallest possible crew. Her shallow draught was offset by her broad beam. Mostly she would be used to transport casks of wine and cords of oak or chestnut from the upper reaches of the river down as far as Libourne or Bordeaux. Like a matron, she could hold her liquor. Like a matron, she would be slow and deliberate but not ungainly.

As they drew nearer, Chaucer also recognized the horse and cart, as well as some of the individuals on board. The horse was Rounce, the cart was a kind of ark containing the wealth of a world, and the individuals were members of Loup's troupe. This boat was evidently the "arrangement" which Jean Cado had mentioned and they were all to travel together. No, to escape together.

"My cousin Arnaud is there," said Jean, gesturing towards the men on deck. "This is his boat."

"And this is well done," said Geoffrey, recalling that Jean had been brought up in these parts. "Thank you, Jean."

There were subdued greetings among the English. Time was short. Chaucer and the others climbed aboard. Cado embraced a man who Chaucer assumed was the master-cousin and who had the shape of the one of the barrels which he regularly transported. There were four or five crew. The players – Margaret and Alice Loup, together with Tom and Simon and the greybeard Martin – were clustered near the blunt bows of the craft. Alice was holding the little dog called Cerberus. In the middle of the boat Lewis was speaking soothingly to Rounce. The horse's ears were pricked against the coming storm and he was shifting uneasily on his hobbled feet. The players' cart, its contents covered with tarpaulins, was roped to blocks set into the deck. Leaning casually against the side of the boat and seeming to belong neither to players nor to crew was another individual whom Chaucer couldn't quite place, although he thought he had seen him before. Where though . . . ?

Fat blobs of rain suddenly started to splatter across the deck and pock the surface of the water. The rising clouds were split with lightning and the thunder came nearer. A great draught of warm air, like a sigh, blew down the alley of the river. Chaucer glanced over his shoulder at the bulk of the Guyac castle. It reared up from the rockface above the shore, asserting its eternal right to outlast summer storms and freezing winters as well as the turmoil produced by mere human affairs.

At once, round the corner, there appeared a group of armed soldiers. It wasn't clear whether they were in pursuit of anyone, but the moment they glimpsed the boat they started to shout and wave. The rising wind and rain carried away their words. They began to run down the slope towards the landing stage. Even before seeing the men, Cado's cousin, who was standing by the tiller, had given orders for the boat to be untied. One of the crew unhitched the last rope from the mooring-post and leapt on board. The others pushed at the river bank with long staves and the craft floated free. There was no question of using the sail in such conditions but, fortunately, the current was vigorous and soon shifted them towards the centre of the stream.

The soldiers – there were half a dozen – lined up along the landing stage. One of them raised his crossbow but in a hesitant fashion, as if waiting for a command to shoot. Whether there was anyone in the party to give the command would never be known for at that instant a curtain of rain drove down the river and obscured them from sight.

Within moments the occupants of the boat were saturated. Water bounced off the deck. It turned clothing into lead, it ran down beards and overflowed boots. Most of the travellers herded towards the tent in the stern but the master remained at the tiller while two of his crew stood in the bows and squinted through the tearing rain on the lookout for snags and sandbanks. Their progress was slow and wavering, despite the current, because the wind was against them. Lewis Loup braved the storm to continue whispering to Rounce, who stood with hanging head and shivering flanks. Thunder crashed almost directly overhead and flashes of sheet lightning imparted a dead pallor to the stretches of river on either side.

There was little space inside the shelter, which was made of canvas stretched over a wooden frame and which, Chaucer guessed, was more for protection against the sun than the rain. He and Caton and Audly huddled with the players. The air was steamy and clammy even while the wind whipped at their legs.

"Only a summer storm," said Jean Cado but he had to shout to make himself heard.

Chaucer wasn't listening. He was gazing at the unknown individual in their midst, the man he'd observed earlier, the one he thought he had seen somewhere before. But, close to, the man's face sparked no memory. Who was he? Then, recalling what Lewis Loup said in the clearing where Henri's body was discovered, he had it. *We have another man come in Bertram's place.* This must be the new player.

The man noticed Chaucer staring at him and smiled. That is, his upper lip rose to reveal prominent dog-teeth. Chaucer would not have liked to see too many of those smiles.

In the village square of Guyac the crowd had dispersed as the rain began to come down in great swathes and the thunder banged overhead. Some among them might have lingered if Matthieu had been dying slowly, and struggling and kicking his way to extinction. But the wild man of the woods was dead. He hung as straight as a plumb line from the tree. Rainwater coursed the length of his body and dribbled from his down-turned feet. Chestnut blossom, torn off by the wind, was strewn on the ground.

Inside the castle, Richard Foix and Gaston Florac were discussing the latest turn of events.

"You are certain that they are gone?" said Florac.

"I tell you, my men saw them – "

"*Your* men?"

"My late master's men if your prefer, it doesn't matter. Chaucer and the rest were seen to depart by boat as this weather started."

"Downriver?"

"Naturally downriver."

"I wish them a happy voyage then."

Why aren't you more concerned? thought Foix but he said, "What shall we do? They must be going to Bordeaux. They are going to report on what has happened here."

Gaston Florac shrugged in that irritating way of his.

"Well, you'd better try and stop them. But don't look to me. I have a widow to console."

16

The storm cleared by early evening. Great tattered rags of cloud hung in the west, shot through with beams of gold. The river flowed smooth and even once more. While they stood warming in the sun, steam rose from their sodden garments. After they had travelled a few miles, Jean Cado's cousin, the tubby master of the vessel, announced that they would moor overnight on one of the islands in midstream since it would be impossible to go any further during the brief hours of darkness. He chose an island almost equidistant from the banks and with plenty of willows and scrub for cover. They took the precaution of tying up on the southern side and ate their supper – salted fish, cheese, bread – cold, so as to avoid the smoke of a fire. Rounce had been disembarked and was stolidly grazing by the water's edge. Cerberus rootled around. They sat on the sandy soil, Arnaud and the boat crew keeping to themselves and the English in a couple of groups. It wasn't exactly comfortable, Chaucer reflected, swatting at a cloud of midges, none of this was comfortable, but it was better than being shut up in a locked room.

He was curious though. He accosted Loup.

"Tell me, Lewis. When did you decide to leave Guyac?"

"Last night. I was all for staying but the opinion of Margaret was that we should leave and the others agreed with her. They were right. We couldn't have competed against a hanging nor would we have wanted to. That place seemed cursed. Three deaths in little more than twenty-four hours. A drowning, a hanging, and one occurring through different means . . . "

He let the sentence dangle in the air.

"And you just chanced across this boat?"

"When he found out that we intended to go, Monsieur Cado told us his cousin was stopping there and that we were welcome to take a passage downriver with him. It is quicker than going overland."

"Generous of the master to take horse, cart and all."

"This is the sum of our wordly goods, Master Geoffrey. We are poor players. We could hardly leave old Rounce behind."

Geoffrey noticed that Lewis had side-stepped his comment. But the remark about poor players gave him an opening.

"So you have not paid for your passage?"

"Cado said it wasn't necessary, that it was all settled."

Chaucer looked across at the deepening shadows on the southern bank without really seeing them. He was tired but anxious. There was an aspect to all this which puzzled him, several aspects in fact. They had escaped, true enough, but there had been a contrived quality to it, quite like something written down in a book.

"What is troubling you, Master Geoffrey? We have got away from the domain of Guyac and Loup's troupe will not be returning there. We should thank God – and Genesius."

"Genesius?"

"Patron saint of us players."

"So what does St Genesius recommend for you next, I wonder?"

"We'll try our luck in the towns."

"With your new player as well?"

"Hubert. Yes, of course, if he's any good."

"You haven't seen him in, er, action yet?"

"We've had no chance. He turned up after our first and only performance of Jacob and Esau."

And Lewis described to Chaucer the circumstances of Hubert's sudden appearance, his account of the rescuing of the dog, his inability to save poor Bertram.

"No one can speak for Bertram now but the dog does not seem very grateful to his saviour," said Chaucer, observing how the terrier was at that very moment skirting the seated figure of the extra player, almost as if he was wary or frightened of him. "And how convenient that this Hubert should appear so promptly, like the Vice in a play. Not only that, it turns out he's a player too!"

"Convenient? Lucky, I should say."

As if divining that they were talking about him, the man called Hubert looked up in their direction. Then he glanced at the sack of grey cloth which sat beside him on the ground. Chaucer wondered what it contained.

Lewis called out, "Hey there, Hubert. There has been such a press of business that we have still to test your mettle. Your playing mettle." Then, seeing as he had not made himself clear, "We want to see what sort of player you are, man."

A expression of irritation seemed to cross Hubert's bony countenance. He wasn't quite quick enough to hide it. Then he rose to his feet and made a swirling sort of bow. Dusk was approaching. A light breeze had risen and shook the willows so that the leaves showed their pale undersides. Everyone had fallen silent and was watching the standing man. Bats flitted above the river, as imperceptible as the blink of an eye. The water running close to the shore gurgled and plopped.

"Very well, my masters."

It was the first time Geoffrey had heard him speak – odd that, since players are normally among the most garrulous of folk. From somewhere in his garments Hubert produced an impressive-looking scroll. He pretended to consult it although the light was scarcely good enough to read by. From time to time he glanced at them from under his brows.

239

"I shall give you the raising of Lazarus and his speech on his return to this fallen world."

Against the dark backdrop of the trees, he hunched his shoulders and drew his hands across his chest as if, newly risen from the dead, he was pulling imaginary grave-clothes about him. Hubert had more than a touch of the cadaver to him, Chaucer thought, appropriate to Lazarus. An ascetic look, as though he fed on little and disdained earthly comforts. Like a monk ought to look (although most monks grew fat in their cloisters these days).

Like a monk . . .

And Geoffrey remembered the monk he'd glimpsed on the deck of the boat carrying them from Dover, the one he'd assumed was from the Maison Dieu in that town. The cowled figure had been leaning against the side, studying a devotional text. That was weeks ago, but he'd recognized the same attitude in Hubert only a few hours earlier when they boarded this vessel at Guyac. It came to him all at once. You can disguise your face with hoods and cowls, you can grow or shave off a beard, but it is very hard for a man to change his posture. Chaucer was sure that the individual now standing before them in the twilight was the one he had glimpsed on the *St Thomas*. And more than that, another memory was teasing at the edge of his brain. Riding through the gate of Dover town . . . the three of them, Audly and Caton and he . . . looking to one side, and seeing a man picking something up from the ground. The same bony countenance, the same upward glance. Dover, the boat, and now on this island in the middle of the Dordogne.

Suddenly Chaucer's tiredness dropped away.

The man called Hubert was beginning to speak his lines as Lazarus.

"Who calls me back from the other side?
Who shakes the bed where I abide?
Who drags me from my peaceful sleep?

Who is it plumbs death's deep?"

He had a dry, rather featureless voice that seemed of a piece with the sombreness of his subject. But then he faltered. There was a rustling sound behind the speaker among the quivering willows. Some animal? Some danger? The dozen or so spectators who were seated on the ground and watching Hubert in the person of Lazarus switched their attention to the gloom of the trees. Some of them stood up. The boat crew fumbled for their knives. Cerberus wriggled from his position on Alice's lap.

A man emerged part-way from the shadows into the open space by the bank. Legs, hands, the upper part of a body. By accident or design, the face remained obscure. To Geoffrey Chaucer, there was something familiar about this shape too. Hubert twisted round to face the man. Close to, he could see more than was visible to the circle of spectators. He let out a sound that was nearer a laugh than a cry, a strange sound. Then, in the space of a second or two, he bent down, snatched up the grey sack from the ground, and crashed off into the surrounding trees.

All this happened so rapidly that nobody pursued him. Nobody moved at all, apart from the dog. Cerberus raced across the stretch of sandy soil and, yapping, pawed at the stranger's legs. The terrier was quite capable of taking on an adversary many times his size without a moment's thought. But on this occasion he wasn't showing fearlessness. For, as the stranger bent down to scoop up Cerberus into his arms, Chaucer and the rest of the company saw that they were looking at Bertram, the player who was meant to be safely drowned in the river.

It didn't take long for Bertram to convince them that he was no dead man returned to the world like Lazarus, but their living and breathing friend. After he'd swallowed some bread and wine – the only thing he'd imbibed for two days apart from quantities of river water and and a handful of mallow leaves – he swiftly recounted how he'd been lured to the water's edge by the individual dressed in a monk's habit. Not a real monk of course but a counterfeit monk, for one thing he wasn't tonsured. Recounted how, in the attempt to rescue his dear dog, he had been shoved into the fast-flowing river by that man – Hubert, did you say his name was? No, he didn't know why the man had done it, either, and he'd been so eager to stay alive that he hadn't had the leisure to ask himself about it.

All he knew was that he had nearly drowned several times over and that, by some miracle, he had found himself clinging to a great trunk of wood which was as helpless in the water as he was but to which he owed his survival since it was at least three times his size. The wood was freshly cut, perhaps tumbled off one of the cargo boats, and so it kept its head comfortably above the water (to say nothing of his own noddle) while it wallowed along in the middle of the stream. It was night by now. Bertram could do nothing except hold on and hope for better times.

Then, just as he was beginning to think he could hold on no longer, it began to grow light and he saw that he – and his log – were being swept past this very island. Fearing that if he didn't act now he would be carried further along the river to a watery grave, he released his grip at the nearest spot to dry land. Somehow he blundered and floundered his way to this sandy stretch of shore. Here he flopped down and slept for many hours. Then he'd been woken by a fine bright sun. He wondered where he was. He wondered whether he had dreamed the murderous, counterfeit monk and the sodden journey downriver. But it was no dream. His clothes smelled of the river and his arms still ached from their desperate grip on the tree trunk. He worried about his fellow players. He thought of his dear old Cerberus. He must get away from here. So he set about hoping for a passing boat. When no boat passed, he started to look more carefully at his surroundings, in search of food or a means of escape. The wooded banks of the Dordogne were only a few dozen yards away on either side but he couldn't see how to traverse the fast-flowing stream. Nor was there any sign of human habitation over there, not a soul whose attention he might attract. He was unable to find anything to eat on the island apart from the mallow, and the tender tips and leaves of that plant served only to exacerbate his hunger. The one thing he had in abundance was water, of which he'd already swallowed an excess when immersed in the river. A little boat floated by but his desperate shouting and waving must have caused its occupants to think him mad, for they did not stop. So, with hunger eating at his guts, he settled down for a second night on the island.

By the next day Bertram knew that he was in real danger of perishing within a stone's throw of the river banks. He'd begun to look for another trunk or log on which he might paddle his way to one side or the other when a violent thunderstorm forced him to take shelter among the trees. And not long after the storm cleared, imagine his joy to see a cargo boat mooring on "his" island, and his even greater joy when he realized that, among the passengers, were Loup's troupe and the Englishmen, together with good old Cerberus. What stopped him rushing out to greet them was the sight of Hubert, the man who'd pushed him into the river in the first place. What was he doing in the company of his fellows? Bertram grew suspicious and more fearful than ever, the effect maybe of not having eaten for a period. He skulked among the trees, trying to eavesdrop on people's conversations. Eventually, however, desperation drove him to show himself. It was pure coincidence that he'd interrupted Hubert as he was about to declaim Lazarus's speech.

All this was recounted in the gathering dusk. Bertram had the player's instinct for the shape of a story and they listened without interruption until the end. Then the only question was: why had this unknown fellow wanted to dispose of Bertram? To take his place among the players? Or for some more obscure reason?

Lewis outlined to Bertram what had occurred at Guyac and the tragic reasons why they were making a quicker exit from that place than they'd planned. Before that, a couple of the armed crewmen were despatched to look for Hubert but it was almost completely dark by now and the search was fruitless. The counterfeit monk might have concealed himself elsewhere on the island, he might have reached the bank if he was able to swim. Geoffrey said nothing about having seen Hubert on at least two other occasions before their arrival at Guyac, but he was convinced that the same individual had been trailing them all the way from England – the fact that Bertram's would-be killer had appeared in a monk's garb was enough to link him to the cowled figure on the deck of the *St Thomas*. And was it not possible that the same person might be responsible for the death of Henri de Guyac?

Explanations and motives for all this eluded him. And there were more immediate matters to attend to. There might be safety in numbers but it wasn't exactly consoling to consider that the individual who'd tried to murder Bertram – and perhaps others besides – was at large in the dark. In the end, since it seemed safer than staying on the exposed shore they withdrew to the boat, where they did their best to sleep and took turns to keep watch through the short summer night. Only Rounce was left on shore.

Geoffrey was on deck with Ned and Alan. They had offered to keep watch together and were peering into the shadowy bulk of the island, talking in undertones. The stars were out and a breeze was stirring among the willows. Quacking and croaking sounds came from the water-level. Alan Audly seemed to be holding a piece of parchment.

"I picked this up from where that fellow Hubert dropped it when he ran off. He was scanning his lines as Lazarus."

Geoffrey took the document. He unfurled it and felt its crinkled surface. There was a seal attached to it. He asked Alan to get one of a pair of lamps that were burning towards the bow of the boat. The lamp gave off a pleasant odour of walnut oil but provided scant light, so Geoffrey had to hold the paper close to the lamp. He examined the heavy seal, which showed a knight on horseback, his left side on view. The writing was in document hand. This, combined with the seal, gave an official look to the paper, which did not appear to be lines of verse from a play. Chaucer bent closer and tried to make out the words. They were in Latin. Then, after a few moments, he straightened up with a snort of amusement.

"It's meant to pass as an official document, I'll be bound. But it looks like a recipe."

"A *recipe*?"

"Which tells us how to cook a goose."

"Is this a joke?" said Ned.

"If it is, I'm not sure who it's on."

"And there's another queer thing, Geoffrey," said Ned Caton. "You know the stirrup-ring that the hanged man stole?"

"He was no more guilty than you or me."

"Whatever is the truth," said Ned, lowering his voice further, "the ring is now in the hands of the master of this boat."

"How do you know?"

"Because I saw it on his finger. He was showing it off to his men. I was as close to him as I am to you now. I saw it plain. When he saw me looking he put his hand away."

Geoffrey was about to say that this wasn't very likely – for why should an item of evidence in a case of murder be found not many hours afterwards in the possession of a boatman who had nothing to do with the crime? – when he recalled the words of Lewis Loup about what Cado had said concerning their passage on his cousin's craft. That it wasn't necessary to pay, that it was all settled. Was the ring the boatman's fee for transporting the English visitors back down the river, out of harm's way? Not on account of any harm that might be done to them but to Foix and Florac and the others. Had he been instructed to return the unwanted guests to Libourne or Bordeaux where they could no longer interfere in the affairs of Guyac? If so, then Cado's barrel-shaped cousin was being very well remunerated for a simple passage, since the stirrup-ring would be worth half a year's wages to him, probably a good deal more. Also, using the ring as payment was a convenient way for Richard Foix to get rid of an embarrassing piece of evidence. And what was Jean Cado's part in all of this?

"What is happening here?" said Ned, echoing Geoffrey's thoughts.

"We're quite in the dark," said Alan Audly, and laughed softly at his own joke.

As he lay uncomfortably on the deck of the cargo boat and watched for the first glimmers of dawn, Geoffrey Chaucer found sleep elusive. They had got away from Guyac but he could not so easily escape the images of everything that had happened there, above all the scene in the clearing where Henri's body had lain.

Someone had murdered Henri de Guyac, he had little doubt. The supposed perpetrator had been apprehended and summarily dealt with, but the bloody hand surely did not belong to Matthieu.

But if not Matthieu's, then whose was it?

In his mind's eye he paraded those who might have an interest in the death of Henri.

There was the death's-head figure of Hubert, if that was the man's real name. He had been on their tail since Dover at least. It occurred to him that Hubert was probably responsible for the attack in the Mouton à Cinq Pattes in Calais and the attempt to fire the inn. If Geoffrey was correct in his speculation that he'd been after the wallet which still hung about his neck like a millstone, then he had failed – but only narrowly. Unable to get so close to him again, Hubert had bided his time until he saw the opportunity of joining Loup's troupe. To achieve this, he had tried to kill Bertram. Life counted for little with him, evidently. Perhaps he enjoyed killing people. Geoffrey had encountered such individuals while on campaign, although in his experience they tended to be found not among the ranks of the ordinary soldiery – who were more concerned about where their next meal was coming from or about getting home un-scathed – but in the files of mercenaries and irregulars.

Yet Hubert was surely not working on his own behalf, any more than a mercenary would be. Presumably his aim was to prevent Chaucer from persuading Henri de Guyac to confirm his allegiance to Edward the Third, either by stealing the wallet or by killing him before he reached Guyenne. Such an act could only be in the interest of one group: the party surrounding the French king, Charles. They wanted to foment war with the English. And if one of the noblemen of Guyenne was wavering in his allegiance then any action which swayed him towards Paris would be legitimate. But if that was truly Hubert's aim, then his mission had been pointless. Henri hadn't shown much mind to be persuaded, and now he was dead anyway. Had Hubert taken the short cut of murdering the Comte de Guyac? But that would hardly have been necessary if the Comte had been intending to join the French party.

Geoffrey's mind – not unfamiliar with that dark arena where diplomacy and intrigue were sometimes joined together and sometimes at odds – put aside the question of whether Hubert, the false monk, had indeed murdered Henri de Guyac. Instead he considered some of the others who might have welcomed the man's death or gone so far as to arrange it.

247

It was painful to think that Rosamond might have been among those wanting Henri dead. Not that she could have killed her husband herself – although she had the strength (he remembered her wielding the boar-sword in the castle garden, he remembered her strong grasp on his wrist in the bedroom) – since she had been in his chamber at the very moment when Henri was involved in the chase. Although, it occurred to him, someone who was familiar with the private exits from the castle as well as the woods around it might have been able to reach the clearing and return again within a comparatively short space of time. She hadn't been present when the body was returned to the castle but had appeared shortly afterwards. It was hard, almost impossible, to think of Rosamond as a murderer but she was a powerful and determined woman. She might have bribed or suborned or seduced another into doing it. Or, at the least, have acquiesced in the result. Her motive was obvious enough if she was in love with Gaston Florac, as the signs indicated she might be. Chaucer recalled that she had once talked with him about the romance of *Nicolette and the Castellan*. In that tale a lady dreams of the violent death of her husband so that she might be free to marry her lover.

And that thought led to its sequel . . . that Gaston Florac might be the murderer of de Guyac. Chaucer hadn't seen much of him but what little he had indicated a man who was used to getting his own way, in an offhand fashion. If he wanted the lady, if he wanted to lay his hands on his neighbour's lands, would he hesitate to act with the necessary ruthlessness when he saw an opportunity? He'd been lost sight of in the forest during the hunt. There was no one to account for his movements, and certainly he wasn't going to be called to account for them himself.

Similarly with Richard Foix the seneschal. It was not so apparent what he would gain from the death of his master but wasn't it possible that he had hopes himself of gaining favour with Rosamond, or that he had been given all kinds of promise of future benefit by Florac? Or, if he was convinced that Henri should throw in his lot with the French king, did he fear his master might be backsliding towards the English camp? Stewards and seneschals were like men invited to a feast but permitted only to taste each dish briefly. They had local authority but they spent their lives in the company of those who wielded genuine power. Some men might grow very impatient in such a situation.

Then there was the strange case of Ned Caton to consider. Ned, seemingly so straightforward and good-humoured. But, Geoffrey thought, suppose that he was right in his speculations that Henri was Ned's father. And suppose that Ned discovered some secret of his parentage only after they arrived at Guyac. Or had an inkling of it before. Had the shock of the discovery driven him over the edge? Had he been determined to avenge some imagined slight on the honour of a beautiful mother? Ned too had been on his own for a period during the hunt. He could have encountered a wounded, exhausted de Guyac and taken advantage of the moment. It was not impossible.

With these thoughts churning around in his head, Geoffrey could resolve only to report on them to John of Gaunt when he returned to England, and heaven knew how far off that blessed moment would be.

Richard Foix was angry with his man Guilheme.

"What do you mean, you can't find them?"

"They have vanished downriver."

"Then take your men and go in pursuit."

"They are most likely out of the domain by now."

"They can only be heading for Bordeaux. You must stop them before they reach the Prince's court."

Guilheme thought for a moment.

"They will have to put in at Libourne," he said. "All the river traffic puts in there."

"Very well," said Foix. "If you saddle up now you will outdistance them. Get to Libourne first and deal with them there. The further away the better."

"By any means, sir?"

"By any means. I just don't want to know the details."

17

They travelled on into the tidal stretches of the river as far as Libourne, which was the limit of Cado's cousin's journey. There they took their leave of the barrel-shaped Arnaud. Geoffrey didn't see the stirrup-ring which Ned Caton had glimpsed on the shipman's finger, the ring which had supposedly belonged to Henri de Guyac and been purloined by the wild woodman. If this had really been a payment made to the cousin to get them out of the way, then the master of the vessel might have grown careful about flashing it around in front of outsiders. Anyway, their voyage with him was finished and they disembarked beside the walled town which lay about twenty miles to the east of Bordeaux. The players, together with their property cart and Rounce, assembled themselves on the crowded quayside. Cerberus ran around, pleased to be on dry land. Ned and Alan helped them to unload. Ned in particular busied himself, hoping to show well in Alice's eyes. Meantime Chaucer despatched Jean Cado to inquire for lodging in the town.

Now Chaucer had a pleasant reunion, for at the other end of the quay he saw a familiar figure. It was the grey-haired master of the *Arveragus*, Jack Dart. He made his way through the people clustered in groups by the waterside, soldiers, traders, idlers. He tapped Dart on the shoulder. If Jack was surprised to see Geoffrey he didn't show it.

"What are you doing across here?" said the lugubrious English shipman. "I thought you had business in Bordeaux."

"My work carried me further afield than I expected. It was inland business," said Chaucer. "And I could return the question. What are you doing?"

"You remember when I said we sustained some harm crossing the bar into the Gironde?"

Chaucer recalled the great grinding and shuddering which had accompanied their entry to the estuary. He nodded.

"Well, worse things happen at sea and my worst fears proved true," said Dart.

"Your worser fears perhaps, for we arrived safely."

"Then we should thank our lucky stars for it. But I will not venture my vessel in the open sea in its current condition. The *Arveragus* will be laid up for a few more days like a man convalescing. The only difference is that the boat's recovery is more assured than yours or mine would be after such a mishap."

"It's a pity that we're not all built of timber. So what are you doing away from your patient?"

"Everything is at sixes and sevens in Bordeaux. War is in the air. Prince Edward is on the move north."

"Why?"

"There is trouble brewing at Limoges. It is in the hands of the bishop at the moment, and he is one of us, but the Prince fears he may surrender to the French. He wants to be in the region to discourage such a move. Accordingly I was ordered to bring some . . . pieces of equipment . . . further upriver so they might be more easily transported overland to the north. I had to take them off the *Arveragus*, then I had to put them on board a river boat and now I've got to take them off again. I'm not used to sailing on a river. I miss my *Arveragus*. That thing is more like a platter for food. It only requires a couple of men to sail it."

Dart gestured over his shoulder at one of the boats moored to the quay. It was similar to the one which had rescued them from Guyac, although with a larger tented area for the shelter

252

of the crew. On the deck, Geoffrey thought he recognized some huddled shapes as the bombards which had originally been transported from Calais.

"The secret weapons?"

"Not secret for much longer. And, if you want my candid opinion, Master Geoffrey, not much use either. We are in for a hiding. The Prince is sick and seems surprised that his black armour does not make him immortal. He must be carried in a litter over any distance. An army led by a sick man is already half defeated. And Gaunt's arrival will make no difference."

"John of Gaunt is here!"

One or two people in the vicinity looked round at Chaucer's words. He hadn't realized he was speaking so loud. It was a measure of his surprise at the news.

"He is in Bordeaux," said Dart.

Gaunt had given no indication that he planned to journey to Aquitaine. His presence was a sign of the seriousness of the situation. Yet, if his employer was already here, then that simplified matters. Geoffrey could report directly to him. Report failure, that is. He was half glad, half apprehensive at the prospect of seeing Gaunt once more.

"I must get to Bordeaux as soon as possible."

"To bring news of the inland wine?"

"Let's drop that pretence now, Master Jack. You saw through it some time ago. But I still need to get to Bordeaux urgently."

"Then you shall return with me – on my platter. We need only to unload our 'secret' items. We'll start back tomorrow at dawn."

"I'm not alone."

"Ned and Alan? I can see those gentlemen talking to a ragged-looking crew. Though there's a pretty girl among them."

"We've grown in numbers. A bunch of players is keeping us company, English too. Loup's troupe, they call themselves. The pretty girl is Alice Loup."

"I've no objection to a spot of mumming. Come one, come all. You may sleep on board if you wish, free of charge. Be my guest. Even if it has to be on a food platter on a piddling river."

"I'm grateful."

"Not that landlubbers would find it so comfortable."

"I'll think on it."

"I can only sleep on water, you see. Sleep properly, that is, though a shipman always sleeps lightly."

Chaucer introduced the members of Loup's troupe to Jack Dart. The shipman took to Margaret and Lewis straightaway and extended his offer of overnight accommodation to the whole band. Lewis promptly accepted, candidly admitting that it would save them the cost of lodgings. Horse and cart would remain on shore, hobbled and secure in one of the outbuildings on the bank.

Later on, as the sun was setting, Geoffrey and Ned and Alan went to inspect the unloading of the bombards. Under their canvas cladding they were revealed as tube-shaped devices made of iron and fastened to sturdy wooden stands fitted with wheels. No longer a secret. One of the bombard-men had no hesitation in telling them everything he knew, which was not much. When asked what propelled the balls, the man clapped his hands, blew out his cheeks and then gabbled on about Greek fire as if he was referring to magic. He pointed to some little canvas sacks piled up in the stern like so many purses.

"Greek fire? You mean gunpowder," said Ned Caton.

"Call it what you like, it is a fearful thing, sir," said the bombard-man. "The noise, the smoke, the stench. Your ears won't stop ringing for half an hour after."

Geoffrey Chaucer doubted that such devices would work effectively. You couldn't bring down a castle, let alone a city, with slugs and stones, however fast and furious they flew. Castles and cities were taken by courageous men on the outside – or by treacherous men on the inside. (And that made him think of the Guyac castle and the treachery within its walls and beyond.) He glanced up at the walls of Libourne, basking in the evening sun. Surely it would require more than a few bombards to breach such a heavily fortified site? Like many of the Gascon towns built by the English during the past few decades it was girdled with stone and, inside, its streets were arranged in an orderly pattern which contrasted with the untidy growth of older places and which seemed somehow un-English to him. More typical was the haphazard assemblage of buildings and store-houses clustered at both ends of the quay.

They watched as the guns were trundled through the town gates by the bombard-men with much sweating and swearing. At the same time Jean Cado emerged from within. With his owlish eyes screwed up against the declining sun, he explained that he'd discovered a spot for them to stay, the best inn in town, a prime position off the market square. He seemed pleased with himself and eager to push his find as *the* place for the gentry. It'll make up for your disagreeable accommodation in the castle of Guyac, he said, not to mention our time on board the barge.

Chaucer had sudden doubts. How much did he really know about Cado? The man had rescued them from Guyac castle but who knew what negotiations or deals lay behind their escape which – aside from the climb down the tower wall – had been surprisingly easy. Besides, if they were staying within the walls of this bastide town, then it would not be so straightforward for them to make their departure early next morning. The town gates would be barred. There'd be a watch to pass through. Chaucer was gripped by the need to get to Bordeaux as fast as possible.

"Thank you, Jean," he said. "But we'd prefer somewhere more out of the way. There, for instance."

He pointed towards a low (in both senses) building at the end of the quayside. An indecipherable, weather-worn sign hung drunkenly from a hook above the door.

"Why, that's for fisherfolk and bargemen and other riff-raff," said Cado.

"Coin is coin," said Chaucer. "Ours is as good as theirs. You stay in town if you prefer."

He half expected Ned Caton and Alan Audly to disagree with his choice but the young men said nothing – perhaps they were finally getting the hang of this life on the road – and followed him to the waterside inn, together with a reluctant Jean Cado. The Gascon shrugged and raised his eyes to heaven, as though despairing at the perversity of these English.

The inn with the unreadable sign smelt dank. The timbers looked as though they had been salvaged from the river. The landlady emerged from the back quarters wiping her hands on an apron covered with fishy blood. But she was welcoming enough, even maternal in her plump way, and treated them as honoured guests. They were offered a droop-ceilinged room with half a dozen lumpy beds, none of which was taken.

It was growing dark outside. The landlady provided a fish stew and fussed around them like a mother hen. The stew was composed mostly of heads, tails and bones but in the opinion of Ned – who had taken a particular shine to the landlady's kindliness – it was the best meal he'd had for weeks. Afterwards they turned in. There was no one else in their room. As usual, Geoffrey found sleep elusive. Every day and every night brought some emergency. What would happen tonight? To distract himself, he wondered what sort of reception he'd get from John of Gaunt. The first thing he'd do was to return the wallet and its contents which still hung, unopened, about his neck. He wondered now whether he'd ever discover what it contained.

How would Gaunt judge him for the failure of his mission? In the larger view, it looked as though the English cause in Guyenne was already slipping away. Even had Henri de Guyac remained alive and thrown in his lot with the English, that would hardly have affected the likelihood of war. Gaunt's very presence in Aquitaine was an indication of how the prospects for diplomacy and persuasion had dimmed. Gaunt had guile, unlike his brother Edward; but he was first and foremost a soldier.

And Geoffrey Chaucer – a man not without ambition – half smiled in the dark to reflect on his connection to Gaunt. Almost a relation, you might say. A relation in a manner of speaking, since his wife Philippa was the older sister of Catherine Swyneford, the lady who had recently become Gaunt's mistress, or so the rumour went in court circles. Chaucer believed the rumour, perhaps because it suited him to. If it was true, Chaucer's sister-in-law had an enviable position in the kingdom since the King's son was devoted to Catherine.

Yet John of Gaunt, Duke of Lancaster, had loved his wife as well as his mistress. Blanche had died at the end of the previous year, only a month after the death of Philippa, Queen of England. Losing his mother and losing his wife, Gaunt was bereft. He was also free. Bereft and free but not likely to be immediately consoled since Catherine was already married. Her husband was about Chaucer's age, and Gaunt's come to that. He was a vigorous man, a fighter, part of Gaunt's retinue. Maybe the Duke of Lancaster had brought his lover's husband down to Aquitaine with him. If anything happened to Hugh Swyneford – which God forbid, of course! – then it would be only a matter of time, Chaucer supposed, before a union between Gaunt and Catherine was solemnized by holy church and all the pomp of the state. He had already written a poem obliquely commemorating the death of Blanche, which he had presented to Gaunt, to the latter's evident pleasure and sorrow combined. In due course he, Geoffrey Chaucer, should surely compose a work to celebrate the second marriage of the King's third son. God willing, he should. It would be a way of atoning to Gaunt for his failure in Aquitaine. It would be good to start writing verse again. He might cast the marriage poem in the form of a dream . . . and thinking this, he must have fallen into dreams of his own.

But it was an unquiet sleep with unquiet dreams. He saw the elongated figure of the false monk Hubert striding through ghostly willows on an island. He saw black-clad figures slipping into murky waters and swimming with the jerky movement of frogs. A storm was coming and the water was pitted with great raindrops. Then came a great crash of thunder, the loudest noise he'd ever heard, and a mighty burst of light.

Waking, he grasped that the thunder was real. There was a lurid, flickering glow across the sagging ceiling of the room. Not again, he thought . . . oh God, not again. There were shouts and screams but they seemed to penetrate from a great distance through the ringing in his ears. He stumbled to the parchment-covered window, dimly aware of the other occupants of the bedchamber milling about behind him.

The river was on fire!

The area by the bank was covered by billowing smoke, tumbling over the edge and black against the coming dawn. The smoke was shot through with flashes of flame.

No, it was not the river on fire but one of the craft moored along the quayside. When they'd arrived it had been high tide. The river had dropped, causing the vessels moored there to sink almost out of view. But now Chaucer saw how the flames threw into relief the low outline of a boat together with figures staggering helplessly hither and thither.

Almost unaware of how he'd got there, Chaucer found himself outside the inn. Great wafts of heat buffeted his face and he was stifled by coils of smoke. He bent double and ran along the quay until he got clear of the acrid clouds and was able to see with less difficulty. He coughed helplessly, while tears came to his eyes.

But his watery eyes confirmed what his instincts had told him. The boat which was on fire and already starting to lurch even lower into the water was the one on which Jack Dart had arrived in Libourne, the one used for the transport of the bombards. And this caused his guts to turn to water. He thought of the individuals who were sleeping on board the boat, of Jack Dart and his men – and the members of Loup's troupe.

The hot air was full of sparks and flaring smuts that drifted down on to the stones of the quay or extinguished themselves in the dark river. To the east the sky was lightening. A confusion of figures was running in different directions, some coming out of the ramshackle buildings on the waterfront, some going towards the town gate while others – the Libourne watch, judging by their dress and weapons – issued from it. Yet there was nothing to be done. The helmeted members of the watch stood at a safe distance. The fire could not be doused now. It was fiercest in the bows of the barge but had spread along the entire length. There was a great hissing sound as the forepart of the boat dipped deeper into the water, at the same time tilting up the stern. The tented area was well ablaze. Other craft were moored on the waterfront but fortunately none was close enough to take fire.

Chaucer looked round. By the fitful light of the flames he saw Ned and Alan nearby. There was a kind of glassy stillness in their faces which he imagined was reflected in his own. Ned opened his mouth to say something but his words were swallowed up in the roaring of the fire. A batch of blackened figures was stumbling towards them along the quay, accompanied by a small dog. To his inexpressible relief, he saw that it was Loup's troupe – or some of them. He counted three, no, four shapes. They were sooty all over and the whites of their eyes showed unnaturally bright. They were bruised and bleeding from assorted cuts and gashes. Their clothes were in tatters. But they were alive.

"Thanks be for that," said Geoffrey, his voice sounding oddly in his ears.

"Where's Alice?" said Ned.

"She got ashore," said Lewis. "I saw her leaping for the bank."

Lewis laughed. It was odd but Chaucer had seen similar responses from men after a battle. At that moment a figure ran past in the direction of the burning boat. He was carrying a great axe high above his head like a warrior going into battle. He put up one hand in feeble protection against the heat and the flying sparks and with the other he brought down the axe repeatedly on the cables which secured the boat to the quayside. There was the clang of steel striking stone. More sparks flew. The man had courage. Chaucer recognized Jack Dart as the frantic figure attempting to release the craft from its mooring. One of the severed ropes, free from tension at last, reared up into the air like a black snake against the yellow flames. Then other men with swords and axes joined Dart in slashing at the remaining ropes. The only course was to let the river take care of the burning vessel, to allow it to sink in its own time.

Now Ned Caton did something unexpected and daring. He too raced forward though not towards the boat which, tethered only by a single cable, was already beginning to ease itself off the bank. Instead Ned teetered on the edge many yards from the departing boat. He half jumped, half slid off the edge and into the water. Geoffrey and Alan ran to the brink. Geoffrey stumbled over a bundle of ropes and flung out his arms to break his fall. Winded, he picked himself up.

The surface of the river was covered with objects, serenely awash and illuminated by the fire. They saw Ned fumbling in the water. He was surrounded by bobbing barrels, chunks of wood still emitting little tapers of flame, waterlogged tarpaulins buoyed up by the stream. And not merely debris but human bodies. Ned Caton was clutching at somebody. He was attempting to keep a pale countenance above the waves with one arm while desperately flailing about with the other. His mouth was gaping like a fish's. He was half a dozen yards from the bank but out of his depth. Though the tide was low this was a deep mooring. In a moment he would sink, taking his burden with him.

Geoffrey cupped his hands and called out to Ned, who twisted his head towards the bank. Retreating a few feet, Chaucer snatched at one of the ropes which lay behind him. The rope snagged on some encumbrance. He shouted to Alan for aid. Gasping for air and colliding with each other, they untangled and straightened the rope with painful slowness, like an action in a dream. The fire roared in their ears. They dragged the rope to the water's edge. But they were too late. Ned had disappeared amid the floating debris. Suddenly he burst above the surface as if he'd driven himself up into the smoke-filled air by main force. He was still clutching at somebody. Chaucer threw one end of the rope into the river, using all his strength to send it out as far as possible. It landed with a silent splash and Ned flailed out with his free hand like a man losing his balance. He missed. Tried again. Struck his arm on a barrel that almost rolled him under. Tried once more. Snatched the end of the rope as it began to sink.

Geoffrey and Alan hauled on the rope and drew the struggling man nearer to the bank. The pull caused Ned to rise half out of the river, holding the individual he'd rescued in a kind of stranglehold. Chaucer saw that the white countenance belonged to Alice Loup. She wasn't moving her limbs but was being towed through the water. When Ned and Alice were directly underneath the quay and about five feet down among the slopping waves, Geoffrey and Alan lay flat on the ground and stretched out their arms. Ned managed to seize Alan's hand, then Geoffrey grasped at his sleeve. Somehow Ned got a purchase with his feet on the slimy stone of the quay wall and, tugged upwards by the others, he slowly emerged from the water dragging Alice behind him. By now others, seeing what was happening, had joined in the rescue.

Ned Caton and Alice Loup were pulled firmly on to the quayside by many hands. Ned stretched himself out face down, spluttering and wordless, rivulets of water pouring off his sides. Alice was laid on her back. Her eyes were shut and her face had taken on a ghostly tinct. Her mouth hung slack and open. She lay with splayed limbs. There was a wail from someone in the group standing around, a man's cry, either Lewis Loup or Simon. Margaret Loup, with more presence of mind, knelt over her daughter. The mother's dress hung off her in rags and her face was smeared with sooty blood. She put her ear to Alice's chest then to the girl's mouth. She pinched and pulled at her cheeks. After an agonizing space, Alice's eyelids quivered. She raised her head, turned slightly and a jet of river water spewed from her mouth. She coughed so violently that her whole frame shook.

"Thank God," said Simon.

"Amen to that," said Lewis. "I thought she was safe on shore but she must have fallen in."

Within a few moments Alice was sitting up, water pooling underneath her. The members of the company crowded about her, patting and soothing. Chaucer and Audly and Caton, who was back on his feet by now, stood to one side. Ned was shivering. It was early on a summer's morning. The first shafts of light were shooting through narrow tiers of cloud in the east. The dawn air, warmed by the fire, was growing cooler again. Behind them lay the walls of Libourne. The town gates were open. Men and women were bustling backwards and forwards, to lend a hand, to watch the spectacle, to see what might be salvaged.

Ned's teeth chattered. Then the landlady of the inn appeared in the company of Jean Cado. She draped a blanket over Ned's sodden shoulders and offered another to Alice. She waddled off and – a true combination of mother hen and angel of mercy – reappeared moments later bearing jugs of wine heated with a warm poker.

"Are you all right, Master Geoffrey?" said Jean Cado.

"I've been better."

The rescuers drank. Chaucer felt life flowing back into his belly. Jack Dart, his creased face all grimy except where it had been washed clean by streaks of sweat, stood nearby, resting nonchalantly on the haft of his axe. After a time Alice Loup was helped inside the inn, accompanied by other members of the troupe and Jean Cado, together with Cerberus. Chaucer noticed that the only one who was missing was Bertram. He was left alone with Alan and Ned.

The three Englishmen looked about them like men wondering what to do next. By now the burning boat had floated many yards offshore and slightly downstream, for the tide was just beginning to turn once more. The forepart was completely submerged and the stern tilted up so that the steering oar was almost clear of the water. Small tongues of flame and wisps of smoke continued to rise from the hindquarters of the barge. A bitter stench hung in the air. The stretch of river between the quayside and the sinking vessel was littered with objects which slowly took on definition in the growing light. Alice Loup had been rescued from the Dordogne but others had not been so fortunate. Among the charred timbers and fragments of canvas were several black-clad bodies floating face down in the water. A small rowboat was launched from the quayside. Two members of the town watch sat in the stern while a third plied the oars.

"What happened, Jack?" said Geoffrey, going across to where the shipman stood on the lip of the quay, still leaning on the great haft of his axe.

The shipman wiped his black brows. He'd lost a vessel. Nevertheless he looked like a warrior after some ancient victory, exhausted but vindicated. Perhaps such disasters were no more than he expected in the run of life. Dart nodded in the direction of the rowboat which was headed for the jumble of flotsam and corpses eddying gently together downstream.

263

"Ask them, you'd better."

It took Geoffrey an instant to grasp that he was referring not to the occupants of the rowboat but to the bodies in the water.

"I don't think they'll be saying much in the future," he said. "Who are they?"

"I don't know. All I can tell you is that they crept on board towards dawn," said Jack. "I was awake though the people in that mumming company were snoring all around me. A shipman sleeps lightly, like I said. I heard the vessel creak and the sounds of scuffling and scraping up in the bows, I heard whispers. Saw some shapes there – four or five of 'em – up to no good, it was obvious straightaway. They were in black and their faces were masked. I was about to confront them when I saw the bastards had fired the boat. They must have brought flint and steel along with them. There were piles of sacking heaped in the bows which took easily. They were crouching round it like men at a camp fire."

Jack Dart paused. He looked at Geoffrey.

"Worse things happen at sea, they say. I may even have said it myself from time to time. But, believe me, a fire is the worst thing of all. That man who is careless with fire on board deserves the noose – and as for the man who starts one deliberately, purgatory would be too kind for him. It can spread so quick, you see, and you've nowhere to go even though you're surrounded by the wherewithal to put it out. My first duty was to get my, er, guests to safety . . ."

"I know you are a brave man, Jack, and now I see that you are a good one too," said Geoffrey. He meant it.

The shipman did not respond with any false modesty but simply nodded at the compliment. He explained how he'd roused the members of Loup's troupe and more or less pushed them down the gangplank to the quayside. Meantime he stood guard with the great axe. The unknown malefactors were gathered at the bow end. There was no gangplank there although they might have leaped for the bank but they didn't move, except to flourish their daggers like desperate men. Maybe they were waiting for the flames to take a proper hold on the timbers of the forepart of the barge. Maybe they were daunted by the sight of the shipman grasping an axe in the stern. Whatever the reason, they didn't shift far although one of them started towards Jack, waving a large dagger. The shipman waved his even larger axe in return and the masked man fell back like the coward he was. Then Jack Dart remembered something which chilled his bones. And, when the last of the players were safely on the quay together with a couple of his crewmen, he ran as if his life depended on it.

As well he did, for no sooner was he on dry land than an almighty explosion burst like a flower from the area of the bows. The people on shore were thrown backwards by a hot wind and scattered like chaff, badly bruised and shaken but still alive. What had happened?

Once again Jack Dart paused in his recitation. Even with his ears still humming and the stench of the explosion in his nostrils, Geoffrey Chaucer admired, from a professional point of view, the shipman's storytelling skills. He waited for the sequel.

"For, Master Geoffrey, what those luckless bastards weren't aware of was that we'd been carrying those secret weapons together with the wherewithal to set the damned things off."

"Greek fire?"

"Gunpowder, they call it. There was a single little sackful of the stuff left behind in the bows by those bombard-men. I saw it after those soldiers had unloaded everything else and made themselves scarce in the town. I was going to tell them about it today. Too late now. It must have gone up. Nothing else would account for the noise and the fire."

The noise, the smoke, the stench, Chaucer recalled the bombard-man saying. *Your ears won't stop ringing for half an hour after.*

265

"So the bad men's lives were forfeit, we were saved and all is as well as can be expected in this fallen world – but you, you've lost a boat."

"Call that a boat if you please, but I don't," said Jack Dart, casting a glance at the barge which was slipping by degrees into the river, its steering oar cocked up at an ever more mocking angle. "We should have been setting off about now. You'll have to use other means to get to Bordeaux."

"We'll find something," said Geoffrey. "I wonder who they were . . . your black-clad shapes?"

He wondered whether one of them had been Hubert, the counterfeit monk. But that individual had struck him as a lone wolf, not one to operate in a band. At that moment the little rowboat started to pull slowly back in the direction of the bank. The sun was up by now and cast a dazzling light almost directly along the course of the river. Chaucer shielded his eyes against the glare. Two of the soldiers were wielding the oars on account of the burden which the remaining soldier was towing behind the boat attached to a kind of grappling-hook. A selection of bodies was bundled together astern like so much rubbish. But one of the corpses – a slight one, wrapped in black rags – had been hauled aboard and lain athwart the bow of the boat, positioned so as to equalize the weight at both ends perhaps. The head hung almost upside down, its hair scorched by the fire. But the dead man's face was largely visible and had been washed clean by immersion in the river. If he'd been wearing a mask then it must have been removed by the salvagers or torn off by the explosion. It was a young-old face, like a disagreeable boy's, and it was covered in dots and blotches which Chaucer at first took to be the marks of fire but which, as the rowboat drew nearer, he realized were freckles.

He couldn't recall this individual's name – wasn't sure that he'd ever known it in the first place – but this was one of the Guyac seneschal's men, the one who'd summoned him under false pretences to the guard-room in the castle. So Richard Foix had not been content to let them escape from the castle but was determined to pursue them down the river. Had he given orders for them to be killed or was he simply trying to slow their journey by burning the boat? Did this dead man, whatever his name was, believe that the entire party was sleeping on board the barge and set out to dispose of them all? He must have seen Chaucer talking to Jack Dart last evening or have spied the company bedding down inside the tent on deck.

"You recognize him?" said the shipman.

The soldiers in the boat had reached the bank by now and, with the help of their fellows, had begun to hoist up freckle-face's body on to the quay. They handled him as uncere-moniously as a dead fish. Chaucer was as certain as he could be that this was the seneschal's man.

"I recognize him," he said.

"This is to do with your inland business?"

"Something like that. One day I will tell you about it. I fear we have brought trouble on you, Master Dart."

The shipman shrugged. He swung his axe in the direction of the other corpses which were now being landed.

"The world is relieved of five malefactors. Count them now."

"There will be others to take their place."

"And they say that I look on the gloomy side of things, Master Geoffrey."

It had been the intention of Guilheme (the dead man with the face full of freckles) to destroy the barge on which he believed Chaucer and the others were sleeping – and to destroy its human occupants as well. Together with his men he had reached Libourne the previous afternoon, confident that they'd outdistanced the fugitives' boat. They had. He had no plan for how to deal with Chaucer and the others but he relied on his wits and whatever means might come to hand. He watched the arrival of the barge carrying the Englishmen and settled down to idle away the evening on the quayside, taking care to be within earshot of Geoffrey Chaucer while remaining unnoticed. He knew from experience that it was easy for him to pass unnoticed. Fortunately, on a fine summer's evening, the quay was crowded with bystanders watching the unloading of the bombards. Guilheme noted the arrival of these weapons and also picked up their ultimate destination: Limoges. It was a piece of intelligence which he would pass on in the right quarters. More to his immediate purposes, he overheard Jack Dart's offer to provide lodging for the travellers on board his barge. He'd listened to Chaucer's courteous reply but – perhaps because he was deaf to the intonations of a tongue which wasn't his own – had not understood that the courtesy was for form's sake.

Accordingly, Guilheme returned to his men, who were drinking the hours away at a tavern just inside the town walls. He told them to expect action later that night and instructed them to dress in the black garb which they'd worn when they ambushed Machaut earlier in the summer. On that occasion he'd met Machaut at Bordeaux and escorted the messenger inland. Gerard had been with him. They hadn't got on with Machaut, hadn't *fraternized* with him. Indeed, the man seemed positively wary of them, as though they were intending to poison him en route or stab him in the back. Poison him, stab him? Not yet, sir, not until we've arrived securely within the domain of Guyac. In truth, Guilheme wouldn't have relished taking on Machaut, even with Gerard's aid. The man looked as though he could take care of himself, was most likely a battle veteran. So the ambush had been arranged for the top of the rise overlooking the castle, the point at which all travellers, whether on foot or horseback, naturally halted to catch their breath and admire the view. This had been Guilheme's idea, although the order to make sure that Machaut – or at least the letter which he carried – did not reach Henri de Guyac came from Richard Foix.

Guilheme was privy to Foix's thinking. The castle seneschal feared that his master was about to jump the wrong way in the war which was surely coming to life again after a period of comparative tranquillity. The future of Aquitaine rested with King Charles of France, Foix was convinced. Those who maintained their allegiance to the English crown – whether out of misguided loyalty or a sense of honour or from stupidity or for whatever reason – they would all be swept away in the new dispensation. The trouble was that a lord did not fall alone. The fortunes of many other lives, more humble ones, would be swept downhill with him. So Richard Foix decided that he would do his utmost to steer Henri away from his inexplicable partiality for the English cause and open his eyes to where his real interests lay. He was comforted by the fact that their neighbour, Gaston Florac, was of a like mind. Though you could never be quite sure what Florac thought, it seemed to the seneschal that he was being encouraged to use what little "influence" he had on Henri de Guyac.

The ambush had succeeded. Guilheme recalled, with a stab of pleasure, the look that Machaut had thrown at him and Gerard when he saw that he'd been betrayed. Got you! The two had hung back and let the others do the dirty work, tumbling down from the overhanging boughs and sweeping Machaut from his horse. The ambushers were, properly speaking, servants to Henri de Guyac. Guilheme had claimed the orders to attack the messenger came from their master but he had deliberately selected from the dross among the castle employees – one man whom Foix had caught pilfering, another who'd been interfering with one of the stable-lads, and so on. They were a desperate little clutch. Guilheme pretended that they might be restored to their lord's favour by doing what he said. In fact, de

Guyac knew nothing of the attack, wasn't even aware of the emissary from England. Richard Foix had handled all the details.

The attackers were wearing masks, not so much to avoid recognition – for Machaut was not due to survive the attack – but because a mask enables its wearer to act with greater ruthlessness. Nevertheless Machaut had put up a good fight, you had to admit it. Afterwards Guilheme had taken possession of the wallet and the letter it contained. He wasn't so curious to discover what was in the letter (not that he could read, of course) or rather he knew that it was safer not to know everything. He handed the letter over to Richard Foix who, in his own typical show of ignorance, asked no questions about the fate of the messenger.

But the English were persistent in their attempts to bring round Henri de Guyac. They'd sent out more envoys, ones not so easily disposed of as a solitary man on horseback. The simultaneous arrival of the players at the castle was another complication. And the greatest complication of all was the death of Guilheme's and Foix's master during the hunt. Looked at in another way, however, Henri's demise was a great simplification. Dead men need no persuading. All that was necessary now was a little mopping-up to ensure that Geoffrey Chaucer and the rest of them did not return to Bordeaux and report to the Prince on what had occurred. For matters were at a delicate juncture. The English were ready to fight in order to hold on to Aquitaine. They mustn't be provoked into a premature move before the forces of resistance were good and ready to face them.

So an accident was required. Death by water, death by fire. Death on a burning boat. The idea came suddenly to Guilheme as he idled on the quayside.

In a corner of the tavern Guilheme outlined the plan to his little band. Wait until the early hours of the morning (for that is the time when men are most off their guard), board the boat, fire it, and release it from its moorings. They'd grinned with the pleasure of anticipation. One of them took out the knife which he'd stolen from Machaut, a substantial thing at least eighteen inches in length, and regarded it fondly. They had taken shelter in a dilapidated warehouse further along the quay. Guilheme forbade them to drink any more so they catnapped until the moment came to don their masks. Crept on board the barge. Made their stealthy way to the bows. Found the pile of canvas and cloth which Guilheme had already observed to be heaped up there. Struck the flint against the steel. Watched as the spark turned to flame, watched as the flame took hold of the dry sacking.

And then things went wrong. There was a great stir from the other end of the boat. The sleepers were being woken! There was a person whom Guilheme recognized as the shipman, the one who'd been talking to Chaucer. He was standing in the flickering light of the flames, wielding an axe. This gentleman held his ground, apparently determined to see that the passengers got safely ashore. The man to Guilheme's right went forward, brandishing his foot-and-a-half dagger, but evidently concluded that discretion was the better part of valour and fell back. The flames were leaping higher now. It was growing unpleasantly warm. Guilheme felt his wits and his courage – never in such large supply as he imagined – draining away. What next? The boat would burn and sink, given time, but their quarry was escaping, was already on dry land. He sensed the others looking at him, waiting for orders.

He opened his mouth to issue some instructions . . . but what? He never knew what he was about to say for, at once, a monstrous blast of heat smote him in the back and a flash of light blinded him and, with his last fragments of consciousness, he was aware of flying through the burning air.

18

It was an easy matter for Geoffrey, Alan, Ned and Jean Cado to hire horses to carry them over the final stages to Bordeaux. This was what Chaucer preferred anyway, rather than completing their journey by boat. He'd had enough of boats. They delayed in Libourne only long enough to check on the well-being of the players. Ned Caton was thanked by Lewis and Margaret Loup in the most heartfelt terms. Alice, thoroughly recovered from her near-drowning, kissed and embraced him. Simon, who might have resented that another man had performed the rescue which should have been his, shook Ned's hand with water in his own eyes. Martin and Tom expressed their gratitude. But the mood of the entire group was shadowed by the death of Bertram. His body had been among those recovered from the Dordogne. He'd been lucky once but the river would not let him go a second time.

The players were bound for Bordeaux also, but they would travel at a slower pace in the company of Rounce and their property cart. Jack Dart too indicated that he'd be returning to the city, although he first had to complete some paperwork for the Libourne authorities on account of the loss of the barge. The general rumour was that the firing of the boat had been a botched attempt to sabotage the transport of the bombards. The men who'd been killed when the remnants of gunpowder exploded must have been agents of the French king, it was openly said. No one bothered to explain why they'd boarded the boat after the bombards had been landed. Still, this was Jack Dart's explanation. If anybody – like Geoffrey Chaucer – knew any different, then it was up to them to come forward and say so.

Chaucer and the other three hired horses and bought provisions for the day's journey. They had scarcely set off for Bordeaux when there was an interlude. They encountered a stream of pilgrims bound southwards for the shrine at Compostela. The parade of men and women passed in front of them at an upland crossroads outside Libourne. Chaucer's little group reined in to let them go by. In truth, the foursome had no choice for the pilgrims rode past with the resoluteness and self-absorption of an army. They were so tight-packed you couldn't have driven a wedge between them. But the day was hot and there was a holiday mood, with plenty of chat and laughter.

Most of the pilgrims were on horseback but there was a clutch of wagons covered with awnings to shelter their occupants from the sun of the plains and the rain which they might meet further south among the mountains. They were passing so close that Chaucer could pick out individual figures among the parade: a full-lipped woman wearing a bright red cloak, which reminded him of Margaret Loup; a sallow-faced man whose eyes constantly flicked from side to side; two attractive young ladies on palfreys, their scarved heads closer together than their horses, exchanging confidences. Alan Audly and Ned Caton tried to attract their attention by waving and smiling but the only person in the procession to respond with a wave of his own was a man who was almost dwarfish but who sat on his horse with great dignity.

There were many people in this party, perhaps nearly a hundred souls, with a couple of guides to the front and several burly fellows bunched towards the end for protection. Seeing the pilgrims ambling along at a pace that was scarcely faster than walking – chatting and laughing, wiping their noses and foreheads with their sleeves, one traveller reduced to no more than her hat and a pair of eyes peering round the flap of a wagon, another near the rear of the column puffing on some kind of bagpipe – seeing the whole of this passing human spectacle, a fugitive idea also passed through Chaucer's mind. He tried to grasp at it but was interrupted by Jean Cado who gestured at the pilgrim stream.

"Those people are travelling on the Limousine way now it is clear for the summer. They will already have been to visit the tomb of the blessed bishop Front in Perigueux and before that St Martial in Limoges."

This crowd didn't appear particularly pious but Chaucer knew that most pilgrims tried to gather up extra points by calling in at lesser shrines on the way to their principal destination. He also knew that lay pilgrims regarded the trip to a shrine, even one as venerable as St James's, as a holiday from everyday life. That's certainly how he would look on it. Only when this lot got within sight of Compostela would they dismount from their horses, assume reverent voices, temporarily discard some of their finery and cover the last couple of miles on foot. The more religious might even go barefoot and the really devout would travel on their knees. Again, some idea connected with a pilgrimage floated through his mind and once again he was interrupted.

"What was that?"

Cado was still speaking to him. "You've been on a pilgrimage yourself, Master Geoffrey?"

"Not yet. When we return home I shall go to Canterbury and the shrine of St Thomas."

"I have visited the sanctuary of the Magdalen at Vézelay – a fine sight that was. I have been to pay my respects to St Foy at Conques. And I have seen Our Lady of Rocmadour and bruised my knees climbing up her steps. Mind you, that was in the years of peace."

"The years of peace? You speak as if they're over, Jean. I'm afraid you're right though, we're likely to be at war soon. But look at this party in front of us. They don't look too bothered about a war."

Jean Cado tapped the side of his nose and looked more than usually owl-like.

"It's a fine morning and they are going about their pious business. Why should they be thinking of death and destruction?"

There was a kind of reassurance in the pilgrim scene, Chaucer thought. Men plotted against each other, they slaughtered each other by stealth or they fell in battle. Towns and villages were razed to the ground and those innocents who lived far from courts and palaces – women and children for the most part – paid the price for the decisions of kings. But life somehow continued. People survived. They themselves had survived a dangerous few days, for example, although he was conscious their own journey was by no means complete.

As the last of the pilgrims rolled by, Chaucer caught sight of Cado regarding him quizzically.

"Something on your mind, Master Geoffrey?"

"I was thinking of our fortunate escape from the domain of Guyac and our voyage downriver. And I was wondering how you got hold of the stirrup-ring which you paid your cousin with."

Cado looked ahead once more. The road was clear now. He said nothing. He might have been pretending not to know what Geoffrey was talking about. He urged his hired horse forward and Chaucer did likewise. Alan Audly and Ned Caton followed. But after a time Cado said, over his shoulder, "It was Gaston Florac gave me the ring."

"Why?"

"He told me to fetch you out of the guard-room and get you away from the castle. It was to look like an escape. He thought you mightn't leave otherwise. The ring was a kind of payment."

"Florac? But it was Foix the seneschal who had us put under guard – for our own protection, he said."

"I don't know what Foix was about but Florac wanted you out of the way altogether. He had other business to attend to."

The Lady Rosamond, Chaucer thought. That was his business.

"You know where the stirrup-ring came from?"

"Yes. I did not wish to keep it so I gave it to my cousin in return for passage on his boat."

There was a quavering in Cado's voice, detectable over the clink of their bridles and the singing of the birds on this bright morning. Chaucer eased his horse forward so that he was riding parallel to Jean. There was some aspect to this affair that was hidden, many aspects hidden perhaps. But one was now growing less obscure.

He recalled various things. That Jean Cado was familiar with the area around Guyac because, according to him, he'd been brought up there. That when the Gascon had first identified the castle of Guyac there'd been a kind of tremor in his voice. That he had seemed especially affected by the hanging of Matthieu – "the unfortunate", "the poor man", he'd called him more than once. Geoffrey also remembered a fragment of his conversation with Richard Foix when he'd been attempting to persuade the seneschal of Matthieu's innocence over the death of Henri de Guyac. The one-armed simpleton had been part of a family, who were compensated for the injury caused by one of Henri's father's hunting dogs. *What happened to his family?* asked Chaucer. How should I know? Foix had replied. *It was before my time. Anyway they were peasants. We do not keep count of peasants.*

Geoffrey glanced back at Alan and Ned. They were ambling some distance behind. Nevertheless when he next spoke it was almost in a whisper.

"Who was Matthieu, the man they hanged?"

"A poor unfortunate," said Cado just as softly.

"Many unfortunates are hanged."

"They say that pity runs soonest in a gentle heart. Aren't I permitted to feel pity, Master Geoffrey, or is it that I'm not gentle or well-born enough for such noble feelings?"

There was a mixture of bitterness and regret in his tone. Chaucer saw that he was close to some truth.

"Your feelings do you credit, sir. Being well-born has nothing to do with it," he said. "But Matthieu was more to you than that. Not a crazed individual who was accused of a crime for which he was almost certainly blameless. You knew his name. You repeated it several times. You *knew* him."

"He was my brother," said Cado.

Chaucer waited. Prompting the man now would be pointless. He was either going to speak or he wasn't.

"Even though I was small and it was many years ago I can remember it as if it was yesterday," said Cado eventually. "We were tenants of Henri's father, not the poorest either. We lived on his land, we grew his crops, we were altogether at his disposal, but it was not such a bad life. One day there was a hunt – nothing to do with us. But my older brother Matthieu, he liked to watch the chase. He would neglect his work in the fields to watch and my father would beat him hard for it. Didn't make any difference. Matthieu took the beatings and went on his own sweet way. He was odd, somehow separate from the rest of us. He liked wandering in the woods too. He spent whole days there, only returning at nightfall. He had a favourite position up in the branches of an oak tree. From there he spied on the chase. He gazed on the riders and the dogs and the men on foot in pursuit of their quarry . . . he liked the colours and the noise, I think . . . he always was a simple soul even before . . ."

"What happened?"

"I was very small as I said, the youngest in our family, too young even to be out working. One day my brother Matthieu was carried in by a pair of huntsmen. They thought he was dead. He'd been attacked by the dogs. He must have tumbled from his perch in the tree or been caught wandering in the path of the quarry, I don't know. His arm was hanging half off him. He had lost a great deal of blood though the huntsmen managed to staunch the wound. I thought he was dead. His face was like chalk and he was stiff and still. We laid him to one side like something discarded. Yet he was not done with. His breathing was shallow and it faltered but it did not stop altogether. We waited for him to die. Yet he did not die – though it would have been better if he had!

"There was a wise woman who lived by herself in the woods not far away from us. She had the reputation for curing those who were at death's door and so she was shunned by us normal folk who believed she was in league with the devil. Shunned by us until we needed her help, that is. My father was all for letting Matthieu pass through death's door without delay but my mother wrapped her scarf about her head and, without telling him, went off to see the old woman. What she promised or offered her I don't know, but the woman visited only when my father was absent. Came and went on several occasions. She poulticed the wound with special ointments. She brought foul-smelling concoctions which she tipped down Matthieu's gaping throat. My mother covered him with a blanket so that my father would not notice the fresh bandaging. She swore me to silence. No one was very concerned however. It was harvest time. Every hand was required in the fields. Each time my father returned from the fields he expected to find Matthieu dead and done with. But each time he found my brother clinging on to life a little more eagerly. Matthieu had lost his arm of course and he had not yet regained the use of his tongue, but it soon became clear that he would recover or at least that he would not die straightaway.

"My father was not pleased – what use was a one-armed mute to him? His attitude only changed one autumn evening when a member of the Comte's household came to our door bearing a little bag which he held out in front of him as though it was something noxious. This person pushed aside the sacking which covered the doorway and stared around him blinking with surprise and distaste, as though he'd never seen such a pitiful hovel before – and most probably he hadn't for even I could tell that this was a *gentleman* by his dress and by the sweet scents which rolled off his clothes. He muttered some words which I didn't understand and more or less threw the bag on to the floor and then stalked away. It clinked. I remember that clearly, the bag clinked. My mother didn't move. My father fumbled with the drawstrings and drew some coins out of the bag. I heard him gasp. He took them outside to examine them more closely. Through the door-frame I watched him holding up the coins so that they caught the fading light, I watched him biting the coins. Then he dropped them, one by one, into the leathern bag. When he came back there was an expression on his face which I'd never seen on it before. There was pleasure there but it was not a pleasant expression, if you see what I mean, Master Geoffrey."

"I understand, Master Jean."

"For the first time he went over to my brother and laid his hand on the boy's shoulder – his good shoulder, that is, the one that still had an arm attached to it. It was as if he was thanking Matthieu. With his other hand he continued to hold fast to the leathern bag. Then he nodded at my mother and walked through the doorway. We never saw him again. We never talked about him either. When I asked once, my mother simply spat on the ground."

Jean Cado paused. He and Chaucer rode on in silence for perhaps a furlong. Behind him Chaucer could hear Alan and Ned exchanging occasional comments. Ahead of them the land swept forward in soft green billows covered with vines. The white track glinted in the sun.

"We stayed in Guyac for a time, a year or longer. As tenants to the lord we weren't free to leave of course and my mother was sharply questioned over the whereabouts of my father. But in the end she must have felt she could no longer stay in a place that seemed to be cursed, even though several men approached her and offered her security if she'd pay them in the only coin she had, which was herself. She had her mind set on better things though. There was a cousin who transported wood and wine up and down the river. He was the father of Arnaud, the shipman of the boat that took us from Guyac. He used to tell her stories of the great towns which lay nearer to the coast. I think he had his eye on her. One day, without telling me what we were doing, she bundled up a few possessions and the two of us boarded at the very spot where we embarked a few days ago. I was all she had left, and that's why she took me with her. She'd had other children but they were dead. There was only Matthieu and me. And like I said, I was too small to be put to work."

"And Matthieu?" said Chaucer.

"When he got better, he took up his old wood-wandering habits again. Only this time instead of coming home when night fell he'd stay away for weeks at a time. When he did turn up, he was like a half-wild animal coming back to his lair. His hair was all matted, his face was covered with cuts and scratches, and he said nothing of course. For all that, he seemed happy in his own private way. He must have found better company in the woods. God knows what he fed on, God knows how he survived but he did. So we left him behind as well.

"My mother and I fetched up in Bordeaux. I had never travelled more than a mile or so from my homeland. The city was another world to me, full of great white houses and clanging workshops and people who walked in the streets without stopping. I did not speak for a whole week, I was so frightened. Like Matthieu, I turned dumb. To cut a long story short, Master Geoffrey, my mother found work in one of those great white houses, a merchant's place. She worked in the laundry. She had borne several children and toiled out of doors all her life, yet she still kept something of her looks. I knew this because as a child I saw the way that men in the city would watch her. And the men in our village as well. But the gaze of the city men was more naked.

"My mother was a favourite of the merchant's. He was a timid little man who the servants used to giggle about behind his back. He spent time in the laundry-room, pretending to be interested in the washing. He was kept in check by his shrewish wife who was forever prowling about the laundry-room on the lookout for her husband. Yet I am grateful to her, for the merchant's wife had no children of her own and she taught me to read and write. So I got other languages, the English you speak and the French they speak in the north. I learned something of the habits of the city too. I was quick to learn and I rose above my origins. And for many years now I have been employed at the Prince's court to translate documents and sometimes to interpret. So there you have it. A civil servant if you will."

"A civil servant. I sometimes think of myself like that," said Chaucer.

"It beats a peasants' hovel, I can tell you."

"And your mother? What happened to her after the laundry-room?"

"Oh, she has been dead these many years."

"So you are the sole survivor of your family?"

"Since Matthieu is gone, I am. And I had ceased to think of him. He was dead to me. I assumed he had long ago perished of hunger or neglect or sickness."

"Why were you eager to return to Guyac? Since it was a cursed place for you."

"I am a city man now, on the business of the Prince's court. My particular errand was to escort important visitors from England to the castle of Guyac. No one there would remember me. I was only a child when we quit the place."

Chaucer looked sideways at Jean Cado as they ambled along the track. The Gascon's face was impassive, his round eyes shadowed under the brim of his hat. Chaucer looked to the front again. In the distance were little clouds of white dust raised by other travellers on horseback. The dust would sometimes be laid by storms similar to the one they'd encountered on the river, but summer had set in like a beseiging army and for the next three months the land would be baked bone-dry.

Geoffrey was interested – and touched – by the story which Cado had told him, just as he was interested in many individual stories. Yet he was aware that there were more questions which needed to be asked and answered. He had to be clear in his own mind about Cado's connection to the death of Henri de Guyac.

"You were in the woods on that day, the day of the hunt?"

"Yes."

"And you saw Matthieu in the wood."

"Yes," said Cado. "I didn't know who he was at first. He appeared in front of me, from out of nowhere. My horse shied and nearly threw me. When I'd recovered from the shock I thought he was some scavenger or hermit. And in truth I do not think I would have recognized the man if it hadn't been for the stump of his arm. He gawped and then he pointed me in a certain direction with his remaining arm. That's when I realized this pitiful woodland creature was Matthieu. He certainly did not know who I was."

"I saw him too," said Chaucer.

"What should I have done, Master Geoffrey? Got off my horse and embraced him as my long lost brother? Exchanged happy memories of our parents? Here was a man who was as close to the beasts as a man can get without losing all trace of humanity. We had nothing in common. In truth, I do not believe I would have been able to dismount from my horse anyway. I was shaking and my legs would have been too weak to support me. I opened my mouth but no words came out of it."

"So you rode on?"

"It seemed to me that he was pointing in the direction of the hunt. But I turned off into another path through the wood. When I looked back my vision was blurred with a kind of red mist. But Matthieu had already gone, I am sure. I did not stop shaking for half an hour after."

"You never went near the scene of Henri de Guyac's death?"

"I rode through the woods. Some of the tracks were familiar to me from when I was a boy, after all. Eventually I circled round and came out once more in the village. It was after the body of the Comte had been returned to the castle. I soon picked up the news and the rumours as well, that his death had not been an accidental one. I heard that Richard Foix was questioning everyone who'd been present. So I came to your chamber to tell you about it."

Chaucer recalled Cado's frantic appearance on that day, particularly when he'd reported on Matthieu's capture. His reaction was not surprising after what he'd seen, the reappearance of a brother he'd long thought dead. Unless, of course, he had seen – and done – rather more than that . . .

The same idea must have occurred at the same moment to Cado for he said, "Henri de Guyac's death had nothing to do with me."

"I never said it had."

"You thought it though."

"Anyone could see that you had reason to . . . feel hostility towards the house of Guyac."

"On account of what once happened to Matthieu? The hunting dogs of a dead lord savage my brother and drive him out of his wits and so I up and kill the dead lord's son many years afterwards. Do you believe that, Master Geoffrey? That I was avenging a wrong done to the 'house' of Cado by killing the inheritor to the house of Guyac? You imagine that someone of peasant stock would have set himself against a nobleman like that?"

"You would not have planned it in advance, Master Jean. But the shock of seeing Matthieu once again after you believed him dead . . . that red mist which blurred your vision, you said . . . and then stumbling across the wounded Henri and having the advantage of surprise."

"So now I am a coward too?"

"That you are not. I recall you were the first to climb out of the tower window in the castle. You showed up us Englishmen."

Cado appeared slightly mollified by the comment but Chaucer could not resist probing further.

"You had a sword with you?"

"What are you talking about?"

"In the woods."

"Naturally I was armed. Woods are dangerous places. But I can only say again that Guyac's death was none of my doing."

"Nor your brother Matthieu's neither?"

"He has paid the price, whether it was to do with him or not. Let the poor man rest in peace. I believed that he was dead. Now he is."

Cado's tone was irritated, almost petulant. Chaucer judged it better to let the matter drop for the time being and they rode on in silence. Yet Geoffrey could not help thinking that, despite his protestations, Jean Cado did have some plausible reasons for hating the house of Guyac. Not that he would necessarily have nursed a grudge over the decades but, as he'd said, the shock of encountering first his brother and then Henri, exhausted after the fight with the boar, might just have tipped him into a course of murder. Cado was an owlish-looking man but he was a tough one. He might refer to himself as civil servant now, one who spent his life behind a desk, but he still had a peasant's resilience. He'd never complained over the hardships and vicissitudes of their journey but had been garrulous and cheerful, at least in its early stages. He had shown a fair bit of courage in climbing first down the sheer wall of the tower. Chaucer did not doubt

285

that, in the appropriate circumstances, Jean Cado might kill someone. Not a calculating killer with his knife hidden behind a smile but one who could commit such a crime in the heat of the moment. Still, he reflected, of how many of us might that be said . . . ? The germ of murder is in our hearts.

They turned aside from the white track and halted for food on the last stretch of grassy upland overlooking the Gironde and Bordeaux. They took the cold meat and bread and a flask of wine which they'd purchased in Libourne from their saddlebags and settled down on the grass. Jean Cado sat slightly apart from the others. They ate and drank without talking. The hobbled horses grazed contentedly. There was no other sound apart from the sawing of the cicadas, no other movement apart from the stir of a warm breeze through the long grasses.

It was hard to believe that armies might soon be trampling across this territory. It should have been easy to put considerations of murder and sudden death to one side. Chaucer did his best to distract himself with the view. Small sails slid along the great river while the distant city walls gleamed in the sun and the flat landscape beyond it was veiled in a summer's haze. Somewhere behind that veil was the sea. Somnolent after wine, Geoffrey lay back and thought of England. The ground provided a comfortable couch. The seed-heavy tips of the grass bent down and tickled his face. The year was advancing. So too was his wife's pregnancy. He sent up a brief prayer for Philippa's welfare and that of her – of their – unborn child, and only then remembered to add Thomas and Elizabeth's names.

He fell asleep. In his dream what had been consciously forgotten returned to haunt him. He was back in the clearing where Henri de Guyac's murder had taken place. He saw the boar lying on its flank by the pond, its side pierced by the spear which stood up like a battle standard. He saw the dogs milling about their quarry, safe from further harm. He saw Henri, fatigued from the fight and bleeding from the wound in his forehead, walking unsteadily towards the clump of bushes on the edge of the clearing. In the margins of Chaucer's vision, in his dream, a hand reached out to grasp at a sword which was lying on the soft, crumbly soil. It wasn't his hand, he did not recognize it as his hand, but he was gazing at it from the vantage point of the hand's owner. In his dream he had become the killer. Which only goes to show, he thought, that it is true, the germ of murder is in our hearts.

The hand, strong and confident, closed round the handle of the sword. Henri de Guyac was looking straight at the bushes now. He'd been alerted by some movement, some sound over here. He moved forward. Chaucer's eyes flicked down again. The hand raised the sword from its resting place. Now Chaucer tried to twist around, to see the face and figure of the person who was holding the sword. But this was a dream and every time he made the effort to catch sight of the murderer in the corner of his eye, the figure moved along a fraction so that it remained out of sight. Only the sword and the capable hand which was clutching it could be seen. All this time Henri was getting nearer and nearer to the bushes, nearer and nearer to the moment of his death. There was nothing Chaucer could do about it. It was preordained. It had already happened. This was all a dream.

A hot gust of wind smote him in the face and he woke up on the hillside. Sweat was pouring off him. How long had he been asleep? No more than a few minutes, to judge by the position of the sun. He sat up and looked around. Alan and Ned and Jean Cado were stretched out on the grass. Such was the force of his dream that, for an instant, Geoffrey thought they were dead. He rose to his feet. It was time for them to go if they hoped to reach Bordeaux before the evening. He felt suddenly uneasy that they had paused this long. They ought to have eaten on the hoof. He felt guilty for having fallen asleep. Who knew what enemies might still be stalking them, even in this peaceful spot? Going over to rouse the others, it occurred to him that – if he really believed that Cado was the killer of Henri de Guyac – then he had been most unwise to reveal his speculations only to fall asleep afterwards in the man's company.

Yet the Gascon was drowsing as soundly as the two English-men. Chaucer went to wake them. To Cado he said, "I am sorry, Master Jean, if I have thrown suspicions on you unworthily."

Cado said nothing but nodded. Chaucer walked over to where Ned and Alan were lying in the grass.

"Pleasant dreams?" he said.

"Ned was thinking of a certain young mummer, I'll be bound, one whose name begins with A," said Alan.

"Better than that fat wife of a Canterbury innkeeper who fills your dreams."

Ned's response was casual, but Chaucer suspected that Alan's comment was near the mark. The rescue of Alice Loup from drowning in the river was a dream in another sense, a young man's chivalrous dream. Just the sort of incident to spark love or, if it already existed, to cause it to burn more steadily. Yet Alice already had her young man. If Ned had truly been a murderous individual now, then he might have taken action against Simon . . .

As they mounted their horses once again, Geoffrey told himself to stop seeing murder and murderers everywhere. If Cado actually was guilty was it likely that he would have been so energetic in helping their escape from Guyac? (Yet, a little voice niggled inside his head, it would have suited Jean to make his getaway as fast as possible too.)

It remained a beautiful day. The sun beat down on their heads as they descended towards Bordeaux. Soon they would be embarking for England. But first he must report on everything to John of Gaunt, Duke of Lancaster.

19

When they arrived at Bordeaux in the early evening, they put up at the hotel of the Twelve Apostles where they had stayed on their first visit. Geoffrey rapidly established that what Jack Dart the shipman had told him was accurate. Prince Edward, the King's oldest son and (in effect) the ruler of Aquitaine, had quit the town and was already moving northwards with his forces in the direction of Limoges. The bishop of that place was godfather to the Prince's son and had hitherto been a trusted ally but he was currently reconsidering his loyalties. He was listening to the overtures of the French and – according to rumour – might hand over the keys to the place at any moment without a fight. A show of strength, backed by bombards and other equipment, might just persuade the bishop to hold fast to the English cause.

Meantime Edward's younger brother, John of Gaunt, had reached Bordeaux. He was now holding court in the Prince's headquarters at the minster of St Andrew's. Chaucer decided to go alone to the minster. What he had to say was for Gaunt's ears only. Travel-stained and weary as he was, he left the others to clean themselves up at the hotel.

The square in front of the minster was full of people even though it was the middle of the evening. There was excitement in their mood but with a touch of anxiety. Voices were too loud, gestures too emphatic. War was in the air, Dart had said, and he was right about that as well. There was nothing much to see

289

but every time a handful of knights and their squires picked their disdainful way towards the minster gates, the knots of people in the vicinity fell silent, only to burst out more noisily afterwards. The sombre dress of priests and friars contrasted with the purples and yellows of the townsfolk. Merchants hung together in clusters, no doubt calculating the likely profits and losses involved in any military action.

There was a guard of archers at the gates to the minster and Geoffrey thought he might have difficulty in passing them. Then he noticed that their pocky-faced commander was none other than Bartholomew, the individual who'd sailed down with them on the *Arveragus*. But Bartholomew proved himself no more amenable than he had on the boat and pretended not to recognize the shabby traveller.

"Piss off," said Bartholomew, slouching against the gatepost.

"I have business with the Duke of Lancaster, I say."

"Like I have business with the Archangel Gabriel."

Chaucer sighed. He was tired and irritated. When he got inside the Prince's quarters, he'd tell Gaunt about his reception. This man would be broken to the ranks. If he got inside, that is . . . Then he saw a change come over Bartholomew's pitted features. Contempt was replaced by a calculating deference. He stopped slouching and stood as erect as his fat frame would permit. Chaucer sensed someone behind him. He felt a hand on his shoulder. A voice he knew greeted him by name. He turned round and looked directly into the face of his brother-in-law.

It had been many months since Chaucer last saw Hugh Swyneford. The man had aged. There were filaments of white in his hair and beard and he wore a haunted expression. Swyneford cast his eyes up and down Chaucer.

"What are you doing here, Geoffrey?"

"I have come to see Gaunt."

"This man was hindering you?"

"Only doing my duty, sir," said Bartholomew.

"Of course you were," said Hugh Swyneford. "Just as you were only doing your duty when I saw you laid out on a bench in the Half Moon giving everyone a view of your gullet."

Bartholomew opened his mouth to say something in response, thought better of it and decided instead on a display of sheepishness.

"Come with me, Geoffrey."

Hugh Swyneford ushered Chaucer through the gates. They walked across the courtyard towards an imposing entrance whose iron-bound doors were thrown open.

"He *was* only doing his duty, I suppose," said Chaucer, whose anger at Bartholomew had evaporated as quickly as it had come.

"With you he may have been, though I suspect bloody-mindedness. He certainly wasn't attending to his duty in the Half Moon last night. Men like him must understand that we are on a war footing now, Geoffrey. There's no room for slackness. Or tolerance, as I suppose you would call it."

This was the familiar Hugh, a professional soldier, rigid but honourable in his outlook. Not for the first time, Geoffrey wondered whether, if he had chosen a lifetime of soldiering, he would have ended up with the same inflexible attitude. The reverse side of that was tolerance – or slackness, in Hugh's book. They were about the same age but Geoffrey always felt like the junior in his presence, waiting for the cue to speak. Nevertheless there was a question he had to ask. He halted, forcing Hugh Swyneford to pause also.

"Hugh, you have heard anything of Philippa?"

"Since we started planning this expedition I have scarcely heard anything from my own Catherine," said Swyneford, "so I don't expect my news is any fresher than yours." Then, softening a little, "But the last I did hear all was well with your family."

"Thank you."

Then the two strode on in silence across the great courtyard.

291

Hugh didn't seem inclined to say anything more to his brother-in-law. Even his conversation appeared to be on a war footing.

They passed more guards and entered a fine hall, through whose mullioned windows the evening sun poured in great handfuls. A scattering of individuals, military and civilian, were standing alone or talking in quiet groups. The atmosphere here was far from the feverish excitement of the town square. At the far end of the hall were several doors. Hugh Swyneford knocked on the first of them. A voice replied from inside. Indicating to Geoffrey that he should stay where he was, Hugh went in and closed the door.

Geoffrey gazed around at the fine oak beams with the royal arms emblazoned on each end. He felt faintly apprehensive at the prospect of seeing Gaunt once more, and not just on account of the failure of his mission. In his mind he traced out the wandering, scarlet-coloured thread which connected them together – John of Gaunt, in whose retinue Hugh Swyneford served; Swyneford's wife Catherine, who was sister to Philippa, Chaucer's wife. Above all, the unspoken link between Gaunt and Catherine. No one knew whether that link was still confined to looks and soft words. Perhaps it wasn't, as the rumour went. Perhaps that would explain something of the haggard look on his brother-in-law's face.

Just as Chaucer was starting to wonder what had happened to him, Swyneford emerged from the room and gestured to Chaucer that he should go in. Then, unexpectedly, he clapped Geoffrey on the shoulder and said, "We are glad to see you again." As Geoffrey was asking himself who comprised the *we*, he found himself inside an ante-chamber. Swyneford remained outside in the hall. Behind a desk sat one of Gaunt's secretaries, Sir Thomas Elyot. He and Chaucer knew each other slightly.

The knight stood up. The light here wasn't as strong as in the hall, but Chaucer thought he saw traces of surprise on Sir Thomas's face.

"You look as though you've been in the wars," he said. Geoffrey scratched his unkempt beard. He glanced down at the stains on his garments. He began to wish he'd delayed and sent out for more clothes at the hotel. By contrast Sir Thomas was finely dressed and well pressed, the complete indoor knight.

"I must apologize for my state," said Geoffrey "but my news is urgent. I come hot-foot."

"I had heard you were dead," said Sir Thomas. "I'm pleased the reports were wrong."

"Not half as pleased as I am," said Chaucer, taken aback by the news of his own demise.

Sir Thomas pointed towards another door in the room and said, "His personal chambers are through there. Turn left. There are guards outside. They know you're coming. They'll let you in."

Chaucer passed through into a stone-flagged corridor. There'd been no need to ask whose private chambers he was being directed to. When John of Gaunt – or Prince Edward – received official guests or supplicants, it would be in the great hall or one of the lesser reception rooms, with their canopied daises and velvet trappings. But when the King's sons wanted to see someone in private, away from all their attendants and ceremony, then they would make use of these quarters.

The corridor was completely enclosed and lit by oil lamps. A pair of guards stood outside a stout door. No slacking here, their postures were steely. The spiked axe-heads on their halberds reflected the flickering lights. Neither man stirred at Chaucer's approach but one of the guards gave an almost imperceptible nod of permission. Geoffrey knocked on the door, heard a familiar voice ordering him to enter.

Within a well-furnished room stood John of Gaunt – the Earl of Richmond and of Derby, of Leicester and of Lincoln, as well as the Duke of Lancaster. He was gazing out of an open window that gave on to a garden full of apple trees. The sun still touched their upper branches. Gaunt turned to look at Chaucer and smiled. Gaunt was his friend but he was also his liege-lord. Geoffrey inclined his head. He was on the point of apologizing again for his sorry appearance, when Gaunt crossed the room and seized his hand.

"I am overjoyed to see you again, Geoffrey, especially after . . ." He paused, then seemed to switch subjects. "But you are tired, I can see. Thirsty too, no doubt. Sit down."

He gestured at a chair, then moved towards a table bearing goblets and a flagon of red wine. He poured out a goblet and handed it to Geoffrey. He took up another from which he had evidently been drinking already. Instead of seating himself in one of the well-padded chairs opposite Chaucer, Gaunt moved back to the window. He pushed his head halfway out and sniffed appreciatively at the evening air.

"They will crop well this year," he said.

Chaucer understood that he was referring to the apple trees. He agreed out loud. What else can you do when the son of a king makes small talk?

"Not that my brother is in a position to benefit from his orchard," Gaunt continued.

"He is away campaigning in Limoges, I have heard."

"Wherever he is he won't be eating apples, poor fellow. He has the bloody flux. Has to watch his diet."

John of Gaunt turned in Geoffrey's direction. Like the King's other sons, Gaunt had inherited his father's looks. A strong aquiline nose separated penetratingly dark eyes. He was uncommonly tall and would have been able to impose himself with a combination of his height and his stare, even if one was ignorant of his royal birth. Yet, like Hugh Swyneford, he too seemed to have aged, even though it was only a couple of months since Chaucer had last seen him. He was dressed in a dark red jupon, sparsely tagged with gold buckles and pendants, relatively informal and a long way distant from ceremonial wear. Nevertheless Geoffrey, sitting in his soft chair, was more than ever conscious of his dusty, stained self. Shouldn't he have taken the time to change before coming to St Andrew's, especially as the news which he had to bring Gaunt was of failure? Only success forgives sweat and dirt.

"You have heard that Henri de Guyac is dead?" he said.

"Yes."

"It was murder."

"So I have been informed," said Gaunt. "The culprit is dead, is he not?"

"They hanged the man who was nearest to hand. I don't believe he did it though," said Chaucer.

"You know who did?"

It crossed his mind to mention Jean Cado's connection to Matthieu but instead he simply shook his head.

"All I know is that I have failed, my lord. I had one interview with de Guyac when he did not show himself much inclined to our cause. I would have spoken with him again the next day but he was dead by then."

"So it was altogether out of your hands, Geoffrey," said Gaunt, leaving the window and seating himself opposite Chaucer. "It was Fortune. Blame her. You're always saying she has broad shoulders."

"Fortune does not wield a knife herself. Humans do that."

"A *knife*. I heard it was a sword that killed de Guyac."

Chaucer understood that Gaunt was well informed. Nevertheless the other now said, "Tell me what happened."

Gaunt filled up their goblets once again. As briefly as he could, Geoffrey outlined the events of the last few weeks following their departure from England to their hasty escape from the castle. He mentioned the mysterious monkish figure of Hubert and told of how he'd been attacked at the Calais inn. He noticed Gaunt's gaze sharpen. He described the explosion on board the barge which had been transporting the bombards. At this Gaunt nodded, as if it was already known to him.

Outside, the shadows in the enclosed orchard deepened and the air stirred by the open window. Within, the room grew gloomier. In a small recess of the chamber a pair of candles were burning. There was another door beside the recess. When Chaucer had finished Gaunt looked down and toyed with his goblet.

"Don't be too harsh on yourself. I fear that even if de Guyac had lived and maintained his allegiance to us, it would have made little difference. Besides I understand that he had already ignored another communication which was brought in the spring."

"Brought by a man called Machaut?" said Geoffrey.

"Possibly," said Gaunt. "As I say, it would have made little difference. By now too many have declared themselves for Paris. The lords of Chauvigny and Périgord, for example. Limoges is falling away. Even if my brother manages to subjugate the place he will forfeit the citizens' hearts while he is breaking their heads. And it looks as though the Ducs of Berry and Anjou together with Armagnac are intending to squeeze us with a double offensive."

"I had no idea that things were so bad."

"Things are worse, Geoffrey. Since you have been away from England, King Charles has formally announced the confiscation of Aquitaine."

"As he did last year."

"That was like a man shooting an arrow into the air to see where it lands. This time he has a mark."

"But we shall fight?"

Until this point Gaunt's tone had been weary. Now he leaned forward and brought down his free hand on the chair arm.

"Of course we shall fight."

"Of course we shall fight, sir."

"You need not repeat my words back to me, Geoffrey, like a councillor. I already know what I think."

Chaucer said nothing. After a time, Gaunt relaxed his grip on the chair arm. When he next spoke, he was more conciliatory.

"Forgive me, my friend. Since I arrived here I've discovered that things are in an even more parlous condition than I expected. My brother has estranged the Gascon nobles by his demands and his high-handedness. He holds court in two palaces and spends for show."

"A prince may do as he pleases, surely."

"The world has changed," said Gaunt. "Princes can no longer act in the untrammelled way of their fathers – but my brother is not intelligent enough to recognize the fact."

Geoffrey Chaucer felt a little uneasy at being the recipient of such confidences. To divert Gaunt, he drew from out of his stained shirt the wallet which he had been wearing for many weeks, it seemed. He handed it over to the Duke of Lancaster, feeling oddly naked without it.

Gaunt opened the wallet without a word and extracted the sealed letter. Chaucer waited. He wondered whether Gaunt would open the letter. But he didn't. Instead he tore it into fragments, which he cradled in his hands and then deposited in the empty fireplace. Gaunt went over to the recess which contained the candles. He retrieved one of them, bent down and applied the flame to the shreds of paper. The flame burnt bright in the relative darkness. The paper shreds flared and curled up.

Geoffrey hadn't been aware it but he was now sitting forward in his chair, gripping hard on the embossed arms.

"What are you thinking, Geoffrey?" said Gaunt. He seemed to have recovered something of his good humour.

I was thinking that a man tried to kill me for that document in Calais and nearly succeeded, he might have said. *I was thinking that I have carried that sealed communication for hundreds of miles, under strict instructions to use it only as a last resort. And now I'll never know what was in it.*

"Now I'll never know what was in it," he said aloud.

"What did you think it was?"

Chaucer could have replied, *The secret of Ned Caton's parentage, my lord. How Henri de Guyac had fathered him on his stay in England many years ago. How you'd intended to send me down to Gascony, accompanied by Henri's by-blow, as a means of getting him back into line.*

But he said none of these things. Instead he said, "I'm afraid I'm too tired for guessing games."

"Well, I suppose it will do no harm now that de Guyac is dead," said Gaunt. He glanced at the blackened fragments of paper in the fireplace. He replaced the candle in the recess. "It is not to go beyond these four walls though. That letter was to remind Henri de Guyac of an incident which occurred many years ago when he was visiting England."

Chaucer felt his scalp tingling. He'd been right!

"Something to do with Ned Caton?" he said.

"Caton? No, not him. I doubt that he was even born when Henri was over there. Why should it be anything to do with Caton?"

"Oh."

"You sound disappointed, Geoffrey."

"Just an idea I had."

"You poets," said John of Gaunt. "Full of fanciful ideas."

"You know us too well, my lord."

"Well enough to detect irony. This, ah, incident was nothing to do with Ned Caton at all. It concerned de Guyac alone. A man died as a result of his actions. In short, he stabbed him to death."

"Who? Why?"

"De Guyac was staying at a certain house in Kent. It belonged to a merchant, the man's name doesn't matter. Henri was trying to negotiate a loan for himself. His father kept him on short commons, you see. In the Kentish house Henri attempted to ravish one of the servants . . . Unfortunately for him, the

298

master of the house intruded on the scene. In normal circum-stances the master would have apologized and gone on his way. He was only a merchant after all while Henri was a Gascon lord, even if he was strapped for cash. But in this case the master seems to have had a partiality for the girl. Words were ex-changed, heated words. In the upshot, de Guyac drew his dagger and stabbed the merchant – fatally."

Geoffrey was shocked. It was true that he'd heard Henri refer more than once to his wilder younger days. Of how the Gascon lord had lived a dissipated life in England until, receiving the news of his father's death, he had at once returned to France. He'd been shipwrecked off the Breton coast and, being saved, had sworn to dedicate himself to a more honourable existence. He had kept his oath, turning his back on his wilder self. Any young nobleman may be excused his youthful behaviour. Leave aside the ravishment, which might be accounted dissipation. But there was a gap between the rape of a servant girl and the murder of a merchant, if murder it had been.

"What happened?" said Chaucer.

"Even an esteemed visitor to England like de Guyac might have been expected to face justice. But at that very moment Henri's father died over here. It was decided at the highest level that Henri should be permitted to return to Guyenne and take up his title. After all, it was only a merchant who had perished. If it had been a knight now . . . And we needed allies in Guyenne then, you see, just as we need them now."

Decided at the highest level. That could only mean the English king.

"This was a long time ago, Geoffrey," said Gaunt. "Like you, I was still being schooled. I knew nothing of the doings of a young Gascon lord – and even if I had they would not have concerned me. But many years later, these things were recalled. It was believed that it might be, ah, helpful for Henri de Guyac to be reminded of certain incidents in a Kentish house."

"Helpful? I admire the diplomatic language. What were you going to do? Expose Henri de Guyac to the world because he had stabbed a rich merchant more than twenty years ago? As you say, my lord, the dead man was only a merchant and not a knight."

"No, it was nothing so crude as exposure. The letter I've burned was sent with my father's authority. It would have reminded Henri that he still remained under an obligation to the English throne, not just a question of fealty and oath, but tied with a more personal bond. King Edward once showed him mercy."

"A politic mercy."

"Do you question my father's actions? Mercy is mercy, wherever it comes from. De Guyac never saw the letter anyway, so the whole matter is dead and buried."

"Dead and buried."

"I say so."

It was half dark outside now. Chaucer considered how wrong he'd been. Ned Caton was not the bastard son of Henri de Guyac and it followed that that cheerful and impetuous young man could have no motive for murder. The letter was important, true, but its contents were quite different from what he'd supposed. Different from what he'd imagined.

You poets, full of fanciful ideas.

He glanced away towards the recess where the candles were still burning. When he'd first looked in that direction he had noticed what appeared to be a pile of cloth on the floor. Now that his eyes were more accustomed to the gloom, he squinted at the pile. Something familiar there. It was not the colour of the cloth, which was grey, so much as the position and outline of the thing. He'd seen that grey sack before, he knew, seen it slumped in a certain place in a half light. But where?

John of Gaunt noticed where he was looking and said, "That contains some interesting items. For example, a flint and steel as well as a devotional book. Also a long cord and a selection of knives."

Chaucer went cold.

"Oh, and a monk's gear," said Gaunt.

On the sandy soil of an island in the middle of the Dordogne. That was where he'd last glimpsed the grey sack. The property of a false monk. He saw Hubert standing up to deliver lines from the Raising of Lazarus . . . Bertram the mummer emerging from the trees . . . skull-faced Hubert turning to see the man he'd drowned . . . picking up his grey bag and disappearing with it into the night.

Suddenly Gaunt called out a name. The door near the recess opened. A figure walked through. It was Hubert. The candle-light seemed to reflect off the sharp planes of his face. But even without those features, Chaucer would have known that bony figure standing erect in the half light.

For his part Hubert didn't seem surprised at Chaucer's presence. But he must have realized that this was his chance, perhaps his only chance, for escape. His eyes flicked sideways towards the still open window. A second later and he was throwing himself towards the window. And a second after that he was sprawled on the floor between Chaucer and Gaunt. Hubert had been quick but the Duke of Lancaster, his reactions honed in battle and tournament, had been quicker. He stuck his leg out and Hubert stumbled and fell.

Chaucer leaped up, knocking over his chair. This man was as dangerous as a snake. But Gaunt had him by the neck-bone and, in another instant, the chamber was full of armed men.

20

Chaucer explained it afterwards to Ned and Alan at the hotel of the Twelve Apostles. He felt he owed that much to his companions, particularly to Ned, although naturally he stayed silent over his speculations connecting him to Henri de Guyac. He wondered where Jean Cado was and was told that the Gascon had departed for his office in the court. It was the following morning. The three were sitting in a private chamber of the hotel with the sun streaming through the windows. Outside, carts trundled past and stall-holders shouted their wares. Inside, Ned Caton and Alan Audly were oblivious to the street sounds as they listened to Chaucer's account.

It turned out that Hubert was an agent already known to the English in Bordeaux. Among those who occupied themselves with secrets he went by the name of Janus. He was not altogether trusted but he'd been useful in the past, ready to spy and to steal for cash. If there was a question about the loyalty of one of the Gascon lords, if it was believed that he might have been in touch with Paris, and you required someone to intercept a letter – even to break into a man's private quarters – then Janus was your man. But he was always treated with scepticism. There was some . . . unsettling . . . quality to the man. Then, scepticism turned to outright suspicion. There'd been a stolen letter that was passed off as genuine and yet proved to be forged, there'd been another agent of the English who voiced doubts about Janus's reliability and was next seen floating face-down in the Garonne. As if to confirm the authorities' suspicions that he'd sold out to the French, Janus had one day vanished off the face of the earth – or at least the gentleman was no longer to be seen around his usual Bordelaise haunts. It was rumoured that he had departed for London.

John of Gaunt of course knew none of these details to begin with. It was not likely that the absent Prince Edward was familiar with the details of his secret operatives, either. All that was left in the hands of secret men who reported to other men, slightly less secret ones. Some word might eventually filter through to a private secretary who would, when absolutely necessary, report to his ultimate master. The actions of spies, with their thefts, stabbings and forgeries, were a long way from the padded courts of Bordeaux and Angoulême. A long way too from the field of battle where knights clashed openly and fought for the sake of honour. But Gaunt, newly arrived in Bordeaux, had made it his business to examine some of the reports of the spies. Then, shortly before the arrival of Geoffrey Chaucer in town, he had been visited by Janus. The man delivered up his tale of what had happened at Guyac where, he claimed, he had been working undercover – and unpaid – for the English cause. He told the story of Henri's murder and the execution of the culprit. Finally he described how he'd witnessed the destruction by fire of the boat at Libourne, and the death of several individuals on board.

"John of Gaunt asked him whether he'd actually seen this for himself," said Geoffrey to the others. "He claimed that he had done but it's more likely he simply heard talk in the town that several corpses had been fished out of the river and assumed it was us. Or hoped it was us. That way, anyone who might have identified him was dead. Gaunt heard him out. He says he was not sure whether to believe him. For certain he didn't trust him. Then it was announced that I had arrived at St Andrew's. I wondered why a couple of people spoke to me as if I'd come back from the dead. Now I know. John of Gaunt gave orders that Hubert – or Janus – was to be kept under guard in a neighbouring room while he talked to me. They were holding a knife to his throat. If he'd uttered a word, the guards were to slit it."

"So this Janus was behind the firing of the boat in Libourne?" said Ned.

"I don't believe so. If he had been he would have paid closer attention to the result. I think it's much more likely that the boat was boarded by men working for Richard Foix, the Guyac seneschal."

"Why?"

"Perhaps to stop us returning to Bordeaux. Foix knew there'd be trouble for him if the full story got back to the Prince. Or it may be that his men exceeded their orders."

"What about the death of Henri de Guyac?" said Alan. "If this, ah, spy is dangerous as you're saying, could he not have murdered Henri?"

"Oh, he is dangerous," said Ned. "Remember that he attempted to drown Bertram in the river."

"I'm certain he was also behind the attack at the Mouton à Cinq Pattes in Calais," said Chaucer. "He was after something, it doesn't matter what. There's no doubt he is dangerous as a snake. But, again, I do not believe he killed Henri de Guyac. Gaunt says that he is working for the French and all the man's acts seem to support that idea. And since de Guyac was likely to switch his allegiance to the French, then they would not have benefited from his sudden death."

"Who did it then?"

"I am not sure."

"But from your tone, you have an idea, Geoffrey."

Chaucer was about to answer when Jean Cado entered the room. After the revelations of yesterday, he seemed restored to his old owlishness.

"Master Geoffrey, you are required at the court – at once."

For the second time in little more than twelve hours Chaucer presented himself at the minster gates. He was sweating with the heat of the morning. The archers were at the gate but the oafish Bartholomew was not on duty. In any case, Hugh Swyneford was once again present to usher his brother-in-law through.

"What is it, Hugh? Why the urgency?"

"A man wants to see you. This is Gaunt's decision."

Nothing more was forthcoming and, knowing Hugh, Geoffrey did not expect it to be. This time Swyneford led Chaucer round to the back area of the minster, where the more menial offices of the court were situated, the laundry and the store-rooms and so on. They reached a barred door. Hugh Swyneford beat on it with his fist, announcing his name. There was the sound of keys turning and bolts being withdrawn. The door opened. Chaucer glimpsed three or four guards in the shadowed interior. Hugh motioned him to step inside. He did so. Almost at once the door was closed again, leaving the other man outside.

Chaucer and the soldiers were standing on a stone platform from which a flight of steps led downwards into near darkness. The upper area was illuminated by smoky torches. Despite the heat of the day, it was cold and clammy in here.

"'E's down 'ere, sir," said one of the guards, taking up a torch.

Geoffrey, having a good idea who the *he* was by now, said nothing but followed the soldier down the steps. A bunch of keys jangled at the man's belt. They emerged into a stone passage with a low, arched roof. He guessed that this had once been part of the crypt or an ossuary. By the flaring light of the torch he glimpsed bricked-up areas, some with small doors set into them. It was even colder and clammier on this level. Already, he wanted to be out in the open air again.

306

At the end of the passage was a larger door with an iron grating at eye-level. Outside were two more guards. They stood straighter as Geoffrey and his escort approached. When they reached the door, the soldier said, "We give 'im the best room, see." He gave a barking laugh and took the bunch of keys from his belt. He selected one by touch and inserted it into the door. He pulled the door open.

There was a rustling from the interior of the cell. For an instant, Geoffrey imagined that the place contained a beast but then reason asserted itself and he made out a figure sitting against the far wall, with its knees drawn up beneath its chin.

"Just a moment, sir. 'Ere you are."

Something heavy and cumbersome was pushed into his hand – what was it? A low stool, yes.

"'E 'as to sit on straw and worse but you can sit in comfort. And you'll want this."

"This" was a little oil lamp, already lit.

"We'll shut the door be'ind you, sir, and we'll close up our ears but we're 'ere on call, remember. And don't go too near 'im. He's all chained up for your safety."

Chaucer wondered how they could close up their ears and simultaneously be on call. He entered the cell, hearing the door shut behind him, hearing the key turn and feeling as much of a prisoner as the occupant. There was already some illumination from a narrow aperture set at a place where the wall met the ceiling. It did not give directly on to the outside but nevertheless admitted a small quantity of light and half-fresh air. Keeping close to the door, Chaucer positioned the oil-lamp on the dirt floor. He felt foolish holding the wooden stool, yet he did not want to sit down on it. After a moment's deliberation he placed the stool near to the light. Then he went and stood with his back to the door, taking care not to block the iron grating. He was doing all this, he realized, in order to avoid meeting the eyes of the man hunched in the dark and to avoid speaking the first word. He was conscious of being looked at. There was a rustle and a clinking sound from the far wall.

"Don't worry, Master Chaucer, you are quite safe," said the man known as Hubert or Janus. "I am securely chained up, as the guard said."

Hearing the flat, featureless voice again, Chaucer felt less uneasy. This was merely a man after all, though one chained like a beast. There were guards only feet away. Hubert could do him no harm. Yet he had no intention of lingering in this place.

"What did you want to see me for?"

"A talk, on condition."

"A prisoner cannot condition."

"He can if he has information to give in exchange," said Hubert.

"There is always torture," said Chaucer. "No exchange or bargain is necessary then. Only that the pain stops."

"I am familiar with pain," said Hubert. He shifted and his unseen fetters chinked.

"Well then?"

"No doubt I would tell you . . . something . . . sooner or later under torture. I am no less than human. But would my words be true, would they be honest, when I did say something? It would be better surely if my words came unforced? Gaunt knows that, he's a wiser man than you. Why do you think he agreed that I see you alone?"

Hubert laughed, the same queer sound which he'd uttered on the river island when he glimpsed Bertram coming back from the dead, like Lazarus. Despite himself, Geoffrey shivered. As if divining his train of thought, Hubert said, "Do you know why Lazarus laughed?"

Chaucer said nothing.

"He laughed because of what he saw on the other side," said the chained figure. His bony face was taking on definition in the feeble light. One side of it was dark with bruises. The jaw opened, somehow independent of the rest of the face. "And what did Lazarus see to make him laugh so? Why, he saw that there was – nothing – there – to – see."

Chaucer turned towards the door. He raised his hand to rap on it.

"What are you doing?"

"I'm leaving this place. I am not interested in your words, whether they are honest or not."

"Why did you come down here then?"

"I was ordered to."

"Well, I am not done yet."

"I am done with you."

"Don't you want to know who killed Henri de Guyac?"

Chaucer paused with his hand in mid-air. He turned about and faced the figure bunched up against the far wall.

"You know?"

"I know. I was in the forest that day. I saw it all."

"How can I be sure you're telling the truth?"

"From my hiding place I witnessed the arrest of that savage man in the woods. I saw how one of the soldiers pretended to have found a ring on him. That is true enough, isn't it?"

"I never believed Matthieu was guilty."

"So if I'm telling the truth about that, why should I lie about de Guyac's murder?"

"You might have done the murder yourself."

"I had no reason to kill him," said Hubert.

This chimed so precisely with Chaucer's own opinion that he said, "Very well, who did do it?"

"You must offer me something in exchange. And don't talk about torture again, Master Geoffrey. Torture doesn't suit you. I can tell from your tone that you are not comfortable with the idea. Leave it to the brutes and the gaolers. What have you got to offer me instead?"

Chaucer considered for an instant. Then he reached inside his doublet. It was clean and fresh on this morning. Why had he thought to transfer from his old clothing the item which he now brought out into the murky light of the cell? Instinct alone must have hinted that he might require it today.

"You left this behind when you ran away from the company of players on the river," he said.

There was another soft chink from the far wall. Chaucer took this as a mark of interest.

"It is a parchment written in document hand. There is a seal attached to the bottom of it. The seal shows a knight riding from right to left."

"That's mine."

"The wording is in Latin. You know what it says?"

"You tell me, Master Geoffrey. You are the educated one."

"It is a recipe for cooking a goose."

At this, the man on the floor laughed. He leaned his head against the damp wall and laughed. The sound was unpleasant, but less so than any other noise he'd made so far.

"Well, cooking a goose. That is appropriate."

"Tell me, Hubert," said Chaucer, "this is an imposing piece of paper – "

"Imposing for the ignorant."

"For the ignorant. Do you use it to pretend that you are on the King's commission? Do you claim that thing?"

Hubert said nothing. Geoffrey experienced a momentary, and childish, glee. He'd struck home. For sure, that was precisely the purpose for which this fettered gentleman employed the parchment.

"It is a serious offence to claim to be on the King's business and to support the claim with a fake document. A capital offence."

"Oh now, Master Geoffrey, you cannot frighten me with that. How many capital offences do you think I've committed in my time?"

Geoffrey sensed the advantage slipping away from him once

more. He turned back to the door before pausing as if a thought had just occurred.

"I can overlook this, ah, document. In fact I can return it for you to do what you like with. Eat it if you prefer. It is a *recipe* after all."

This time Hubert's laughter was a sarcastic sneer. Yet Chaucer could tell that he was interested.

"What do you want in return? Let me guess though."

"You have it,"said Chaucer. "All you have to do is tell me who murdered Henri de Guyac."

Hubert shifted about on his bony haunches. He paused, pretending to consider the matter. Eventually he nodded, a single downward and upward movement of his skull.

"Very well," he said. "I will tell you, Master Geoffrey."

21

The damage to the *Arveragus* wasn't as bad as Jack Dart had hinted at to Chaucer. The repairs on the boat were finished soon after his return to Bordeaux. Dart himself arrived on the afternoon of the day that Geoffrey had his gaol conversation with Hubert. He had travelled overland with Loup's troupe, since a kind of bond had been forged between the shipman and the players after the firing of the boat at Libourne. Their progress had necessarily been slower than that of Chaucer, Caton and Audly, because they were moving at the pace of their Rounce-drawn property cart, but even so they had no great distance to cover.

When Geoffrey and the others encountered the players once more, he found them with long faces on account of the death of Rounce. Lewis Loup took Chaucer aside and, with water in his eyes, explained how the poor old horse had expired at the very moment they had been ferried across the river and reached the city walls. It was too much for Rounce, this last fatiguing journey and all. Yet Loup was not as soft-hearted as his incipient tears suggested. He had swiftly come to an arrangement with the ferryman to dispose of Rounce's corpse, against the protests of Alice and Simon. They feared that the horse would be eaten, until the ferryman told them that the eating of horse-meat was proscribed by the church in these parts. Loup wasn't altogether sure whether to believe the ferryman – not about what the church proscribed but about whether the Bordelaise had lost their taste for equine flesh on the pope's say-so. But what does my daughter expect, he said? That we should give the beast a Christian burial?

Anyway, the expiry of their horse and the drowning of Bertram had encouraged them to return to England and – thanks to their new friendship with Jack Dart – it was arranged that they should all take ship when the *Arveragus* was ready.

Geoffrey saw Gaunt once more in his private quarters. The Duke of Lancaster was preoccupied with the next stage in the campaign. If it wasn't yet open war it was certainly not peace. Gaunt was consulting a sheaf of letters. He complained to Geoffrey that his forces were too small – five hundred archers and little more than half that number of men-at-arms. He was waiting for reinforcements to arrive under Sir Walter Huet. Then he planned to join his brother Edward who, en route to Limoges, had stopped at his Angoulême court. Gaunt seemed relatively uninterested in Chaucer's account of his dialogue with Hubert.

"The man can wait until I return," he said. "A few weeks in the vaults under this place will do him no harm."

Chaucer suspected that Gaunt was preserving the man because he might be useful in the future. A foolish course, in his view.

"He is a dangerous man, my lord."

"Fettered and guarded, no man is that dangerous. What did he have to say to you?"

Chaucer hesitated. "Nothing of any significance."

"He shed no light on the death of Henri de Guyac?"

"No."

"Very well, Geoffrey. Your work here is finished. You have your quittance from me. And my thanks. Take those two young men with you and return to your wife and family in England."

When Geoffrey seemed reluctant to leave, he added, "Oh, you do not want to be involved in this campaign. Go home and write some more verses for me. You are a desk-man and I would not have you stray far from your books. Do you still carry your Boethius with you?"

For answer, Geoffrey tapped the volume inside his doublet.

"We may all need the consolations of philosophy if things go as I fear. Bear my greetings to Philippa – and to her sister if you should see her," said John of Gaunt. And with that he bent over his letters once more and the interview was over.

Later that week, Chaucer and Audly and Caton set sail from Bordeaux in the *Arveragus*, under the command of Jack Dart. They were part of a convoy, again headed for Calais to pick up more soldiers and supplies. Most of the coastal traffic was from north to south these days, but the *Arveragus* carried a few items of cargo as well as some civilians, including the players.

At about the same time as Chaucer and his party embarked from Bordeaux, Hubert decided that it was the moment to act. The discomforts of his cell, with its cold and darkness and stench, meant next to nothing to him. But he had picked up from the talk of his gaolers that John of Gaunt had recently departed the town for the north.

Hubert was not exactly afraid of Gaunt but – during his interrogation by the King's son and before Chaucer's un-expected appearance on the scene – he had felt himself subdued by the man's unrelenting gaze and hard questions. It was as if Gaunt doubted him. And this was most unfair! He had gone to the minster of St Andrew's, where he was known as Janus, in the expectation of being rewarded for his information. It was true he'd been working for the French when he attempted to retrieve the letter which Chaucer was carrying but Hubert saw no reason to confine his efforts to one side.

Speedily, and surprisingly, he had been ushered into Gaunt's presence to tell his tale. He'd honestly believed in the accuracy of most of what he'd recounted: the account of de Guyac's death and its aftermath (although with some details omitted); the description of the explosion on board the barge at Libourne and the presumed death of its occupants. It wasn't his fault that Chaucer and the rest were still alive, he thought later. If he, Hubert, had had anything to do with the matter, they wouldn't have been . . .

He'd more or less finished his story when one of Gaunt's underlings had bustled into the room with whispered news. And the King's son had looked in his direction with a renewed hostility and suspicion. When Gaunt had given the command for him to be bundled into the adjoining room, it had been almost a relief to be out of his presence and in the hands of the common soldiers, even if one of them held a knife pressed to his gullet and others were pinioning his arms.

Hubert was used to having his way with ordinary men and women. A look, a smile, a comment was usually enough to bring anyone round to his point of view. If not, he depended on his cunning or the sharp edge of his hands. But, with Gaunt, the boot was on the other foot. He would be . . . reluctant . . . to be seen by him again. Accordingly Hubert decided that it would be an opportune moment for him to quit his accommodation underneath the Prince's palace while Gaunt was out of town.

Hubert was fettered like a common criminal round the ankles. He could move a few feet to exercise his limbs or to relieve himself but he could go no further. Nevertheless his hands were free. That was their mistake. No doubt they believed that gyves, locked doors and armed sentries were enough. Their mistake again. He made a rapid survey of his weapons. His grey sack, containing the flint and steel, the daggers and the rest, had been removed from him. However, he still possessed his hands and his cunning. They are weapons which no gaoler can confiscate.

He had these things, together with one other item. For Geoffrey Chaucer had left behind the document – the "King's commission" – in exchange for a true account of the person who'd murdered Henri de Guyac. In telling this story, Hubert had not lied any more than he had lied with John of Gaunt. Rather, he had informed Master Geoffrey of what he witnessed in the woods, leaving out no significant details. Let the plump civil servant do what he wanted with the information. It was no concern of his. In return, he had received the parchment, which turned out to be a recipe for cooking a goose! He had originally acquired the document and its imposing seal from a man in Southwark who specialized in such items. If he returned to London – no, when he returned to London – he would have a word with the gentleman. In the darkness of his cell Hubert smiled.

When the key next turned in the cell door to admit the gaoler carrying a food bowl, Hubert said to him in a suppliant's tone, "I have been thinking, sir."

"'Ave yer now."

The gaoler, his keys clinking at his belt, deposited the bowl containing some slop at a little distance from Hubert. He was wary of the prisoner and stretched out his hand with the food, as one might with a chained mastiff. Hubert had heard the others call him Allen.

"I am unjustly kept here," he said.

"That's what they all say," said the gaoler.

"In my case it is true, Allen," said Hubert. "Look."

He held up the scroll with the seal so that it reflected the minimal light. In spite of himself, the gaoler's attention was caught although he still kept his distance.

"Don't take my word for it, man. Examine it for yourself."

"Can't read, mate."

"Then go look at that seal. Go on, move by the door where you can see better."

The gaoler took hold of the proffered document. He retreated to the cell door. Outside were at least two other guards.

The flaring gleam of a torch penetrated the half-open door. The gaoler applied his eyes to the parchment. He inspected the seal, he felt it with his fingers.

"I am on the King's business," said Hubert.

"In 'ere?"

"Even here."

The gaoler said nothing. He continued to finger the document as if it would impart some secret to him. Hubert knew that he had the man, almost. His spirits rose.

"All right in there, Allen?" came a voice from beyond the door.

"Yeah, yeah," said the gaoler.

"The King's business," repeated Hubert softly.

"'Snogood. I cannot read."

"It is in Latin, my man. What other tongue would you expect the King of England to write in?"

"The King, 'e wrote this?"

"None other."

"Still can't read it."

"Then bring it back over here. I can point out the words and explain what they say. But first push the door to. What I have to tell you is for your ears alone."

The gaoler called Allen pushed at the door with his heel and moved towards Hubert, who kept very still. The man squatted down on his haunches. Near enough. Hubert took back the document. He pointed to a random word. "This says king, Allen. The Latin word for it is 'rex'."

Even as Allen was nodding, Hubert flung the bowl of slop-food in his face. Instinctively the gaoler raised his hands to his face and threw his head back. Hubert struck at his exposed neck with the edge of his hand. The man toppled sideways, with a wheezing sound. Only his keys jingled.

"All right?" came the same voice from outside.

"Yeah, yeah," said Hubert in passable imitation of the dead man.

It took him a few moments to locate the key which would unfasten his fetters. Then he was up and flexing his stiff legs. Just as well he was up and ready, because at that moment the two guards who'd been outside decided to enter the cell and ascertain that everything really was all right.

They never stood a chance.

22

It took Geoffrey Chaucer time to nerve himself to confront the person who had murdered Henri de Guyac. When he did so, the *Arveragus* had cleared the Garonne estuary and was heading for the open seas. The boat was comparatively empty yet it was difficult to seize an unguarded moment when no one else was in earshot. He even contemplated doing nothing with his knowledge, just as he had chosen to keep silent before Gaunt. Yet some imp of justice whispered in his ear that he could not keep silent for ever. Murder was murder. And murder will out, they say . . .

In the end, Margaret Loup came to him, by chance it seemed, though he'd earlier hinted to her that he would welcome a word in private. It was the evening. Fine barred clouds lay to the west. The sea was calm with a gentle south-westerly breeze. The other half-dozen boats in the convoy were scattered across the sea.

Chaucer was sitting on the forecastle using a barrel top as a makeshift table. He had a notebook in his hand which he'd purchased in Bordeaux. The other hand held a quill. He was aware that, to the onlooker, he must appear like the posed picture of the writer, and a slightly ridiculous one at that. Yet he did not care. Gaunt's casual words – *Go home and write some more verses for me* – had reminded him of his true trade, a trade that had gone by default for these several months. Yet the page in front of him remained obstinately empty apart from a few jotted words.

Loup's wife climbed the ladder which led from the lower deck and strode towards Chaucer. She was a large, powerful woman with a decisive tread. Geoffrey recalled her hands gutting the rabbits in the clearing by the Dordogne. He thought too of the competent hands he'd glimpsed in the dream, grasping the sword handle.

"What do you write, Geoffrey?"

"A story."

"One of your own?"

"No. Few of the tales that poets tell are their own. We borrow and steal from other men."

"And this one. What is it about?"

"It's a story of revenge."

"Revenge?"

"Carried out many years after the offence which prompted it."

Margaret's large brown eyes held his in a steady gaze. The wind ruffled the strands of greying hair which escaped from under her headscarf. She was wearing her red dress.

"It's a man's subject," she said finally.

"If there were time," said Geoffrey, "we might debate which sex is the more steadfast in seeking revenge. Men may take revenge straightaway but women are more capable of storing it up in their hearts, wouldn't you say?"

"I think you've already made up your mind," she said.

"In this story which is forming in my head now, there was once a young servant girl who lived in a merchant's house in, let us say, in Surrey."

"Why Surrey? Why not say Kent."

"The place is immaterial, but Kent if you prefer. The merchant is a wealthy man. He is accustomed to receiving visitors, important ones. Some of the visitors are looking for favours . . ."

"For favours!"

"I mean that they are looking for money, for loans. One day

a visitor, who comes from this part of the world, from Aquitaine in fact, arrives at the merchant's house. The nobleman is after money as well but while he is staying in the house the servant girl takes his eye. The nobleman pursues her, against her desires. But what can she do, a humble member of the household? In short he has his way with her."

Chaucer paused. He hadn't been watching Margaret Loup while he was speaking but now he risked a glance. Her face was set, unreadable.

"While they are . . . engaged in this fashion . . . the master of the house discovers them. He has always had a partiality for the servant girl – "

"Like a father's partiality," said Margaret Loup. "There was nothing dishonourable about him. He never spoke an improper word, he never laid hands upon the girl."

"I am glad of it," said Geoffrey. "Glad of it. But nevertheless he is roused to fury by what he sees. There are heated words between the merchant and the visitor from Aquitaine, a violent argument. In the upshot, the Gascon draws his dagger and stabs the merchant."

"Who had no weapon. Who was unarmed." Margaret's tone was bitter. "A harmless man, a good man. Yet he died."

"The nobleman might have faced justice but he had influential friends who procured his freedom. He returned to his homeland, thankful for his escape and vowing to lead a purer life in future."

"I know nothing of that," said the woman. "All I know is that he killed a harmless man who was as a father to me."

"Many years afterwards," said Chaucer, speaking more rapidly as he approached the crisis of his story, "the girl, now a mature woman with a husband and a daughter of her own, found herself in the very territory which belonged to this nobleman. Yet she seemed to be travelling there quite willingly, even happily, and I don't understand that. This is a problem in my story. Didn't she know where she was, whose land she was on?"

"That's easily explained," said Margaret Loup. "When this man was in the merchant's house he went by another name, since his business there was so delicate. The servant girl never knew his real identity. What concern was it of hers? Nothing from beginning to end. She was entirely in the hands of men. When she arrived in his domain and saw him, she got the shock of her life. He had changed, grown older in the intervening years, yet there was no mistaking him."

"And that is when the woman felt the first stirrings of revenge."

"Have you ever stoked a fire that seemed to be out, Master Chaucer? You thought all life had departed from it, but a single stir brings back the flame and soon it is crackling merrily for one last time and giving out more heat than ever."

"So the woman begins to plan her revenge. She hears that the lord is to go out hunting the next day."

"Maybe she hears too that he is a daring huntsman, one who goes off by himself after the quarry," said Margaret.

"Yes, she sees an opportunity given her by Fortune. I'm not sure what she does next . . ."

"Steals a hunting sword perhaps."

"Steals and conceals it. But she tells no one?"

"She tells no one," said Margaret firmly. "This is her quarrel alone."

"I thought so," said Chaucer. "I was baffled when this woman's husband first roused my suspicions at the scene of the murder and I see now that he was completely ignorant of her plans."

"Completely ignorant."

"So she wears voluminous clothing, ample skirts at all times, good for the concealment of a weapon. She takes care to wear her usual red that day. It reflects the fire in her heart. She is tough and strong, accustomed to striding many miles in a day. Events seem to fall into her lap. Together with the others she wanders into the wood where the hunt is taking place. She separates herself from her companions. Drawn by the noise of the kill she comes upon a clearing where the nobleman is about to give the death-stroke to his quarry. It is as if Fortune itself has directed the woman to this place and now delivers her enemy into her hands. Perhaps Fortune will do her job for her and the nobleman will be killed by his quarry."

"Part of her wants that," said Margaret. "But another part wants him to be left alive."

"And he does survive but his quarry is good and dead. Now she crouches on the edge of the clearing and waits for her quarry to approach. He does, and then she leaps out – "

"As he had leapt upon her all those years before. As he had attacked the good, harmless man all those years before."

"What does she feel when the deed is done?"

"Satisfaction and despair."

"Satisfaction and despair. And so it is finished."

"No," said Margaret, "and you know it is not. For even though the man who you call noble escaped justice in the first place, there is no such escape for the woman."

"Perhaps she thought she'd got away with it."

"For a time she did."

"A man died on account of the killing. An innocent man."

"I need no innocent man to prick my conscience, Master Geoffrey. I have not slept soundly since," said Margaret. "I expected hourly to be unmasked, disclosed. When Alice nearly drowned and was brought out of the river as if dead, I thought that was the beginning of my punishment, inflicted not on me but on those dearest to me. It was not, God be thanked. Yet who knows what the future holds? Who may yet be punished for my crime?"

All this time they had been opposite one another on the forecastle. At some point Chaucer found himself on his feet. He and Margaret Loup were standing face to face. Now she turned towards the side of the ship to face the setting sun, turned as casually as if she wanted to look at the view. This upper area of the *Arveragus* was a little like a castle turret, with shields for battlements. She leaned her ample hips against the bulwark between two of the shields. And at that moment her husband Lewis Loup appeared at the top of the ladder which led from the lower deck. He called her name. She looked surprised. She twisted sharply and seemed to lose her balance. Slowly, almost deliberately one might say, she toppled from the edge of the ship into the calm waters.

23

So Margaret Loup is gone, but what happens next to some of our other characters? To Hubert or Janus, for example. Well, that gentleman has escaped from the vaults under the Prince's court in Bordeaux. At present he is wandering at large in the territory of Aquitaine, and waiting to see what opportunities the coming war will provide. Let us pray he comes no closer to any of us.

And Richard Foix, the seneschal of Guyac? He has heard of the disaster at Libourne and the death of a number of his – or, more properly, of de Guyac's – men. He gave those instructions about halting Geoffrey Chaucer and the others only because he believed he'd had the hint for action from Florac. Yet now Florac wishes to know nothing of it. Foix fears that he is in bad odour with Gaston Florac who, he is almost certain, will marry Rosamond de Guyac after a short period of mourning. He fears that Florac may seek to sacrifice him if there is trouble from Bordeaux, which looks likely.

As for the story of Rosamond de Guyac and Gaston Florac, we'd best turn to romance for that. It's not quite reality but it wraps things up nicely since Rosamond and Gaston *will* wed in time and live quite happily. There are many incidents in the story of *Nicolette and the Castellan* – incidents such as battles, dreams and debates – but this is how the romance draws to a close.

One day Nicolette's husband and the castellan of Domfront were out hunting, in the company of the lady. Although both of them loved the lady greatly, their love for the hunt was almost as great. They were in pursuit of a white-footed hart and had endured many checks and setbacks in their day-long chase. The hart had been long talked of but never glimpsed until this day. Following the cry of the hounds they came together by the banks of a mighty river. They looked up and beheld the white-footed hart on the far side. The river flowed fast and deep, and the two men wondered at the courage of the hart which had swum to the opposite bank and now stood regarding her pursuers with grave and gentle eyes. No dog would dare to cross the stream and even the bravest horse would balk at the attempt.

Without any words the two men dismounted from their horses. Their meinie urged them not to attempt the crossing, entreating them to abandon their quarry and return home. For, they said, it is plain that the white-footed hart is no living being but a goddess who has taken that shape for her own purposes. No mortal animal could have swum that stream and lived. Harm will surely come to you if you continue this pursuit. Nicolette herself added her pleas. But Nicolette's husband and the castellan of Domfront turned their backs on the wise words of their retinue and the lady and, clad as they were, plunged into the quick waters.

They battled against the stream and, for all their strength, were carried far from the bank and out among sharp rocks. Halfway across, the husband of Nicolette called out to the castellan, "Help me, my friend, for I am injured and sinking and I am like to drown." Yet the castellan was not in such a dire taking as his fellow and might have swum on to the far shore. Nevertheless he turned back and, with a mighty effort, he saved his fellow from the waves. Together they clambered on to the bank where their meinie was waiting. All this while, the white-footed hart continued to regard them with her grave and gentle eyes. When she saw that they had reached safety, she turned and vanished into the darkness of the woods, never to be seen again.

The followers gave thanks to God for the rescue and praised the castellan of Domfront for his selfless deed. Yet all was not well with the husband of Nicolette. For he had been wounded to the heart by one of the sharp rocks in the middle of the river and now his life's-blood was pouring out of him as he lay on the grassy shore. His wife took his hand but she was so overcome by grief she was unable to speak and wept instead. The castellan knelt down beside him and said, "I am sorry to see you in such a taking. You shall be borne home with all speed." His friend said, "I am not long for this world, and my only carriage henceforth will be a bier." The castellan too began to weep but the husband told him to dry his eyes and to listen carefully to his words. "For," he said, "I have long known that you are in love with my lady here. Nay, deny it not if your love be honourable, for my time is short." So the castellan acknowledged that what he said was true. "As for my dear Nicolette, I do not know how she will bear herself when I am gone," continued her husband. "Only this I know, that none is so worthy to be loved as she. If she should think of becoming once more a wife, then I ask her to remember you." And with those words he expired.

Many tears were shed at the death of this man. Nicolette was beside herself with grief and the castellan of Domfront, seeing her distress, truly regretted that he had not been the one to perish in the stream. The dead man's body was borne homeward on a bier, as he had predicted, and many days of mourning followed. The funeral obsequies were the most splendid ever seen in that place. Yet all things human have their period, even great grief, and after the due time of mourning, Nicolette recalled her dying husband's words and looked with favour on the castellan of Domfront and the two were wed with the agreement of their counsellors. From that day onward, Nicolette and the castellan lived in harmony with never a word of jealousy or strife.

Geoffrey Chaucer and Alan Audly and Ned Caton eventually found themselves back on their native soil. They had parted from the players at Dover, after disembarking from the *Arveragus*.

Lewis Loup was almost inconsolable at his wife's death but grimly determined to go on the road again with his players, now reduced by two. Chaucer observed Ned Caton's sadness at leaving the company of Alice Loup. For a little while, that young man would carry her round in his heart. And then she'd fade from it, as Rosamond de Guyac had faded from his.

Geoffrey said nothing of Margaret's confession but claimed that they had been talking of stories (which was true in its way). The wife had gone to look at the declining sun and had somehow lost her footing on the deck and fallen overboard. Her husband had witnessed her final moments, had heard the splash. He and Chaucer had rushed to the side but there was nothing to be seen amid the calm blue swell.

Chaucer felt some scruple about Margaret's death. Yet, he told himself, she had chosen to die by "accident". Conscience-stricken, she might have believed that others would pay for her offence unless she first destroyed herself. Certainly, drowning was preferable to the humiliation of the public execution which would have been her fate had Chaucer revealed to anyone else the account which Hubert gave him. He might, of course, have kept silent. Yet murder will out . . .

And what of Chaucer? Well, he finished the story which he'd begun telling to Audly and Caton on the way down to Bordeaux and then taken up once more in the guard-room at Guyac. The three men were nearing Canterbury, when some remark prompted Ned to demand the rest of the story.

"Story?" said Chaucer.

"Yes," said Ned and Alan, almost together. "The rest of that story. The one about the woman on the cliff-tops who saw her husband drown."

Drown? He thought of the player Bertram who had drowned twice over in the Dordogne, he thought of Margaret Loup's last moments.

"Ah, that story," said Geoffrey Chaucer. "Where was I?"

"The young man had rescued someone from the waves," said Alan.

"Or was about to rescue someone," said Geoffrey. "You asked me as we were arriving in Bordeaux whether the story would end happily, Alan. Judge for yourself."

He paused to gather up the threads of his narrative. It seemed a long time since he'd embarked on the tale.

"Where was I? The lady Dorigen marries the knight Arveragus who goes away to fight in England. She awaits his return, only to see his ship shattered on the rocks within hailing distance of home. Aurelius the squire has long nursed a passion for Dorigen, now a widow, and he throws himself on her mercy. Will she have him? Taking pity on him, she agrees but only if he retrieves her husband from the sea, so that she can give Arveragus a proper burial. It's an impossible task of course. Arveragus's bones must be scattered across the sea-bed by now. Aurelius is plunged into a new gloom. One day he's walking on the cliff-tops when he sees a little fishing boat in trouble. Like Arveragus's great boat, it too breaks up on the rocks. Scarcely thinking of what he's doing, Aurelius runs down the steep path to the shore."

"That was where you finished," said Ned. "A dramatic moment."

"There's an art to storytelling," said Chaucer, with a touch of complacency. "So Aurelius the squire plunged into the water. He could swim. But not in those waters. No one could swim in those waters. His breath was snatched away by the cold and the turbulence of the waves. Perhaps in his misery he was determined to put an end to himself rather than trying to rescue any survivors from the sinking fishing vessel. Then as he struggled to keep afloat no more than a few arms' lengths from the shore – because instinct is a great force, and whatever his intentions he couldn't compel himself to go under for good – he was suddenly buffeted in the back by something. He assumed it was a spar from the shattered vessel, or an object thrown from the deck. But it was a man, already drowned perhaps. He was floating face down, rocked violently backwards and forwards by the motion of the waves.

"Without knowing whether this individual was alive or dead, Aurelius tried to grab hold of him. The body slipped out of his reach. Flailing about, he made another attempt. Once again the body eluded him. On the third try Aurelius managed to grasp the man under the arms and, kicking out with his legs and struggling to keep his mouth and nose clear of water for a few seconds at a time, he pushed back towards the shore. Whereas five minutes earlier Aurelius hadn't cared whether he lived or died, now he was desperate to bring this burden back to land. And still he did not know whether he was lugging a corpse or not!

"It took an age but eventually as his strength was running out Aurelius felt the shelving beach. His feet skidded on the stones, more than once he slipped back underwater, borne down by the weight of the man he was staggering beneath. Then at once he was on the shore. He rolled away from the body and lay exhausted, oblivious to the pebbles digging into his back, indifferent to the clasp of his sodden clothing. The man he had rescued lay, still face down, next to him. By this time some others had arrived, drawn by the wreck. Shore folk. They carried Aurelius into shelter, a place used to store fishing gear. They dried his clothes in front of a blazing fire, a beautiful girl held a cup to his lips and warmed him with spiced wine.

"When he'd recovered his wits – which didn't take long, he was a fit young man for all his misery and melancholy – Aurelius gazed round. He was lying on a makeshift bed covered in a rough blanket. The man he'd saved was also lying close to the fire but on the floor. He'd been covered with a blanket too with only his face exposed, a heavily bearded face, still slick with water and green fragments of weed. His clothes were being dried. Aurelius didn't think they were worth salvaging. They were poor, thin garments, scarcely adequate for a fisherman. Then he saw that the blanket was rising and falling in the region of the man's chest. He was still breathing! And now the girl – daughter of one of the folk who lived near the shore – was bending over him and tipping a little of the spiced wine into *his* mouth. The man spluttered. His eyes opened.

"It was a miraculous recovery from the waves," said Chaucer, thinking of the story of Henri de Guyac's recovery from the waves. Thinking of how Margaret Loup had been lost.

He continued, "The door to the hut opened and in walked the lady Dorigen. She hadn't witnessed the wreck herself but she'd heard that someone had been rescued from the waves. Furthermore she knew that Aurelius was the rescuer. Perhaps she came to compliment him, to commend him for his selfless bravery. The folk who used the hut drew back in the presence of a lady.

"Dorigen looked at Aurelius. He was conscious of his nakedness underneath the rough blanket. She said nothing. But she smiled at him, as he had never seen her smile before, and for the sake of that smile Aurelius felt that he would have risked death again, risked it a thousand times over. Then she moved to examine the man lying on the floor. His eyes had closed once more. Perhaps he was surprised to find himself alive after all. A trickle of the spiced wine had run sideways into his clotted beard.

"Aurelius heard a gasp. He looked at Dorigen. She was white in the face. She stretched out a hand and, if she hadn't grasped hold of one of the timber supports of the hut, she would have fallen to the floor. Her mouth gaped but no further sound came out. She kept her eyes fastened on the man. The eyes of the man on the floor fluttered open. He gazed up at the woman. He made to rise up although he didn't have the strength. He fell back again but a bare arm emerged from under the blanket and reached out in Dorigen's direction. He mouthed some words, inaudible words.

"You've guessed who the man was of course. It was Arveragus, her husband, come back from the dead. Later, when they'd all returned to their castle and Arveragus had recovered from his ordeal and Aurelius had been properly thanked for his selfless rescue, the full story came out. The knight had not been aboard the ship which Dorigen had seen destroyed on the black rocks, the ship with a great golden lion on its sail. He had been wounded while campaigning in England, so badly wounded that his companions despaired of his life. He gave instructions that not a word of this should reach Dorigen and told his companions to sail homeward without him. Once arrived, they were to break the news to her gently, stressing that he would return as soon as he was fit again. He didn't expect to recover but he thought that at least in this way her heart and mind would be prepared for the worst – or less unprepared for it.

"Yet he did recover. It took a long time but eventually he was able to rise from his bed and move again. Straightaway, weak but in high spirits, dressed in the nearest garments which he could lay hands on, he took the first available boat to Brittany. It was a fishing vessel. As he drew closer to the cliffs of home the wind began to rise and the sea grew rough and the little boat was driven towards the black rocks. He did not know the original fate of his own fine craft, the one with the golden lion. News did not travel so quickly in those days. Arveragus had no idea that his fighting companions had been lost at that very spot many months before. If he had, he might have reflected that there is no avoiding destiny. The death which he had eluded then was now staring him in the face. Him and the crew of the little boat.

"The boat broke up on the rocks, as you've heard, and Arveragus was flung into the water with the others. He struggled against the waves but he was as helpless as a baby. When he was going down for the third time, his thoughts were of Dorigen. She would be a widow after all. The next thing he knew he was spluttering while someone tried to pour warm liquid into his mouth. There was a great heat on his left hand from the fire and he was conscious of the throbbing of an old wound in his side, the one he'd sustained during his time in England, the one that had almost destroyed him. Then he became aware of someone standing over him and he opened his eyes to see his wife. She turned white and put out a hand to steady herself. She made to speak but no words came out. She was more shocked to see him than he could understand.

"Once the explanations were over and done with, a great joy and relief took hold of Arveragus's household. The knight had been snatched from the jaws of death, twice. Dorigen had believed that he was lost to her for ever and yet here he was, lying in her arms and promising her that he would embark on no more campaigns or quests – at least not for the time being.

"But what of Aurelius? He was grateful for the knight's gratitude of course. He'd saved a man from drowning. He was more than grateful for the smiles and graceful words with which Dorigen showered him. Yet even as she was saying how she'd never be able to thank him enough, saying it for the hundredth time, he sensed that she wished to be left alone with her husband, miraculously restored to her arms. He departed for his own more humble dwelling. He was exhausted from his own narrow escape from drowning yet he could not sleep that night. Instead Dorigen's old pledge went through his head like an arrow. She had promised herself to him, on condition that he retrieved her husband from the sea. Wasn't that exactly what he had done? The fact that Arveragus was alive rather than a scatter of bones was a minor consideration and, if looked at in the right way, ought to be a cause for even greater thankfulness on Dorigen's part. As far as Aurelius was concerned he had more than fulfilled *his* side of the contract. Now it was up to Dorigen to fulfil hers and to surrender to him. As the night wore on and sleep remained as far away as ever he worked himself into a state of righteous indignation. Was it likely that Dorigen would remember her promise? Probably not. Wasn't it much more likely that she would forget it, either deliberately or simply because she was overwhelmed with delight at Arveragus's fortunate rescue? Why should everyone be happy apart from him?

"At daybreak he got up and wrote her a letter It was couched in the most courtly terms, although it came hot from his brain. He said that he was glad her husband was restored to her. He gave thanks to heaven for their joint rescue from the waves. He reminded her of their conversation in the garden and of her pledge. The rest he left up to her. She was a lady after all. He could not enforce anything on her. But behind everything the idea beat through his mind and heart, *Why should everyone be happy apart from him?*

"The following day Arveragus discovered his wife in tears. A letter lay in front of her. She hastily put it out of sight. He pressed her with questions. What was wrong? She tried to pretend that her tears were simply the overflow of joy on his safe return. He embraced her and asked again what was the matter. Dorigen, shaken by so many turns of fortune, soon confessed everything. The conversation in the garden, the pledge. She had promised to give herself to Aurelius if her husband was recovered from the waves so that she might give his bones a proper burial. And Aurelius had kept his word. What was she to do?

"Her husband looked grave. He turned away in grief. When he looked once again at Dorigen his expression was resolute. He told her that she had given her word and that she could not break it. She must go to Aurelius and keep her side of the bargain. It was a question of honour. 'But,' he said, 'for heaven's sake, wife, say nothing of this to anyone, for the sake of our house and its good name. And request of Aurelius that he too keeps silent over this matter.' Then, seeing her distress, he clasped her once more and said, 'All may yet be well, do not fear.'

"With a heavy heart, Dorigen made her way to Aurelius's house. When the knock came at his door he was surprised. He hadn't been expecting her. Firing off the letter had cooled his passions. Seeing the pain which was written on her face, a different emotion coursed through his veins. It was pity. For you know that pity flows most easily in the noblest hearts, and though a mere squire Aurelius possessed true *gentillesse*. Soon he had established how things stood with Dorigen and Arveragus. It had never occurred to him that Dorigen would tell her husband of their agreement. He was amazed at the sense of honour displayed by both the knight and his lady. He listened while Dorigen repeated in a subdued fashion her husband's request that no one, outside the three of them, should ever know of this business.

"Before Dorigen was able to finish her story, pity had overwhelmed Aurelius. He could scarcely speak, his tongue was so heavy. He could scarcely see through his tear-filled eyes. He said to Dorigen, 'Lady, return to your husband. I hereby release you from our agreement, every particle of it. You have both demonstrated such loyalty to your word of honour that only a wretch could take advantage of you. I am not that wretch. Go now and live happily with your husband. I am honoured too in having recovered such a fine gentleman from the clasp of the sea and in having returned him to his noble wife.' She made to speak but he said, 'No, not a word further,' and with that he chastely embraced Dorigen and just as chastely kissed her. It was the first and the last time they would ever touch.

"She departed from Aurelius's humble house and went back to Arveragus. Her own heart was full of emotion. Somewhere between grief and joy she informed her husband of what had happened. Arveragus was lavish in his praise for the good squire who had preserved him and his lady, both in body and reputation. And then he consoled Dorigen whose suffering in his absence and afterwards had been as great, perhaps greater, than his own. From that time forward they lived as a knight and his lady should, in perfect peace and friendship."

Chaucer paused. Dusk was nearing. A sudden gust blew a scatter of leaves across their path. He could see the walls of Canterbury in the distance. They'd reach the town in time for supper. Tomorrow morning, early, as he'd promised himself, he would visit the shrine of St Thomas to give thanks for their safe return. Hundreds of miles away a war might be in the offing. For certain, there would be death and skirmishes in Aquitaine. Yet he did not feel that this was his campaign. Why, John of Gaunt had as good as instructed him that it was not his concern. *Go home and write.* Very well, he would. Go home. Write. Within a day or two he ought to be inside the gatehouse at Aldgate. Back with his wife and family. And a new baby imminent. What should they call him? Chaucer had no doubt it would be a him. Call him Lewis perhaps . . .

He remembered travelling this route a few months earlier. Then, though none of them had known it, they'd had Hubert on their tail. Evidence of that, if he'd required more, had come when they collected their horses from the Maison Dieu in Dover, the religious house where they lodged on the way out. Asking for the ostler Peter, Chaucer was informed by Brother James that the lad was dead and buried, killed after falling from a ladder in the stables. That was apparently an accident but the discovery a day or two afterwards of the body of a member of the order – Hubert by name – in the copse of trees which stood by the Maison had been plain murder, for which no one had yet been called to account. Chaucer might have said that the man who'd most likely been responsible for both deaths was safely under lock and key in the Prince's palace in Bordeaux.

Nevertheless he kept silent out of the desire to avoid delay and complication. It was one more item to pass on to John of Gaunt in time. Perhaps Gaunt would have second thoughts about the wisdom of keeping alive such a dangerous man as the counterfeit monk.

Anyway there was no need for secrecy on their journey now. They would put up at one of the better inns in Canterbury, not the Phoenix. Chaucer smiled to himself at the bad behaviour of his companions on the outward journey, their bedding of the innkeeper's wife and daughter. He hadn't seen the funny side at the time. Well, it was no more than Master Sampson had deserved perhaps, and it would make a good story to tell in the future, suitably polished and decked out with a bit more detail. He'd have to change people's names and trades of course. Innkeeper Sampson might become a carpenter . . . no, a miller. Everyone knew what millers were like, a by-word for sharp practice. While the two young men should be . . . students, cocky students, deserving to be taken down a peg or two. That meant shifting the place away from Canterbury to Oxford or Cambridge . . .

"Is that it?" said Ned, breaking into his train of thought.

"Is what it?"

"In your story. What about Aurelius?" said Alan.

"Ah, Aurelius," said Chaucer, who had already put the tale of Dorigen and Arveragus behind him and was thinking of his next story.

"You cannot leave him so dissatisfied," said Ned.

"But Aurelius *is* satisfied. He has shown himself capable of great bravery and generosity. He has earned the heartfelt thanks of a knight and his lady. He's shown that he possesses true *gentillesse*. What more could he want – or you want for that matter?"

"You know what we mean," said Alan.

"Oh, very well," said Chaucer with feigned weariness but

pleased to be pressed to complete his tale. "You remember that when Aurelius was recovering from his near-drowning he was sheltered and warmed in a hut on the shore. A girl – the daughter of a couple of the shore-folk – was refreshing him with a little spiced wine. She was beautiful even if he'd only been dimly aware of it at the time. For her part, she was full of admiration for Aurelius's courage. She was overwhelmed with pity for this brave and handsome young man. Straightaway she had lost her heart to him though naturally she said nothing. They met again, by chance, several weeks later on the cliff-tops. He had not seen her clearly at their first meeting in the hut – he was only thankful to be still alive, and then he was distracted by the arrival of Dorigen and everything which followed on from that. By now he had resigned himself to a loveless existence. But fortune has a way of overturning our resolutions. Read Boethius for that."

"What was the girl's name?" said Ned.

"I don't know," said Chaucer. "The old stories don't say."

"Old stories? I thought you'd made this up," said Ned.

"I don't make anything up," said Chaucer.

"There was a boat in our convoy on the way back," said Alan Audly, "called the *Agnes*. We might call the girl that, following our principle of name-giving."

"Agnes? Why not?" said Geoffrey Chaucer, amused at the *our*. "Anyway, this Agnes was eager to find out from Aurelius more details of his daring rescue of Arveragus, and the squire, though modest, was happy enough to tell her. 'How brave,' she kept on saying, 'how brave of you.' Modest Aurelius lowered his eyes repeatedly but each time he looked up he was struck more forcefully by Agnes's beauty. She, for her part, could scarcely look at him for shyness. But then she didn't need to. Every feature of him was stamped on her heart while his voice alone was music to her ears. It was growing cold and windy on the cliff-top and the two went to seek shelter and to continue their conversation inside. And since we're going to be inside the city walls in a moment and in shelter ourselves, I'll bring this drawn-out tale to a close. It ended the way it should. The love that Aurelius felt for Agnes – which wasn't stewed and simmered for years like his feelings for Dorigen – sprang into life as if from nowhere. We cannot hold on to two passions at once. The stronger or newer will push out the older. It was as if Dorigen had never been."

"Oh, shame," said Ned.

"But it is so," said Chaucer, wondering whether Ned was thinking of Alice Loup. "It is so. Therefore these two – Aurelius and Agnes – fell in love. They married. Like the knight and his lady they also lived in perfect peace and friendship. So our tale is done, and God bless us all."